PRAISE FOR GLENN MEADE

"The Irish-born author teeters on the edge of genius and sacrilege with this thriller [*The Second Messiah*] . . . Fans of Davis Bunn or Dan Brown won't bat an eye at Meade's unblinking look at the Vatican and the religious secrecy that fuels such novels. With a plot that screams, a controversial edge, and characters with attitude and something to prove, this has all the makings to be the next *Da Vinci Code*."

—*PUBLISHERS WEEKLY*

"Dan Brown meets Tom Clancy—Glenn Meade sure knows how to get your pulse racing. I was gripped from page one. . . . You know you're in safe hands with Glenn Meade—*The Second Messiah* is a rollercoaster of a thriller that lifts the lid on the inner workings of the Vatican and leaves you wondering just how much of the fiction is actually fact."

—STEPHEN LEATHER, author of *Nightfall*

"A thrill a minute. A cross between Indiana Jones and Dan Brown. Thriller readers will love this book."

—*MIDWEST BOOK REVIEW*

"Reading similarly to both a Thoene novel and *The Da Vinci Code*, bestselling author Meade's *The Second Messiah* will keep readers on the edge of their proverbial seats. . . . *The Second Messiah* reads quickly and will hold the reader's attention with its many plot twis⁺ Recommended for readers of Joel C. Rosenberg."

—*CHRISTIAN RETAILING*

MORE PRAISE FOR GLENN MEADE

"... keeps readers on the edge of their proverbial seats with multiple plot twists."

—*CHARISMA*

"Meade knows how to entangle, and untangle, an exciting array of characters and plots guaranteed to keep the reader hooked ... a talented storyteller, he sets the scene quickly before taking off on a rollicking ride that keeps the pages turning."

—*CROSSWALK.COM*

"Meade's research is so extensive yet unobtrusive ... that it is often easy to forget you're reading fiction and not history."

—*THE WASHINGTON POST*

"A writer of powerfully built and skillfully executed plots. Immerse yourself in his intricately woven intrigue and explosive action, and enjoy them thoroughly!"

—*OLEG KALUGIN*, former head of the KGB's First Directorate

"Fast, sly, and slick, this thriller delivers the goods—tension, action, plot twists—until the smoke clears on the last page."

—*BOOKLIST*

ALSO BY GLENN MEADE

Brandenburg
The Second Messiah

THE
ROMANOV
CONSPIRACY

A THRILLER

GLENN MEADE

HOWARD BOOKS
A Division of Simon & Schuster, Inc.

NEW YORK   NASHVILLE   LONDON   TORONTO   SYDNEY   NEW DELHI

Howard Books
A Division of Simon & Schuster, Inc.
1230 Avenue of the Americas
New York, NY 10020

First Howard Books paperback edition June 2013

HOWARD and colophon are trademarks of Simon & Schuster, Inc.

For information about special discounts for bulk purchases, please contact Simon & Schuster Special Sales at 1-866-506-1949 or business@simonandschuster.com.

The Simon & Schuster Speakers Bureau can bring authors to your live event. For more information or to book an event, contact the Simon & Schuster Speakers Bureau at 1-866-248-3049 or visit our website at www.simonspeakers.com.

Designed by Jaime Putorti

Manufactured in the United States of America

10 9 8 7 6 5 4 3 2 1

The Library of Congress has cataloged the hardcover edition as follows:

Meade, Glenn, 1957–
    The Romanov conspiracy : a thriller / Glenn Meade.—1st Howard Books hardcover ed.
      p. cm.
    1. Romanov, House of—Fiction. I. Title.
    PS3563.E16845R66 2012
    813'.54—dc23

                        2012002718

ISBN 978-1-4516-1186-1
ISBN 978-1-4516-6945-9 (pbk)
ISBN 978-1-4516-1189-2 (ebook)

FOR KIM AND LUKE,
AND ALL THE KILGORES AND REDMONDS
WITH LOVE

AUTHOR'S NOTE

All stories find their own lover.

I fell in love with this one when I visited the village of Collon, on Ireland's northeast coast, in the distant shadows of the majestic Mountains of Mourne.

It was in the burial grounds of the village's Presbyterian church, dating from 1813, with its beautiful stained glass windows, where I found the forgotten graves of a group of Russians who fled to Ireland during their homeland's October Revolution.

And it was here that I heard the first echoes of a remarkable plot to rescue the Russian tsar and his family in 1918, an event still shrouded in some secrecy. This was one of the most difficult stories I've researched, for it proved to be a deeply rooted enigma with many tendrils.

What began in St. Petersburg in the fevered days of the Russian Revolution ended in a cluster of graves in an Irish country churchyard. In between are long-lost clues to an intricate conspiracy, one that may well answer the twentieth century's most enduring mystery.

Many of the characters named in this book existed, as did the shadowy order sometimes known as the Brotherhood of St. John of Tobolsk.

Much of what you are about to read is true.

The rest, but a small part, is fiction, part of the mosaic of storytelling that a writer must employ to bring life to his tale.

But as to which part is truth and which small part is fiction, I will leave that for you to decide.

My dear Maria, history may never reveal what truly happened to all of the Tsar's children. The answer is so secret that for now I cannot speak of it.

—LENIN, IN REPLY TO HIS SISTER IN JULY 1918, AFTER SHE INFORMED HIM THAT SHE HAD HEARD RUMORS OF THE ROMANOVS' EXECUTIONS

Anna Anderson is part of a much deeper mystery than any of us can comprehend, for she left behind so many unanswered questions. One of the most startling questions is this: how could a supposedly simple, deranged peasant woman manage to confound the world's brightest and most respected legal and investigative minds for over six decades? In this regard, I'm reminded of a saying that I once heard: "There are always three sides to every story. There's your side, there's my side. And then there's the truth."

—GREGORY ANTONOV, ON ANNA ANDERSON, ONCE REPUTED TO BE THE TSAR'S YOUNGEST DAUGHTER, ANASTASIA, WHO ALLEGEDLY SURVIVED EXECUTION AT THE HANDS OF HER CAPTORS

THE PRESENT

1

I believe that the greatest secrets lie buried and only the dead speak the truth.

And in a way that was how I came to be in the woods that morning when we found the bodies. It was raining in the City of Dead Souls, a heavy downpour that drenched the summer streets.

"Traffic isn't bad this morning. Thirty minutes, no more," my Russian driver said as our Land Rover skirted imposing granite buildings, the remnants of a grander civilization long since past.

I sat back and watched the old imperial city flash by. Named in honor of Catherine the Great in 1723, Ekaterinburg lies in the shadow of the Ural Mountains. The landscape resembles the rugged beauty of Alaska—thick woods filled with wolves and bears, deep ravines and snowcapped peaks. Rich ore mines contain the greatest treasures in the world: platinum and emeralds, gold and diamonds honeycomb the soaring mountain ranges that lie beyond this sprawling Siberian city.

As my Land Rover left Ekaterinburg and drove past heavily forested birch slopes, I snapped open the leather briefcase on my lap and plucked out a file. The label on the blue cover said:

PRELIMINARY FINDINGS: EKATERINBURG FORENSIC
ARCHAEOLOGICAL DIG
DR. LAURA PAVLOV, FORENSIC PATHOLOGIST,
JOINT DIRECTOR

I reviewed the thick clutch of pages, the results of my work for the last three months. This was my first visit to Ekaterinburg and our team came from all over: forensic archaeologists, scientists, and students from America, Britain, Germany, and Italy; and of course our host, Russia. The brief of our cooperative venture was simple—to dig in the forests for evidence of mass executions during the Russian Revolution's Red Terror.

Many thousands perished, not least the Romanovs, the Russian royal family—the tsar and tsarina, and their four pretty daughters and their youngest son, thirteen-year-old Alexei—shot and bayoneted to death, their skulls smashed by rifle butts and their corpses doused in sulfuric acid.

The Ipatiev House, where they were held captive, was known locally as the House of Dead Souls. But the Reds executed so many victims, their bodies dumped in mine shafts and unmarked graves in the vast forests outside Ekaterinburg, that the locals coined their city a new name: the City of Dead Souls.

What I hadn't counted on was the heat and the mosquitoes. Siberia is an icebox in winter but during its brief, hot summer the temperatures can soar. The forest comes alive with flies and mosquitoes. The heat makes the trees drip with sweet-smelling resin and the fragrant perfume drenches the air.

The rain stopped as my driver turned onto a narrow, worn track, rutted and muddy from the movement of heavy vehicles. The Land Rover headed toward a collection of temporary huts and heavy canvas walk-in tents erected in the middle of a clearing in a birch forest. A painted wooden sign said in English and Russian:

THIS SITE IS
PRIVATE PROPERTY
NO UNAUTHORIZED ENTRY

Something else I hadn't counted on that summer's morning as we pulled up beside one of the tents. I came to these resin-scented woods to exhume the ghosts of the past. Yet absolutely nothing could have prepared me for the bizarre secret that I was to stumble upon when the frozen Siberian earth offered up its dead.

For with the dead came truth.

And with truth came the first whispers of the most incredible story I have ever heard.

I stepped out of the car and tore open the entrance flap into my tent. I went to sit behind my work desk as my dig supervisor, Roy Moran, came in. "Hey, baby."

Memphis Roy we call him, and he always called me *baby*. In Memphis, everyone calls everyone else *baby*. The fact that a woman was in charge of the dig didn't make any difference—if I'd been a man, Roy still would have called me *baby*.

Roy's a big, bony, no-nonsense guy and one of the best in the business. I tore open my briefcase, ready to attack some paperwork, and said, "I thought you were supposed to be digging shaft number seven this morning."

"Baby, I sure am." Roy stood there, hands on his hips and a little out of breath. The look on his face was a cross between excitement and puzzlement. He raised the grimy Tigers baseball cap he always wore, wiped sweat from his forehead, and grinned. "Turns out seven may just be our lucky number."

"Spit it out."

"We went down as far as we could and hit a peaty layer of near permafrost. But we've found something, Laura. I mean *seriously* found something."

I threw down my pen. Roy wasn't a man to get wound up about anything. But at that moment he seemed energized, delight bubbling from him like an excited twelve-year-old. "Tell me," I said.

"Hey, baby, you really need to see this for yourself."

I followed Roy through the scented woods. He walked slowly, his muscled legs picking a way through a path of rain-drenched ferns and old fallen trees. He said, "The shaft mouth goes down about sixty feet. It's pretty deep."

The entire clearing was crammed with mining equipment, wooden staves, and scaffolding, and dotted with a bunch of trucks and SUVs.

"Why do I feel an *and* coming on? You still haven't told me what you've found."

Roy grinned, not changing his pace, his excitement infectious. Beads of sweat glistened on his forehead and his eyes sparked. "Baby, it's a woman. We believe there may be another body down there, too, but it's too deeply buried to see what we've got. Who knows? There might even be more."

I felt excited as we moved between clumps of silver birch trees and halted at the mouth of a mine shaft. I smelled the rich, earthy brown scent of peat. The shaft was a hole in the ground, about eight feet square, the sides buttressed with thick wooden planks. One of several mines we explored during the dig, looking for any evidence we could find of artifacts from the Romanov era, when much of this region was a killing ground.

On the night of July 16–17, 1918, in Ekaterinburg, the Romanov family—then the world's wealthiest royals—vanished. Eyewitness accounts suggested that the entire family was massacred.

But for whatever reasons the Bolsheviks chose not to confirm their deaths and rumors persisted that some if not all of the family had escaped execution. There were even suggestions of secret plots to rescue them from their imprisonment in Ekaterinburg. Reports flourished for years that one or more of the tsar's daughters and their brother, Alexei, had escaped death.

The family had sewn precious stones—diamonds and other gems— into their underclothing, in the hope that such valuables would come in useful in the event of their escape. It was believed those same precious stones had impeded or prolonged their deaths.

Such stories had held me spellbound in childhood. No matter what the truth, like so many others fascinated by the mystery I *wanted* to believe Anastasia and Alexei escaped.

The mystery deepened and decades later on separate occasions, digs outside the city uncovered the remains of six adults. Among them was believed to be the tsar, his wife, and two of his daughters. DNA tests affirmed the likely identities by a possible blood connection to the British royal family.

But the discovery was shrouded in some controversy. Many experts believed the bones belonged to the Romanovs. But just as many didn't, citing among other reasons the fact that countless royal relatives were executed in the region and that the bones could have been theirs.

A later dig in a forest pit west of Ekaterinburg discovered two more sets of human remains. DNA tests suggested that they belonged to the tsar's missing daughter and son, Anastasia and Alexei. But one of the sets of remains was never completely proven to be those of Anastasia—a *probability* existed, but it couldn't go beyond all doubt. And so the tests were branded as being inconclusive by some scientists and hardened doubters within the Russian Orthodox Church. It left a nagging feeling that the mystery persisted, that the puzzle was somehow still unsolved.

Above the shaft mouth our engineers had rigged up a motorized winch with an old harness chair, driven by an electric generator. The scent of peat wafted up. I said to Roy, "You mean bones, or a complete skeleton?"

"I mean a woman. She's complete, mummified in the permafrost, and she's perfectly preserved by the bog peat and the cold."

I felt a raw tingle of anticipation down my spine. I leaned my hand against one of the silver birch trees, the bark bleached white by the sun. "How old?"

"At an educated guess and from the way she's dressed, we're talking the Romanov period."

Roy went down first. He descended with a wave of his hand as the motorized harness whirred him down into the dark pit. A few minutes later the harness returned empty. I climbed aboard and strapped myself in.

For the last month working at Ekaterinburg we'd unearthed a bunch of material: rust-covered Mosin-Nagant rifles, green-corroded copper coins, spent ammunition cases, a pair of eyeglasses, even several caches of silver and gold tsarist ingots, along with personal effects and jewelry. So many wealthy families with tsarist connections had fled here during the revolution, hoping to escape the bloodshed, but the Reds caught up with them.

Not all the victims were wealthy. My own past lies buried in these woods. Long before I saw Ekaterinburg I knew about this city by the snaking, broad banks of the Iset River, where my grandmother Mariana lived as a young girl. She was eleven when the October Revolution's Red Guards invaded her city. Her family were hardy *mujiks*—tough Russian peasants—who worked backbreaking hours digging ore from the icy permafrost, the rock-hard peaty Siberian earth that remains frozen even in summer.

Three of Mariana's brothers were executed in the forests beyond the town, including her beloved Pieter, barely fifteen. Their crime? They protested when the Reds seized their small mining company, a ragged enterprise that barely fed their family of twelve. Lenin didn't believe in personal ownership.

Everything a man possessed now belonged to the Soviets. If anyone protested, they were imprisoned. If they protested still, they were shot, all part of the brutal Red Terror that swept Russia once Lenin seized power.

Fleeing for their lives, my grandmother's family traveled across the frozen landscape one malignant winter and boarded a rusty steamship in St. Petersburg, bound for America. The only memories they carried in their cloth bags were some faded sepia family photographs and postcards of Imperial Ekaterinburg, the brittle pages yellow with age and smelling of wood smoke. I still recall that peaty wood smell when as a child I would leaf through the family album, filled with the faded images from another world.

Once, as a child, among the album pages I found an old black-and-white photograph and next to it a crushed handful of dried flowers, kept in an ancient fold of greaseproof paper, the edges stained with age.

"What's this, Nana?" The photograph showed an imposing railway station, decorated with fluttering Imperial Russian flags. On the steps of the station stood the unmistakable image of the Romanovs: the tsar and his wife waving to a crowd, next to them their son and daughters. I recognized Anastasia wearing a white dress and shoes and a simple bow in her hair, a bouquet of flowers clutched in her hands.

"That was the day in 1913 when the tsar and his family came to visit Ekaterinburg. Before the war, before everything turned bad in Russia." Her blue eyes watered, as if she recalled some long-cherished memory.

"And the flowers?"

"Of all the royal family, Anastasia was the most rebellious, the most sparkling. That day on the station steps she threw her bouquet to the children in the crowd. You can imagine there was such a rush, I was almost killed, but I managed to grab some of the bouquet. I've always cherished it."

I looked down at the photographic images and gingerly used the tip of my fingers to barely touch the fragile handful of dried flowers. "You *saw* Anastasia? She actually *threw* these flowers?"

"She was an imp, that one, full of life, a real tomboy, and we children loved her. The family affectionately called her *Kubyshka,* meaning 'dumpling.'"

And now here I was, part of an international archaeological dig, spending my summer in jeans and grubby sneakers in a walk-in tent on the outskirts of Ekaterinburg. Absurdly, it seemed as if my family's past had come full circle.

My curiosity eating me, I pressed the harness control block. The motor whirred. The harness lowered me into the pit and I was devoured by shadows.

At first I descended into blackness, but after about twenty feet the shaft's sides were lit by electric lightbulbs. Here and there, I kicked against the walls with my worn Reeboks to keep from hitting the sides.

Below me I saw a blaze of light and suddenly Roy gripped the harness. "Okay, baby, you're at rock bottom."

I let go of the rope and my feet hit a floor of muddied wooden planks. I maneuvered out of the harness and shivered. It felt intensely cold. I rubbed my arms. A cube of aching blue light shone down from the shaft mouth.

Nearby, a couple of powerful halogen lights illuminated the chamber floor, which expanded for at least twelve feet in all directions, wider than the shaft. Some of the chamber was lost in deep shadow and it felt eerie. Roy had engineered a lattice of struts and beams to prevent a cave-in but that didn't comfort me—I hated enclosed spaces, especially tunnels, which in my profession didn't help.

A heavily built man with a thick gray mustache and wire-rimmed glasses was busy hacking away at the icy peat of one of the chamber walls, using a lump hammer and a broad chisel. He stopped hammering and grinned. "Hey, Laura, how's it going?"

Tom Atkins, from Boston, had a toolbox open at his feet and his breath clouded in the chilled air. He wore a thickly padded Columbia ski jacket, heavy woolen gloves, and earmuffs. Next to him was a trestle table covered with an assortment of tools and brushes, as well as a couple of powerful electric flashlights. He removed the earmuffs.

"You came prepared, Tom." I nodded toward a pile of unopened Budweiser and Heineken beer cans stacked in a corner.

"Hey, don't knock it, this place is better than my refrigerator."

"So what have you two found besides the perfect place to chill beer?"

"Take a look over there first." Tom nodded to a wire sifting tray.

I picked it up. In a corner of the tray was a collection of badly tarnished military brass uniform buttons. I saw some copper kopeks and silvered rubles and could just make out the dates: 1914, 1916, and one 1912. There was a yellowed comb made from ivory and the remains of a luggage clasp. The sight of a child's hair band sent a poignant shiver down me.

During the Red Terror—the revolution's purge designed to keep a grip on power and instill fear—the Bolsheviks were known to execute entire families. I shook my head. "Sad, but interesting."

"The real jackpot's over here." Tom jerked a thumb toward the side of the chamber he was working on. "Better take a deep breath, Laura."

"Why?"

"It's kind of uncanny. Macabre almost."

I picked up one of the flashlights from Tom's table and moved deeper into the chamber. I shone a powerful cone of light onto the frozen soil and experienced a moment of pure terror. A human hand protruded from the permafrost. The flesh was intact, bleached white, the fingers lightly caked in mud, the fist tightly clenched. It appeared to be clutching something. "What the . . . !"

"You ain't seen anything yet. Look right there." Roy pointed to the permafrost wall.

And then I saw it. Connected to the hand was a body—a woman's face stared out grotesquely from the peaty earth. Her clothes were exposed, some kind of pale-colored blouse and a dark woolen top that looked from another century. *"Jeepers."*

Tom said, "Creepy, isn't it? The permafrost's acted like a deep freeze."

Roy added, "Baby, it doesn't surprise me. They've found woolly mammoths intact in this kind of soil. Take a look over to the left."

I did, and saw the remains of a dark, coarse jacket protrude from the rich brown earth, about a foot of the cloth exposed, and what appeared to be the vague shape of a small human torso underneath the fabric.

Roy said, "There's another body in there. We can't be sure if it's a child or an adult, but it'll take us some time to get it out. We'll concentrate on the woman first."

I turned my attention back to the woman, shivered, and peered closer. The preserved head was plainly visible. Her eyes were closed. I could see her nose and lips, ears, and cheeks, locks of dark hair curled across her features and forehead. She had good cheekbones. I shone the flashlight on her alabaster face and it was a disturbing experience. I knew I was looking at one of the most remarkable finds ever discovered at Ekaterinburg. "It's astonishing. I wonder who she was?"

"Heaven only knows. But there's something else," Roy offered.

"What?"

"Take a look at what's in her hand."

I shone the light on the still clenched bones, held firm for how many decades? It appeared that she was clutching some kind of metal chain. "What is it?"

"Looks like a piece of jewelry," Tom said.

"I'll take your word for it. Anyone want to try to pry the hand open?"

Roy grinned. "We thought we'd leave that to you."

"Thanks a bunch."

"You're the boss, baby." Roy handed me a pair of disposable surgical gloves.

"Here, hold the flashlight while I try."

Roy held my light and shone it on the clenched hand. I slipped on the gloves, steeled myself, closing my eyes a moment, and then I went for it. I gripped the index finger and the wrist and pulled gently, trying to open the hand.

The flesh felt marble cold and solid.

I was afraid that I might tear the skin apart or the entire hand would shatter like delicate porcelain. To my surprise, the bones uncoiled silently, just a fraction, but enough to see what it held. "Aim the torch here."

Roy shone it on the open hand. In the palm's bleached white furrows I saw a chain and locket.

It looked nothing extravagant or expensive like some of the jewelry found at Ekaterinburg, hidden away by royal relatives or the wealthy merchants who were executed here. I lifted out the locket and wiped it gently with my fingers. I could see it had some kind of raised image on the front, but the locket was part covered by peaty earth, the chain fragile.

Roy offered his penknife. "Here, try this."

I took the knife and scraped away caked dirt. There was no mistaking the raised Romanov family seal in gold, inlaid in front. It showed the double-headed imperial eagle. I could tell there was an inscription on the locket's rear, but it was obliterated by corrosion. My heart skipped.

Tom said, elated, "You think we got lucky?"

"Great minds think alike. I wish I knew."

Roy said, "Hey, baby, you think maybe we've found Romanov remains?"

I didn't reply, just stared at the locket, mesmerized.

Tom rubbed his frozen hands as if trying to set them on fire with friction. "Who knows? But we better inform the Russians. We'll have to cut her out of the permafrost. Hopefully a closer look can tell us if her body suffered any trauma and how she likely died."

The Russians had control of the dig. An inspector came out every other day from Ekaterinburg to check on our progress. But that was barely on my mind as I stared at the locket, my mind on fire. "*No,* don't do anything, or inform anyone officially. Not just yet."

Tom frowned, and Roy said, "Why not?"

I stared again at the remains of the two bodies and I felt stunned, filled with excitement. I looked up toward the gaping mouth of the shaft. The blue light that shone down at me that moment felt like an epiphany. I clutched the locket. My heart raced.

Roy must have seen the excitement in my face and said, "What's wrong?"

I crossed back to the harness and strapped myself in. "Someone get me photos of the body. I want them from every angle. And get a hair sample; we need to carry out a DNA test. I want to know if this woman could be a Romanov, or a blood relative." I pressed the motor control switch and the seat began to ascend.

"Hey, where are you going, baby?" Roy asked, confused.

"To book a flight. And don't ask me to where. You'd never believe me."

Some events in our lives are so huge in their impact upon us that they are almost impossible to take in. The birth of your first child. Or a hand slipping away from yours as you sit by a loved one's deathbed. The mystery of the bodies in the permafrost was on the same seismic scale. For the next eighteen hours my mind was a blur and I hardly slept. What I do remember is that after flying from Ekaterinburg to Moscow it was the afternoon of the following day when I landed at London's Heathrow airport.

The first thing I did was check the phone number written in my diary and I called it again from my cell phone. The number rang out. I tried again six more times, but with the same result. A generic voice asked me to leave a message. It was my sixth since that morning.

I felt exhausted but I hoped that the answer to the enigma of the Ekaterinburg bodies was another short flight away.

Dublin is barely a sixty-minute skip out over the Irish Sea and as my Aer Lingus plane began its descent, I saw the bright green Irish coast, spattered with huge dark patches of rain cloud.

By the time I'd hired a car and consulted a map, another hour passed. I drove north through relentless heavy rain showers, eager to reach my destination.

Sullen bands of charcoal clouds did their best to keep the sun at bay, but soon after I passed a huge modern bridge near a town called Drogheda, the sunlight burst from behind the cloud. Farther on I saw the Irish coastline and the rugged Mountains of Mourne, a striking patchwork of intense green shades, the colors so vivid my eyes ached.

All I had to do now was find the village I was looking for and the man I hoped would help solve the mystery.

The signpost said Collon. I pulled my rented Ford into a village square. It was deserted, neat, and tidy, with hanging baskets of flowers. It looked quaintly Victorian, an old blacksmith's premises with a horse-shoe-shaped entrance dominating the square.

I crossed the street to a local grocery store and asked for directions and found the red granite Presbyterian church and graveyard at the southern end of the town. Below the bell tower was chiseled in stone the year it was built: 1813.

The burial ground looked even older, the church magnificent, the stained glass windows works of art. I wandered between the grave sites, some of them hidden by undergrowth and wild bramble. I glimpsed a rusted metal cross with an inscription dated 1875—*Elizabeth, aged three and Caroline aged six, their sweet and gentle presence never forgotten, they have gone to lie in the arms of the Lord.* My heart felt the haunting echo of a long dead grief.

As I moved on, my cell phone rang and the harsh jangle of music seemed to violate the silence. I answered my phone, half-expecting a call back from the number I'd tried to ring. "Laura?" It was Roy, the line clear despite our distance. "Where are you?"

"Ireland."

"Ireland?"

"It's a long story. I don't want you to think I'm crazy dashing out on you, but I may be on to something. It has to do with the bodies and the locket. If it pans out, I'll let you know."

"Baby, you've got me interested. And if it doesn't?"

"This could be an enormous waste of time and money. What about the DNA?"

Roy wasn't getting all the answers he wanted and I could hear his frustrated sigh. "They're working on it. I can tell you from the preliminary forensics it's likely that the woman was Caucasian, between seventeen and twenty-five. We haven't even got to the second body yet, we've been too busy with the first."

"Anything else?"

"She hasn't thawed out enough to tell what trauma she might have suffered, but remember the coins we found? The latest was 1916. We think we're dealing with roughly the same period, give or take a few years. The woman's dental work suggests she was reasonably well-to-do. So we're in the right ballpark for the Romanovs. Any luck with the inscription?"

With great care I plucked the locket from my purse and turned it over in my palm. I'd spent most of the last nine hours of flying time studying it and managed to clean away more of the dirt. But the rest of the inscription was eaten with corrosion and stubbornly defied deciphering. "I still can't make out what it says."

A cautious tone crept into Roy's voice. "The Russians aren't going to be happy. They're already asking where you've gone. I told them some urgent family business came up and you had to leave. *Gee,* Laura, taking a piece of their history could be construed as theft. I don't even like talking about it over the phone. What if they throw you in prison when you get back?"

I carefully slipped the locket into my purse. "Don't worry, the locket will be returned. I've only borrowed it in the hope that I can identify its origin."

"How?"

"We'll talk again."

"Hey, baby, don't keep me in suspense."

"Sorry, I've got to go. And don't worry about the Russians, I'll handle them. Call me as soon as you have anything."

I flipped off my phone as I saw an old man come toward me among the graves.

He halted near a cluster of tombstones. I noticed that they were Russian-style crosses with double crossbeams and Cyrillic inscriptions, and they looked odd among a landscape of Anglo-Christian and Celtic crosses.

The man waited by one of the graves. I could make out the name inscribed in Russian on the polished granite stone: Uri Andrev.

The man stood studying me as he rested his right hand on a blackthorn walking cane. His skin was a jaundiced yellow and looked thin as crepe paper. He stood tall and dignified but with a slight stoop, and he spoke English but I thought I detected a Russian accent. "So, you came at last. It's Dr. Pavlov, isn't it?"

I stared back at him. "How did you know?"

"I finally got your phone messages. I never carry a cell phone, as you Americans call it. Forgive me, but I've been a hospital patient these last few days."

"Nothing serious, I hope?"

He offered a faint smile. "The usual problems of old age, I'm afraid. Forgive me, I didn't call you back but your message said you'd meet me at the church. I had my housekeeper drive me and saw you from the road. I recognized you from your photograph in the professional journals. You're an outstanding scientist, Dr. Pavlov."

"You're too kind."

The man offered his hand, the backs of his palms freckled with liver spots. "Michael Yakov. It seems we share an obsession, doctor."

"Pardon?"

"The Romanov era. I've long been interested in your work."

"And I'm suddenly very interested in yours."

"I believe your message said you found the woman?"

"Yes, Mr. Yakov. We found her. Just as you predicted. There may be other bodies, including what could be a child, but at this stage I can't tell you any more than that."

Yakov sucked in a breath, as if my confirmation had struck a nerve. "I very much hoped that you'd find her. You dug in an area where I believed she might be buried."

As I stood there listening to this old man talk, I couldn't help but think how absurd all of this was.

I had never met Michael Yakov, but he wrote to me constantly over a period of about a year. In fact, for a time I started to think he was stalking me. His letters came every few months, inquiring after my work in Ekaterinburg. And now here I was, hoping he'd solve my mystery.

"Mr. Yakov, ever since it became public knowledge that I intended to work at Ekaterinburg, you've written to me at least a dozen times. In almost every letter you suggested that I might find the remains of a young woman in the sectors where I was digging, and if I did, to contact you. You seemed particularly anxious to mention the woman."

He nodded. "Yes, I did."

I looked him in the eyes. "You even mentioned the possibility of finding the locket in your correspondence. But you never once offered to explain the woman's identity. And when I wrote to inquire why you were so interested in this dig, and why you seemed so convinced that I might locate the bodies, I received no reply. To tell you the truth, I had you down as a crackpot. Which is why I stopped answering your mail months ago.

"Until yesterday. Yesterday, when we found the woman, I began to wonder if you were a clairvoyant. Do you mind telling me what's going on?"

Yakov let out a sigh that almost sounded like a cry of pain and his eyes watered. "It's a very personal story, Dr. Pavlov. One that was told to me by my father."

"It's personal for me, too. You've involved me."

Yakov didn't reply as he reached out to touch the polished headstone. His fingers caressed the granite, then he blessed himself with a sign of the cross, as if paying his respects to the dead.

I said, "It seems a strange place for a Russian to be buried—among Celtic crosses."

"Do you know this country?"

"I've visited Celtic sites here on several occasions."

Yakov glanced around the cemetery, as if he was familiar with every stone and plot, every overgrown bush and blade of grass. "Quite a number of Russians are buried in this region, which is not as strange as you might think, Dr. Pavlov."

"Why?"

"There was once a strong commercial trade between Russia and Ireland, in flax and horse-breeding. Many Russian families came to live here after the revolution, some of them in this area, about the same time as the Irish fought for their independence from the British. They went straight from the frying pan into the fire, so to speak."

"I never knew. Was this man one of them? Did you know him?"

Yakov's fingers caressed the grave's smooth granite. "You could say that. I met him shortly before he died. Uri Andrev was a truly remarkable man, Dr. Pavlov. Someone who changed history. What's even more remarkable is that hardly anyone knows of him. His name is lost in the fog of time."

"I don't get it. What's it all got to do with the remains of the woman?"

Yakov looked back at me and his watery eyes blazed with a sudden zeal. "It has everything to do with it. In fact, perhaps it's fitting that we should begin our meeting here, in this very graveyard, Dr. Pavlov."

"Why?"

"Because we are standing among secrets and lies, and all of them need explaining."

Briar Cottage faced the distant sea and must have been well over a hundred years old. An oval-shaped metal sign on the wall by the front door was painted black, the name inscribed in decorative white lettering.

The cottage was obviously once part of a large country estate, for to get to it we passed through a pair of ancient granite pillars, each topped with a carved stone lion, their limestone features weathered by the elements.

Across some fields I noticed the ruins of a huge manor house and the crumbling stone walls of what looked like an orchard. We drove along a gravel road that wound through a meadow dotted with massive oaks before we finally arrived at the whitewashed cottage.

It all looked very quaint, with a blue-painted door bordered by a trellis of roses. It commanded a view of the countryside and was protected from the sea winds by rolling hills, rich with the fragrant coconut scent of thick yellow gorse.

It started to rain again as I parked my rented Ford on the gravel outside, next to a dated blue Toyota sedan. A few straw remnants of the cottage's original thatch stuck out from under the black slate, looking like a roughly fitted wig.

I followed Yakov to the door. He was surprisingly agile for his age but I could see the years were taking their toll, his hips giving him trouble. The door was split into an upper and lower stile, as you still sometimes see in parts of rural Europe, and he fumbled with the lock and led me inside.

The cottage was unexpectedly large, with a beamed ceiling and a breathtaking view of the Mountains of Mourne sloping to the sea.

The place looked in disarray. Books, newspapers, and magazines were strewn everywhere, some scattered on a large coffee table in front of the limestone fire mantel, stained black by the years.

Wooden shelves lined the walls, filled with books and stuffed with collections of yellowed newspapers tied together with string. A selection of briar walking sticks were stashed in an umbrella stand in a corner, two ancient armchairs either side of the fireplace; on one of them the fabric on the arms looked paper-thin from wear. A wicker basket was piled high with logs and turf.

The room was a bit cold but a fire was still going. Yakov removed the screen, rattled the sparking embers with a fire iron. He tossed on a few logs and some chunks of turf, replaced the screen, and rubbed his hands.

"The older you get, the more you appreciate a little warmth. Sometimes a summer's day here can be a touch chilly."

"How long have you lived here?"

Yakov went to boil an electric kettle with fresh water. "Over three decades. At first I rented the cottage, then I bought it when the owner died. A nice lady comes by to cook and clean for me." His smile widened, good-humoredly. "We have an arrangement. She cleans my clutter, and when she's gone I make a mess again. Tea?"

"Tea's fine." I noticed black-and-white photographs on the walls. Judging by the clothes worn by the men and women in the images, I guessed the era to be about the time of the First World War, or soon after.

One of the photographs was of a couple. I stepped closer to examine it. A handsome, Slavic-looking man wearing a cloth cap and a striking young woman with long dark hair. They looked happy. The woman's arm linked the man's and they struck a casual pose as they relaxed, smiling, outside a whitewashed property.

At the bottom of the photograph was written in blue ink: *Uri and Lydia, taken by Joe Boyle at Collon, July 2nd, 1918.* My eyes were drawn to the white-painted property behind the couple. The photograph could have been taken anywhere, but then I noticed its half door and a rose bush trellis and I recognized the property I was standing in, Briar Cottage.

Yakov measured three spoonfuls of dried tea leaves into a ceramic pot and blended in the steaming water; a rich aroma filled the room. "In case you're wondering, the cottage was once part of an estate owned by a Russian businessman and his wife, a well-known stage actress from St. Petersburg who found fame before the First World War. Her name was Hanna Volkov—perhaps you've heard of her?"

"I'm afraid not."

"Do you mind if I ask where you got your interest in Russia, Dr. Pavlov? It seems very strong and personal."

"My grandmother came from Ekaterinburg, so I grew up hearing stories about her homeland. Every time she watched the movie *Doctor Zhivago* she'd cry for a week afterwards, if that explains anything?"

Yakov offered a faint smile. "I've heard it can have that effect. Beneath what can seem like an icy exterior, Russians are a deeply emotional people."

"She always said that Lenin's revolution was a fight for the soul of

Russia. That it was a battle between good and evil, between God and the devil, and that for a time the devil won."

Yakov rubbed a hand thoughtfully on his jaw. "Perhaps she was right. It was certainly a brutal battle."

The room spoke of Russia and so reminded me of my grandmother's home. A gleaming lacquered onion doll decorated a bookshelf. A polished nickel-plated samovar stood in a corner and gilded religious icons hung from the walls.

Even the books on the shelves told a story: Waldron's *The End of Imperial Russia*, King's *The Court of the Last Tsar*, Fischer's *Life of Lenin*. I noticed among the shelves countless volumes about the Romanovs, and just as many about Anna Anderson, the mysterious woman whom some claimed to be Anastasia, the tsar's youngest daughter.

"What brought you to Ireland, Mr. Yakov?"

"Many things, all of them personal. I first came as a guest lecturer to Trinity College many years ago and never returned to Russia. But that's another tale." He swept a hand toward the shelves. "I'm happy with my books and my papers for company. It's a quiet life but an absorbing one."

"May I?" I gestured to the bookshelves.

"Help yourself."

I plucked down one of the books and studied the cover. *The Lost World of Nicholas and Alexandra*. I flicked through the pages and glimpsed photographs of a Russia that my grandparents knew, complete with black-and-white photographs of the tsar's family, including his beautiful four daughters and handsome young son. I selected another book, one of the many about Anna Anderson. "You seem to have a keen interest in Anna Anderson, Mr. Yakov."

"No doubt you're familiar with her story?"

"Of course. She was a mentally unstable woman with no papers to identify her who was pulled from a Berlin canal in 1920 and admitted to a psychiatric hospital. She refused to say who she was, but she seemed to have such an intimate knowledge of the Russian royal family that her supporters always claimed she was really the tsar's daughter, Anastasia, who survived the Romanov massacre."

I flicked idly through the book and added, "She also inspired films, a Broadway musical, and numerous books, if I'm not mistaken."

Yakov nodded, hooking his thumbs into the pockets of his waistcoat. "Correct. She was a mysterious, fascinating woman whose existence raised more questions than it answered. Some say those questions persist."

"She was certainly a puzzling character, I'll give you that." I slid the book back and next to it I noticed an ancient copy of Yeats's poems, the tan leather binding scuffed with age. I took it down, opened it, and saw it had been published in 1917. I flicked open a page that was marked with a long thread of brown silk, the page well thumbed. I read some lines.

> *When you are old and grey and full of sleep,*
> *And nodding by the fire, take down this book,*
> *And slowly read, and dream of the soft look*
> *Your eyes once had, and of their shadows deep;*
>
> *How many loved your moments of glad grace,*
> *And loved your beauty with love false or true;*
> *But one man loved the pilgrim soul in you,*
> *And loved the sorrows of your changing face.*

Yakov said, "Do you like Yeats?"

I looked up. "I like this, if only I knew what it meant."

"It can mean whatever you want it to mean, but as always with Yeats there are themes of love and loss, memory and longing. They're melancholic traits the Russians and Irish share, as well as a passion for poetry."

I closed the book, replaced it. "Have you family, Mr. Yakov?"

"There's only me, I'm afraid. My wife and I were never blessed with children."

"You never lost your Russian accent."

"Russia was my home for much of my life. Please, take a seat, Dr. Pavlov." He gestured to one of the worn armchairs by the fire, then filled two glass cups with fragrant, steaming tea.

"Do you need help?" I asked.

"I've managed for many years on my own, since my wife died. I shall manage until my health defeats me. Sugar? Milk? Or cream, as you Americans say?"

"No cream, one sugar. When are you going to unravel this puzzle for me, Mr. Yakov?"

He added sugar to both our glasses and included a few more spoonfuls for himself. Yakov handed over my glass. As I took my seat he slid into the armchair opposite, groaning as he sat. "First, I should tell you more about my background, Dr. Pavlov. My father was Commissar Leonid Yakov, recorded in the history books as a high official in the Bolshevik secret police, the Cheka. Perhaps you've heard of him?"

I went to sip the hot tea but instead lifted my eyes in surprise. "Yes, I have. He had quite a brutal reputation, if I remember correctly."

"For a time my father was among the most feared men in Russia. And with just cause. He did many terrible things." Yakov sipped from his glass and added, "In fact, the grave you just saw, of Uri Andrev."

"What about it?"

"He and my father had a very close personal bond."

"What kind of bond?"

"One that went far deeper than either of them could have imagined. A dark family secret that they unknowingly shared."

"Family secret? I don't follow."

"Andrev's father and Leonid Yakov's mother . . . they once had a relationship. They came from very different classes, you see, but they found great comfort in each other. In fact, they had a child together, named Stanislas, a brother to my father and Uri Andrev, though it remained a secret."

"I'm sorry, you've lost me. Can you explain?"

"All in good time, doctor. You say you found the body?"

"Yes. Along with the locket you mentioned in one of your letters. It was clutched in the woman's hand."

Yakov shook his head and his pale lips trembled slightly. "I'm both relieved and amazed by your discovery, doctor."

I put down my cup. "I can't wait to hear how you knew about the woman. I brought the locket."

His eyes rose. "Did the authorities allow that?"

"Actually, I didn't tell them."

"Dr. Pavlov, surely you know that theft of any artifact in Russia—"

"Is a serious offense, yes, but trust me, I intend to take it back. First I thought you'd want to see it for yourself. I've also brought head-and-shoulder photographs we took of the body, right where we found it."

Yakov said anxiously, "May I see them?"

I handed across a padded manila envelope filled with photographs.

Yakov's yellowed hands trembled as he slid out the color forensic snapshots and carefully spread them on the table. He slipped on a pair of thick reading glasses and picked up the snapshots delicately, one by one, as if they were precious.

He registered the images of the woman's body, shot from different angles. When he finally looked up, his eyes were moist. "May I see the locket?"

I offered it across. "It has the raised Romanov Imperial eagles on the front, as you suggested. There's an inscription on the back but it's corroded and I haven't been able to decipher it. But seeing as you knew about the locket I'm hoping that maybe you can help me there. Do you know what else it says?"

Yakov took the locket almost reverently, as if it were a sacred thing. He studied the corroded metal, turning it over in his palms, the fragile chain cascading down, and this time Yakov's eyes really did fill with emotion.

"Are you okay?" I asked.

"Yes, Dr. Pavlov." His voice sounded hoarse.

"Our discovery at Ekaterinburg obviously means something to you."

"I think you could say that."

"Tell me, how did you know about the locket?" I probed.

"The same way I knew about the woman's body. My father told me."

A thought hit me like a hammer blow and my pulse quickened. "Did your father have anything to do with the Romanovs' execution?"

I remembered seeing Leonid Yakov's name mentioned in the history books, but never in that regard.

To my surprise, his son nodded. "Yes, he did. He was secretly directed by Lenin to supervise their execution. And I must tell you that I've never made that admission to a soul until now."

"Do you know what the rest of the inscription says?"

"I believe I do, Dr. Pavlov."

"Then for heaven's sake, tell me."

Yakov looked away, into the distance, as if he was trying to see something in his mind's eye. But whatever it was, it must have been deeply personal because he didn't speak. And then for no reason at all that I could fathom he began to cry. Deep, convulsed sobbing that made his shoulders shake. He took out a handkerchief, wiped his eyes. "Please, forgive me."

"Mr. Yakov, there's nothing to forgive. What upset you?"

"The memories of an old man."

"I don't understand. Who was the woman? And what does she have to do with the grave we just saw? There's a connection, isn't there?"

Yakov suddenly looked frail and troubled, completely alone, like an old man close to death and fearful of the prospect. A second later his face changed, and something in his sad expression suggested a small boy who's suddenly gotten lost without his parents. He said quietly, "You're an expert on the Romanovs, aren't you, Dr. Pavlov?"

"More a professional interested party than an expert."

"Then I'm afraid you'd never believe what I have to say."

"Why not?"

Yakov's voice lost its frailty. "Because the accepted history of what happened the night the Romanovs died is a huge conspiracy."

"That's a very bold statement, Mr. Yakov."

"I can prove it."

I looked at him, bewildered. "If that's true, have you ever discussed this claim of yours before now?"

Yakov's eyes blazed with fervor. "I've tried to many times, but no one would believe me. No more than *you* would believe me without evidence. But now that you've found the bodies and the locket, you have the evidence. I'm an old man, I can't have a whole lot of time left, so I want you to hear the real story, Dr. Pavlov."

"What real story?"

"Of what happened to the Romanovs on the night they disappeared, all those years ago. It's not the story the history books will tell you. There was terrible bloodshed that night, unbelievable brutality and death, that much is certain." He paused. "But there were too many vested interests for the real truth to come out. And when I'm done the entire mystery of Anna Anderson, the woman they called Anastasia, will be explained."

I stared dumbfounded at Yakov. He added, "In fact, if this story began anywhere it began in St. Petersburg in 1917 with an American spy named Philip Sorg."

"I've never heard of Sorg."

"Few people have. Sorg's an enigma, a young man who was in love with the tsar's daughter, the royal princess Anastasia. The couple you saw in the photograph taken outside this very cottage, Uri Andrev and a woman named Lydia Ryan, they were part of it, too. They spent time here together in this very house before traveling to Russia for the rescue."

"What rescue?"

"To save the tsar and his family."

I must have looked shocked as I met Yakov's gaze. "I read about a number of rescue plots, but surely they all came to nothing."

"Believe me, this one was different." Yakov's face ignited. "This one the history books do not record, and with good reason. For you are about to discover something that I did, Dr. Pavlov."

"What's that?"

"That as far as the Romanovs are concerned, the real truth lies hidden beneath mystery, myth, and lies."

PART ONE

THE PAST

2

JANUARY 1918

It was the coldest winter in twenty-five years.

In Paris, a foot of snow fell in a single night and fourteen homeless vagrants perished, their frozen bodies stuck to the city's sidewalks. The tragedy forced the capital's mayor to throw open the metro stations to shelter the destitute from the cruel weather.

Parisians joked grimly that the winter would claim more fatalities than the German shells. The bloody war that raged all over Europe had already claimed seventeen million lives and was being made even more brutal by the freezing climate.

A newspaper reported that on the Western front, ravaged by battles and snowdrifts, a squad of German artillery cut off for three weeks without rations roasted their horses to survive. When the horse meat was devoured, the soldiers boiled and ate their leather saddles.

In Siberia, where the temperature was twenty-five below, Uri Andrev was fighting a different battle as his hunters closed in for the kill.

Shouts and *cracks* of rifle fire echoed as shots ripped through the trees left and right of him. They smacked into the birch trees and kicked up tiny exploding puffs in the snow, but Andrev kept moving, his body racked by exhaustion, his weary legs like rubber in the bone-numbing snow.

He struggled through the woods, fighting for his life, the sound of dogs growing louder, yelps and barks as the animals picked up his scent.

He sucked in frozen lungfuls of air, his chest ablaze, and with every agonizing step he prayed that he would reach the train track. His coarse prison uniform and boots, his only protection from the freezing cold, rubbed like sandpaper against his skin.

A rifle cracked, then another, and shots zinged inches from his head. Gasping for breath, Andrev glanced back. At least two dozen armed guards zigzagged through the woods behind him.

Up ahead he saw the rail tracks curve through a bend in the woods. The shrill whistle blast of a train sounded. Andrev focused on the tracks as the whistle screamed louder. He was less than a hundred yards from the line. He knew that the train was his only hope of freedom. If he could only clamber aboard when the engine slowed rounding the bend.

Eighty yards.

Seventy.

Shots buzzed past him like crazed bees.

Sixty.

Fifty.

Andrev kept moving, each footstep an agony in the heavy snow, his body on fire with so many pains that it felt as if a thousand daggers slashed at his flesh.

Another volley of shots slammed into the trees to his right.

And then it happened.

One moment Andrev was running, the next his legs threaded air as the ground disappeared beneath his feet and a vast hole appeared in the earth. He let out a cry, lost his balance, and sank into the abyss like a rock.

He landed hard on his shoulder in an open pit and heard the crack of bone. Andrev's shoulder was on fire with raw pain. He struggled to untangle himself from what felt like branches of deadwood.

To his horror Andrev saw that the tangle of branches was a mass of frozen human corpses.

He was lying in a huge pit where the camp guards disposed of the dead—hundreds of rotting bodies, their limbs meshed in an obscene tapestry. He struggled to haul himself out of the pit as the forest again thundered with gunfire and barking dogs. As he climbed out, agony in his shoulder, Andrev again heard the shrill whistle.

A black train with a huge red star on its front belched steam as it thundered round a bend in the woods, like a massive steel snake on tracks. His heart lifted and he started toward the tracks.

Behind him in the woods he never saw the guard kneel and take aim.

A rifle exploded and the bullet punched Andrev like a hammer blow, sending him flying forward into the gruesome pit, and then there was only darkness, silent, empty, painless darkness.

The black train with a red star painted on the front and red flags fluttering from its carriages screeched to a halt with a squeal of brakes.

Steam billowed from its engine as one of the carriage doors snapped open. A stern-faced man with hard blue eyes and blond hair jumped down, brandishing a Nagant revolver. He wore an ankle-length leather trench coat, scarf, gloves, and an officer's leather peaked cap.

He saw the guards run forward out of the woods, readying their rifles as they approached the pit. One was a brutal-looking sergeant with a Slavic face, a Cossack *nagaika* whip coiled from a leather uniform belt around his waist. He aimed his rifle at the unconscious prisoner and his finger fastened on the trigger.

The officer brought up his right hand and the Nagant exploded once, hitting the sergeant in the left arm; the rifle snapped from his grasp.

"Stop firing. That's an order." The officer raced up to the sergeant and barked, "You idiot. What's your name?"

"Sergeant Mersk, Commissar Yakov." The sergeant wore a grubby sheepskin hat and had a drooping black mustache.

"I gave strict instructions that the prisoner was to be taken alive."

The sergeant, a big, powerfully built Ukrainian, clutched his bloody arm and struggled to his feet, examining his flesh wound. "I—I'm sorry, Commissar. I thought he would escape."

"If he's dead you'll pay with your life." Yakov thrust the Nagant back in his holster and trudged over to the pit's edge. The prisoner was sprawled in the snow among a tangle of rotten corpses. His eyes were closed and fresh blood seeped from a bullet wound in his side. In his filthy prison clothing, his body emaciated and his face unshaven, he was a pitiful sight. Yakov noticed a faint cloud of breath rise from the man's lips.

He snapped at the guards, "He's alive. Get him out of there and be careful. If he dies I'll hold you all responsible."

Half a dozen guards slid down into the pit, their breaths fogging as they lifted out the prisoner and laid him on the snow. Yakov knelt, felt the man's faint pulse. He said to a guard, "Give me your trouser belt."

"Commissar?"

"You heard me. And someone give me a bayonet."

The guards obeyed the order and Yakov used the bayonet to cut away the prisoner's clothing, exposing a bleeding wound. Yakov tore the scarf from his neck, folded the cloth neatly in a square, and used it to compress the bullet wound; then he tied the belt around the prisoner's torso to stem the bleeding.

He snapped his fingers at the sergeant, saying, "Take him back to camp on board my train. And find the medical orderly. I want this man kept alive."

The Ukrainian sergeant sourly clutched his wound. "But the prisoner tried to escape. That's a crime punishable by death."

"I'll say whether he lives or dies. Obey the order or it's you who'll get a bullet."

"Yes, Commissar Yakov."

The sergeant instructed his men and they carried the wounded man to the train. Yakov stared back at where the prisoner's blood stained the snow. He knelt, touched the crimson with his gloved fingers. Anger flushed his face as he stood up again.

The confused sergeant said, "I don't understand, Commissar. Why did you intervene to help this traitor? He's nothing but trouble."

Yakov watched as the man was lifted on board by a group of Red Guards from the train. "The prisoner has a name."

The sergeant's eyes flashed with contempt. "Uri Andrev, an Imperial Army captain and convicted enemy of the state. Do you know him, Commissar Yakov?"

"You could say he's my brother."

3

GERMANY

Nearly two thousand miles away that same morning, the entire north coast of Bremerhaven was smothered by a curtain of mist.

The young woman looked striking as she stood on the bow of cargo frigate *Marie-Ann* and it chugged out of the fog into Bremerhaven harbor.

With her long auburn hair down around her shoulders, in another age Lydia Ryan might have passed for a pirate queen standing at the prow of her ship, were it not for the sensible, warm clothes that she wore—a long, black woolen skirt, leather boots, and a waist-length jacket and blouse that hugged her figure.

She had the Spanish look you see so often in the west of Ireland— pale skin and green eyes. An interesting throwback to the Basques from northern Spain, who settled on the country's western shores thousands of years ago.

The *Marie-Ann* prepared to dock, its propeller dying as the captain cut the engines. The harbor was sealed off by German army troops. Lydia Ryan's work that morning required complete secrecy.

She spotted Colonel Horst Ritter, of German military intelligence, as he watched from the harbor wall. He was about fifty, dressed in an immaculate pressed uniform and pigskin gloves, his knee-high boots polished like glass. Ritter took a deep breath of salty air, twirled his waxed mustache, and allowed himself a smile as he waved to her.

Lydia waved back.

Ritter gave a signal and two trucks with canvas tops reversed toward the edge of the harbor wall. German soldiers jumped down, rolled up the canvas tops, and unloaded wooden crates of arms and munitions onto the quayside.

As the *Marie-Ann*'s crew docked, Lydia climbed up onto the harbor wall using a ladder of metal rungs. "Colonel Ritter, don't they ever give you a holiday?"

Ritter clicked his heels, all charm as he took her hand and kissed it. The young woman had a firm figure and a vivacious look that Ritter always found enticing. "Not when I have important work to do, such as helping you Irish republicans defeat the British. A great pleasure to see you again, Fräulein Ryan."

"The pleasure's all mine, Colonel."

Ritter's English was impeccable and he sighed good-humoredly. "Ach, if only that were really true and I was thirty again. You had a pleasant voyage?"

"Not exactly, considering we spent five days changing flags to avoid the British navy. Still, it had its moments."

"No matter, you made it safely. Your cargo's ready. Two hundred rifles and a hundred thousand rounds of ammunition. There are even a half-dozen Bergmann machine guns thrown in for good measure. Compliments of the Kaiser."

"Colonel, I could kiss that man. I'm even tempted to kiss you."

Ritter threw back his head and laughed. "And I might be inclined to accept, fräulein."

A youthful crew member from the *Marie-Ann* clambered up the metal rungs, clutching a bottle of Jameson whiskey. He had the same handsome dark looks as Lydia and he was no more than eighteen, his cloth cap set jauntily on his head, his cheeks spotted with freckles. He handed the bottle to Lydia. "Paudie says we shouldn't be long loading. Ten minutes at most."

"Good. Go help with the boxes, Finn."

The youth scrambled back down the ladder.

Ritter said to Lydia, "There's a certain resemblance, if I'm not mistaken?"

"My youngest brother." She handed Ritter the Jameson. "A small gift by way of saying thanks. I hope you like Irish whiskey, colonel?"

Ritter examined the bottle and gratefully touched his cap in salute. "I certainly do. I'll enjoy it." He nodded toward an empty stretch of the harbor, his face more solemn. "You're in a hurry so I'll not detain you long. Will you join me for a brief stroll?"

"If I didn't know better, I'd say that invitation sounded a touch ominous."

Ritter took her arm. "I'm afraid so. I have some bad news."

Lydia allowed Ritter to escort her along the harbor. There was no breeze, the sea mist lingering, and suddenly she felt very tired, the stress showing in her face.

Ritter removed his pigskin gloves. "After a week of sharing cramped quarters with a crew full of men, you must be longing for a hot bath and some privacy."

"You read my mind, Colonel."

"This is the third smuggling run you've carried out in seven months. I'm surprised you've lasted this long without being caught by the British."

"You know us Irish. We'll risk taking weapons from the devil himself."

Ritter smiled. "Not that we Germans can complain. Your rebels will tie up British troops and keep them from our front lines."

"What's this bad news, Colonel?"

"I've received reports from our Kriegsmarine that the Royal Navy is very active in the Irish Sea. The British appear to be working even harder to prevent you from smuggling arms."

"Don't worry, our captain is used to playing cat-and-mouse with their navy."

Ritter slapped his pigskin gloves in his palm. "I'm sure. But remember what happened to your comrade Roger Casement when he smuggled our rifles?"

"The British hung him as a traitor."

Ritter nodded. "They'll do the same to you if you're not careful, and it won't matter that you're a woman. They may not even give you the benefit of a trial—just a bullet in the back of the neck to simplify matters."

"Why the sudden concern?"

"I don't want to lose you, Fräulein Ryan. Neither, I'm sure, do your fellow republicans, or that young brother of yours. So I've arranged for one of our submarines to shadow your vessel all the way to the Irish coast. If you encounter trouble, the U-boat captain will do his best to take care of it."

"I appreciate it, Colonel, as I'm sure the crew will." Lydia Ryan observed that the *Marie-Ann's* cargo was almost loaded. "And now, if there's nothing else?"

"Actually there is. It's about the prisoner you asked me to check on."

Lydia Ryan halted, her expression changing instantly. "What about him?"

"I checked our lists of British forces prisoners-of-war in at least two dozen of our POW camps and so far there's no report of an Irishman named Sean Quinn among our captured enemy. Or at least no one who matches the age, background, and description you gave."

"You're certain?"

"Absolutely. I'm truly sorry, fräulein."

Lydia's face was crestfallen. "Not your fault, Colonel. At least you tried."

"I take it the man was a close friend or relative?"

"Yes."

Ritter frowned. "I don't understand. He's British forces, yet you're a rebel fighting the crown?"

"A long story, Colonel, one meant for another day. And now, I really better be getting back."

As they turned to walk toward the *Marie-Ann,* her cargo loaded, Ritter said, "Please. I have a gift for you, too. One good turn deserves another."

He slipped a hand into his uniform pocket and removed a small, shiny black Mauser pistol with polished walnut grips. "Something to help you if ever you find yourself in a difficult situation."

Lydia accepted the pistol. "I'll take all the weapons I can get. You certainly know how to impress a lady, Colonel. Most men do it with flowers or chocolates, but you Germans are nothing if not kind *and* practical."

Ritter touched her arm fondly, then stepped back, clicked his heels. "I mean it, I'd hate to lose you. Bon voyage, until the next shipment."

"If the devil doesn't get me first."

Ten minutes later, from the stern of the *Marie-Ann*, Lydia watched Ritter standing on the harbor wall. He gave her a final wave before he disappeared like a ghost into the sea mist. She shivered, a hollow ache in the pit of her stomach after hearing Ritter's news.

A noise sounded above the brittle clanking of the engine and she turned. Her brother stepped out of the wooden wheelhouse, where the captain was busy steering his way out of port.

Finn came up beside her and removed his cap to reveal a head of thick black curls, innocence in his youthful features that made him so appealing to the girls. "Well? What did the German officer say? It was about Sean, wasn't it?"

"Is it that obvious?"

"It's written all over your face. Did he have any news or hold out any hope?"

"No news. But there's always hope, Finn."

Her brother shook his head. "He's not coming back now, Lydia. You have to face up to it. I know Sean was the love of your life, but he's been missing in action for over three years. You'd have heard by now if he was a prisoner." He touched her arm, more than genuine fondness in the gesture, a reverence almost. "You have to move on with your life."

"Sean was reported as missing, not dead. They'll find him one day, I know they will."

"But Lydia—"

A sudden anger rose up inside her and combined with all the pent-up tension of the last week at sea. "No, I won't accept the worst. We know nothing without the proof. Now go tell Dinny that we'll have a German U-boat shadowing us all the way home; it'll be a comfort. And be quick about it."

Finn hesitated. "You really need to get some rest, you know that? You're on edge. You haven't had a proper night's sleep in almost a week. Go down below and try to shut your eyes while you can. One more thing."

"What?"

"I love you, Lydia Ryan, despite your faults. You're still *mo cushla,* as Dad always says." Finn winked impishly, using the old Gaelic term of endearment that always softened her heart. *Mo cushla*—"You're the breath of me, the beat of my heart."

She smiled back despite herself, her anger diminished. "Go on with you. I'll be along shortly."

Finn moved toward the wheelhouse. She watched him go and was immediately sorry for her outburst. There was a time when her heart was large and gentle and kind, but the war, of course, the war with all its ravages and deep valleys of hurt, had made her temper quicker and her heart much smaller and harder.

She became aware of something heavy in her right hand—it was the small black Mauser that Ritter gave her. She hitched up her skirt, exposing her legs, and tucked the Mauser into the top of her right ankle boot.

Just then the *Marie-Ann* cleared the harbor and a wind gusted out of nowhere, making her shiver.

The fog disappeared and the infinite gray enormity of the Baltic stretched to the horizon. For some reason she felt utterly and completely alone. "Where are you, Sean Quinn? Curse you for not being here when I need you most."

As quickly as it came, her grieving plea was snatched away by the wind, lost in the cold, uncaring vastness of the Baltic.

Lydia wiped her eyes, straightened her skirt, and went down below.

4

***

The city looked like hell on earth, a place gone mad.

It was spring but winter's glacial hand still clutched the streets of the ancient settlement built by Peter the Great—huge, dirty chunks of frozen water clogging every avenue and pavement.

There were plenty of signs of war, of course, and Philip Sorg missed none of them as his hired horse-drawn droshky headed west, past the chaos of St. Petersburg's sprawling slums and their endless lines of dirty gray laundry hanging from balconies.

Sorg took mental note of the piles of sandbags outside important public offices and the propaganda posters that adorned lampposts and walls. He paid attention to which streets were pockmarked with holes from artillery shells and where the bloodred flags of revolution fluttered from the tsarist buildings that once managed the vast Russian Empire, stretching from the Baltic to the Pacific.

He observed the number of motorcars and trucks—very few apart from those commandeered by rowdy gangs of Red Guards—and the numbers of dead horse carcasses and bodies on the streets. He counted people in queues outside grocery stores—they always numbered in the hundreds, if not thousands. He even noted slogans daubed on walls: "Land and Freedom." "Long Live the Workers." "Victory or Death."

In a country in the grip of revolution's turmoil, racked by fighting between Bolshevik Reds and tsarist Whites, each trying to gain supremacy, Sorg noticed that children avoided school just as much as civilians avoided making unnecessary trips, for there was more than the occasional boom of artillery and the crack of sniping in the streets.

Sorg noticed such things. He was far more observant than the average foreign businessman who had made St. Petersburg his home in hope of prospering in the chaos of a civil war.

But then Philip Sorg was no ordinary businessman.

"Less than two hours if we're lucky, sir." The coach driver cracked his whip on his horses' flanks as they picked their way along the slushy highway leading out of the city, the snorts of the huge animals misting the air.

"Thank you, comrade." Sorg tipped his Trilby hat and pulled up the thick collar of his long black Chesterfield coat against the freezing March morning.

His journey should have taken no more than forty minutes by steam train but the previous night the train drivers' union declared a strike until midafternoon, so Sorg was forced to hire a carriage for the outward journey. As it passed a bakery with a long queue of hungry people, his attention was drawn by screams and shouts of angry pain.

Sorg stared in horror as two starving women tried to kill each other over a loaf of bread. The brawl lasted only long enough for the women to punch and bite, and tear out hair, until the pitiful loser left the street in tears, clutching a sore head and dragging her two crying children behind her.

They were gone into the crowded backstreets before Sorg could climb out of the carriage and pursue them—he wanted to give the pitiful woman a handful of coins. Everywhere in Russia, it seemed, starving people were scavenging for survival.

It was easy to understand why. A pound of butter cost a day's wages. A loaf of bread—if you could find a bakery open—cost almost as much. Trams ran only intermittently. Among a hungry population, prostitution and theft were rife. Sorg included all this in his secret reports to Washington, the minute and intimate details of a city's life, the kinds of things that mattered to a spy in a foreign country.

Unusual things—like the fact that despite the revolution, or because of it, foreign visitors were everywhere. The hotels and backstreets were crowded with an odd assortment of people—well-intentioned aid workers come to help alleviate food shortages, and international revolutionaries and communists desperate to offer their support. Still others were newspaper correspondents or foreign businessmen hoping to make a quick profit in the turmoil.

Over an hour later as Sorg's carriage *clip-clopped* past a huge village mansion he witnessed more turmoil—the building being ransacked by a looting mob. Peasants dragged out their spoils: chairs and paintings, tapestries, even plumbing. One cackling old woman hauled out a wooden toilet seat, wearing it around her neck like fair-day prize, while the crowd fell about laughing.

It was common knowledge that Scandinavian antique dealers scoured the city for bargains as the great houses of the rich were plundered. The wealthy former occupants were gone, fled into exile with whatever jewelry and valuables they still possessed.

Those who didn't care and still had money whiled away their time in the beer halls or nightclubs where gypsy bands played, or in smoky gambling casinos. St. Petersburg and Moscow had taken on decadent, wild atmospheres.

"We're here, sir."

Sorg came out of his daydream as the horses snorted and the carriage drew to a halt. He looked around him. Tsarskoye Selo never failed to awe him.

Whenever he thought of Russia, Sorg thought of this city built by Catherine the Great. It was a testament to her vanity, a stunning concoction of imperial grandeur. Cobbled lanes, postcard-pretty wood-framed houses painted amber and duck-egg blue, gilded Orthodox churches with cupolas. The kind of fairy-tale Russia his father used to get sentimental for when he drank too much vodka. This despite the fact that Sorg's mother was only too glad to leave Russia when the tsar's brutal pogroms slaughtered Jews wholesale and made countless millions of them homeless refugees.

At the end of a broad avenue Sorg spotted the pièce de résistance— the grand Alexander Palace, the tsar's summer residence, sixteen miles from St. Petersburg, with its magnificent wedding-cake colonnades.

So close, so very close.

He clutched his worn leather Gladstone bag, climbed down from the cab, and handed the driver a silver coin. "Thank you, comrade."

The driver took it, kissed the silver, and grinned as he tucked it in his pocket. "Thank *you,* and good day, sir." He snapped his reins, turned his carriage round, and the horses' *clip-clop* faded in the mushy snow.

Sorg began to perspire with a rush of adrenaline.

He was slim, of average height, with quick brown eyes and a well-trimmed beard. The one imperfection to his neat figure was his left leg. It was an inch shorter than the right. Sorg suffered the usual cruel childhood jibes: *Rabbit, Jumpy, Clubfoot.*

But he remembered the day when he was four years old that his father, a music hall musician and a practical-minded man, employed a remedy: seated at the kitchen table, with a sharp knife and a block of leather, his dada shaped an inch-thick sole and nailed it to his son's left shoe. It moderated his limp but ironically made the physical imperfection appear more like a swagger, because Sorg's hip had shifted to counter his deformity. Still, it was a trait Sorg came to gratefully prefer.

"How does that feel, Philip?"

"Much better, Dada. I feel like a real boy now."

Years later, Sorg was certain he deciphered the watery reaction in his father's eyes that day: love and pride, and pity that all he could do to ease his son's affliction was add an inch of leather to his shoe.

Sorg adored his father.

Another childhood memory haunted Sorg.

He was ten. One winter's evening a group of men in dark uniforms smashed down the door to his parents' one-room apartment. They were led by a sinister-looking thug with a milky stare in his left eye and a shiny bald head, his skin so pale that it looked bleached white. He wore a long black overcoat and seemed to enjoy inflicting punishment. In his right hand he gripped a brutish-looking brass knuckle-duster.

To this day, Sorg remembered the sneer on the man's hate-filled face after he kicked in their door and flashed his identity card. "Kazan— secret police, the Ochrana. Keep your hands where I can see them, you Jewish socialist muck. We'll teach you to raise trouble."

Forever after, Kazan's face lived vividly in Sorg's nightmares.

His expression was a study in pure evil, and he laughed as he savagely beat Sorg's father with the knuckle-duster, then dragged him away despite his mother's desperate pleas. Sorg's mother was beaten, too. Her pregnant stomach kicked, her body pummeled with blows.

Sorg never saw his father again.

Ahead of him now was a broad avenue with wrought-iron gaslights that led up to Alexander Palace, a brisk ten-minute stroll away. His lodging house was less than that. Carrying his bag, Sorg began to walk.

It was hard to believe that the Romanovs—the tsar, his wife, young son, and four princess daughters, including Princess Anastasia—were prisoners here. But Sorg was about to change all that, and the irony wasn't lost on him.

He was going to help rescue the tsar, the very man his father despised.

As Sorg walked east, the elegance of the graceful streets faded and he came to a deserted, cobbled courtyard of wood-and-brick townhouses.

The homes were once occupied by minor court officials. Here and there they bore the bullet-mark scars of civil war. Some were in ruin and boarded up.

He saw a big, fleshy-looking man with hunched shoulders shoveling snow from the footpath of one of the townhouses. He wore a fur-collared coat and gloves, and he slinked over. "Mr. Carlson, you're back. Keeping busy, I hope?"

"I'm trying to. And you, Mr. Ravich?"

The landlord grinned crookedly. "It's hard to get help these days, Mr. Carlson. My groundsman left me to join the Reds. By the way, the council may turn off the water supply for a time to carry out repairs."

"I'll remember that."

The landlord had bad teeth, a long, thin nose, and crafty eyes. He had once been an officer in the tsar's navy, or so he told Sorg, and boasted that he owned four of the townhouses along with valuable commercial property in St. Petersburg. Sorg was his last remaining tenant in the crescent and the landlord seemed fearful the Reds would seize his property.

Sorg didn't trust him, was convinced that he was some kind of degenerate. "I better catch up on work," Sorg suggested.

"Of course, Mr. Carlson. Back to the salt mines for me also. Any problems, let me know." The landlord returned to shoveling snow.

Sorg climbed half a dozen steps to one of the townhouses, took a key chain from his pocket, and opened the two locks on the solid oak door. He stepped into a cold, sparse hallway.

The two-room apartment with threadbare lace curtains comprised a front room that doubled as a bedroom, and a grimy kitchen. The dwelling was shabbily furnished, lacked a woman's touch, and the air's damp smell suggested it hadn't been lived in much. It was perfect for Sorg's needs.

The landlord believed that he was a Swedish antiques dealer who traveled for most of the week. In fact, much of the time Sorg was a guest in one of St. Petersburg's few remaining decent hotels, the Crimea.

He stepped into the kitchen, put down the Gladstone on a rickety old table. He turned on the water faucet and let it run before filling the kettle—at least the pipes hadn't frozen. He struck a match and ignited the gas cooker. While the kettle boiled, he undid his Gladstone bag and removed a screwdriver.

He turned and opened a green-painted cupboard door. His eyes settled on a wood panel at the back of the cupboard. Using the screwdriver, he removed four screws and pried out the panel. Behind was a cubbyhole. He slipped both his hands inside and hefted out two canvas waterproof bags.

He undid the slim ropes that bound one of the bags—inside were stacks of banknotes, Russian rubles, English sterling, Swiss francs, and American dollars. His stash looked intact. He retied the bag and replaced it in the cubbyhole.

He carried the second canvas bag into the front room, laid it carefully on the table, and untied the rope. Nestled in a gray blanket was a complete brass Kriegsmarine spyglass—the Germans made the best telescopes. The spyglass was at least thirty years old but a perfect piece of workmanship. Sorg screwed together the tripod legs and attached the spyglass on top.

He heard the kettle boil. He returned to the kitchen, made a pot of tea, and poured steaming amber into a glass, using a spoon to stop it from cracking, and then moved back to the front room. Pulling up a chair beside the tripod, he opened his overcoat and sat, placing a packet of cigarettes and a cheap metal ashtray on the floor beside him.

Beneath his coat he wore a dark wool suit, his high stiff collar and slim tie covered by a thick wool scarf that didn't stop him from shivering. He rubbed his hands, then gently parted the window's lace curtains no wider than his palm.

The striking scene that spread before him was the reason Sorg had chosen this lodging. The room had a clear view of the Alexander Palace. He lined up the telescope to face the palace's rear gardens. Adjusting the focus, he saw bare birch trees, the grounds deserted apart from a few armed guards idly strolling the snowed paths.

Sorg took a leather-bound notebook from his pocket and laid it on the floor. He always used his own coded shorthand, so if anyone else read the pages they would read gibberish. A sharpened lead pencil was ready in his top pocket alongside a black fountain pen. He removed the pen, balanced it in his palm.

The six-inch fountain pen was a remarkable device—the nib made of Toledo steel, sharp as a scalpel, a covert weapon supplied by the State Department. Remove the cap and you had a lethal edged blade that could write exquisitely just as easily as it could slit a man's throat.

Sorg tapped the blade against a silver band he wore on the second last finger of his left hand. The ring flashed in the light: a small symbol was inscribed on the bottom of the band.

A reverse swastika—an ancient Tibetan mark of good fortune. But the simple piece of jewelry symbolized so much more.

Sorg replaced the pen and checked his pocket watch: 11:45 a.m. Soon he could begin his work. He felt anxious.

As he put away his watch he felt the bulge in his pocket.

He rummaged and removed a small brown pharmacy bottle with a glass stopper. Laudanum tincture. A blend of nine parts alcohol to one part cocaine, commonly sold in pharmacies without prescription. It was becoming harder to find in Russia these days, along with everything else.

It would be tempting to take a few drops to settle his nerves but he resisted. He needed to conserve his supply. Tea and cigarettes would have to do. He replaced the bottle in his pocket.

He lit a cigarette, sipped his tea, and settled down to wait.

And his mind turned to the first time he visited another Romanov palace and encountered the most spirited young woman he had ever met . . .

5

Sorg would never forget the gala evening at the Peterhof Palace.

The ballroom was full of so many desirable, beautiful women, and they looked stunning in their jewels and fine silks. He found so much beauty almost intimidating, and clutching a glass of Burgundy and dressed in his formal evening suit with tails, he left behind the sound of Strauss waltzes and wandered through gilded palace rooms.

Chandeliers sparkled from a thousand reflections, and centuries-old Bokhara rugs and oil paintings adorned the walls.

Tall negro servants, wearing colorful turbans and robes, came and went carrying silver trays of food along richly carpeted corridors.

It struck Sorg as an obscene irony—streets away in St. Petersburg existed the most deprived slums. Huge tenement blocks where families paid a third of their wages to landlords. Where factory workers lived ten to a room. Men who worked twelve-hour days, with only Sunday afternoons to rest.

Sorg wandered along a corridor dripping with chandeliers. After he'd spent a month in the capital, his palace invite was arranged with the help of the American ambassador. It was meant to be an intelligence-gathering exercise as much as a way of introducing Sorg's face to St. Petersburg society.

Such sumptuous events attracted the usual crowd—dukes, duchesses, princes of royal blood, ambassadors and diplomatic staff, wealthy businessmen with muttonchop whiskers, and the idle champagne set—including the sinister monk, Rasputin.

Sorg spotted him swanning around drunkenly with a bunch of titled married women in tow. The monk's bad teeth, long greasy hair, and coarse laugh didn't seem to deter the ladies' fascination.

As he passed a room Sorg heard the sound of music and stepped in. A young woman was seated at a gleaming Steinway, playing the opening movement from Tchaikovsky's First Piano Concerto.

Dark auburn hair trailed down her back in waves, her pale classical beauty complemented by the modest, pastel blue silk dress she wore. A lush figure seemed ready to blossom beneath the silk's sheen. She looked ravishing. Sorg guessed that she was no more than sixteen or seventeen, but with her high cheekbones and determined mouth, she had a self-assured look.

She played with such joyful intensity that Sorg felt himself captivated. She must have sensed his presence, for she stopped and turned to face him. Sorg put his glass down and clapped.

The young woman eyed him uncertainly and fingered a simple pearl choker around her neck. "I can't believe that deserved applause. Do you like Tchaikovsky?"

Sorg said, "If you'd asked me five minutes ago, I would have said no. But I think you've made me a convert."

Her eyes were striking, cornflower blue. He was never good with the opposite sex, always found them a challenge, but for some strange reason this young woman made him feel at ease. Maybe it was the spark of mischief he saw in her eyes.

She swung round on the piano stool and smiled. "You're far too kind. Conrad says I need to practice more."

"Conrad?"

"My piano tutor, but he's an idiot. He's threatening to leave Russia, says it's getting far too dangerous with all the rioting."

Sorg joined her at the piano, making a deliberate effort to mask his gait. "He could have a point."

The young woman considered. "He also says that the tsar may soon be a prisoner in his own palace while the Reds and the Whites fight it out in the streets. Would you agree?"

"I'm afraid I wouldn't know. Does such a thought worry you?"

"It's certainly troubling. Do you *really* think I played well?"

"Yes, but you could always do better. Try a little more *allegro con spirito*. You can't do Tchaikovsky justice without as much passion as possible."

A spark glinted in the young woman's eyes but vanished just as quickly, as if she was amused by the slim young man in front of her who walked with a cocky swagger. "You're an expert, are you?"

"That's debatable. May I?" Sorg leaned across and played the same movement with a flourish, his fingers moving deftly over the keys, before he ended the piece with remarkable vigor. He looked down at the young woman and smiled. "Why don't you try playing it that way?"

His face was close to hers and he could smell her lavender fragrance. She looked impressed. "H—how on earth did you ever learn to play like *that*?"

Sorg picked up his wine and sipped. "Lessons from the age of four helped."

"Can you give me any other advice?"

He smiled. "Always make sure that the lid over the keyboard is open before you start to play."

She giggled. "Now you're being funny."

"My father used to say that."

"Was he a musician?"

He nodded. "Most of my family, too. Poor ones, though. They worked the music halls of Moscow and St. Petersburg."

"That must have been interesting. But four seems awfully young."

"I think we try to make up for our shortcomings in different ways. Maybe I wanted to impress."

"Pardon?"

"I'm just prattling. I was invited to join an orchestra after music college. I managed to stay a year until it taught me a valuable lesson."

"What was that?"

Sorg smiled. "That living the rest of my life as a member of an orchestra would bore me to tears. So business replaced the piano, I'm afraid. It's a lot more interesting."

The young woman stood and put a hand gently on his arm. He felt a stab of electricity at her touch.

"What a shame, it was obviously music's loss. Could you teach me how to play like that?"

As their eyes met, Sorg felt a flash of attraction. It was absurd. He was at least ten years her senior but felt captivated. With her auburn hair, blue eyes, and vivacious personality, he thought she was the loveliest creature he had ever seen.

"Why not? But you'd have to put in the effort."

"Don't worry about that. My sisters say that I'm the wild one in the family and do everything with a passion. By the way, your Russian is excellent, but is that a slight accent I detect?"

"I'm an American citizen. My mother and I left Russia when I was a child."

"My papa says the Americans are going to be the most powerful nation in the world someday. What's your name?"

"Philip Sorg."

"I insist on hearing you play again, Mr. Sorg. In fact, seeing as my tutor's lost his nerve and thinks Russia is doomed, I want you to teach me how to play as well as you did, assuming you'd consider giving lessons."

"I'd consider it an honor."

She noticed the silver ring on his finger. "Are you a married man, Mr. Sorg?"

"No, a bachelor."

A door opened and a young woman stepped into the room. Sorg saw a striking family resemblance—the same lush hair and porcelain features. The woman said, "There you are, you imp! Mama says you're to return at once to the ball. People are asking for you."

"Tell her I'll be there soon."

The older girl offered Sorg an exasperated grin. "Whoever you are, sir, will you promise me that you'll make sure my sister returns to the ball at once?"

"I promise to do my best."

"Just remember, or Mama will get cross." The sister left.

The young woman smoothed her dress. "Don't mind Olga, she's a bossy boots. Still, I better be getting back. May I have your business card, Mr. Sorg?"

Sorg rummaged in his waistcoat pocket. "Won't you have to ask your parents' permission to allow me to tutor you?"

"They'll give it once I tell them what a brilliant pianist you are. But first they'll have your credentials investigated."

"Investigated?"

Mischief flickered in her eyes. "Tell me if you have done any bad things or that you are wanted by the police or suchlike, Mr. Sorg."

"Not that I know of." He handed over a handwritten copperplate business card.

The young woman studied it and moved to the door. "It says your address is the Hotel Crimea and that your business is import and export?"

"Mostly in precious metals, but I deal in anything that turns a profit. May I ask your name?"

The young woman's smile broadened. She looked lovely when she smiled. "Call me Anastasia," and with a flourish she was gone, racing down the hall.

6

Sorg snapped out of his daydream. Four armed guards stepped out through a pair of French doors onto the snowy palace lawns.

He tensed, watching through the telescope. Behind the guards came the Romanov family. Sorg's heart twitched, as if someone slipped a dagger between his ribs.

The last to appear was Anastasia. She clutched the family's black-and-white pet dog, Jimmy, before she let it down to romp in the snow. Her hair fell about her shoulders, a white scarf bundled at her neck. Sorg should have recognized her that day from royal photographs he'd seen but she seemed so much older: the girl in the images looked like a child. Up close, Anastasia looked like a young woman.

Her piano tutor Conrad's prediction had come true. Within months, the tsar abdicated and his family was placed under armed guard, confined to the Alexander Palace at Tsarskoye Selo, while Kerensky's government clung to power by a thread, embattled on all sides: socialists, Mensheviks, and Reds jostling to seize control as the country veered toward bloody civil war.

Sorg watched now as Anastasia and her elder sister, Olga, made snowballs and threw them at their sisters, Tatiana and Maria. Anastasia wore what looked like one of her father's coats. It was at least several sizes too big for her and it made her look vulnerable.

Sorg tore away his gaze as the former tsarina and her husband strolled toward a bench and sat. As usual the ex-tsar carried his thirteen-year-old invalid son, Alexei, in his arms. He settled the child on his knees, holding him close.

Anastasia told Sorg once that her family was in constant fear of Alexei bleeding to death. Her family—except her father—believed that Rasputin miraculously helped lessen Alexei's blood disease. Sorg found it impossible to accept that the mad, drunken monk at the ball could help anyone.

But Rasputin was dead now, poisoned and shot by his enemies, and then dumped in the Neva River.

Sorg watched Nicholas tenderly stroke his son's hair. The man seemed such a contradiction. Sorg could never forget the newspaper photographs his father showed him of Jewish children, infants among them, butchered during the tsars' pogroms. Sorg's own relatives were victims. Was it hardly surprising that the revolution was led mostly by Jews, Lenin included?

Sorg shifted his focus back to Anastasia. She and her sisters play-fully cavorted in the snow. *It's so absurd,* Sorg reminded himself. He was a grown man of twenty-six, a cynical Brooklyn Jew who scoffed at love. Anastasia Romanov was sixteen, a deposed Romanov princess. Was it wrong for him—a grown man—to care for someone so young? But even if he despised everything her father stood for, this young woman aroused in him the warmest of feelings.

As he watched her, he thought: *I didn't foresee this happening. I didn't foresee falling helplessly in love. I never thought that I would need your company, long to kiss you; ache for you to come and lie beside me at night. I never imagined that I would be terrified of never seeing you again.*

It troubled him to think what his own father would say. A man who hated royalty with a vehemence.

Yet Sorg recalled that after each of his piano lessons, he found him-self more and more looking forward to his palace visits.

It didn't matter that he used the visits as much to gather intelligence information as for his own pleasure. Sorg convinced himself that much more than a glimmer of attraction passed between him and Anastasia during their first meeting. And as much of a tomboy as she was, he sensed her vulnerability.

As if despite her privileged upbringing—or because of it—she didn't fit in anywhere. That weakness made him want to protect her.

Sorg came alert as the guards ushered the Romanovs toward the palace.

Their exercise period was over. The last to enter the French doors was Anastasia. For a moment she hesitated, as if she was searching for something in the grounds but wasn't quite sure what, and then with a turn of her pretty head she moved back inside the palace doors and was gone.

Sorg's heart sank like an anchor, as it always did whenever he lost sight of her. He tore his gaze from the telescope. What kept his spirits up was his hope of rescuing Anastasia; that was his mission. He cared nothing for her father. In truth he loathed the tsar, but he had a job to do and it included the ex-tsar and all his family.

He wrote up his notes, recording the time and the family's general appearance along with his impressions. He would wire his encoded report to Helsinki. In due course, via the undersea cable from London to New York, his message would be telegraphed to Washington.

Sorg put away his notebook and pencil and began to disassemble the telescope. He heard a faint sound like a creaking floorboard and turned.

The landlord, Mr. Ravich, stood in the doorway. He wandered in with his crooked grin, removing his gloves, finger by finger. "Ah, Mr. Carlson, I just came to check if everything's all right with the plumbing?"

Sorg asked hoarsely, "How long have you been standing there?"

Ravich tucked his gloves into his pocket. In an instant he replaced them with a revolver that he pointed at Sorg.

"Long enough. I've learned that a surprise visit to new tenants is often enlightening. It does seem I chose my moment well. I hope this experience has taught you something, Mr. Carlson?"

"To keep my door locked in the future."

Ravich's grin widened. "The gun's loaded, by the way. And I'm well able to use it. Are you armed?"

"No."

"We'll see." The landlord circled Sorg, patting down his clothes.

Sorg felt sweat rise on his forehead, his mind turning somersaults.

Ravich finished, then his free hand caressed the shiny brass telescope. "A fine instrument. German, if I'm not mistaken? Are you enjoying a spot of bird-watching, Mr. Carlson, or is it something more interesting?"

"What do you want?"

Ravich pulled back the net curtain. "The view is one of the reasons why I bought this property. I hoped one day it might add value to my investment. Alas, the mess that Russia is in, I fear my hope may be a lost cause."

"What's your point?"

Ravich wandered across the room and peered in at the Gladstone bag on the kitchen table. "I keep asking myself what a man like you is doing with a spyglass pointed at the palace grounds. An innocent act perhaps, but . . ."

"But what?"

"I've kept a discreet eye on you since you rented these rooms. After seeing what I've just seen I'm tempted to presume that you're a spy."

"You presume a lot, Mr. Ravich."

Ravich jerked the gun. "Don't take me for a fool. I worked in naval intelligence for years. You're watching the palace where the Romanovs are imprisoned."

"Where's this all leading?"

Ravich's eyes flashed greedily. "I really don't give a curse who you are or who you're working for. Only that you're sensible enough to come to an arrangement." The landlord rubbed his thumb and fore-finger together in a universal gesture. "You carry on doing whatever it is you're doing and I turn a blind eye in return for a little generosity."

"How do I know I can trust you?"

"You don't. But I think we'd agree things could get messy for both of us by involving the police."

"I have cash in the other room."

Ravich motioned with the gun toward the kitchen. "I'm very glad to hear it. But I warn you—try anything and I'll blow your head off."

Ravich pressed the revolver into the back of Sorg's neck and they stepped into the kitchen. "Where's the money?"

Sorg pointed to the open cupboard and the unscrewed panel lying by it. "In there, in a canvas bag."

"Remove it. Slowly."

Sorg hefted out the canvas. He went to open the bag but Ravich said, "Stop. Place your hands above your head and step away."

Sorg did as he was told.

Ravich used his free hand to loosen the bag string. He rummaged and plucked out a wad of rubles and American dollar bills. Sweat rose on Ravich's brow. "How much is in here?"

"Seven hundred rubles in different currencies."

Ravich licked his lips and his hand dug greedily into the Gladstone. "It's not enough. I'll want more. Much more."

At that exact moment Sorg's fingers grasped at the pen in his breast pocket. Before he could remove the top off the steel nib, Ravich brought up the revolver and it exploded once.

The shot cracked past Sorg's shoulder. He dropped the pen and grabbed for the gun, his adrenaline pumping. The weapon detonated again, gouging plaster from the wall. Ravich was a big, beefy man but Sorg caught him off balance and pushed against him with all his might. Ravich toppled and Sorg fell on top of him and they rolled on the floor.

Ravich gave a pained grunt, rage in his eyes. "I'll kill you!"

Sorg struggled to get control of the revolver, using all his weight to twist the gun toward Ravich's head and slip his finger inside the trigger guard. The gun exploded again, Ravich's skull snapped back, and his eyes rolled open.

Sorg caught his breath. A pool of blood spread behind Ravich's skull. He twitched violently and fell still. Sorg retrieved his pen from the floor and pushed himself up to a kneeling position, his face bathed in sweat.

He examined Ravich. A gaping bullet hole was drilled above his left eye, exiting at the back of his head. Sorg pried the gun from Ravich's fingers. His legs weak, he staggered into the kitchen and threw up into the sink.

When he could vomit no more, he turned on the faucet and rinsed away the mess, and as much of the blood spatter as he could from his clothes. His overcoat and scarf would cover the rest. He opened one of the drawers.

It contained a box of wax candles and a couple of dishcloths. He grabbed a cloth and wiped his mouth. He listened to his heart hammering furiously. It was the first time he ever killed and it made him feel scared, yet exhilarated that he survived.

His survival instinct kicked in and Sorg crossed to the window and stared beyond the curtains. The street was empty. He moved to the front door, opened it gingerly with shaking fingers. The courtyard was deserted.

Ravich had swept it of footprints, except for his own. Sorg's mind worked furiously. If he simply left the body where it lay and disappeared, perhaps Ravich had relatives who would search for him. Sorg couldn't be certain of anything, but knew that he had to move fast and without panic.

He stashed the spyglass telescope and banknotes in the canvas bags and tucked both inside his Gladstone. He screwed up the cubbyhole panel. In the kitchen, a blood pool still blossomed around Ravich's skull. Sorg removed a wax candle from the drawer, took a dinner plate from another cupboard, and returned to the front room.

He struck a match, lit the candle, and dripped enough wax to stick it to the plate. He left the plate on the edge of the table. Sorg wedged open the kitchen door with a piece of folded newspaper. Finally, he buttoned up his coat and donned his Trilby hat. He opened the valve in the cooker, hearing the snake hiss of the gas flow.

He picked up the Gladstone and stuffed Ravich's revolver in his coat pocket. He exited by the front door and when he hit the cold air, Sorg was already drenched in sweat.

Minutes later and a hundred yards along the street, he heard the massive boom of the gas explosion, sending a spear of bright orange flame shooting into the air, the shock wave striking his back with the force of a punch, almost knocking him over.

Sorg held on to his hat and kept walking.

7

The blond-haired man with hard blue eyes and a pockmarked face sat beside Uri Andrev's bed. He wore an ankle-length leather trench coat with a scarf and black leather gloves, his polished boots shining, a Bolshevik party badge on his lapel.

Andrev looked at him as he became conscious and the man's features settled into focus. His face looked older than its twenty-eight years and his coarse skin told of a poor upbringing. Old scar tissue puckered his face, not unlike a boxer who had gone too many rounds in the ring.

They stared at each other with the easy silence of two men who knew each other a long time, until the blond smiled. "Hello, Uri. It's been far too long. Two years at least." His accent was working-class St. Petersburg.

"Leonid. It's good to see you."

"And you." Leonid Yakov studied Andrev, whose dark hair was cropped close to the skull, his face unshaven.

Red welts from malnutrition covered Andrev's face, his skin blotchy with bruises inflicted by the camp guards.

The room was freezing despite a blazing woodstove in a corner, and the blond removed his leather gloves and blew on his hands. Near the door stood two guards in overcoats and fur-lined hoods, rifles slung over their shoulders. One tall, the other a squat, robust figure with bow legs, both their faces hidden by headgear.

Andrev's brow felt on fire, an agonizing throbbing in his left shoulder and side. He was in the camp's sick bay. Sick bay was a joke. It was no more than a filthy wooden shack with a dozen rusting metal beds, vomit-stained floors, coarse blankets, and sackcloth pillows. Disinfectant and rotting bandages stank up the air. A patched sheet hung from a line of rope, all that separated Andrev from a handful of other ill prisoners, their coughing and sputtering a constant background.

"I've got something that might help your pain." Yakov produced a pewter hip flask from his coat pocket. "Here, have some vodka to warm your belly. Put some sunshine into you."

Andrev gratefully accepted the flask, touched it to his cracked lips, and sipped. "What are you doing in this godforsaken place?"

Yakov stood. "All in good time. Some friends want to see you. Zoba, you first."

He beckoned the squat little man with the fur hood. When he came closer, Andrev recognized his dark, Georgian features, a hint of the Asiatic in his wrinkled eyes and powerful physique. His good-humored face was set in a permanent grin. "Hello, Captain."

They shook hands warmly. "Zoba. What are you doing here?"

The Georgian's grin broadened. "I keep asking myself the same question. Four years in the trenches and still able to laugh—the commissar here reckons I need my head examined."

"I'm glad to see you."

"We had some good and bad times serving together, us three." He nodded to Yakov's flask. "Seeing as this is a reunion, I won't say no to some sunshine."

Yakov handed him the flask. "Any excuse."

Zoba grinned, swallowed a mouthful. "There are places in the world a man can die of thirst. In Russia, you're born with one."

Yakov said, "I have another surprise, Uri. Come here, little brother." He beckoned to the other guard, a fair-haired, shy-looking youth who barely looked in his teens, his uniform at least a size too big for him. The young man stepped over and removed his fur hood. "Hello, Uri."

Andrev beamed, his pleasure obvious. "*Stanislas . . .*"

The youth said proudly, "I joined the Red Guards, Uri. I'm a soldier now."

"You can't be, you're not old enough."

"I'm almost seventeen, old enough to carry a rifle for Comrade Lenin."

Andrev said with genuine affection, "What's the world coming to when boys start taking up arms? Come here." He grasped the youth's hand warmly and hugged him. "The last time I saw you was at my father's funeral. You looked as if you were still playing with toys. Now look at you."

Stanislas brandished his rifle. "This has replaced my toys, Uri. All my friends have joined the revolution. Lenin's our God now. Tell him why we're here, Leonid."

Yakov slapped a hand on his brother's hair and ruffled it. "You talk too much, Stanislas. You and Zoba go find something to eat. It'll give Uri and me a chance to catch up."

"I hope you get well soon, Uri."

Andrev fondly gripped both their hands and then Stanislas and Zoba left. When they closed the door, Andrev's face was sober. "How could you let Stanislas join the army, Leonid? We've both seen the horrors of war."

Yakov sat and took a swig from the flask. "I couldn't change his mind. He's like me, impetuous and headstrong."

"Don't let him serve, I beg you."

"I know Stanislas has always been like a kid brother to you. Don't worry, it's why I had him transferred to my unit, to have him under my wing. I'll keep him out of harm's way. Here, drink some more."

"Are you trying to get me drunk?"

"Vodka is all there is to numb your pain, I'm afraid. We ran out of chloroform. *Drink,* it'll help you forget that we're on different sides."

Andrev swallowed a few gulps of the scorching liquid and coughed.

Yakov smiled. "It's the best Siberian vodka, a hundred proof. Here, they use it to fuel storm lamps. The lamp stays alight even in the worst blizzard. The trouble is putting the lamp out afterward."

"Are you trying to kill me?"

Yakov's smile faded and he picked up a damp cloth, dabbed sweat from Andrev's brow. "The sergeant, Mersk, said you were troublesome. He looks like a nasty piece of work."

"Mersk despises everyone. He claims escape from here is impossible."

Yakov shook his head with amusement. "So you decided to give him a run for his money? You always did like a challenge, Uri. Live dangerously, carefully, was always your motto. Remember when we broke out from the German prison camp?"

"I made you trudge for three nights without sleep through heavy snow."

Yakov nodded. "As if that wasn't bad enough, you made me sing those rowdy Cossack marching songs we knew in childhood, just to help me stay awake. You kept me alive, Uri." Yakov added, "By the way, the drunken idiot who calls himself the camp medic tells me that the bullet went clean through flesh. I've dressed it as best I could and used vodka to clean it. But I think your shoulder's dislocated."

Andrev stared at Yakov's black leather coat, a Communist Party badge on his lapel. "Since when did you start working for the secret police, Leonid?"

"I was appointed to the Cheka by Comrade Lenin with the rank of commissar."

"I'm impressed. You never said what you're doing here."

Yakov avoided the question. "Let me take a look at your arm." He examined the limb. "It's definitely dislocated. I'd keep the orderly away, he'd probably make things worse."

Andrev winced. His brow felt feverish, his shoulder scorching with pain. "Set the bone for me."

"You trust me?"

"You saw my father set enough bones in his day."

"True." Yakov tightly twisted the cloth and thrust it at Andrev's mouth. "Here, bite on this and roll onto your good side."

Sweat beaded Andrev's face as he clenched the cloth between his teeth and rolled onto his right side.

"Bite hard, dear friend." Yakov gingerly felt the injured arm, probing for the bone's joint. When he found it he shifted all of his weight onto Andrev's shoulder, grunted and pushed hard.

The bone snapped into place with a sharp crack.

A surge of pain detonated through Andrev's body, and then his eyes rose to the ceiling and he passed out.

■ ■ ■

Yakov crossed to a sink in the corner, grabbed a zinc bucket, and filled it with icy water. He took the cloth from Andrev's limp mouth, drenched the towel in the chilled water, and slapped it onto his face. Andrev came awake, sputtering, his eyes filled with pain. "That hurt, darn you."

"With luck, you'll still be able to play the accordion." Yakov winked and tore the filthy sheet from the rope, all that offered them a curtain of privacy. It exposed them to the patients in the other beds, a half-dozen skeletal-looking prisoners, ill and unshaven. They stared over at the black Cheka uniform. Yakov barked, "What do you think you're looking at?"

The fearful patients looked away. Yakov ripped up the sheet to make a crude sling and draped it around Andrev's neck and under his arm. "It'll have to do for now."

"The train I saw is yours?"

"It's how I travel now, on Lenin's orders. People say I'm his right-hand man. Would you believe it? Me, entrusted by Lenin himself."

"To do what?"

"Hunt down and shoot enemy agents and spies, speculators, and counter-revolutionaries, and anyone who challenges Lenin's authority." Yakov picked up two worn gray blankets from an empty bed nearby and placed them around Andrev. "That should keep the heat in."

"What are you doing in a prison camp miles from anywhere? This can't be just a coincidence, Leonid."

Near the door was a dented wheelchair with a square of rough-hewn wood for a seat and two wheels with rusted spokes. Yakov's face was solemn as he crossed the room and pushed the wheelchair over to Andrev's bed.

"Do you feel up to talking? It's cold outside on the veranda, I know, but at least it's private."

"What's bothering you, Leonid?"

Yakov removed an envelope from his pocket, snapped open a page from inside. The document was authorized at the bottom with an offi-cial-looking red-inked stamp and a scrawl. He lowered his voice. "I've been given an order by Lenin that concerns you, Uri."

"What order?"

Yakov handed him the page. "It's for your immediate execution."

8

Yakov pushed the wheelchair onto the veranda. He sat on the edge of the wooden rail and took a dented metal cigarette case from his coat pocket. "Smoke?"

Andrev silently accepted a cigarette.

Yakov lit them both. He tossed the match in the snow with a faint hiss. They sat in the silence a long time, smoking, their breaths cloudy as they stared out at the camp's ragged jumble of watchtowers, rusting barbed wire, and wooden huts. Wisps of wood smoke smoldered from chimneys; guards marched past with clusters of frail, exhausted prisoners, some in prison garb, others in tattered military uniforms of the tsar's army.

Andrev scratched his stubble and said finally, "Am I permitted to know why I'm being executed? Or do you Reds need reasons these days?"

Yakov blew on the hot tip of his cigarette and stared out at the camp, all around them a wilderness of snow. "A White army battalion is only twenty-five miles away near Perm. They could liberate the prisoners to fight another day. Lenin sees army officers of your caliber as a threat if you're liberated."

"No trial, no military tribunal, just a firing squad. Is that it?"

"You Whites show no mercy to our men, either, Uri. This war is savage."

"Will Lenin execute the tsar as well?"

"He and his family are under house arrest, but their day will come, too."

"You'll kill *all* of them? The entire family?"

Yakov said, "It's inevitable. The party wants to be certain the Romanov bloodline can never hold power again."

"So, you Bolsheviks are even killing children now?"

"Sometimes unpleasant things are necessary for the common good. But it's no more brutal than the behavior of the tsar's secret police in their day."

"You know I despised that kind of thing. I was no blind lover of the tsar."

"Yet you fought for him."

"I was a serving officer. But take my word, your Bolsheviks will destroy this country."

Yakov's face twitched as he removed a photograph from his tunic pocket. "I found this among your clothes. You'll want it back."

Yakov handed over the photograph. Andrev tossed away his cigarette and eagerly clutched the picture of a woman and a young child.

Yakov said quietly, "Nina seems well. And little Sergey looks like you. Family is important to a man."

Andrev looked up from the photograph, as if trying to fight his emotions. "You never remarried?"

Yakov flung away his unfinished cigarette, glanced out at the thick forest that rolled in all directions, and smiled. "An ugly sod like me? What woman would have me? Besides, the party is my mistress."

"And your daughter?"

"Six next birthday, would you believe? The day we stormed the Winter Palace, her mother was one of the first to perish."

"I heard. I'm sorry."

"We all have our crosses. Since then, Zoba's wife helps to look after her."

Andrev studied the photograph of his wife and son and his eyes moistened.

Yakov said quietly, "Answer me a question, Uri?"

Andrev stared back, as if he had trouble holding himself together. "What?"

"If I asked you what would make you happy, what would it be?"

"I think you already know my answer." Andrev looked past the camp, to where the thick woods faded like phantoms. "That I could be with my wife and son again. That I was a free man. That I could wake up every morning next to them, in a place full of hope and not despair."

"What else?"

"Isn't that enough? What was it Chekhov once said? 'We live for love, and for hope and dreams, and for the small things that please us and for little else.' It would be pleasant too if the snow was gone and it was spring again."

Yakov's lips creased. "You're still a romantic, Uri. No doubt you still read poetry. You haven't changed."

Andrev met his stare. "But you have, Leonid. This revolution of yours is a misguided experiment that won't last. It's taken a brutal turn."

"Tell me what revolution hasn't shed blood."

"Lenin promised freedom and liberty, and yet I and countless others are in chains. He swore he'd rid this country of the secret police, yet he creates his own. That isn't a man I can trust. All he craves is power."

"What's your point?"

"People will soon realize that it's all one huge, bloodthirsty mistake. You Reds will kill more innocent people than all the centuries of tsars put together."

Yakov shook his head fiercely, and his face flushed. "On the contrary, I believe that this will be Russia's finest hour."

"Then we must differ, Leonid. A man believes what he wants to believe."

Yakov's smile faded.

Andrev clutched the photograph, his voice thick with emotion. "Sergey is three. Yet I could count on one hand the number of times I've seen my son since the war began."

Yakov softened, put a hand on Andrev's arm. "This battle's been hard on all of us. But what if I told you that you could have all those things you want? What if I told you that you could walk out of this camp a free man? Be with your wife and son and start your life afresh?"

"I'd say that you've been drinking too much."

Yakov said, "I didn't just come here to deliver your death sentence. You and I, we've long been like brothers. We served in the same trenches. My loyalty to you is as strong as ever even though we've chosen different sides in this war. It's a war that has turned the best of friends into the bitterest of enemies, but I refuse to let it do that to us."

"What are you trying to tell me, Leonid?"

"The moment I learned that you were to be executed I went to Lenin. I told him how proud I was to have served with you. I told him how your father was a man of the people, a good doctor who never took a penny from his patients who couldn't afford it."

"Leonid . . ."

"I know, I'm impetuous, but hear me out. Your father was one of the finest men I've ever known. He fed my family, made sure Stanislas and I had proper schooling. He fought hard to save my mother until the TB took her, and then he cared for us like his own after she died. I told Lenin I owed you my life and I begged for yours in return."

"What are you saying?"

"That I came here to offer you your freedom. Lenin agreed to pardon you from execution. But on one condition."

"What?"

"That I convince you to join the Bolshevik cause."

"Join the Reds? Are you insane, Leonid?"

"You don't have to do it with a passionate heart. Pretend if you must. You can be one of my staff. I simply want you to survive. Others have changed sides. Surely you can agree if it means saving your life and that you can be with your wife and son again."

"What about my men?"

A flurry of icy wind blew snow across the compound. Yakov pulled up his coat collar and shook his head. "I was ordered to force-march the prisoners to another camp, two days' walk away. There's nothing I can do for them."

"But for heaven's sake, Leonid, they only have the rags on their backs. They'd never survive the march in this weather."

"I believe that's the idea. Bullets cost money, shoe leather is cheap. Comrade Lenin insists his orders are to be obeyed. He ordered that this camp be burned to the ground when we leave."

Andrev considered. "How did you learn I was to be executed?"

"Nina heard that your lines were overrun near Perm and you and your men were captured. She could find out nothing from the authorities so she made contact with me. When I inquired, I learned about the execution order. Then I went to see Lenin."

Andrev fought his emotions. "How is Nina? And Sergey?"

"Things are not easy for them, naturally, with this war. But your wife and son are surviving. I'll try to help them, with food, or whatever I can."

"I'm grateful." Andrev fell silent for a time. When he spoke again, anguish braided his voice. "How can I turn my back on my men, Leonid? How? They've fought alongside me for years. It's not just my uniform I'd betray, it's my own honor."

Yakov grimly tugged on his cap, leaned close into Andrev's face, his hand on his shoulder. "I know you're a principled man. I know you're loyal. But please, this time you must think of yourself. Think of your family, I beg you, Uri."

"How long have I got?"

"You're to be executed at dawn."

9

Andrev sat on the bed, snow falling beyond the window. He stared at the photograph of his wife and son that lay on his sackcloth pillow.

Not a day passed when he didn't recall when it was taken. He was home on leave one summer and he and Nina took Sergey on the train to Neva beach, outside St. Petersburg. Sergey was a year old and fascinated by the sound of the train's whistle, and every time Andrev mimicked the noise his infant son broke into a fit of giggling.

It was the same day Sergey took his first faltering steps in the sand and collapsed on his bottom, a huge smile of triumph on his face. Nina was so overjoyed that the three of them danced together in the sand. Later on the promenade, they bought ice cream and some stuck on Sergey's nose, which made him laugh, and they had a beach photographer take their snapshot.

It was a happy time.

He and Nina had married a year after he completed his cadetship in the St. Petersburg Military Academy. For him, marrying Nina seemed a natural progression after knowing her since childhood. She always seemed to him like a child in a woman's body. He couldn't help but feel protective of her.

Once he was promoted to first lieutenant he became entitled to a small but comfortable redbrick house in the officers' quarters of his barracks. After two miscarriages, Nina gave birth to Sergey three years later.

A blond-haired boy who had his mother's good looks, he came two months premature. For a time it didn't seem as if he would live, his lungs underdeveloped, but by some miracle he managed to cling to life and thrive.

Fatherhood came easy to Andrev and often while Sergey slept he would stand over his cot and watch him breathing, awed by the powerful bond nature forged between him and his son. But within a month the war came. It was followed by revolution, and the world was turned upside down. The tsar abdicated, the Reds seized power, and Russia was thrown into a bloody turmoil.

The war against Germany had gone badly and hundreds of thousands of Russia's best young men were slaughtered by better-equipped German forces.

The tsar's army split almost down the middle, one half supporting the Whites loyal to the former tsar, the other half siding with the various socialist splinter groups that sprouted all over Russia. One of those minority parties, the Bolsheviks—or Reds—led by Lenin, cunningly chose their moment to seize power and Russia became locked in a civil war. Lenin held Moscow but the rest of the country dissolved into chaos as the White armies and the Reds embarked on a savage guerrilla war.

Andrev felt his emotions rise now and touched the photograph of his wife and son as if it were fragile. Nina's merchant father indulged his only daughter's almost every whim, and her world collapsed once the Reds grasped power and her husband was captured.

Andrev knew that his imprisonment, and not knowing if she would see him alive again, took its toll. He was not even allowed to write to his wife. But the cracks began to show in their marriage soon after he joined his unit.

It was clear Nina wanted a husband, not a soldier who spent more time with his men than he did with his wife. Their intimacy waned; their arguments grew more frequent. Whatever love once existed faded to a ritual that owed more to friendship than passion.

Worse, since the Reds grasped power they seized every White barracks and forced army families out onto the streets.

The last Andrev knew—in a letter he received from Nina before his imprisonment—she and Sergey were living in a cramped one-room flat with damp walls and a communal toilet in a slum building in St. Petersburg. She eked out a living on what little money her father could afford to give her.

It broke his heart not to be with his family. But he wasn't alone. Anyone who opposed Lenin—men, women, entire families—were either executed or sentenced to hard labor in the frozen wastes of Siberia's penal camps.

The average survival rate for camp prisoners was eight months. Many lasted fewer than four, their health broken by grueling work chopping timber, tunneling into dangerous ore mines, or slowly starving to death on a miserable diet of watery soup made from rotten vegetables and gristle. The irony was that the same penal system Lenin once so vehemently denounced, he now used to crush his enemies.

Andrev stared at the image of Nina and Sergey. The question that never left his head returned to haunt him: *What is to become of us?*

He was a long way from the simple, happy life he once knew in St. Petersburg.

When he could bear the pain no longer he tucked the photograph inside his shabby uniform. Somewhere off in the distance he heard the whistle of one of the trans-Siberian trains that passed the camp most days.

It made him think of that summer's afternoon when he and Nina took Sergey to Neva beach, when the ice cream stuck on Sergey's nose and made him giggle, and the simple joy in their hearts as they danced with their infant son in their arms.

The sick bay door burst open and snapped Andrev out of his trance. Two men came in wearing ragged military uniforms. Captain Mikhail Vilsk was a lanky infantry officer, his uniform threadbare, his lips a mass of encrusted cold sores. His left leg had been shattered below the knee by a German bullet and he walked with the aid of a cane.

His companion, Corporal Abraham Tarku, a former jeweler in civilian life, was a battle-hardened soldier from Kiev, who wore wire-rimmed glasses, one of the lenses cracked into a few shards but still in place. A couple of his fingertips were missing, the stumps bearing the blackened telltale signs of frostbite.

Vilsk hobbled over to the bed, taking in Andrev's bandaged wounds. "We thought you'd be nailed into a box by now, Uri. Instead we hear that the guard who wounded you was shot by a Cheka officer. Is it true? How are you?"

Andrev nodded. "I could be a lot worse. And yes, it's true."

Corporal Tarku stepped over to the window, rubbed the fogged glass with the blackened stump of a fingertip. He squinted out through the snow flurries. "The Cheka officer is Leonid Yakov, isn't he, sir? I'd recognize him anywhere."

"Yes, it's Yakov."

"I saw him step down off his train when it pulled into the camp siding, before they took you off on a stretcher."

Vilsk raised an eyebrow. "It seems you've found yourself a guardian angel, Uri. How do you know him?"

Andrev got up from the bed and moved to the window, ignoring his pain. "Yakov served in our unit. He was my sergeant, and a good one."

Corporal Tarku spat on the floor and wiped his mouth with his sleeve. "That was before he went over to the Reds. I heard he's a commissar now. Travels all around the country in that armored train of his, on Lenin's orders, slaughtering our men or sending them to the camps."

Vilsk frowned at Andrev. "Why did Yakov intervene to spare you?"

Tarku added, "He and the captain were once close friends, almost like brothers, isn't that true, sir?"

Andrev rubbed his jaw and thought furiously, snow still falling out on the camp. "That's not important right now. I have dire news and I want your solemn promise you'll keep it a secret for now. You'll understand why when I tell you."

Both men gave their word and when Andrev explained, gloom darkened their faces. Vilsk rummaged in his pocket and found a cigarette butt he had been saving all day. "So, we're all marked for death, aren't we, Uri?"

"It seems that way."

"What about the deal Yakov offered?" Vilsk used a birch twig to light the cigarette from the woodstove, and stuck it between his blistered lips.

"I can't leave my men to die," Andrev replied.

"Yakov's turned out to be a right swine," Tarku said bitterly. "He'd sell his soul for Lenin. And he holds a grudge. The Cossack officer who gave the order to shoot into the crowd storming the Winter Palace when Yakov's wife was killed, he paid the price."

"What are you talking about?"

"They say Yakov hunted him down and killed him with his own sabre."

Andrev peered beyond the snow flurries and could make out Yakov's black train parked in a siding beyond the main gate. "If we could reach Perm and alert our troops, we could lead them back here and storm the camp before dawn, surprising Yakov and the guards."

Vilsk said, "Are you out of your mind, Uri? How do we get to Perm in this weather, let alone escape? It's thirty miles away."

Andrev used a finger to draw a rough map on a fogged pane of glass. "What have we got to lose? The train from Omsk ought to pass here shortly after midnight, weather permitting. It slows as it comes near the camp because of the track's curve. If we could climb on board it would take us within a five-mile walk to our lines in less than an hour."

Vilsk said, "Getting on board the train's impossible. Guards are always posted where it passes near the camp's west gate."

Andrev said, "Leave that to me. I've got a diversion in mind. Just the three of us, though. We don't want a mass breakout alerting the guards."

Tarku said fiercely, "If we can turn the tables and make contact with our troops, we'll hang that swine Yakov."

Andrev said, "Leave him to me."

Vilsk tapped his knee with his cane. "Better go without me, Uri, I'd only be a hindrance."

"Tarku?"

"I'm with you, sir, if you're sure you can hold up."

Andrev came away from the window. "So long as we can get on board the train, a five-mile hike won't kill me. Try and find extra clothes to keep us warm. And weapons of some sort, a knife or cudgel. See what you can find."

"When do we go?"

"Before midnight, when the guard changes. Then we'll take our chances."

10

In his long black overcoat, and with his bald head and black hat, even a glance from Inspector Viktor Kazan could make a man feel guilty.

His left eye was milky white—he'd lost sight in the eye to an anarchist's bomb—which gave him a frightening stare, but his good eye missed nothing as it swept over the fire scene like a searchlight.

In his right hand he clutched and unclutched a heavy brass knuckleduster.

Kazan's nostrils flared, overpowered by the stench of burnt human flesh as he covered his fleshy jowls with a handkerchief. Wearing a high shirt collar and thin black tie, he picked his way toward the burnt-out kitchen, a mess of debris.

In the growing darkness, the inferno's dying embers smoldered orange. The horse-drawn fire-tenders finished their work and now the blaze was replaced by just a few black plumes of lazy smoke.

A young police captain in a pale blue uniform and dark blue overcoat accompanied Kazan and said, "The gas engineers have turned off the supply at the mains and made everything safe, Inspector."

Kazan stared at the charcoal-blackened corpse. It appeared the body was slammed against a kitchen wall with the force of the blast. It lay on its side, partly fused to the wall and the concrete floor, which was drenched with water from the fire hoses.

Kazan nudged the corpse with the tip of his boot and flakes of charcoal broke away. "Do you know the victim's identity?"

"We think it may be the property's landlord, a retired naval officer named Ravich. Two of his neighbors last saw him shoveling show outside here about noon today."

Kazan wrinkled his nose at the horrible stench, the body unrecognizable, not a shred of flesh uncooked. "Who rented the house?"

"One of Ravich's neighbors said he'd told him that the tenant was a foreign businessman. He arrived about six weeks ago."

"Age?"

"Mid-twenties. The neighbor didn't know his nationality. And there are no signs of other remains within the ruins. In fact, he seems to be something of a phantom, this man."

"A phantom?"

"He kept to himself. No one saw him apart from Ravich and the neighbor."

"Do you have his name?"

"No, Inspector, but we can try to find out."

Kazan removed his hat and wiped his brow with a handkerchief, his pale bald head smooth and shiny. "Trying isn't good enough. I want a name and I want a description." He scanned the nearby Alexander Palace, like a predator trying to pick up a scent, his right hand busily toying with the knuckle-duster. "So, you think it was all a dreadful accident, Captain?"

The captain recalled that Kazan, a former secret policeman with the tsar's Ochrana who now worked for the Bolshevik Cheka, had a brutal reputation. Kazan was savage in his pursuit and known to beat obstinate prisoners to death. Hundreds if not thousands of the tsar's former secret policemen were retired, fired, or killed by revengeful mobs. But not Kazan.

He made sure his cunning and expertise were useful to the Bolsheviks.

The captain said cautiously, "Well . . . yes, Inspector, it really does look that way. It wouldn't be the first gas explosion in cold weather. However, my colonel thought it wise to inform you of the blast in case there was more to it, especially as the property is near the palace."

"How very wise of your colonel." Kazan slipped the knuckle-duster into his pocket. He knelt and examined a congealed tarry substance that coated the concrete floor near where the corpse was slammed into the wall.

He took a pinch of the black substance and rubbed it between thumb and forefinger. It was brittle and flaky. He sniffed a morsel, licked it with his tongue. He dusted his hands and stood. "The black mess is blood."

"How do you tell, Inspector?"

"Thirty years of experience." Kazan scanned the floor, kicking away burnt debris, before he made a steeple of his gloved fingers, touched them to his lips. "The victim may have committed suicide, but I doubt it with this much blood *and* a gas explosion. It's more likely that a killer may be trying to cover his tracks."

The captain thought, *Dear God, help the criminal if Kazan picks up his scent.*

Kazan studied the Alexander's vast, snow-covered lawns. "Did Ravich's neighbors notice any strangers in the area?"

"No, we asked them."

"But the tenant is missing."

"The explosion occurred only four hours ago. He may turn up yet."

Kazan snorted. "And he may not. Intuition tells me there's more to this, happening so close to the palace. There are royalist spies who'd like nothing better than to rescue the tsar, so let's not take any chances."

The captain thought, *That's rich.* Kazan didn't take long to change allegiance.

Kazan spotted something in the ashes, bent down, and picked up a small brown glass bottle with ribbed sides. It was covered in ash and the rubber screw-stopper had melted. Kazan cleaned off the ash and sniffed around the top of the bottle.

"You found something," the officer asked.

Kazan's nose wrinkled at the bitter smell. "Laudanum."

"Pardon?"

"A narcotic used to treat many ills. Pain, anxiety—the list is long."

Kazan slipped the bottle in his coat pocket. "Check with the local cabbies and lodgings. Find out if any strangers arrived recently. Watch the railway stations and the roads leading out of town. Circulate the tenant's description."

The exasperated captain said, "But, Inspector, my men are busy . . ."

Kazan's good eye drilled into the captain's face as the milky one stared into nothing. "You'll do as I say. If our phantom's out there, I'm going to find him."

"Can you halt a few minutes?" Sorg asked the cabbie. "Nature calls."

They were on the outskirts of Tsarskoye Selo, on a slight rise covered in thick pine woods, a frozen stream snaking through the trees.

The cabbie reined in the two sturdy horses, their breaths snorting in the freezing air. "Certainly, citizen. Take your time."

Sorg pulled the blanket off his legs, climbed down, and moved into the woods, taking his Gladstone bag with him.

The snow hadn't penetrated under the pines, the needles soft and damp, his journey silent, and soon he came out on the far side of the woods. A view of Tsarskoye Selo spread out before him.

Sorg took the spyglass from his Gladstone and leaned the muzzle against a bare birch tree, its bark the color of tarnished silver. It wasn't difficult to spot the house. The smoke plume was blacker and thicker than any other rising into the winter air.

Sorg focused on the horse-drawn fire carriage, painted red and blue, figures standing around as smoke curled from the ruins.

He noticed two men talking. One wore a long dark coat and a broad-rimmed black hat. When he removed it to wipe his brow, a bone-white bald head was revealed.

Sorg turned ashen. He felt as if someone had frozen his heart. A surge of fear coursed though him. Sixteen years had passed, but the man was still frighteningly familiar.

Kazan.

He looked older, fleshier, but Sorg never forgot the image of the man who had dragged his father away. *What's Kazan doing here?*

The Ochrana was disbanded. Was the Cheka making use of his brutal talents? It made a warped kind of sense.

Sorg shivered, as if someone had walked over his grave. Then he began to sweat. He rummaged in his pockets for the Laudanum tincture, thinking a few drops would calm his anxiety.

The bottle was gone. He must have lost it in the struggle.

He swore.

Snapping shut the spyglass, he pushed it into the Gladstone. Then he walked back through the woods and climbed into the carriage. He pulled the blanket over his legs, shaking now.

The cabbie smiled. "Your business is done?"

Sorg thought, *I have a feeling it's just begun.*

11

At eight that evening Yakov was seated behind his oak desk, looking through some papers, when he heard a sharp knock on his carriage door. "Come in."

Zoba entered, the Georgian rubbing his hands together, stamping his boots, his face frozen and the wind whistling. "It's as cold as an Eskimo's kiss outside. My feet are like ice blocks."

Yakov stood up from his desk and took a tin cigarette case from his pocket. "Throw another log in the stove and get some heat into you."

Zoba crossed to a tiled woodstove in a corner, opened it, and was greeted by a blazing furnace of heat. As he threw in a log someone banged on the door.

This time a soldier entered and a gust of icy wind raged in before he managed to shut the door. He snapped off a salute. "Duty Officer Malenkov reporting. A night to keep warm, Commissar. A bad storm's brewing, I'd say."

"Isn't it always in this godforsaken place?" Yakov saw the duty officer's eyes dart about the luxury carriage. A half-dozen comfortable seats were upholstered in bright red velvet and a nickeled samovar bubbled in a corner, a whiff of charcoal scenting the air. Nearby stood a side table with a bottle of vodka and some glasses. "You look impressed," Yakov said to the man.

"We don't see much luxury in these parts, comrade." The duty officer peered past an open door and saw a private bedroom in another part of the carriage. It looked more sparse, with a soldier's simple metal cot.

Yakov struck a match, lit a cigarette, and blew out smoke as he crossed the polished walnut floor to the stove blazing in the corner. "Tell him, Zoba."

"You're standing in the former private carriage of the Grand Duke Andrew, which now rightfully belongs to the Soviet people. We carry a hundred and fifty troops on board, and two special carriage stables to transport a dozen of the finest cavalry horses for our mounted scouts."

Zoba rapped his knuckles against one of the steel-hinged plates hanging by each of the windows, gun ports cut into the metal. "We've added steel shutters and machine-gun turrets for extra protection. When Comrade Lenin travels with us, he calls our train his 'Kremlin on wheels.' It has its own kitchens, troop sleeping quarters, and plentiful stores of arms and munitions."

Yakov said to the duty officer, "Well, what do you want?"

"I picked the firing squad. They'll be ready to carry out the execution at dawn. The remaining hundred and sixty prisoners will be force-marched to the Soborsk camp."

Yakov inhaled on his cigarette and sighed. "Hopefully the captain's execution won't be necessary."

"Comrade?"

"Not your business. How has Captain Andrev been since he arrived here?"

The duty officer shrugged. "He's a resourceful man. The last time he broke out he reached a village thirty miles from here before we caught up with him. Sergeant Mersk beat the captain to within an inch of his life for that. How he lived I'll never know."

Yakov tapped his cigarette in an ashtray. "Because Andrev is a born survivor, that's why. The kind this revolution needs."

"Now it seems his luck's run out."

"We'll see. I take it he hasn't asked to see me yet?"

"No, he's still in the sick bay."

Yakov stubbed out his cigarette in the ashtray. "You may go. Find my brother, Stanislas, and send him here."

"Yes, comrade."

The man left and Zoba said, "Good luck convincing the captain. Something tells me you're going to need it."

Yakov's face was solemn as he opened a desk drawer and removed a wooden frame containing an old photograph. It was an image he always cherished: of his mother and Stanislas, Uri, and his father, all of them together, taken in a St. Petersburg studio. He showed Zoba.

"The day it was taken, my mother was growing steadily worse with TB. Uri's father took us all by carriage to a fair in St. Petersburg. I think he thought it would cheer up my mother and give Stanislas and me a happy memory with her. He had our photograph taken—so we'd always have it to cherish. Uri's father was that sort. A good and thoughtful man."

Zoba rubbed his hands together as he prepared to step out into the cold night. "I hope his son makes the right decision, Leonid." He left.

Yakov consulted his pocket watch: 8:05. He opened the top button of his uniform tunic, poured a vodka into a shot glass, knocked it back in one swallow, and slapped the glass on his desk.

He looked again at the images in the photograph. "Come on, Uri, get sense. You don't need to be a martyr."

It was bitterly cold outside, a blustery gale tossing snow flurries against the windows. The snow fell thicker and thicker. Yakov stood staring out at the swirling flakes as if hypnotized. It was on a cold winter's night like this that he and Uri Andrev first met. A night of birth and near-death, in which their lives were forever intertwined.

Yakov closed his eyes tightly. How could he ever forget the slums of the Black Quarter, the anguished screams and drunken cries that echoed like church bells in his mind? He recalled the despair of his childhood, the filthy stench of poverty that never left his nostrils. And in an instant his memories flooded back . . .

12

With its glorious Winter Palace, broad boulevards, and leafy parks, St. Petersburg was one of the most beautiful cities on earth, the Paris of the north.

But there was another St. Petersburg, a squalid capital of filthy backstreets, crime, and poverty, where hundreds of thousands of working families were crammed into crumbling tenements owned by rich landlords.

It was into this world that Leonid Yakov was born, in the harsh, dangerous district known as the Black Quarter. His father worked as a deckhand out of St. Petersburg docks, a cruel, bearded man whose breath always stank of alcohol.

Yakov loved his mother. She was a proud, strikingly handsome woman who found work as a cleaner in the houses and gentlemen's clubs of St. Petersburg's wealthy. It was backbreaking labor that often lasted from dawn until dusk and paid a pittance, and then she came home to kneel and scrub their own lodgings, determined to keep her family scrupulously clean despite the squalor all around them.

Every night she would read to Leonid, from a children's book or from the newspaper. She always kept books by her bedside: Dostoyevsky, Tolstoy, even Karl Marx. Big, thick, well-thumbed books and a worn dictionary that she studied every day. Yakov never forgot that.

And he never forgot the haunted look in his mother's eyes. A look that he in time realized was a mixture of exhaustion, hunger, and later the gnawing tuberculosis that ravaged her body with fits of coughing. One in five children died in Russia from hunger, neglect, or disease, and Yakov had already lost his young sister, Katerina, to TB in the harsh winter of 1901.

He recalled the sunny day in February he helped his mother carry the bony, stiff corpse wrapped in a tattered blanket to the paupers' cemetery. When they said their prayers for the dead, when they had held each other tightly and clung together, crying, Yakov climbed down into the open pit to bury the tiny body. No gravestone to dignify his sister's existence, just a plain wooden marker he cobbled from firewood, and which recorded her brief life.

There was something else Yakov never forgot that sunny morning as he comforted his mother—the images of the tsar's power and wealth that seemed to mock their poverty and suffering, and sent a powerful flood of anger surging through his veins.

When he heard the bells of St. Isaac's Cathedral ring out and he looked across St. Petersburg's rooftops, he saw the city's shining golden domes, the many splendid mansions of the rich, and a thousand glinting windows in the tsar's vast Winter Palace.

It was that winter his mama's belly became heavily swollen again. The same winter his drunkard father went to work on a steamship to America and never came back.

A few months later he remembered climbing the tenement stairs and seeing bloodstains leading to their room. Shocked, Yakov ran inside and found his mama lying on the bed, clutching her swollen belly, screaming with pain, livid fear in her eyes. "Leonid, fetch help! Go to the hospital and ask for Dr. Andrev—hurry! Tell him that your mama's ill; her baby's come early."

Yakov's heart chilled as he watched in horror the crimson clots staining the bedclothes between his mother's legs. A neighbor came and used a towel to try to stem the bleeding. "Fetch a doctor fast, boy!"

Yakov ran furiously to the city hospital, four streets away, as snow began to fall. Breathless, he halted outside the entrance and saw a shining black horse and carriage with the leather hood pulled up.

Seated in the carriage was a coachman and a neatly dressed boy about Yakov's age, ten, with a thoughtful face and big dark eyes.

Beside him sat a girl, a year or two younger. She was beautiful, with big, slate-gray eyes and perfect skin. She wore a pastel blue coat, a scarf, and mittens, her blond curls peeping beneath her woolen hat.

A tall, distinguished gent strode down the hospital steps and went to climb into the carriage, joining the coachman and the children. He wore a gray hat and he carried a doctor's black bag. He looked tired as Yakov ran up to him. "Please, I'm looking for Dr. Andrev, I need his help."

The coachman went to raise his horsewhip at the scrawny waif pestering his client. "Get away, you scumbag. The doctor's just come off duty."

"I need the doctor." Yakov was defiant and grabbed the bridle to stop the horse from moving. "Didn't you listen to me, you idiot?"

"Why, you little—"

The doctor grabbed the coachman's raised arm. "No, don't touch him—don't I know you, child? You're Mrs. Yakov's boy."

"Yes, sir, Leonid. My mama said to find you. Please, sir, she's dying."

"Get up here. Coachman, drive as fast as you can."

A breathless Yakov rushed the doctor and the young boy up the tenement stairs into the room while the young girl and the coachman remained out in the carriage. Crowds of neighbors parted to let the doctor through.

One of the women said, "She's bleeding badly, sir. We can't stop it."

The doctor examined the patient and said to the woman, "Get me hot water, lots of it, and soap, quickly. Everyone else get outside, now!"

The clot of neighbors melted as the woman ran to fetch water. The doctor removed his overcoat, rolled up his sleeves, and opened his black bag. Leonid Yakov's eyes were wet. "Is my mama going to die?"

The doctor said busily, "I can't answer that question. My son, Uri, will take you outside while I tend to your mama."

Yakov said fiercely, "No, I'm not leaving her."

But the doctor stood no nonsense and ushered Yakov out the door.

"Your mama's hemorrhaging badly; she's a very sick woman." The doctor snapped his fingers. "Uri, go outside and you and Nina keep this young man company and out of my hair."

Yakov stepped down onto the pavement, lit by gas lamps. The pretty girl in the pastel blue coat stepped out of the carriage. "May I join you, Uri?"

"Papa says we're to keep Leonid company, Nina."

Yakov thought that Nina looked as perfect as a porcelain doll. Mesmerized by her beauty, he felt his heart beat faster. She had long dark eyelashes and the softest skin Yakov had ever seen. The working-class dung pile threw up the occasional rose, but none as beautiful as this girl.

The dark-eyed boy beside him was tidily dressed and well scrubbed. He didn't look snooty like some rich kids, but Yakov resented him. He resented *all* the rich and their children. "What's your name?" Yakov demanded.

The boy said politely, "Uri. And this is Nina."

"I'm Leonid Yakov." He stared up at a filthy window, shadows dancing from a flickering oil lamp. "I hope your father's a good doctor, Uri Andrev."

"Why?"

"Because if my mama dies I'm going to kill him."

The boy ignored the threat. "My papa's one of the best doctors in St. Petersburg. He might be bad-tempered sometimes, but that's because he gets angry with the world, and thinks it's so unfair." He studied the gaslit street, a confident look about him despite his age. "What's it like living here?"

"What do you think?" Yakov was full of frustration and fear and he prodded a finger in the boy's chest. "Where do you live?"

"Neva Boulevard."

"Those big houses? You're the son of a rich doctor. You've probably never been in a place like this before, have you?"

Nina said, "Of course he has. Tell Leonid, Uri." Her eyes lingered on Uri with a look of admiration.

"My father delivers babies all over St. Petersburg," Andrev answered defiantly, "and we're not rich. So prod me like that again and I'll punch you."

Something in the boy's tone said he meant it. He wasn't some pushover wealthy brat. Yakov hated to admit it but he was beginning to admire Uri Andrev for standing up for himself. He had spirit.

Nina looked at him, her blue eyes pools of concern. "Why are you so angry, Leonid Yakov?"

The girl was so beautiful that Yakov could barely look her in the eyes and he thought, *If you were poor and lived in the Black Quarter you'd be angry, too,* but she had no idea of the harsh life around her.

From above, they heard a baby's cry. Yakov darted up the tenement as fast as he could run and pushed in the door.

His exhausted mother lay on the bed, sweat drenching her face as she clutched a bundle in her arms. The neighbor was cleaning blood off the floor while the doctor scrubbed his hands in a bowl of soapy hot water.

His face was drenched in sweat but the tension was broken by the baby's cry filling the air. The doctor beamed. "Good news, Leonid Yakov. Your mother's going to live, and you have a baby brother."

That night, snow falling beyond the window, Yakov rested by his sleeping mother. The doctor, Uri, and Nina were gone, and he was obsessed with worry.

His mother was unable to work, so they couldn't eat. He fretted as he stared at his infant brother's tiny pink face, mesmerized by its helpless beauty as he rocked him in his arms. Strange how a baby could make you feel so protective and loving.

What can I do to help? He was almost eleven, but children as young as nine worked in factories, bakeries, and markets, or as chimney sweeps and delivery boys. He was bright in school—he could read and write—but from now on he would have to forget about school. He made up his mind that if he couldn't find work, he would steal food, but the worry consumed him.

A little after midnight he heard the soft clip-clop of a carriage out in the street. Footsteps ascended the tenement stairs. Someone rapped on his door. Yakov stopped rocking his brother and placed him by his still-sleeping mother. He crossed the room and cautiously opened the door.

The doctor was back. This time he carried two straw-made luggage baskets, a baby's cot, and some bedding. He looked tired, dark circles under his eyes. "May I come in, Leonid Yakov?"

"Yes, sir."

The doctor laid down the luggage baskets, cot, and bedding and removed his hat, placed it on the rickety table, then crossed to Maria Yakov and her baby. He studied their faces as they slept, then felt the mother's brow. "Her temperature's normal again. With God's grace, your mother will be fine."

"And my brother?"

The doctor nodded tiredly. "He came a month early but I think he'll come through this. The cot once belonged to Uri. I thought your mother would find it useful. I have no need for it, Leonid."

"Thank you, sir."

"You met Uri. He's a good lad, kind and honest, as his mother was. I hope you liked him?"

The doctor's breath smelled of plum brandy. Yakov recognized the smell from his father. The doctor wasn't drunk but he had definitely been drinking. Yakov nodded and said honestly, "Your children didn't seem spoiled like other rich kids."

"My son and I are not rich, Leonid. I understand it may seem that way to you. But I'm just a busy doctor with far too many patients and too little time. Then again, perhaps if I didn't drink so much and insisted that my patients pay their bills, I might have more money to my name. But life isn't all about money."

"Sir?"

The doctor smiled vaguely. "Nothing. As for Uri being unspoilt, you're right, and I can thank his mother. She came from a military family. A simple, moral life was something she insisted on." The doctor rubbed his eyes tiredly. "And Nina isn't my child. Her parents are my good friends who asked me to pick up their daughter from music lessons." There were only two chairs in the room and the doctor selected one. "Sit down, Leonid."

Yakov sat.

The doctor took a packet of cigarettes from his pocket. "Forgive me, but I had a busy night. After I left Uri home and took Nina to her parents, I had to return to the hospital to operate on a patient. Then I went home, poured a plum brandy, gathered some things before I came here, and . . . well, you know the rest." The doctor lit a cigarette and for a long time he gazed again at Maria Yakov, then at her child, deep concern in his eyes.

Finally, he studied the stark room. His mouth tightened, as if he was angry or moved by the grimness around him, Yakov couldn't tell which.

"How does my mother know you, sir?"

"I'm the doctor who delivered you, Leonid." He smiled faintly. "As I recall, you were a spirited little boy even then. Impatient to greet the world with a loud, angry voice."

"My mother never told me, sir."

"After your father left, I found her some work at my doctors' club. Did she tell you that?"

Yakov shook his head.

The doctor's eyes settled on well-worn books by the bed. "Your mother's a kind and honorable woman, Leonid. A caring woman. In a fairer world and with the proper education, she could have done well for herself. But this world we both live in is not often fair, as I'm sure you know."

"Yes, sir. Why are you helping us, sir?"

"What are we if we can't help others? We are nothing. Have you thought of a name for your new brother?"

Yakov's gaze shifted toward the bed. The tranquil image of a sleeping mother and child would always bring out the tenderest feeling in him. "My mama said we would name him after you, because you saved the baby's life. What's your first name, sir?"

"Stanislas."

"That's what we will call my brother, Stanislas."

The doctor looked touched, almost embarrassed. "That . . . that's kind of you both. Very kind. Be sure to help your mother, Leonid. She's had a difficult birth and almost died. Be good to her."

The doctor patted Yakov's head fondly, then he stood, handed him a small brown bottle. "I'll come by tomorrow. Meanwhile, have your mother take just one of these pills if she feels pain. If you need me, summon me night or day, at any hour. I'll come at once."

The doctor took one last look at Maria Yakov, still sleeping, then ran a finger delicately across the spines of her bedside books. "Your mama reads a lot?"

"Every night, sir."

He picked up one of the books. "Your mother likes Tolstoy."

"Yes, sir."

"May I tell you something Tolstoy once wrote, Leonid?"

"Yes, sir."

"He wrote about our duty to each other as human beings. That whenever we're offered love, we should accept it, with gratitude. That wherever we encounter tenderness, we should embrace it. And wherever we find a soul in need, it's our duty to help lessen that need. Do you understand, Leonid?"

Yakov didn't, but he nodded vaguely. "Yes."

The doctor gave a tiny smile and placed an envelope on the table. "Perhaps not completely, but I hope that someday you will. Please accept this also, Leonid. I'll say good night. Take care of yourself and your brother."

The doctor left, his footsteps echoing down the stairs, and then came the sound of the carriage horses pulling away into the snowy night. Puzzled, Yakov dragged open the luggage cases and gasped.

Inside were tinned meat, jams, tinned herring and sardines, an entire *sack* of potatoes, dried corn, spices, flour, dried milk powder, a big tin of tea, and a huge jar of tiny pickled cucumbers. And clothes for him and his mother—sweaters, a pair of thick woolen scarves, shirts, and socks—some of them new, others used, but they were warm clothes, freshly pressed, and there were blankets and baby clothes and fresh sheets that smelled of lilac. Yakov buried his face in the sheets and inhaled the clean, perfumed smell. He felt overcome, and tears drenched his eyes.

When he tore open the envelope he found fifty rubles, more money than his mother could earn in months. And a note, in copperplate handwriting, with an address.

Some provisions to help you, Leonid. You're a very brave boy.
Please don't worry about the future, I'll be there to help.

Dr. Andrev

There was another note in a child's neat handwriting that said simply,

It was good to meet you, Leonid Yakov. I'm glad your mama is
well and you have a baby brother. I wish I had one. Perhaps we
can share yours? Perhaps we could all be like brothers? I hope we
meet again. Nina sends her good wishes.

There would be so much more Yakov would feel grateful for to the doctor in the years to come, but that night, staring at the two straw cases overflowing with food and warm clothes, at his exhausted mother and baby brother sleeping, Leonid Yakov could only weep, deep fits of sobbing that racked his body with a wonderful warm feeling of relief and gratitude, and a newfound faith in human kindness.

13

The door burst open and jerked Yakov back into the present. A gust of wind howled into the carriage as Stanislas stepped in, looking such a child in his oversized uniform, and over sixteen years passed in the blink of an eye. "You sent for me, commissar?"

Yakov warmed his hands by the stove. "Relax, you're not on parade, little brother. Are you still on picket duty?"

Stanislas joined him at the stove, rubbing his palms. "Until midnight, and it's freezing out there. Any word yet from Uri?"

"No. That's why I wanted to see you. I'd like you to talk to him."

"Why would Uri listen to *me*?"

"Because he's always had a soft spot for you. Uri treats you like a kid brother. He trusts you."

Stanislas's face tightened with worry. "You know that neither of us could bear to see him executed. You said you had a plan, Leonid."

"If I can call it that. Remind Uri of his duty to his wife and son. Hammer that home. Try to appeal to his common sense. It's worth a try."

"What if he still refuses?"

Yakov said, "Tell him I'll transport all of his men to the camp on board our train. No one will have to walk and no one will perish. He has my word on that if he agrees. That's my plan—it ought to appeal to Uri's strong sense of duty to his men. Go see him after your watch ends."

"But you'll be disobeying Lenin's orders. You could be shot."

Yakov put a hand on his Stanislas's shoulder. "That's my problem, little brother. Just make sure that you talk to Uri."

■ ■ ■

Just before midnight Andrev heard two double raps on the window. The dimly lit room was filled with the sound of the other prisoners snoring. Uri got up off his bed, his blanket still draped over his shoulders, and felt his way to the window. He tapped a reply on the frosted glass, then crossed to the sick bay door and lifted the latch.

Corporal Tarku stepped in, squinting through his glasses, wearing his fur hat, woolen scarf, and mittens. He had on two overcoats, his boots crusted with snow, and he carried an armful of garments. He whispered, "Captain Vilsk donated an overcoat, sir. And I've given you one of my sweaters. You better keep your blanket with you. It's freezing out there."

Andrev shut the door and accepted the clothes. Tarku helped him place the coat over his shoulders and tie the sweater around his neck, using it as a scarf. "You're sure you'll be able to manage with your wounds, sir?"

"I'll have to. Any trouble getting here?"

"None. The guards are busy changing the picket." Tarku produced a ferocious-looking butcher's knife from his coat, the steel flashing in the wash of light that filtered into the room. "I have a weapon. I'm a jeweler, sir. It cost me a valuable gold ring I managed to keep hidden."

"I won't ask where. Remember, don't use the knife unless you have to."

"What's the plan, captain?"

"A simple one. You and I are going to walk out the front gates."

The corporal's face dropped as he tucked the blade back into his pocket. "You've got to be joking, sir."

"We'll have to gauge it just before the Omsk train is set to pass the camp, so that we'll have time to jump aboard."

"How do we do that?"

"Yakov's carriage is parked in a siding near where our train passes. He's expecting to meet me to discuss his proposal. If we can get the guards to take us to Yakov's carriage, we'll judge our moment to jump them and climb on board the Omsk train."

"But Yakov only wants to see you."

Andrev moved to the door. "Leave that to me."

"It sounds risky. What if the alarm's raised and Yakov follows us in his train?"

"It'll take at least fifteen minutes for Yakov's engine to get up steam, even longer to catch up. We'd have a head start. Even if he telegraphs ahead to the next station, we'd have left the train by then and be on our way to Perm."

Andrev silently lifted the door latch, peered out. A few voices soared in the snowy darkness, the sounds of guards talking as the picket changed. The camp appeared asleep, the snow no longer falling, the horizon ink-black. The moon was out, bruised clouds marching across the silver lunar light.

Beyond the camp gates stretched endless acres of impenetrable forest as black as night.

"It's time, and don't forget a prayer," Andrev said, then jerked his head for Tarku to follow as he stepped out.

As they trudged in the snow toward the west gate's barbed-wire perimeter, they saw storm lamps illuminate the sentry hut. Andrev said, "See that pinprick of light on the horizon beyond the gates?"

Tarku squinted through his broken glasses and could just about make out a faint dot that looked like a low, twinkling star, but he knew it was a locomotive's powerful headlamp. "The Omsk train is right on schedule."

"We've got about ten minutes before it passes the camp." Andrev approached the perimeter gates, crisscrossed by barbed wire. Two guards leveled their rifles. "Halt, who goes there?"

Andrev spoke up. "Prisoners Tarku and Andrev to see Commissar Yakov."

The door of the nearby guard hut opened and the big Ukrainian with the mustache, Sergeant Mersk, stepped out, wearing his sheepskin hat. His left arm was bandaged and he was in foul mood. "What do you think you're doing here, Andrev? I could shoot you for breaking curfew."

"You'd be making another mistake, Mersk. The commissar wants to see me."

The Ukrainian's face twisted with anger as he strode over. In his right hand he carried a short, brutal-looking Cossack whip, the *nagaika*, a metal tip braided into its end. He thrust the whip handle into Andrev's face. "Don't think you're going to get away with the trouble you caused today, you piece of royalist muck. What business do you have with Yakov?"

"Ask him yourself."

"I'm asking you." Mersk's hand came up and he struck Andrev a blow with the whip handle.

Andrev fell back and Mersk said, "You've always been a trouble-maker." He tossed away the whip, drew his Nagant pistol from his holster with his good hand, and there was a click as he cocked the hammer and aimed the barrel at Andrev's head. Mersk grinned and said to the guards, "He tried to flee and I shot him, right? You'll both back me up?"

The men readied their rifles. "Whatever you say, Sergeant."

Mersk's grin widened. "I say we kill these two traitors for attempting to escape."

There was the sound of a rifle bolt being cocked, and a voice said, "If I was you I'd drop your revolver, Comrade Sergeant. Unless you want to face a firing squad."

Stanislas stood with his rifle in his hand, his breath fogging in the icy air. He stepped closer, pushed his rifle barrel into the Ukrainian's neck. "I said drop the revolver. My brother wants to see the captain."

The Ukrainian grimaced, tossing his Nagant in the snow. "You ought to show more respect to your superiors, Yakov."

"Really? I thought one of the reasons we started the revolution was to put an end to all that 'respect for your superiors' nonsense." Stanislas kept his rifle aimed at the Ukrainian and said to Andrev, "Who's your friend, Uri?"

"Corporal Tarku. I need him with me when I speak with Leonid."

Stanislas considered, then stepped back and pulled open the gate for them. "Both of you come with me." He grabbed one of the oil lamps hanging near the guard hut and said to Mersk, "I'll borrow the lamp if

you don't mind. In the future, I'd be more careful and follow the commissar's orders. Good night, Comrade Sergeant."

Mersk watched as the three men retreated toward the siding where
Yakov's train was parked. Hatred blazed in the Ukrainian's eyes, the
kind that went beyond all reason. He picked up his revolver, replaced
it in his holster, and retrieved the *nagaika* whip. "Who does that little
troublemaker think he is, talking to me like that? Just because he's
Yakov's brother."

One of the guards grinned. "Still, the kid put you in your place,
Sergeant. Are you going to let him get away with that?"

The Ukrainian's whip suddenly cracked and snaked around the
guard's neck. The man let out a tiny gasp as Mersk reeled him in close.
"Who asked you what to think?"

The guard wheezed. "You . . . you're choking me."

"Next time I will." Mersk pushed the man away, releasing the whip.
He opened the gates and glared at Yakov's train parked in the siding. A
dangerous look flashed in his face as he slapped the butt of the *nagaika*
into his thigh. "Someone needs to learn a lesson. If anyone asks, you
two never saw me, or so help me I'll skin you alive, understand?"

The guards nodded. And with that the big Ukrainian slipped out
between the gates, fury in his face as he disappeared into the darkness.

14

As they walked together toward Yakov's train, their feet crunching in the snow, Andrev said, "I owe you our thanks, Stanislas."

He grinned. "The Ukrainian didn't like being outsmarted. It's just as well I came to fetch you."

"Mersk's the kind who enjoys inflicting pain. A word of warning, Stanislas. An animal like Mersk is trouble. Watch your back from now on, I beg you."

Stanislas waved his rifle. "I can look after myself. And I'm a good shot, Uri. Tell your corporal to walk a dozen paces ahead, where I can keep an eye on him."

"Why?"

"We need to talk. Please, no arguments."

Andrev heard a faint rumble of a train and peered into the darkness ahead but couldn't see the engine's headlamp. "Move ahead of us, Tarku."

The corporal's eyes flicked wildly with concern. "But, Captain . . ."

"Do as I say for now, Corporal."

"Yes, Captain." Tarku sighed and reluctantly moved ahead.

Stanislas slowed his pace and whispered, "Leonid's worked hard for your release. He's desperate to help you, Uri."

The train rumbled louder as its headlight appeared and sped closer. Andrev guessed the engine was no more than three or four minutes away. Tarku anxiously glanced back at him.

Stanislas noticed and said, "Your corporal seems on edge."

Andrev tensed. "He's always on edge. Don't think I'm ungrateful for Leonid's help."

"They say my brother's ambitious, and he is because poverty lit a fire under him, but he's a man worth being loyal to. Zoba and I idolize him. We know what he went through when his wife died, and when our mother passed. You know that he's not one usually to show his feelings. He keeps things inside. But I know he cares about you, Uri."

"I know."

Stanislas put a hand on Andrev's arm. "That's why there's something he wanted me to tell you in private, an offer he wanted to make you . . ."

As the train's light sped closer Tarku suddenly spun round in a panic. The knife appeared from inside his coat and the blade flashed in the lantern's light. "We haven't got time, Captain—"

Tarku lunged toward Stanislas but Andrev blocked him and pried the knife from his corporal's fingers. "No, don't harm him!"

A confused Stanislas dropped the lantern and raised his rifle. "What . . . what's going on here?"

Andrev slapped his hand over Stanislas's mouth, catching the cry in his throat. He spun him round and slammed the youth face-first against the nearest carriage. Tarku stepped in quickly to snatch the rifle from his hands.

Andrev whispered, "Listen to me, Stanislas. Much as I hate it, I'm going to have to knock you out." He leaned in close, their frosted breaths mingling. "When you come to, we'll be long gone. I'm sorry I have to hurt you, little brother."

Andrev applied pressure to the neck artery, and the youth struggled and grunted, then his eyes flickered as he began to pass out.

Andrev said, "Don't fight it, Stanislas."

A gruff voice said from behind, "I knew you two scum were up to no good. Now you're going to pay."

Andrev spun round as Stanislas slumped to the ground. The Ukrainian sergeant held the *nagaika* in his good hand. Malice and anticipation shone in his face.

Tarku aimed the rifle. There was an instant swishing sound and the *nagaika* cracked. It struck Tarku's hands and he cried out and dropped the weapon. The *nagaika* cracked again, coiled around Tarku's neck. The big Ukrainian dragged him closer, head-butted him, and the corporal went down like a sack of flour, unconscious.

The Ukrainian grinned. "Your turn now, Andrev. I'm going to enjoy teaching you a lesson."

Andrev went to sidestep but the *nagaika* cracked and struck his injured shoulder. He yelled in agony, feeling a stinging jolt.

Mersk sneered, tossed aside the *nagaika,* and withdrew a frightening-looking double-sided Cossack dagger, the blade flashing. "It's time I finished this once and for all. I'm going to skin you alive, Andrev."

A train whistle shrieked as the Omsk train came round a bend near the camp. The headlight wasn't more than five hundred yards away, a plume of smoke blowing from its funnel. Mersk saw the oncoming engine. "Is that what you were up to, Andrev? A fast ride out of here? Too late. You'll never make it."

Stanislas groaned, dazed, and staggered to his feet. Mersk said to him, "Where do you think you're going, you little rat?"

The youth was barely conscious, hardly able to stand. "My—my rifle."

As a dazed Stanislas went to pick up his rifle the Ukrainian's blade swung down hard and the hilt buried in his back. Stanislas grunted as his body arched and then went stiff, horror blazing in his eyes. He slumped to the ground as the Ukrainian withdrew the blade and wiped it on his coat sleeve, still grinning.

"No!" Andrev said hoarsely, his cry of disbelief trapped in his throat.

"Now it's your turn, Andrev."

"You evil animal!" Andrev exploded as he stared in horror at Stanislas's body. He moved quickly and his fist came up and struck the Ukrainian hard on the jaw. The big man staggered back, dazed, but only for a second and then the blade appeared again and slashed through the air.

"Say hello to the devil, Andrev, you're about to meet him." Mersk thrust with the dagger but Andrev dropped to the ground, sliding forward on his feet, kicking Mersk's ankles and making him lose his balance. The Ukrainian's legs went from under him and he toppled into the snow.

As he struggled to get up Andrev slid his good arm around the sergeant's neck, placed his knee against the man's back, and pulled. The Ukrainian struggled and gasped, then all the breath went out of his body and he slumped and fell still.

Andrev staggered to his feet, his shoulder in agony.

He tried to catch his breath as the Omsk train powered toward him, puffs of steam clouding the night sky, and then came a piercing engine whistle. He leaned over Stanislas, whose eyes were open wide. He felt his neck for a pulse but there was none.

"You poor, innocent boy." Overcome, Andrev's eyes welled with tears as he used his fingers to close Stanislas's eyelids, then he rocked him in his arms, shaking his head, disconsolate. "Why him? *Why?* He was only a child, for pity's sake . . . only a child."

When he heard the train's whistle again he wiped his eyes, laid the body down gently in the snow, and pulled Tarku up by the lapels, and shook him. "Wake up, wake up, do you hear?"

Tarku came awake groggily and it took him a moment to adjust his glasses and recognize the bloody carnage around him. "What—happened?"

"Later. The train, Tarku. Run for the line."

"Did . . . did you kill Mersk?"

"I don't have time to find out. Run!"

The cargo train came closer and suddenly it was on top of them, its whistle shrieking like a banshee, the rumbling carriages shaking the ground beneath their feet as it slowed rounding the bend.

Andrev took one last, grief-stricken look at Stanislas's corpse, then grabbed Tarku by the scruff of the neck and started running toward the train.

It was past midnight when Yakov heard the banging on his carriage door. He was dozing in his bedroom cot, still wearing his boots and overcoat, and he clambered to his feet as the banging grew louder. "I'm coming, hold your horses."

He rubbed sleep from his face, strode out, and snapped open the door. Two of his Red Guards stood there, an ashen-faced officer beside them.

"Commissar, I—I need you to come with me at once."

Yakov jumped down and pulled up his collar to keep out the cold, his greatcoat billowing around his legs. He joined the officer and men, their feet crunching as they hurried in the snow toward the rear of the train.

"What's going on here?" Yakov demanded. The camp was alive with light and noise, prisoners being roused from their huts, beaten with rifle butts, and herded out into the snow. The guards formed them into rows and counted heads.

The officer quickened his pace. "It seems Andrev and his corporal escaped. The guards say both came though the west gate with your brother, on your orders. Now we can't locate them."

Yakov's jaw tightened. "*What?*"

"We fear the prisoners scrambled aboard a train that passed here not five minutes ago. We're carrying out a head count to check if they were alone."

Yakov fumed. "Someone's going to pay dearly for this. A firing squad if need be."

"Commissar, we're stoking the engine as we speak. Your driver says he can have a head of steam up within the next fifteen minutes."

"He better work bloody faster than that if we're to catch up."

They came toward the end of the carriages and Yakov saw a circle of his Red Guards, a few carrying kerosene lamps. Some appeared dumbfounded, dread on their faces as he approached.

Yakov stuck his hands on his hips as he fixed them with a livid stare. "Why are you all standing around like dolts?"

The officer spoke. "Commissar, Andrev attacked two of our men when he escaped. One was Sergeant Mersk; he was almost strangled. The second man was stabbed to death."

The circle of guards parted to reveal Mersk, who stood holding on to a carriage for support, looking pale as death and massaging his neck. Then one of the guards lowered his storm lamp, and the yellow light washed over a dead body lying twisted in the snow.

"Stanislas . . ." Yakov uttered his brother's name in disbelief, and his heart jolted as he felt a lump in his throat that almost choked him.

A crimson wound stained the back of his brother's greatcoat, his face lifeless.

Mersk babbled hoarsely, "It was Andrev who did this, Commissar. He tried to strangle me and I almost passed out. Andrev took my knife and stuck your brother like a pig, then he and Tarku escaped."

For a few brief moments Yakov looked numbed, an unreality to it all, and then he fell to his knees, clasped his brother to his chest, and rocked him back and forth in his arms. "Dear God. No . . . !" his voice cracked.

And then it sounded as if a terrible wound had opened and Yakov threw back his head and screamed, a haunting shriek of anguish that came from the very depths of his soul and seemed to echo without end in the frozen darkness.

PART TWO

15

It was raining that morning and still dark as the uniformed guards waved the dark green Rolls-Royce through the gates of Buckingham Palace. The car tires sloshed over rain-drenched cobble as the chauffeur drove toward the rear and halted within a private courtyard.

The driver climbed out and opened the back passenger door, and a small, sickly-looking man with bug eyes and an oversized nose stepped out into the rain.

Wearing a top hat, an elegant long black overcoat, and a silk scarf, he looked up at the distant night sky over London's East End, his gaze drawn to two huge German zeppelins, their silver cigar shapes suspended in the glare of searchlights. The air erupted with the deafening explosions of British anti-aircraft artillery and the shriek of air raid sirens.

The zeppelins usually came during darkness to drop their bombs before they scuttled back across the North Sea.

Explosive flashes lit up the night as a palace aide, a plainclothes Guards' officer, came forward and escorted the man into an oak-beamed hall. The officer helped him remove his overcoat, hat, and scarf. "Good morning, Mr. Ambassador. Another air raid, I'm afraid. It's good to see you again, sir."

There's nothing much good about it, the man thought. "Is the king awake yet?" His accent was unmistakably American. North Carolina to be precise.

"Yes, sir. Allow me to take you to him."

He followed the officer along a warren of passageways until they came to a paneled door. The aide stepped inside, flicked on an electric table light, and gestured to a nearby armchair. "I hope you'll be comfortable, sir. I doubt that His Majesty will keep you waiting long."

The officer withdrew, closing the door. The American slumped into the armchair and coughed, clearing his chest, clogged as usual from a ten-a-day cigar habit. He was in an anteroom to the king's study, heavy with period furniture and oil paintings.

On a dais was a bronze bust of a drab-faced Queen Victoria, the walls adorned with paintings of kings and queens long dead, their portraits adding gravitas to the monarch's office. The visitor had waited here on many occasions but none so early as this cold, wet May morning.

Walter Hines Page, U.S. ambassador to the Court of St. James's, was beset by anxiety. He heard footsteps, slipped on a pair of wire-rimmed glasses, stood, and checked himself in one of the wall mirrors.

His bespoke dark suit with tails and his waistcoat were immaculate, his body smelling faintly of soap after the steaming shower he'd taken soon after being wakened by a transatlantic telephone call. The report he received during that ten-minute call had carved deep worry lines into his skin.

He looked down at the black leather attaché case handcuffed to his right hand, and which was the cause of his distress. By nature a restless man, Page felt sweat rise on his brow as he thought about the contents. Glancing up, he saw the bronze bust of Queen Victoria stare back at him. Her dour face seemed to scold him for what he was about to deliver. *The bad news is not my fault, ma'am, I'm only the messenger.*

Outside, he heard the distant cracks of more explosions as the door opened and the officer reappeared. "His Majesty will see you right away, Mr. Ambassador."

16

They were seated in the paneled study, a log stove blazing, the king at his desk, the Union Jack in a glass-and-wood frame on the wall behind. It was a battle-tattered flag that Page was sure had some historical significance, but that morning he didn't care a hoot to ask.

The king wore a crumpled silk dressing gown and his sad, hound dog eyes looked puffy from lack of sleep. The uncanny likeness of King George V to his cousin Tsar Nicholas of Russia always unsettled Page. The men could have been twins—with identical features, matching beards and mustaches.

A silver tray with china cups, milk, sugar, and pots of fresh coffee and tea were placed on the desk. The king was in good spirits despite the air raid and dug a hand into his dressing gown pocket as he glanced beyond a leaded window, the night sky sparking with muffled explosive flashes.

"Take a seat, Walter. It sounds as if our anti-aircraft boys are having a busy night of it. Coffee or tea? Help yourself."

"Coffee, thank you. I do apologize for waking you, Majesty," Page replied in his mannerly southern twang.

"Your call to my aide said it was most urgent." The king noted the handcuffs locked to the briefcase. "A bit dramatic, the bracelets, aren't they, Walter?"

"I think you'll understand when I explain, Majesty."

Page unlocked his attaché case with a key from his waistcoat. Removing an envelope from the case, he unfolded the single page inside. "I received a phone call from President Wilson at two a.m. Our conversation concerned a secret coded telegram the president sent to my office prior to his call. He ordered me to reveal the contents to you personally, along with his instruction to discuss with you certain grave matters. I have here the decoded telegram. Perhaps you might care to read it, Majesty?"

The king frowned, took the page, and read:

FROM: PRESIDENT WILSON. REPORT URGENTLY TO HIS MAJESTY:

OUR AGENT CODE-NAMED DIMITRI CONFIRMS THAT THE TSAR AND HIS FAMILY—WIFE ALEXANDRA, DAUGHTERS OLGA, MARIA, TATIANA, ANASTASIA, AND SON, ALEXEI—WERE REUNITED IN THE SIBERIAN CITY OF EKATERINBURG ON MAY 23RD, AFTER BEING SEPARATED AT TOBOLSK.

DIMITRI SECURED INFORMATION FROM A TRUSTED HIGH-RANKING SOVIET OFFICIAL, WHO BELIEVES THE BOLSHEVIKS INTEND TO EXECUTE THE TSAR AND HIS FAMILY, DESPITE SECRET NEGOTIATIONS WITH THE ALLIES. INFORM HIS MAJESTY OF OTHER POINTS TO BE DISCUSSED. AWAIT CONFIRMATION INSTRUCTIONS HAVE BEEN FOLLOWED.

The king looked up, his voice husky. "You're sure about the message concerning Nikki and the family? You know how notoriously unreliable the telegraph can be."

"The message was resent three times to avoid ambiguity."

The king sighed and handed back the page. "If you don't mind my asking, who the devil is Dimitri?"

"Our top agent in Russia. He managed to get close to the Romanovs for a time, by befriending Princess Anastasia before the Bolsheviks imprisoned the family."

"He must have a death wish, dashing around Russia at a time like this."

The United States, like Britain and Germany, had its share of spies in Russia. Since the Bolshevik uprising, nations had sent dozens of their intelligence operatives into the country to keep them abreast of the looming civil war.

The king sipped from his cup. "Not that I'd know much about our own agents. Sometimes I think my prime minister deliberately keeps me in the dark, fearing I'll interfere. But if it's true about Nikki?"

"I'm told we can take it as gospel, sir. Lenin's fraught, his regime is being battered on all fronts. And desperate men take desperate measures. Besides, our agent's reports have proven highly accurate in the past. His intelligence gathering is absolutely first-class."

"That disturbs me. Nikki may not be the wisest of kings, but I've always known him to be a good man."

Page didn't care all that much personally for the Russian tsar—his own opinion was that recent events were chickens coming home to roost. Among most diplomats, the tsar had a reputation as a decent enough man. But Page considered him a weak fool who had allowed himself to be manipulated by Russia's corrupt elite for their own ends.

Millions of working-class citizens had been kept in check by the Ochrana, the state's brutal secret police: dissenters were purged, exiled to Siberian penal camps, tortured, or shot, while the tsar stood by like a dolt.

Page said, "I'm pretty sure it will disturb everyone, sir. But we face greater dangers. Since Lenin seized power we've all been biting our nails. We know that he's in negotiations with the Germans to pull Russia out of the conflict. That would be devastating for us. The Germans could free up their divisions from the eastern front and move them west. The war could drag on for years."

The king sighed and put down his cup. "You hardly need to remind me."

"And then there's the gold."

"I was wondering when you'd get to that."

Page said, "Britain accepted millions in gold bullion from the tsar for safekeeping, to make sure Russia's reserves didn't fall into Red hands if they seized power. A wise move as it turned out."

Russia had the largest gold reserves in the world. Over sixty million pounds in gold bars had been shipped to vaults in Britain and Canada for safekeeping—a vast amount. Another forty million was deposited in Swiss banks.

The king took a silver box from the mantelpiece and lit a cigarette with a match. "We need that gold, Walter. Without it, the expense of the war will ruin us. But what's your point?"

"Now that the Reds are in power, and they've found the coffers almost empty, they'll want the gold back. This leaves America in something of a dilemma."

"Go on."

"We've loaned Russia millions to buy weapons for their war effort. They don't just owe us, sir, but everyone. Look at France, for heaven's sake. Half of all French households have purchased tsarist bonds. But the Reds could refuse to pay us all back. Or tell us to go to Britain instead and take it out of the gold."

The king balked. "They could do that?"

"Lenin's already discovered that his country's in hock up to its ears. It's bound to be part of his strategy. If Britain doesn't pay, there's a risk the American banking system would collapse under the strain."

"It's a complete mess."

"And a two-edged sword. Give back the gold and you help the Bolsheviks and create a huge financial crisis in Europe. The simple fact is that Britain won't have enough bullion to match its paper money. Your country will be bankrupt. How will you pay for munitions, weapons, your troops' wages?"

"All right, don't rub it in."

Page stood. "Those are the simple facts, Majesty. We both know that Prime Minister Lloyd George is gravely concerned. However, my president has some thoughts on the subject and wanted you to hear them in private, without involving the prime minister."

"What thoughts?"

"We know that the Reds haven't got a firm grasp on power just yet and that the White royalist forces still haven't given up the fight. We know that British troops will soon control several northern Russian ports and that American marines will join them shortly, to try to put a stop to the Reds' gallop."

The king warmed his hands at the stove and picked up his cup. "Your point being?"

"The game is still to play for. If we could get the Russian royal family out of the country, help bolster the Whites with weapons and training, and cut off all support to the Bolsheviks—create a stranglehold if you like—then it might be possible to defeat Lenin."

The king looked horrified. "You know that I can't publicly take sides. The Romanovs are a thorny issue—Lloyd George warned me not to grant my own relatives asylum. He claims that international propaganda has been mounted against the Romanovs by militant socialists. If I take a hand in their rescue it would cause street riots."

"I'm talking about hidden hands, sir. Nothing to do with the politicians. But it would have to be kept totally secret and it would have to be done fast. We must find the right people who are daring enough to devise a rescue plan and execute it swiftly. My president wanted me to convey to you that any suggestions you might care to make would, of course, be treated with the utmost confidence."

Page waited for a response but he didn't get the one he expected. Instead, the king actually smiled and put down his cup. Page said in his charming North Carolina lilt, "I'm afraid I fail to see the humor, sir."

"Tell me, do you believe in coincidence? My wife believes in all that rot but I didn't. Not until now."

"I don't understand."

The king stroked his beard. "You've heard about the rescue of the Romanian royals from Odessa some months ago, as well as the actress Hanna Volkov?"

"Of course. They were spirited out of Russia but no one knows quite how."

The abduction of members of the Romanian nobility and a famous Russian stage actress from a hotel on the Black Sea had made international headlines. Held prisoner by a gang of Odessa Bolsheviks, the entourage was mysteriously freed from under their captors' noses, only to reappear unharmed in Bucharest.

Page added, "I was relieved Hanna Volkov was freed. Didn't she retire from the stage and marry some filthy rich Russian?"

"Yes, but knowing Hanna it had to be for love, not money. And the truth is she retired only when the Reds started to tell theater managers what plays to stage. Hanna didn't like that; she's a true liberal."

"I saw her on Broadway once. She's a gifted actress."

"She's much more than that, Walter. You don't know the half of it."

"What do you mean, sir?"

"I'll arrange for you to meet her. And the man responsible for her rescue. He's quite a character. Definitely one of life's adventurers. And able to think on his feet like nobody else I know."

"Majesty?"

The king put a hand on Page's shoulder. "Let's take a stroll. I think it's time I told you about a very remarkable but possibly insane Irish-Canadian named Joe Boyle."

17

IRELAND

Ten miles north of Dublin, sheltered on one side by dramatic three-hundred-foot cliffs topped by a white-painted lighthouse, lies the busy fishing village of Howth.

A trading port since the fourteenth century, it attracted fierce invaders down through the centuries: the Vikings, the Normans, and finally the British. The latter's occupation of Ireland had already lasted for over six hundred years, every successive Irish rebellion met with swift and harsh resistance by the mighty sovereign empire.

That same morning just before ten, two fit-looking men in civilian clothes sat in a covered black Model T Ford. They watched the bustling harbor as dozens of brightly painted trawlers chugged into port with their day's catch, followed by noisy flocks of seagulls.

"Any sign of her yet?" Jackson, the taller of the two, wrinkled his nose, the harbor stinking of dead fish. He had a sharp, devious face, a black pencil mustache, and wore his hair brilliantined, the butt of a Webley revolver just visible in a shoulder holster under his overcoat.

His companion, Smith, his hair cut razor-tight under his cloth cap, was an ape of a man, a former bare-knuckle fighter from Manchester who had once beaten a man to death in the ring. He sat in the driver's seat and watched the harbor with binoculars.

Both men were British military intelligence working out of Dublin Castle, their task to keep a check on Irish republicanism. It was a job military intelligence often carried out with extreme brutality, and worse was yet to come when Churchill freed legions of hardened criminals from British jails, promising them a pardon in return for helping to crush the Irish uprising.

Smith said, "I see it, Captain. A blue and white trawler with a black funnel a mile or so out to sea and heading our way. It's the *Marie-Ann*, I'd take bets."

Jackson raised his own binoculars and scanned the waters beyond the harbor. He spotted the vessel trailing a plume of muddy gray engine smoke as it powered its way toward port. "Good. Let's go fetch Boyle."

"Speak of the devil, sir," Smith said.

Jackson turned to look toward the road that ran along Howth harbor. It was peppered with fishmongers' shops, guesthouses, and tearooms, all dominated by an imposing white-painted hotel, the St. Lawrence. A tall, striking-looking man stepped out of the lobby, side-stepped a moving trolley bus, and strode briskly toward them. He was about fifty, tall, with broad shoulders, his tailored suit crisply pressed, and he wore a brown felt hat.

Smith watched him approach. "What exactly is Boyle up to, sir?"

Jackson selected a cigarette from a silver case, an irritated look on his face. "The devil only knows. He's of Irish background, with a name like that. And if I'm to believe London HQ he's a lieutenant colonel in the Canadian army. The title's honorary, mind you. Apparently, he formed his own machine-gun battalion to fight on the western front, volunteers all of them."

Smith cracked his knuckles as he watched Boyle approach with a purposeful stride. "He's a right cocky sod, acting like he's running the bloody show. Who does he think he is?"

Jackson tapped his cigarette and lit it with a match. "If London's telling us to extend him every help we can, Boyle must have friends in high places. He could be liaising with Scotland Yard for all I know, seeing as he's got a special license to carry a firearm."

"I've heard a rumor from one of the NCOs serving in Dublin Castle, sir."

Jackson blew out smoke. "Spit it out, Smith, I'm listening."

"He claims he heard of Boyle in Belfast, and he still has relatives up north. That his family were piss-poor and emigrated to Canada, where the young Boyle became a bit of a legend."

"Go on."

"He says Boyle has as many talents as backgrounds. Amateur heavyweight boxing champion of the USA, former Yukon gold miner. Not to mention that he's a millionaire, with business interests in America and Russia. I think that covers most of it."

Jackson stroked his mustache. "If all that's true then he can't be here on police work, can he? And it still doesn't tell us what Boyle is up to with Lydia Ryan. He has to know she's one of the rebels on our wanted list."

"Where did he get his information, sir? He knew exactly when the *Marie-Ann* was due to arrive and told us Ryan would be on board. Then he orders us not to arrest either her or her mates, but just to follow them. I don't get his drift."

Jackson offered Smith a conniving grin as Boyle approached. "Neither do I. But I think it's time we showed Mr. Boyle who's boss in this neck of the woods, don't you? You briefed the men?"

"Yes, Captain. They're ready for the ambush."

"Good. We can't have a dangerous rebel like Ryan running around the country, doing as she pleases. She's for the hangman's noose if I have my way." Jackson took a fierce drag on his cigarette, picked up the binoculars again, and studied the trawler eagerly as Boyle finally joined them, tipped his hat, and climbed into the back of the Ford.

"Gentlemen, good morning to you." He had a boxer's physique and a ferocious energy about him, and although his voice sounded North American there was a hint of Ulster in Boyle's tight-lipped demeanor. His left eyelid was half closed—the result of a scar that looked like a badly stitched wound, which gave him an odd, grinning expression. "Well, any sign of her yet?"

Jackson tossed him the binoculars. "The blue and white trawler on its way into harbor. It's the *Marie-Ann*. You'll see some people moving about, and one of them appears to be a woman."

Boyle took the binoculars and studied the vessel. He saw a couple of men moving about on the prow. When he glimpsed a raven-haired woman by the cabin his heart skipped. "That's Lydia Ryan, all right, I'm pretty sure of it."

Jackson said, "We're not ungrateful for your intelligence, Boyle, but look here, you must know that Ryan's wanted for arms smuggling and shooting dead two of our comrades. They were personal friends of mine."

Boyle tipped back his hat and watched as the *Marie-Ann* glided toward the harbor. "Your friends should have been more careful. What do you know about Lydia Ryan?"

"Very little. Our information on her is scanty."

Boyle put down the binoculars and almost laughed. "No wonder you lot are making a mess of Ireland. Ryan's American-born, with an Irish father and English mother. Her folks returned to Ireland when their daughter was twelve and bought a stud farm in County Kildare. She was engaged to a local man who enlisted with the British but he was posted as missing in action at the beginning of the war."

"Am I supposed to feel sorry for her, Boyle?" Jackson said.

"No, I'm just filling in the gaps. Ryan was never political but after 1916, when your lot executed the Irish republican leaders, that's when she and her brother, Finn, decided to throw in their lot with the rebel cause."

Boyle peered through the binoculars once more and added, "On occasion she's a driver for Michael Collins, one of the republicans' top men. She's also one of his best gun-runners. It's no secret the Irish are hoarding guns in case they take on the British army again. In fact, Miss Ryan's got a weapons cache on board, destined for her republican friends."

Jackson licked his lips and began to perspire, as he always did when the scent of trouble was in the air. He took back his binoculars and studied the trawler as it came in to dock. "So, she could be caught red-handed. What else do you know about her?"

"Enough to write a book. But that's plenty for now. Are your men in place and ready to follow her?"

Jackson nodded. "Yes, we've got relay teams. The penalty for arms smuggling is hanging, Boyle. What do you want with her?"

Boyle observed the *Marie-Ann* prepare to dock, the crew ready with their tie-up ropes. He winked, tapped the side of his nose. "My business, I'm afraid. And there'll be no one caught red-handed, Jackson. Just follow my orders."

Jackson bristled. "I'm not sure I like the tone of your voice, Boyle."

"I'm not too fond of yours either, but you have your instructions. Observe and follow, that's the order of the day." Boyle removed a Colt pistol from a shoulder holster under his coat and checked that it was loaded.

"Are you planning on using that thing?" Smith asked him.

"Not if I can help it. As I told you, gentlemen, this is an intelligence-gathering exercise. I want to know where Ryan goes. And your men better keep well back when they're tailing her, or I have a gut feeling that the lady's liable to kill us all. On that point, just one more thing."

Jackson looked irritated, raised an eye. "And what's that?"

Boyle smiled, looked from Smith to Jackson, an infinitely danger-ous look in his eyes as he tipped back his hat with the Colt. "Harm a hair on her head and I'll personally shoot you both."

18

Lydia shivered, feeling cold but invigorated as she stood at the prow of the *Marie-Ann,* her face washed with salt spray. The trawler chugged through the waves into Howth, dozens of brightly painted fishing vessels crowding the harbor.

She wore a man's donkey jacket with leather elbow patches, coarse wool pants, and waders, her raven hair hidden under a cloth cap. A strong breeze wafted down from the craggy headland and for a moment it overpowered the smell of salt air and fish, and instead the air was exotically scented with fragrant yellow gorse, smelling like coconut.

The wheelhouse door snapped open and Finn joined her. "You look miles away. What are you thinking?"

Lydia wrapped her arms around herself as if to keep out the chill and nodded toward the lighthouse, the huge cliffs scattered with shrieking gulls. "Do you smell the gorse? It's a scent I never forgot. Sunday afternoons Sean and I would take the tram to Howth Head for a stroll and a picnic."

Finn grimaced and nodded at their night's work, the fish catch in the hold, covering their arms cargo. "Me, I'm thinking be grateful we're home. I couldn't stand another night stinking of fish, or I'd be liable to kill someone."

Lydia scanned the town's harbor. "We're not home yet, Finn. Start saying your prayers that there's no trouble waiting. Where's Dinny?"

"On his way."

The wheelhouse door opened and the captain stepped out. His beer belly overhung his leather belt, and he had a stubbled face and a wild head of Celtic hair that looked as if he'd seen a ghost. He came over to join them, clutching a pair of binoculars.

"Well, what's the story, Dinny?" Lydia asked.

The captain peered through his binoculars before resting them on his belly and pointing to a granite building on the harbor road. "The green curtain's closed in the top left window of the chandler's office, our signal from the lads there's no sign of trouble onshore."

Lydia shielded her eyes and saw the window's drawn green curtain, then she borrowed the binoculars to study the other harbor buildings. "You're sure about the harbormaster's staff?"

"The senior clerk is one of ours, so he'll make sure no one bothers us taking the goods from the harbor. The British patrol the port a few times a day but it looks all clear to me. If there were any patrols about, we'd get the signal and head back out to sea until they've gone."

Lydia handed back the binoculars. "Why do I have the feeling that it all sounds too good?"

Dinny grinned. "Because you're as cautious as a week-old lamb, Lydia Ryan. And rightly so, but I think we're fine to chance it."

"Once we dock we need to get those crates on board the trucks as fast as we can. I want them well concealed by the catch and everything covered with the tarpaulins."

"It'll be done, Lydia." The captain tipped his cap and turned back to the wheelhouse. The trawler men began uncoiling ropes, preparing to tie up.

Before Lydia knew it the harbor wall came up to meet them and she felt a sharp bump as the *Marie-Ann* ground against the buffers. The crew shouted orders and ropes flew through the air as the boat was pulled alongside the harbor wall, next to the rungs of an iron ladder.

Lydia checked that the shiny black Mauser was loaded before she replaced it in her pocket. She put an open palm to her brother's face, let it linger a moment. "If there's even a sign of trouble, you keep well out of it, Finn, do you hear?"

He looked as if his pride was hurt. "So you always tell me. But I can fight as well as any man, Lydia."

"Of course you can, but you're worth far more to the movement alive than dead, Finn Ryan. Now, start getting that fish out of the hold so we can unload the rifles."

And Lydia winked and patted him fondly on the cheek before she clambered up the metal rungs to the harbor.

When she reached the dockside it thronged with people. It was Friday morning and trawlers big and small were unloading their catches, buyers from the Dublin fish markets swarming all over the harbor.

A Ford truck with a canvas rear cover and laden with boxes of chipped ice reversed down the dockside. It came to a halt and two men jumped out, wearing greasy oilskin aprons and capes. One of them kept watch on the dock as the second, a strapping fellow with huge hands, red hair, and freckles, strolled over and tipped his cap at Lydia. "You made it, boss. We were beginning to think you'd forgotten all about us."

"Save the chitchat until after we're done, Mattie."

The man snapped at his comrade. "Let's get shifting, Paddy."

They went to work, aided by the trawler crew who removed the crates of ice chips. They filled them with fish while several crew members maneuvered the arms crates onto the dockside and loaded them on the back of the truck. Then the crates of iced fish were stacked on top before the stinking, oily tarpaulins were thrown over the cargo.

The job done, Lydia slid into the truck's cabin. Finn joined her, followed by the burly, red-haired young man, who moved into the driver's seat and started the engine while his comrade sat on the truck tailgate.

Lydia studied the dock. It thronged with dozens of trucks and horses and carts. Near the coast road a tram trundled past on its way up to Howth Head, sparks exploding like fireworks from the overhead electric lines.

"What's up?" Finn asked.

Lydia shook her head. "Not a Tommy in sight. It's almost too perfect. There's not even a cloud in the sky. Call it intuition, but all of a sudden I've got goose bumps."

The red-haired driver smiled. "That's the Celt in you, always looking for an omen. But if the Brits are waiting they'll get more than they bargained for. We've got a rifle and a Bergmann machine gun behind the seats."

"There'll be no shooting, Mattie, not unless I tell you. Rifles are replaceable, lives aren't." Lydia touched the driver's arm. "If the Brits are going to try anything, they'll probably do it as we leave the harbor, so keep your eyes peeled."

Across the street from the harbor, Joe Boyle observed the truck exit the port and turn onto the main Howth road that led toward Dublin, Lydia Ryan seated in the cabin.

Jackson tossed away an unfinished cigarette. "Just following Ryan makes no sense, Boyle. We need to arrest her. What's your bloody game?"

Boyle kept his eyes on the departing Ford, the suspension weighed down with the heavy cargo. "That's privileged information, Jackson. All you have to do is obey orders. Now stamp your foot on that pedal before we lose them."

19

Ten minutes later on the road to Dublin, Lydia began to relax. She removed her cap and let her hair down just as they approached a junction with a signpost that said Sutton Crossroads.

Suddenly a Triumph motorcycle with a sidecar overtook the truck. The driver and passenger wore helmets, scarves, and goggles, and they waved and tooted their horn in good spirits as they roared across the junction at high speed.

Finn said, "Now there's a pair in a hurry. Someone's likely to cause themselves an injury."

A mile farther on their truck rounded a curve in the main coast road, the salty marshes of Dublin Bay stretching away to the left. Ahead of her Lydia saw the motorcycle and sidecar lying on its side in the middle of the road, the rear wheels still spinning. The driver lay sprawled on his back and the sidecar passenger knelt beside him. When he saw the truck he frantically waved them down.

Finn said, "I told you. Dance with the devil and you'll pay for the tune."

Mattie tensed as he slowed the truck. "This isn't our problem, Lydia. What if it's a trap? Do you want me to drive round them?"

Lydia was uncertain as she observed the stricken man, his passenger waving desperately. Her conscience played at her but she took no chances as she felt for the Mauser in her pocket. "Pull up about twenty yards ahead of the motorcycle. Keep the engine running and be alert."

Mattie skirted round the accident scene and braked to a halt. Lydia cocked the Mauser, tucked it into her palm, and rolled down her shirt sleeve to conceal the weapon. She scanned the road front and back but it was empty. "Stay here while I see what's up."

"Be careful, Lydia."

"I intend to."

Mattie reached behind the seat, ready to grab the Bergmann as Lydia stepped down from the cabin and approached the passenger.

He was about thirty, with chopped blond hair and blue eyes. He looked worried, his accent Irish. "Thank heaven you stopped. We were going a bit fast and the bloody bike went out of control as we came round the curve. I think my friend's back is broken."

Lydia looked over at the driver sprawled on the pavement. He was groaning, his eyes closed behind his goggles. "Have you tried to move him?"

Lydia heard a soft, distinctive click as the man prodded something in her side.

"Yeah, but he's a right lazy sod." The blond was grinning at her now, his accent suddenly London Cockney. He clutched a Smith & Wesson revolver in his hand and kept his back to the truck so that the occupants couldn't see his weapon.

"All right, you Fenian cow, do exactly as I say. Walk toward my mate. Try to signal your friends and we'll plug you. Not that anyone can help—we've got you ambushed."

Out of the corner of her eye, Lydia saw a flash of khaki uniforms crouched behind a wall across the road. She tried to gauge their chances but knew the odds were poor. She saw Finn and Mattie stare back at her, unaware of what was going on, but uncertainty in their faces.

The blond jabbed her with his revolver as they approached the man on the ground. "Kneel down like you're taking a look at my mate, then call your friends out of the truck, tell them you need help. Try anything and you'll all get plugged, you hear?"

Lydia heard a snigger and glanced down at the motorcycle driver, who remained still. She noticed a small revolver hidden in his gloved hand. "Blimey, get on with the act, Benny." He smirked up at Lydia. "I like the trousers, love, they really show off your backside."

"Go to the devil," Lydia replied.

The blond grinned, his back still to the truck, his gun trained on her. "Bloody heck, but we've got a right martyr here, Frank. Don't worry, darling, we'll part those legs of yours back at Dublin Castle—a good night in the bed will put manners on you, and I'm the man to do it."

A steely look ignited in Lydia's eyes. "There's one slight problem."

"Yeah, and what's that?" the blond grinned.

"You'll never live long enough."

Lydia's right hand came up, and the Mauser cracked once as she shot the blond through the left eye, killing him instantly.

She turned to the second man, frantically raising himself from the ground as if struck by electricity. He raised his gun. "You witch . . ."

Lydia shot him twice in the chest, punching him back across the pavement. She spun round and shouted to Mattie and Finn, "Ambush, troops across the road, get out of the truck!"

In an instant Mattie hauled out the Bergmann machine gun from behind the seat but a shot rang out, hitting him in the chest, his body jolting and then it fell still.

Finn jumped out of the cabin clutching a pistol just as Lydia raced to join him, shots exploding, bullets hammering the truck, the man on the tailgate tarpaulin struck in the arm as he clambered for cover.

Lydia managed to drag the Bergmann from under Mattie's body and ducked down behind the vehicle. "Keep your head low, Finn, or you'll lose it!"

A volley of shots rang out from across the road and Lydia hefted the Bergmann in her arms. Choosing her moment, she stepped out from behind the truck, squeezed the trigger, and the machine gun danced in her hands.

As Boyle approached Sutton Crossroads, the Model T slowed. He heard sharp cracks of gunfire, followed by the distinct *rat-tat-tat* of a machine gun. "What the blazes . . . ?"

Instinctively he reached for his Colt in its shoulder holster but next to him Jackson already had his Webley out and he stuck it in his ribs. "There's been a change of plan, Boyle."

"What are you talking about?"

Jackson grinned. "We had an ambush waiting for Ryan and her friends. They're outnumbered, so it shouldn't last long. I'm making it my business that Ryan's going to hang."

"You stupid idiot," Boyle said through clenched teeth.

Jackson struck Boyle across the mouth with the Webley, drawing blood. "You'll keep a civil tongue in your head when you're talking to an officer of the crown, Boyle. Relieve him of his pistol, Smith."

"With pleasure." Smith grinned, leaned over, and snatched Boyle's Colt.

A dangerous look sparked in Boyle's eyes, something dark and deep that was infinitely threatening. "You'll pay for your stupidity, Jackson. You've no idea what you've just done."

Jackson scoffed. "We'll see about that. My superiors are going to be bloody pleased when they learn I've captured a bunch of republicans." He checked his pocket watch. "We don't want to walk into a crossfire, so we'll bide our time until the firing dies."

The barrage rose in intensity, the rattle of machine-gun fire mixed with the crackle of small arms. Boyle sat with his fists clenched, barely able to control his fury.

Jackson grinned. "Relax, Boyle. This shoot-out's going to be over soon. With luck we won't have to bother about hanging Ryan."

Five minutes later there was a lull in the shooting, then it started up again with ferocious intensity. Johnson impatiently consulted his watch. "What's the bloody delay? It ought to be over by now."

The sound of a motorcycle engine ruptured the air and a rider appeared, driving at speed through the crossroads. He skidded to a halt in front of Jackson.

The rider pushed up his goggles. "They broke through our ambush, sir. They had a machine gun and kept our men pinned down with fire and made their escape."

"What?"

"But they didn't get far. We'd set up another blockade round the next bend and caught them again. Two of the Fenians are dead and the other two are wounded. We're taking them to Dublin in one of our trucks."

The motorcycle rider roared off and as Jackson and Smith turned back to the car, Boyle stepped out. He glared at them, his hands resting on his hips, fury in his eyes.

Jackson said, "You're under arrest, Boyle. You're not going any- where."

Without warning, Boyle's left hand came up and tore the revolver out of Jackson's hands, breaking two fingers in the process.

He screamed and Boyle's right fist smashed into his jaw, a cracking sound like bone shattering as the force sent Jackson flying across the car's hood.

Smith watched, grinding his teeth, as if relishing the fight to come. He crouched into a fighting stance, tucked his head, and balled his big fists. "Plucky, aren't you? Let's see you fight someone your own size."

He came in swinging with his fists but Boyle sidestepped, kicked Smith hard below the kneecap, and then slammed his fist into the back of Smith's neck.

Smith staggered, grunting in pain, but quickly regained his balance and went to grab his gun.

Boyle brought up the Webley, cocked it, and aimed at Smith's fore- head. "Stay out of it, son, unless you want a hole drilled in that thick skull of yours. Toss your gun on the ground. Hand me back my Colt, the butt first, nice and slow, then step away."

Smith did as he was told, then raised his hands and stepped back.

Boyle crossed to Jackson and said, "I thought I told you not to harm the woman."

Jackson was still on the ground, clutching his jaw, but a raging defi- ance blazed in his eyes as he glared at Boyle. His speech was slurred, as if his jaw was dislocated. "With any luck Ryan's dead. Just who do you think you are, you bloody Irish pig?"

"That's easy. I'm the man who's going to teach you a lesson."

And with that Boyle raised the Colt and shot Jackson twice, once below each kneecap.

20

Three hours later Boyle was pacing outside a secure room in Dublin's Mater Hospital on the north side of the city.

Two armed Royal Irish Constabulary detectives guarded the corridor, a part of the hospital often reserved for recovering republican prisoners from nearby Mountjoy Jail.

Boyle turned as the door opened and a nun wearing a crisply starched white gown and wimple came out. She carried a stainless steel surgical dish and some bloodied gauze. "You can go in now, sir. But the doctor said for no more than a few minutes."

"Thanks." Boyle stepped quietly into the room. It was softly lit and smelled of disinfectant. Rain drummed against the window, which had thick metal bars. An armed constable with a bushy mustache sat nearby, reading a newspaper. He folded it away when Boyle entered and gave a silent nod.

Boyle moved over to where an elderly nun with a wrinkled face and bony hands stood over Lydia Ryan's bed, taking her pulse. One of Ryan's wrists was handcuffed to the metal frame despite her bandaged wounds, and she was sleeping, her long hair fanned out on the pillow, looking as if she were floating on water. "How is she, Sister?"

The elderly nun scowled at him, her skin the color of old parchment. "Resting after surgery. You can't question her, if that's why you're here."

"I didn't intend to, Sister. I wanted to see how she's doing."

"It's Matron to you. Are you the scoundrel who shot her?"

"No, I shot the British officer in the ward down the hall, the one with the shattered kneecaps."

The matron looked confused, taking in Boyle's accent, uncertain as to where his loyalties might lie. He tossed his hat on a metal locker by the bed. "It's a long and complicated story, Sister, don't ask me to explain. But take my word for it, this woman was never meant to be harmed."

The nun's face lightened. "May God forgive me for saying so, but maybe you did right shooting that army thug. His kind has ruined this country."

Boyle stared down at Lydia Ryan's sleeping face, her long eyelashes dark against her pale skin. "What's the prognosis?"

"A gunshot wound to her left shoulder. There's no serious damage, so she'll recover. Her brother's a different matter. Bullets shattered his left leg. He'll be lucky to walk again."

Boyle studied Lydia. Her face looked incredibly peaceful in repose, a familiarity about her dark looks that was almost uncanny, and without thinking he gently placed a hand against her cheek. In the silence that followed he became suddenly conscious of two things: the rain drumming hard against the glass and the nun's stare. He drew his hand away.

"Do you know her, my son?"

Boyle's gaze returned to the patient. "We've never met, but she reminds me of my dead daughter."

"I'm sorry to hear that." The nun blessed herself, took a set of rosary beads from her habit, and shuffled them in her bony hands. "Prayer always helps, you know."

Boyle's face tightened with a flash of remembered grief, an infinite sadness there. "You know what they say about God. Once you lose a child, then all the angels you can dance on the head of a pin mean nothing. It makes it hard to believe in him."

The nun put a hand on his arm and he felt its bony grip. "But he still believes in *you,* my son, always remember that."

Struck by the pious strength in the nun's words, Boyle picked up his hat. "Any idea where I can find a cabbie to take me to Sackville Street? I've got an appointment to keep."

"There's a rank outside the hospital's main entrance, but on a wet

night like this you may have a while to wait." The nun searched Boyle's
face, as if he confused her. "Who are you, sir?"

Boyle tugged on his hat. "Funny, that's a question I've been asking
myself for years. But keep those rosary beads moving, Sister, they may
help me yet."

21

Twenty minutes later a cabbie dropped Boyle outside the Gresham Hotel on Dublin's Sackville Street. The rain was coming down in sheets as he went to his suite on the top floor.

When he let himself in, Hanna Volkov was already there, seated on a red chaise longue, the fire lit and blazing, the room decorated with heavy velvet curtains.

She looked younger than her thirty years and with her splendid figure and finely chiseled Slavic cheekbones, she had a presence made for the stage. She exuded calm and elegance, her sapphire blue eyes wide and expressive.

He shook his wet hat. "Rain's the one thing you can always be sure of in this country. I'm beginning to think that every child born on this island ought to be given an umbrella at birth."

Hanna smiled and stood. "You Irish seem to have a fixation about the weather, Joe." Her voice was soft but husky, her English perfect but with a noticeable Russian accent.

Boyle removed his overcoat and hung it on a stand by the door, along with his hat, before he crossed to a liquor cabinet. "Only because it's so lousy. Having said that, there's many a day when you can witness all the seasons in a single hour. Drink? I could certainly do with one."

"Wine would be good."

Boyle poured her a red wine and a Bushmills whiskey for himself, then joined her by the fire. She seemed tired and anxious that evening. Her black pencil dress complemented her figure and she wore little jewelry, just a plain gold ring and a simple necklace from which hung the Russian eight-point cross.

Boyle handed across her glass, sipped his whiskey, and sighed. "I'd propose a toast except the news isn't good. She's going to need time to recover."

"How much time?"

Boyle sighed. "I'm not sure. I've arranged to talk to her doctor tomorrow. It's an accursed nuisance. Lydia Ryan was perfect, had every qualification for the job. It's going to be impossible to find a replacement so late in the game."

Hanna put down her wine. "There's no one else?"

Boyle swallowed his whiskey. "Not unless you count a female clerk who worked in the tsar's private office, and the elderly wife of a royalist officer. I don't think either would be up to the job. Only someone like Ryan has the kind of nerve to pull off what we intend."

Hanna Volkov crossed to the window that overlooked Sackville Street, as two trucks manned with Lewis guns and British troops trundled past in the rain. "How long do we have?"

"No more than seven days to send our couple in, if they're to have any hope of reaching Ekaterinburg in time."

A hint of despair crept into Hanna's voice. "Tell me it will work, Joe."

Boyle ran a hand over his face. "I promised you I'd do my utmost, and I'll keep to that. But we're running into trouble. Even if Ryan agrees to help and is in the full of her health, she'll face a perilous journey."

Outside in the streets came the distant crackle of gunfire. Boyle moved back to the liquor cabinet and splashed more Bushmills into his glass. "After six hundred years of failed rebellions, this time the Irish are really going at it with a vengeance."

"By the way, you upset our friends in London. They phoned to suggest you keep that gun of yours firmly in its holster. They said this country's already like the Wild West without your adding to it by maiming one of their own."

Boyle yanked shut the curtains. "Jackson deserved it. His stupidity's messed up our plans."

"What about Uri Andrev?"

Boyle turned to a metal travel chest with a padlock in the corner of the room. He opened the lock with a key from his waistcoat and removed a paper file. "He's still our best choice for lots of reasons. He once served in the tsar's bodyguard and knows the royal family by sight. He knows that part of Siberia—the camp he escaped from wasn't far from Ekaterinburg. He's also used to getting himself out of tricky situations."

Hanna said, "If there's one thing I learned working on the stage it's that every character has a flaw. What's his?"

Boyle consulted the file. "Only one, and not so much a flaw as a gap in our knowledge. When he arrived in London he was interviewed by a White liaison officer working with His Majesty's immigration. Andrev told him he escaped from a Red prison camp and eventually made it back to St. Petersburg and briefly reunited with his family. But what happened soon after that, we're not really sure, except that he went on the run."

"What do you mean?"

"Something happened to him in St. Petersburg, some kind of confrontation with the Reds. It seems he barely escaped with his life and had to abandon his wife and son. The officer who interviewed him said Andrev appeared to have been deeply traumatized but refused to talk about it. The question is, will he be prepared to risk his life and go back?"

Boyle tossed the file on the coffee table. "Tomorrow ought to provide us with the answer. Speaking of which, you better get some sleep. You've got a seven a.m. start if you want to catch the mail boat to Holyhead."

Hanna picked up her purse. "Good night, Joe."

Boyle led her to the door, her own suite just across the hall, and he took her hand and kissed it. "Have a safe crossing, and good luck convincing Andrev in London."

She hesitated at the door, concern in her eyes, uncertainty in her voice. "Do you honestly believe we can save them, Joe?"

"We have to. The last thing we want on our conscience is the deaths of five innocent children."

22

The bedsit in Whitechapel was in a terrace of butter-brick Georgian houses. Uri Andrev heard the knocking on his door and came awake with a headache, raised himself from the bed and groaned.

The window in the bedroom was closed but beyond the curtains streaked sunshine, the din of voices, and the hooting of traffic. He heard Madame Bizenko's footsteps retreat down the stairs, then he climbed out of bed, stretched his arms, and examined himself in the mirror. His eyes were swollen and bloodshot and with good reason. He'd been drinking vodka in one of London's rowdy Russian émigré clubs and the night had lasted until one a.m.

Andrev shaved, washed with cold water and a flannel cloth, and toweled himself dry. There were thick welts in his skin where his wounds had healed. Then he dressed in an open-collar shirt, a dark suit of coarse cloth, and a peaked cap. When he went downstairs Madame Bizenko was in the kitchen making tea. She was a cheerful, gray-haired Jewish woman from Minsk with a high-pitched, girlish laugh. She had a fondness for playing both the violin and poker. Thick cuts of bread were stacked on a plate, next to a dish of butter and a bowl of hard-boiled eggs.

"Good morning, Mr. Andrev. You look a bit under the weather this morning. Like you were dragged backward through a hedge, if you don't mind me saying so."

Andrev smiled. "Too much vodka last night, I'm afraid."

"The curse of the Russians, but there's always the antidote—strong black tea."

There was a small garden out the back with a table and chairs and as it was a pleasant spring day, he said he'd have his breakfast out there. He went out to the patio, taking his tea, a cut of bread, and two hard-boiled eggs.

The boardinghouse in Whitechapel in London's East End was run by Madame Bizenko and her husband, a small nervous Londoner who chain-smoked and always deferred to his wife. The neighborhood was a teeming mass of immigrants: Russians, Balts, Slavs, and Irish, tough men who worked as laborers in the factories and warehouses or on road construction. Andrev shared the digs with four other men.

The two he shared a room with, an Irishman and a Scot, worked shifts in an armaments factory so he hardly saw them. The other two were Russians and he was convinced that at least one of them was an anarchist.

Despite Madame Bizenko's cheerful nature the house had a soul-less air, with faded wallpaper and peeling paint, but he was glad to call it home. For the first month in England he was penniless and had to sleep rough on park benches and in alleyways, with only a filthy gray blanket for warmth. For food, he scavenged among the bins of hotels and restaurants, or stood in line at the charity soup kitchens run by the émigré clubs.

But he was lucky to find work in a printing works and now Andrev had a steady job, the relative comfort of Madame Bizenko's digs, and the luxury of two meals a day.

Last night, his boss, Ivan Shaskov, told him to take the morning off, telling him he'd been working far too hard lately—until ten most nights—and afterward Andrev visited one of the émigré clubs. He didn't make a habit of frequenting the clubs in the evenings but he was starved for news from home and the boisterous clubs were hives of gossip.

Andrev sat in the sunshine and found a day-old newspaper some-one had left on the table. As he sipped his tea and ate his bread, he read the pages.

The news confirmed the rumors he had heard last night. Lenin was desperately trying to cling to power. He may have signed a treaty with the Germans at Brest-Litovsk, but German troops were already within firing distance of St. Petersburg. The treaty had cost Russia a third of her population, 61 million, and one-quarter of her territory. Japan had invaded in the Far East, and the Russian defenses everywhere had all but collapsed.

Andrev tossed aside the paper in dismay. The futility of it all sickened him.

"Good news, Mr. Andrev?" The landlady came out to clean away the plates.

"They're still killing each other. This stupid, endless war goes on."

Madame Bizenko shook her head. "Idiots, all of them. Maybe when they're tired of shooting at each other they'll eventually get sense and stop."

"I wouldn't hold my breath." Andrev drained his tea and stood. He didn't want to be too late for work.

As Andrev rode his bicycle through Whitechapel's busy streets, the sidewalks were crowded with shoppers and soldiers in uniform; the crush of bodies and the smell of engine fumes were almost overwhelming. The worn black Raleigh bicycle was a gift from his boss and he was glad of it.

He was surprised that London was so international. Aside from tens of thousands of troops, Britain's capital was host to every nationality: White and Red Russians, French, Belgians, Serbs, and Italians, to name but a few.

Hundreds of thousands of foreign refugees had crowded into the city since war began. Many of them were unable to return home because of the hostilities, and the sidewalks were a babble of languages. The restaurants and bars, cafés and lodging houses, all seemed full to overflowing.

As Andrev cycled toward the center of Whitechapel he saw the blackened ruins of buildings, scorched by fire and explosions.

Despite the war and fuel being rationed, merchant shops thronged and market stalls were laden down with fresh food and vegetables. Street vendors sold chestnuts roasted over charcoal embers, while Italian-run fish-and-chips shops did a brisk business. For four pence, you could have a good meal of fish and thick-cut chips, wrapped in old newspaper.

Yet there were still deprived backstreets full of barefoot urchins. The war put many to work but poverty prevailed in the gaunt faces inhabiting London's tenements, rampant with prostitution.

As he cycled on a footpath that cut through Hyde Park, Andrev dismounted. A brass band was playing on a covered rostrum. It reminded him of the military bands that played in St. Petersburg's parks in summer. It was over four months since his escape from the camp, but it seemed like another life. So much had happened to him in between.

The brass medley ended and the air filled with the lively strains of a waltz.

It was music Nina loved and at once made him think of her and their son. His eyes welled up and he closed them tightly. A flood of questions troubled him. *How are you coping, Nina and Sergey? What are you doing? Are you safe and well?*

Then a dark wave swept in and memories flooded his mind—of Stanislas's brutal death. That image never left him. Or the horror of those days after he escaped and made his way to St. Petersburg to find Nina and Sergey, pursued at every step. It pained him to think that Leonid Yakov would believe he killed Stanislas. As he stood trying to shake off his anguish, he saw a young mother stroll through the park, a small boy with blond curls clutching her hand.

Andrev stared at the mother and child until they disappeared along a path. His heart swelled. He felt overwhelmed, completely and utterly alone. A crushing memory troubled him, of the last time he saw Nina and Sergey—alone in a cold, dilapidated St. Petersburg slum, trying to stay warm with his old army coat draped over them.

Andrev forced back his tears. This pain couldn't go on forever, he told himself. Sooner or later, he had to get a grip.

23

He turned down a littered side street and dismounted his bicycle outside a ramshackle redbrick factory building: the office of the Whitechapel Metal Printing Works. Some of the broken windows had been replaced with newspapers and wooden planks. A couple of scrawny-looking children played in the dirty street, skinny-ribbed dogs barking and yelping at their heels.

Andrev locked his bicycle in the hallway and climbed two flights of stairs. The office he stepped into was large and busy, a printing press clanking away noisily in a corner. A couple of printers were working at the press, their aprons covered in ink, and they waved to him as he took off his coat.

Ivan Shaskov stepped out of a nearby office. A ruddy, cheerful, middle-aged man with a broad Russian face, his boss always wore a fresh flower in his suit buttonhole. "Hello, Uri."

"Ivan."

Shaskov looked worried as he put an arm on Andrev's shoulder. "I just want a quick word. Come into my office, take a seat."

Andrev followed his employer into a cluttered room littered with files, old wooden boxes overflowing with assorted lead fonts, and stacks of newspaper pamphlets tied with waxed string.

The printing works published a weekly newspaper and dozens of anti-Bolshevik pamphlets aimed at the émigré White Russian community in London. An empty vodka bottle poked its head above the debris, testament to his boss's occasional late-night binge when working into the small hours.

Shaskov anxiously twiddled a pencil with both hands. "I thought I'd ask how you're settling in at Madame Bizenko's."

"Well enough, thanks. Is something the matter, Ivan?"

Shaskov forced a smile but it quickly faded, and he dropped the pencil on the desk and crossed to the window. London's ocean of rooftops stretched beyond the glass. As Shaskov stood staring absently at a pair of pigeons floating like gray rags in an air pocket, Andrev was reminded of their first meeting.

It was April, his second month in London. He knew no one and slept on park benches and in alleyways. He slept with a blanket a kind old lady near Charring Cross gave him and on good days he managed to survive by scavenging scraps of bread and meat from restaurant bins.

On bad days he starved. On one of those occasions Andrev felt so weak from hunger he had to stop to sit on a park bench. A dapper little man with a goatee beard and a white carnation in his buttonhole stood feeding pigeons with thick crusts of bread left over from his sandwich. Andrev's ears pricked up when he heard him call out to the birds in a Moscow dialect. "Excuse me, are you Russian?"

The man looked up warily at Andrev's disheveled state. "Yes. From Moscow. And you?"

"St. Petersburg." Andrev eyed the crusts the birds devoured.

The man's eyes missed nothing. "Are you hungry?"

It was almost three days since he last ate and whether it was pride or fatigue, Andrev didn't know, but he felt speechless. The man dusted crumbs from his hands. "My name's Ivan Shaskov. I run a printing works nearby. Come."

He led Andrev two streets away to an untidy redbrick terraced home in Friar Street, where the man's elderly wife ran Andrev a hot bath and made him a hearty dinner of steak, fried potatoes, and eggs, which he wolfed down. Shaskov came back with a suit. "That ought to do you for now until you get yourself settled. Here, take this."

Shaskov handed him a ten-shilling note. Andrev felt moved to tears. He hadn't a penny in his pocket. "I—I don't know what to say . . ."

"Say nothing. It's a loan, not charity. Pay me back when you can."

"But I have no job."

"You do now." Shaskov smiled and slapped him on the shoulder. "How's your English? Is it good?"

"I believe so."

"Don't worry if you know nothing about printing, you'll soon learn. You start work tomorrow."

The little man was like a guardian angel to him, but now, on this morning, deep frown lines creased Shaskov's face.

"What is it, Ivan? You seem troubled."

"Did you hear the news in the club?"

"It's full of new rumors every day. What news are you talking about?"

"That now Americans intend landing in north Russia and Siberia, just like the British, to threaten Lenin's grip. And that the tsar and his family have been moved to Ekaterinburg."

"Yes, I heard."

Shaskov sighed and dug his fingers into his waistcoat pockets. "Speculation is wild that the tsar may be killed. Not only him but the whole family. I'm no lover of the tsar's regime—it was corrupt and ineffective—but if they murder the family, Russia is lost, Uri. Those godless Bolsheviks will turn the country into a graveyard and there'll be no going back for any of us. It seems this is a morning for bad news."

"What do you mean?"

Shaskov opened a drawer and withdrew an addressed envelope with blue Finnish stamps. "The letter that you gave me. My brother Felix managed to reach St. Petersburg from Helsinki and make inquiries about some of my family still in Russia. I had Felix personally try to deliver your letter and money, as you asked."

"Go on."

"Felix wrote to me when he returned to Helsinki. He said that Nina and your son are not at the address anymore. They've gone, Uri."

Andrev sat forward anxiously. "What do you mean, 'gone'?"

Shaskov shrugged. "My brother said that Nina is no longer living there."

"Did he speak with any of the neighbors?"

Shaskov nodded. "One of them claimed that she saw Nina leave the tenement building late one night, carrying a small suitcase. She never saw her since."

"What about Sergey?"

"The neighbor didn't mention a child; she only saw Nina."

Andrev said worriedly, "What if something happened to him? He should have been with his mother."

"Don't torture yourself, Uri. It's a mystery, I know, but there's an explanation. Russia's a mess, law and order have broken down, people are fleeing every day. My brother managed to locate Nina's sister through one of the neighbors."

Andrev said eagerly, "Tell me."

"She gave him an address in Moscow. It's an apartment house Nina's father used to own on Kolinsky Prospect."

"I know it. What else?"

Shaskov hesitated. "I don't know how to say this, Uri."

"Say it, for heaven's sake."

"She told my brother that Nina had divorced you."

"What?"

Shaskov said sympathetically, "She said that Nina hardly saw you for most of the war. That you hadn't been a proper husband and father." He paused. "The woman may just have been venting spleen. I know none of that is your fault. That you're a victim of war as much as anyone. But you know women, they're emotional creatures. Besides, my brother seemed to think Nina may have had a different motive."

"What?"

"Haven't you heard? Lenin's imprisoning the families of White officers, to instill even more terror. Perhaps divorce was a clever tactic to help her avoid arrest. At least they stand a chance of surviving."

Andrev's hand trembled as he held it out. "May I see the letter?"

Shaskov offered it across and Andrev devoured the contents.

Shaskov said, "Has Nina enough money? Will she be able to cope?"

Andrev barely managed to keep his emotions from spilling over. "We didn't have much. Her father helps what little he can."

Shaskov put a hand on Andrev's shoulder to comfort him. "I'm sure that your family's safe. That's all that's important right now. My brother left the letter and the money you gave him with Nina's sister to forward it to her. Please don't worry. We'll think of some way of contacting Nina again."

Emotionally battered, Andrev couldn't focus on that prospect. He needed answers *now,* but with Russia in chaos it took weeks for a letter to reach Moscow, and weeks more to get a reply. Most of the time mail wasn't delivered at all, which was why he sought Shaskov's help.

Andrev felt hollow. "It's very kind of you, Ivan."

"What are friends for?"

"I better get to work." Andrev stood, trying to hide his emotions; he went to take off his coat but Shaskov shook his head.

"No, leave it on. Someone wants to meet you."

"Who?"

"I believe a very nice lady would like to buy you lunch."

24

That same afternoon a carriage pulled up outside St. Constantine's Greek Orthodox Church in Whitechapel.

The blackened oak entrance doors were firmly shut, but a judas gate set in one of them was ajar. Hanna Volkov climbed down out of the carriage. "Wait here, Francis, I won't be long."

The coachman tipped his hat. "Yes, ma'am."

As she went up the granite steps she was moved by a pitiful sight— dozens of disheveled men and women lining up outside a soup kitchen at the church refectory. She entered through the judas gate, holding on to her hat as she ducked inside.

It was very peaceful in the church, London's harsh bustle reduced to a hush. Incense scented the air, candles flickered. The walls were decorated with gilded icons, infused with rich colors: azure blue, crimson red, pale turquoise. There were no pews, just a few wooden chairs and benches set around the walls.

An Orthodox priest wearing a long black cassock and a greasy leather belt blessed himself in front of the altar. He turned, his features lit by sunlight that splintered through the stained glass windows. He was a tall, striking figure, powerfully built, his face half-hidden by a long beard.

Father Eugene Doneski smiled as he padded across the marbled floor in his sandaled feet. He grasped Hanna Volkov's gloved hand and kissed it lightly. "Hanna, how good to see you again."

"It's just a brief visit, Father."

"No matter, you are always welcome."

Hanna produced an envelope with sterling banknotes from her

purse and pressed it into Doneski's hands. "To help you with your work, Father."

The priest protested. "But you give so much already. Our kitchens could barely exist without your charity."

"Please, my husband would have wanted it so."

"You are too kind." Father Doneski slipped the envelope into his cassock and flicked a look toward the oak entrance doors at the back of the church. "You said you needed privacy. I'll see to it that you're not disturbed, Hanna."

She sat in one of the benches facing the altar. A noise startled her and she turned.

A man stepped in through the judas gate. He wore a coarse woolen suit and carried a tweed cap in his hands, a scarf tied loosely around his neck. He genuflected before he walked down the center aisle, his footsteps echoing.

In the background Father Doneski padded toward the doors and bolted shut the judas, the noise booming like a gunshot.

The man startled and looked back in time to see the priest disappear into the shadows. When he reached Hanna and halted, she stood and offered her hand. "You must be Uri Andrev."

He accepted her firm handshake and inclined his head before he moved onto the bench beside her.

Hanna studied Andrev. He was reasonably handsome, his manner pleasant. He appeared calm and in control, but a steely look glinted in his restless dark eyes. "My name is Hanna Volkov. Have you ever visited St. Constantine's before, Mr. Andrev?"

He took in his surroundings with a grateful smile. "It's been a welcome refuge from the rain on more than one occasion. And Father Doneski's kitchen kept me from starving now and then. Why do you ask?"

Hanna looked toward a glass window in a corner of the church. Through it she could see the line lingering from the soup kitchen. "I don't know where we'd be without selfless men like Father Doneski. Thanks to Lenin, millions of destitute Russians have crowded into Europe."

Her eyes swung back toward her visitor. "May I tell you a secret, Mr. Andrev? I was never overly fond of churches as a child. They always seemed dark and cheerless places. But the older I get, the more I appreciate that there's a certain peace here that you find nowhere else."

"I can understand that."

She regarded the gilded altar. "Perhaps Chekhov was right when he said that a house of God is one of the few places in this world where we can begin to sense the tranquility of his embrace."

"I take it you didn't ask me here just to talk about religion, Madame Volkov. Or Chekhov's writing, for that matter, though I'm sure you're familiar with it."

"You know who I am?"

"I once saw you onstage and recognized your face from the newspapers. But I'm mystified as to why St. Petersburg's most famous actress would want to meet me."

"You have a good memory, Mr. Andrev. But the truth is my husband was murdered on Lenin's orders after the Reds seized power and I haven't stepped onto a stage since."

"I'm sorry to hear that. Murdered for what reason?"

"Because Lenin's a bloodthirsty killer. My husband opposed him and paid with his life. That's the way it is in Russia these days. Dissent is crushed."

She stared into Andrev's eyes. "They told me that something bad happened to you before you fled Russia, Mr. Andrev. That you had some kind of confrontation with the secret police and that you were forced to abandon your wife and child. Would you care to tell me what happened?"

"That's not your business."

"You're right, but it may have a bearing on an offer I'm about to make to you."

"What offer?"

"A very interesting one. Please answer."

Andrev's face tightened, his eyes caverns of pain. "I was hunted by the Cheka soon after I escaped from a camp. I managed to reach St. Petersburg and make contact with my wife and son. We didn't have much time together, a few minutes, no more, because our home was being watched."

He faltered. "I had to leave quickly so as not to endanger them. That's when I encountered the Cheka commissar hunting me. There was a confrontation. I shot a couple of his men and barely managed to flee."

"Do you still care for your wife and son?"

"My wife divorced me. But of course I care. And how could I forget my son?"

"Why did your wife's feelings change toward you?"

Andrev betrayed a heart-wrenching look. "War changes us all. It changed Nina more than most. Are you going to tell me what this is about?"

Hanna stood. "There's a small restaurant not far from here that serves a half-decent borscht. If you've no objection, I'd like to buy you lunch. The people I represent have an interesting proposition to put to you."

"What people?"

"That will be explained in time. We'd like you to return to Russia. It would be highly dangerous. But we can offer you something in return."

"What on earth are you talking about?"

"How would you like to bring Nina and your son to London?"

25

Two thousand miles away it was blustery and threatening rain that same afternoon as the olive green Fiat truck pulled up outside a shabby tenement building at the southern end of Kolinsky Prospect.

Built a century previous, it housed twelve families in sixteen rooms, with no electricity and dilapidated, stinking communal toilets on the ground floor.

Yakov climbed out of the Fiat, carrying a bulky brown-wrapped parcel tied with string. He wore his leather jacket, cap, and high boots, his holstered Nagant pistol by his side. "Wait here and keep an eye on the truck. I want to speak with Andrev's wife alone."

In the driver's seat, Zoba smiled, the Georgian's dark eyes slanting at the corners. "You really think they'd steal a truck belonging to the Cheka around here?"

"In desperate times like these, people will do anything."

When Yakov knocked, she came to the door.

She carried an armful of washing and looked strained, wearing a frayed dress, stitched in places, her blond hair down around her shoulders.

"Hello, Nina. May I come in?"

Beyond the door Yakov saw a shabby room sparsely furnished with a rickety table and a pair of wicker chairs, the peeling wallpaper speckled with mold patches. In one corner was a woodstove, some blackened pots on top. An ancient wrought-iron bed was pushed against one wall and she'd obviously done her best to decorate the room, the rotting sash windows draped with blue curtains, a handful of white lilies in an old vase.

She appeared tired and ran a hand anxiously through her hair. "Sergey's asleep. I'd ask you to be quiet."

Yakov saw the boy sleeping in the bed, covered in old coats and blankets, his blond curls damp on his forehead. He was a handsome child who bore a strong resemblance to his father. He gave a hacking cough and turned over in his sleep. Yakov saw he had a sickly pallor. A bottle of medicine and a teaspoon were near the bed, next to a kerosene lamp.

"How have you been, Nina? How's the boy?"

"Sergey's been ill. His chest has always been weak, ever since he was born. But the damp here doesn't help matters."

"What does the doctor say?"

She pushed a strand of hair from her face. "What doctor? The best ones have fled the country, and you Reds have conscripted most of the others. For the last six months I've had to deal with a quack who barely knows what he's doing and charges a fortune."

"I'm sorry to hear that."

Nina plucked a frayed child's sweater from the washing and laid the rest by the back window.

It overlooked a communal rear garden, a patchy grassed courtyard filled with rows of clotheslines flapping in the breeze. She sat at the table clutching the sweater, beside her a darning needle stuck in a roll of wool.

Yakov removed his hat and laid the bulky parcel on the table. "Some food and condensed milk for you and the child. And some clothing for him. I know it's a struggle."

She fixed him with a resolute look. "I told you before, I want nothing from you, Leonid."

"Can't you forget your stupid pride? If not for you, then take it for the boy."

"Nothing," she replied fiercely. "I'll take nothing from you and your kind, not while my parents are rotting in prison. They did no wrong yet they're accused of being enemies of the people. What's that supposed to mean?"

Yakov saw the bitter resentment in her face and said, "I told you I'm working on it. These things take time. But that's not why I came."

"No doubt it has to do with Uri. I told you all I know. The last time I saw him for only a few minutes before he had to leave. You and your men were watching the house. You know the rest. Uri escaped. I have no idea where he went. And if I did I wouldn't tell you—surely you must know that?"

Yakov considered her reply and looked over at the child, then back at her. She noticed the look in his eyes. "Accept my word and don't even think about asking Sergey; he has enough to deal with, missing his father. It's difficult. He used to talk about Uri a lot; now he just cries if his name is mentioned."

Yakov stood and peered out into the street as the rain started. "A revolution is difficult for everyone. It can't be won without sacrifice and suffering."

"And what's yours, Leonid? You seem to thrive on all this drama."

He didn't answer for a moment, and then he said, "No one escapes this war's hardships unless they're clever enough to flee."

"What does that mean?"

Yakov joined her at the table. "Uri's gone. Escaped to France or Britain, most likely. Somewhere White émigrés can find a shoulder to cry on, or murderers escape their punishment."

"How do you know this?"

"Deduction. If he were still here he would have contacted you by now. But I know Uri. He's not the kind of man who's going to leave you and your son alone in squalor. Whatever your differences, at some point he'll try to rescue you from this, if only for Sergey's sake. And once he does, this time he won't escape, I promise you that."

She shook her head. "I can't believe that Uri committed the crime you accuse him of."

"That's your opinion. War changes people. It changed you; it changed him. What he did to Stanislas I wouldn't have done to a dog. Besides, there was a witness."

"Uri loved Stanislas like a brother. He wouldn't have harmed him. Not ever."

"Do you know the horror I carry around in my mind day and

night? Of Stanislas, his broken, bloodied body lying in the snow. He was sixteen, for pity's sake, still a child."

"For heaven's sake stop it, Leonid. Let things rest in peace and end this madness before it destroys you."

A savage expression lit Yakov's face and he got to his feet, scraping back the chair, hatred erupting in him like a storm. "Never. That won't happen, not while I have a breath in my body."

The child shifted in the bed, cried out before he fell back to sleep.

Nina rose from the table. "You won't listen to me, will you? I'm wasting my time. If you have nothing else to say I'd ask you to leave before you wake my son."

Yakov picked up his cap. "Do you still love Uri?"

"What I feel for Uri is none of your business. No more than our differences are. He and I were once man and wife, now we're not, that's all there is to it."

Rain lashed the window. Yakov studied the shabby room before he looked at her. Something close to pity stirred in him.

Nina didn't speak as he stepped toward her, cupped her face in his hand, and said, "Don't look at me as if you despise me."

Nina stared back at him. "I've never despised you. I've always liked you, Leonid. But you're not the person I once knew. That Leonid was decent and had a good heart. This one is bitter and merciless. What's changed you? It's not just Stanislas's death. It's more than that, isn't it?"

He looked into her eyes but didn't reply.

She went to turn away but he pulled her toward him, his lips moving hungrily on hers. She fought him, pushed him away, and slapped him across the face, blood appearing on his lips. "No, Leonid . . . !"

Yakov wiped the streak of crimson from his mouth, stared at it. He glared back at her with a kind of tortured smile. "It only proves what I've always known. The poor can't possess beautiful things."

"I was never beautiful, Leonid, if that's what you mean."

"You sell yourself short. Sometimes at night I used to close my eyes tightly and imagine what it might be like being married to you. To love you and be loved by you in return. But of course, I had no hope.

Someone like me could never dream of possessing someone like you. I was too poor and ugly to ever hope for that."

"Leonid . . . you mustn't speak that way."

"Why not? The first time I saw you the night Stanislas was born, I could have curled up at your feet like a puppy. A childish love, an infatuation, of course, but to me it was love nonetheless. Do you know what's sad? I've never felt that way about another woman. Not even my daughter's mother."

Nina flushed.

Yakov dabbed his bloodied mouth with the back of his hand. "This revolution will change everything. People like you and your kind won't be safe. Life will be harsh for you. Cruel even. But someone like me can be your protector. I can make sure you and your child come to no harm."

The child stirred again in his sleep and coughed. Nina picked up his parcel, thrust it at his chest. "Please, leave now."

"Take it, for the child's sake."

"I want nothing from you, Leonid. *Nothing.*"

He regarded the shabby room. "It doesn't have to be like this. It doesn't have to be grim and hopeless. I could have you assigned better living quarters, proper food. But most of all I can give you something you desperately want."

"What?"

"Your life back. Just tell me the moment Uri contacts you again."

"And if I don't?"

"Then I'm certain Lenin will exile you and your child to a Siberian prison camp."

She heard his boots clatter down the stairs moments later.

She crossed to the window and looked out, saw Yakov climb into a truck before it drove away. She watched it go and let the curtain fall back into place, and then she went to stand over her son, Yakov's threat fresh in her mind.

She looked down at Sergey's sleeping face, at the tiny beads of perspiration on his brow, his plump cupid lips and delicate skin, the damp blond curls she loved to run her hand through. She stroked his face gently with the back of her hand as she heard his labored breathing.

When she could bear it no more, she turned her face away, her eyes welling up with tears as she stumbled over to one of the wicker chairs.

Then, with her head cradled in her arms on the table, she cried: for her parents, for her child, for the secret she kept and had promised never to tell, for the husband she'd forsaken, and for the whole sorry mess her life had become.

26

The carriage turned into Hyde Park and the horses trotted toward one of the fountains. The sun was out, the day hot, and Cockney vendors on bicycles sold ice cream from boxes of crushed ice.

The carriage halted and Hanna Volkov climbed down, hoisting her sun umbrella over her head as she approached the fountain.

A sickly-looking man in his sixties stood smoking a cigar and staring at the surge of water as he leaned on his cane. He was dressed in a formal suit and hat and looked an odd figure with his bug eyes, pasty face, and fat nose.

He turned as Hanna approached, and tipped his hat to reveal his balding head, his accent unmistakably American southern. "Why, Hanna, it's wonderful to meet you again."

"And you, Mr. Ambassador."

Walter H. Page replaced his hat and looked out at the sun-drenched grounds busy with strolling couples and playing children. "Would you mind if we walked? This old man needs to stretch his legs." He gestured with his walking cane to the path that led past the fountain.

Hanna saw a beefy man in a bowler hat and mustache follow in their footsteps twenty yards behind. He looked uncomfortable in his brown suit. She guessed that he was the ambassador's bodyguard.

"I take it you put our proposition to Mr. Andrev?"

"Yes, I did."

Page tapped his cigar. "Then before I ask the all-important question, I'd like your opinion, Hanna."

"Mr. Ambassador?"

"Having met Mr. Andrev, would you trust him? I mean, completely trust him never to breathe a word about our scheme to a soul, at risk of his own life?"

She hesitated for just a second before she said, "Yes, I would."

"Forgive me, but I sense a slight doubt, Hanna."

She looked toward the fountain. "It's not a doubt, more a concern."

"Tell me."

She told Page some of the details of her meeting in the church that morning. "I think Uri Andrev has been through some kind of personal hell. Something awful happened to him after he escaped from the camp."

"What do you mean?"

"It's obvious to me that he's suffered a shock of some kind. If you want my opinion, he's hurt and he's confused, maybe even close to broken."

A worried look flashed on Page's face. "Broken?"

"Not quite. But I think he's a man on the edge. And yet, he's got strength about him that you can almost touch. It's most strange."

"What exactly happened to him?"

"He wouldn't say. But I sense he's been deeply affected by something other than the problems with his family."

Page considered before he sucked on his cigar, blew out smoke. "I'm old enough to recall as a boy seeing General Sherman's troops march into our town and torch our family home. It affected me greatly. Civil war's a brutal experience, one that leaves deep scars and divides families and friends. . . ."

"You're going to ask me if I think Andrev's been too deeply affected by the war to be of use to us?"

"I simply wondered if his distress would impair his ability to carry out his tasks."

"I honestly don't know, Mr. Ambassador. But I don't think we have much choice at this late stage, do we?"

Page took another puff of his cigar, and Hanna could almost hear his mind whirring as he weighed her answers. "I suppose not. So, Boyle is still in Ireland, working on Miss Ryan?"

"He hopes to have her answer by today."

"Then I guess only a single question remains. Is Mr. Andrev with us or not?"

Five minutes later Hanna Volkov's carriage turned out of Hyde Park and joined London's busy traffic.

Walter H. Page stood there a minute longer, watching the carriage go, lost in thought as he finished his cigar, then crushed it with the heel of his shoe. He walked a short distance to his own waiting coach, climbed in, and the driver snapped the reins and the horses trotted toward the park exit.

A hundred yards away a thickset, middle-aged man with a coarse peasant face sat on a bench, leaning against the crossbar of his bicycle, sweating as he licked the remains of an ice cream.

He observed the coach belonging to the balding, odd-looking little man move out into the traffic after Hanna Volkov's. Next to the woman with striking good looks, the little fellow looked ugly. "Beauty and the Beast," he called them, smirking to himself.

The thickset man finished the ice cream and tossed away the remains of the wafer cone, wiped his mouth with the back of his sleeve, and mounted his bicycle. Sweat prickled his face as he tried to decide whom to follow from now on—the Beauty or the Beast?

And then he made up his mind and started pedaling like mad.

27

Across the Irish Sea it was raining that same day, a summer downpour that drenched the city's streets.

Rivers of water pelted the windows as Boyle sat by Lydia's bed in the Mater Hospital. Perspiration bathed her face and she muttered something in her sleep.

The doctor said to Boyle, "She's going to need a few more days before she gets her strength back, so try not to tire her too much."

"I'll do my best. And otherwise?"

"She's young and healthy, and ought to fully recover." The doctor left, closing the door softly.

A little later the rain stopped and sunlight flooded the windows. Boyle waited patiently and saw Lydia's eyes flicker. She blinked drowsily, took in her surroundings, and then her confused gaze settled on her visitor.

"How do you feel, Miss Ryan?"

Her voice sounded slurred. "Tired and sore. Who are you?"

Boyle smiled and fetched a wheelchair left in a corner. "You'll be glad to know that the doctor says you'll be fine. Here, let me help you into the chair."

Lydia came fully awake. "Why? Where are you taking me?"

"For some fresh air. You and I need to chat."

"Who are you?"

"I'm the man who's going to save your life."

The tiny park behind the hospital was filled with flower beds and overlooked a row of eighteenth-century Georgian houses. Boyle halted the wheelchair by a wrought-iron bench.

The granite watchtowers of nearby Mountjoy Prison poked their heads above the hospital walls. Boyle produced a packet of Player's Navy cigarettes and said good-humoredly, "I hear smoking's all the rage among women ever since Mrs. Pankhurst threw herself under those Derby horses for the sake of equality. The suffragette newspapers are calling cigarettes 'the torches of freedom.'"

"Is that meant to be a joke?" Lydia asked.

"No, just my way of saying that I won't be offended if you'd like a cigarette."

"I wouldn't. Are you going to tell me who you are?"

"The name's Joe Boyle." He lit his cigarette, cupping the flame in his hand before he shook the match and tossed it away. "A terrible habit, one I've begun to indulge in only occasionally recently. Perhaps it helps me over the hurdles. You're giving me a mighty suspicious look, Miss Ryan."

"It's your accent that confuses me. What are you doing working alongside British intelligence murderers?"

Boyle took a drag. "Now that's where you'd be wrong. But I am a colonel in the Canadian army, unofficially. Just don't ask me to explain; my story's complicated."

"I don't understand."

"Let me keep it simple. I want your help, Miss Ryan, and I want it badly."

"To do what?"

Boyle took another drag and blew out smoke. "You really are a remarkable young woman, do you know that? There aren't many with your background. Your father ran a successful horse-breeding business in St. Petersburg, where you were educated at St. Benedict's Convent and learned to speak Russian like a native."

"I fail to see what any of that has to do with you."

"Let me finish. Your parents retired to Kentucky, and seem to think that you and your brother are safe in your uncle's stud farm in Kildare. They know nothing about your involvement in Irish republicanism or his, for that matter. If they did they'd have a fit and want you on the next boat to America."

"You seem to know a lot, Boyle."

"I make it my business. Before you met your fiancé you worked as a governess to the Russian royal family. That must have been quite an adventure for a young woman of nineteen."

Lydia said, "The House of Romanov employed hundreds of foreigners as governesses and tutors. I was only one of many."

"True, but didn't the children consider you one of their favorites? The tsar sang your praises after you helped save one of his daughters from a near drowning in the grounds of Peterhof. What was it he called you—his 'Irish good luck charm'? Though I'd hazard a guess that you're not exactly an admirer of royalty since you turned republican."

Lydia's patience waned. "Take me back inside, Boyle. This is tiresome."

She raised herself from the wheelchair but Boyle gently pushed her back. "Hold your horses, we're just getting to the interesting part."

"What is this, Boyle? A short summary of my life before the British execute me?"

"Let me tell it to you straight. The people I represent intend to rescue the tsar and his family."

"What?"

"You heard me. If all goes as planned, we intend to snatch the Romanovs from under their captors' noses."

Lydia stared at him, then she laughed. "Are you mad, Boyle?"

Boyle said with mild amusement, "Calling someone mad—why that's almost a compliment in Ireland. And don't you know that there's a strange law of the universe that says fortune always favors the brave?"

"You're really serious, aren't you?"

"Too right I am." Boyle placed a foot on the rain-soaked bench in front of Lydia and leaned on his knee. "It would mean a hostile journey to Russia and back. You'd travel in the company of a man and use the cover of husband and wife. Once you reached Ekaterinburg, you'd have specific tasks to perform to ensure the family's safe rescue. It's a solid, workable plan."

Amusement sparked in Lydia's eyes. "Have you got my funeral planned afterward, too, Boyle?"

"I know what you're thinking. If you're caught you'd be considered a spy, and spies are shot. But I'm confident our strategy will work. Otherwise I wouldn't be throwing my own hat into the ring. I'd be going in with you."

"Who *are* you, Boyle?"

"We may get to that in time, once I have your answer. There's also another very special reason why I picked you, but we may get to that, too."

Lydia said with fervor, "Do you really want to know what I think? You're right, I have absolutely no interest in monarchies, or anyone connected to them. In fact, I've grown to despise them. Because of royals like the tsar, millions have perished in this and countless other wars. And for what? Some pompous idiot who believes he or she has a God-given right to rule?"

Boyle took a long drag on his cigarette and exhaled. "I take it you met the tsar when you worked for his household."

"Of course I met him. He's a pleasant but not too bright man who should have given up power years ago. I also think he's a fool for ignoring the warning signs. He made his own bed. Let him lie in it."

"And his children?"

Lydia paled and stared silently back at him, as if a nerve was struck.

Boyle said, "I hear that you were particularly close to Anastasia. It was she you helped rescue at Peterhof, wasn't it?"

"That was five years ago, Boyle. A lot has happened. I'm a different woman. We live in a different world."

A wry smile curled Boyle's lips. "Obviously, now that you're smuggling German arms. But we're still talking about five helpless children. Would you turn your back on them?"

Lydia said nothing.

Boyle said, "Our intelligence tells us the Reds intend to execute the entire family, which means we need to act with haste. There'd be a few days' training before we'd send you on your way. You're a woman who's able to handle herself in a difficult situation and that kind of qualification is hard to come by, Miss Ryan."

"I'm not the woman you need, Boyle, I'm really not." Lydia met his stare. "And don't think it's because I don't have feelings for the children. I do. But this is not my battle. I already have a cause."

Boyle tossed away his cigarette and sighed. "You're not making this easy for me, are you?" He snapped the wheelchair round, facing Lydia in the opposite direction. "Let's see if I can change your mind."

28

Boyle maneuvered Lydia's wheelchair through the hospital. He pushed her along a white-tiled corridor until they came to a room where two uniformed policemen stood guard. "What have they told you about your brother?"

"Nothing, except that he's alive. Why?"

Anxiety showed in her face as Boyle nodded to one of the policemen, who opened the door.

Boyle wheeled her inside. Her heart almost stopped when she saw Finn lying unconscious in a metal bed, his head to one side, his arms bruised and bandaged, one of them manacled to a rail of the wrought-iron headboard. He looked so young and vulnerable.

And then Lydia noticed the hollow in the covers where her brother's left leg had been. "Finn . . . ," she cried hoarsely.

Boyle wheeled her closer. "They had to amputate his limb this morning. The lad's had a tough time of it. He's still unconscious after the anesthetic."

Fear spread on Lydia's face. She went to speak but her words caught in her throat.

Boyle said, "He's not out of the woods yet, but the doctors say he'll live."

Lydia struggled with her emotions. Boyle maneuvered her nearer Finn's bed. She reached out and brushed hair from her brother's forehead.

"Finn, can you hear me?" She squeezed his hand but he didn't respond. She stroked his arm, her eyes wet as she said to Boyle, "What's going to happen to him?"

He met her gaze. "That depends on you. Refuse to help me, and the

British will execute you both. Wasn't it one of your republican leaders, James Connolly, who was carried to the firing squad on a stretcher? They'll make no exception with Finn."

"But he's just a child."

Boyle's voice softened. "I'm not the executioner; I'm simply telling you how it is."

Anger flared in her reply. "What exactly do you want of me, Boyle?"

"Your complete cooperation."

"I want details."

"We're tight for time so we'll need to get things under way smartly. We'll have the use of a cottage on a private estate north of Dublin. It's secluded and perfect for our needs. We'll spend a few days going over your cover story to give it the ring of truth, while you and your traveling companion get acquainted. Then we'll send you on your way. There's a cargo ship leaving Belfast docks bound for the Baltic and St. Petersburg in six days' time and we'll be on it."

"Who's the companion?"

"A Russian army officer, a former member of the tsar's bodyguard who escaped from a Bolshevik prison camp. And don't worry, your brother will get the best of care in your absence. When you return you'll both be free to sail home to America."

"Assuming I return."

"I'd be lying if I said that your journey won't be dangerous."

Lydia stared down at her brother's sleeping face, at his shackled arm, then she looked up and said furiously, "You're a callous, cold-hearted brute, Boyle."

"You want the truth? I was lucky to get the British to agree to this. Be grateful that you and Finn at least stand a chance."

"You can go to the devil."

She went to strike him across the cheek but Boyle had a boxer's reflexes and he caught her arm. He met her stare, saw torment in her eyes, a terrible anguish, and something in him softened as he relaxed his grip. "I'll give you an hour to think about my offer. After that, it's out of my hands."

29

It was surprisingly chilly that morning in June, and Father Doneski was lighting another candle at the altar of St. Constantine's.

He heard footsteps come down the aisle and turned. A thickset man with a coarse, peasant face full of cunning stood there. "Hello, priest," he said in Russian.

"What do you want?" Doneski demanded, bristling.

The man smirked and tipped back his cap. "Just a quiet chat between friends."

Doneski blew out the taper he was using to light the candles. "You and I will never be friends. And remove your cap in God's house before I tear it off."

The man's smirk widened. "Getting very brave, aren't you, priest?"

In an instant, Doneski crossed the gap between them and ripped the cloth cap from the man's head. The visitor was no match for the priest's powerful physique and could only watch as his cap was flung to the floor. "In my church, you will do as I say," Doneski raged.

The man picked up his cap with a sullen look and dusted it in his hands. "I'd be more respectful if I was you, or someone's liable to suffer."

Doneski seemed at once in torment, his jaw twitching. "I told you everything I know."

The visitor stuffed his cap in his pocket. "Not everything, priest. I followed Hanna Volkov all day yesterday. She's staying at the Connaught Hotel. It turns out she met with the American ambassador. Before that, she met with a man, here in the church. I followed him to a printing works in Whitechapel. What's going on? What's that bourgeois witch up to?"

Doneski fell silent.

The man said, "Have you forgotten our agreement?"

Doneski's fists balled in anger and he found it hard to keep himself from strangling the man. "I always said that you Reds were the devil incarnate."

"You wouldn't like your dear old mother or your relatives in Moscow to be harmed, would you? Tell me about Volkov before I change my mind and they're left to rot in their cells."

Doneski's shoulders seemed to sag and he knew resistance was hopeless. "The man Hanna Volkov met with, his name is Andrev, he's a Russian émigré. I've seen him before at our soup kitchen."

The man grinned. "Excellent. Now scour that mind of yours and tell me every little thing you know. Don't leave out a morsel."

Just after six the following evening the thickset man boarded the overnight train for Edinburgh, leaving King's Cross. He carried a sailor's duffel bag and a third-class train ticket.

By early next morning the engine crossed the Scottish border and finally chugged into Edinburgh Station.

The Russian slept little and was exhausted, the information he memorized fueling his nervous excitement. He visited a telegraph office in the city and sent a brief coded cable to Paris, from where it would ultimately find its way to Moscow.

He stopped at a grocer's and used his ration book to buy some jam, tinned ham, dried biscuits, and sardines for his long journey ahead. He also bought a bottle of buttermilk and some fresh bread and cheese for his breakfast and ate them ravenously as he walked to the docks.

The Russian presented his ticket and boarded the *Baltic Prince* just before noon, his Swedish passport in the name of Lars Westens checked and found in order.

It was a pleasant enough crossing, the North Sea like glass and the Northern Lights shimmering in the bright Arctic night sky. Four days later the Russian disembarked in Helsinki and took a tram to the Market District, where an elderly female party member ran a safe house.

She supplied him with a hot bath and a meal, a small sum of cash, fresh travel documents, and a train ticket for Moscow.

After several delays at the Russian border while the Red Army guards scrupulously checked every passenger's papers, his train finally reached Moscow seventy-two hours later.

By 9:15 that morning the man presented himself at the Kremlin's Troitsky Gate, a curious little white round tower connected to the main fortress by a bridge over an old moat. He handed over his papers and an arrogant-looking officer examined them. "What business do you have here?"

"Private business. Now telephone Comrade Lenin's secretary and tell her that Semashko is here from London with urgent news. Be quick about it."

The commander resented being spoken to by an unshaven, bleary-eyed vagabond in crumpled clothes carrying a sailor's bag, but something about the man's tone told him it might be wise to obey the request.

He made the call and soon a pretty little hunchbacked girl, wearing a thick gray woolen skirt and black cardigan and flat brown shoes, shuffled down the cobbled path from the Kremlin. Maria Glasser was Lenin's private secretary. She shared the Red dictator's innermost secrets and was totally trusted by him.

The man with the sailor's duffel bag called out, "Maria! Tell these idiots to let me pass."

The secretary said to the commander, "I can vouch for this citizen, comrade. Let him enter."

As Maria Glasser led the way up toward the Kremlin, she addressed the visitor like the old comrade that he was. "Lenin read your cable. He's been anxiously awaiting your arrival. But we better hurry—he's got an important meeting in the War Ministry at ten."

"Do yourself a favor and just cancel Lenin's meeting, Maria."

"What?"

"Once he hears my news he won't be going anywhere."

■ ■ ■

Two miles away in Moscow's Arbat District, Yakov stepped out of the Fiat truck.

In the driver's seat, Zoba said, "Maybe you could spend some time with her at my place. My wife can make us all dinner."

"There isn't time. I have an appointment at the Kremlin in an hour."

"You have to make time where children are concerned, Leonid. Do you know why Trotsky summoned you?"

"I'll worry about that when I get there." He picked up the brown-wrapped parcel from the truck's floor and tossed it at Zoba. "I've a job for you. Find another way to get food and clothing to Nina Andrev."

He removed a heavy leather purse full of rubles from his pocket and left it on the front seat. "She'll need medicine for the child. You can only get that kind of thing on the black market these days, and it's expensive."

"But she's already refused your help."

"Use a local priest, or the doctor who tends her child. Have them say it's to help her plight. Make it sound believable. I don't want her to suspect it came from me."

It was two o'clock and the public schoolyard was filling up, some of the younger children coming out to meet their mothers.

Yakov walked up to the wire fence.

The dark-haired girl came out moments later. She would soon be six years old and was wearing a worn blue dress and stout leather shoes. Nothing remarkable about her, a plain little girl with pigtails, but her big, expressive eyes were her mother's and they made her look incredibly innocent.

Ever since the first day he held her in his arms as a newborn, he felt touched by her. He'd named her Katerina, after his dead sister, and she seemed to be his only real connection to the world, now that Stanislas was gone.

She searched the waiting crowd anxiously, and then Yakov saw Zoba's wife appear, a smiling, big-bosomed peasant woman.

She picked up his daughter in her arms, hugged and kissed her, then led her away by the hand, the child skipping happily.

Yakov felt a terrible urgency to go after his daughter, to take her in his arms and smother her with kisses, see her childish smile and those big innocent eyes light up her face, but he desperately fought the need.

He had the party's work to do. Personal needs came second.

"A revolution is difficult for everyone. It can't be won without sacrifice and suffering."

He recalled Nina's reply. "And what's yours, Leonid . . . ?"

He was staring at the answer to that question, as Katerina skipped away.

For a long time Yakov stood at the wire, silently watching his child, until he felt his eyes moisten and he turned back toward the truck.

30

Yakov hated the Kremlin.

There was something sinister about its twelfth-century bloodred walls, the site of the original wooden stockade where Ivan the Terrible liked to impale his victims.

He drove his dark green truck into the Armory courtyard.

A Red Army aide was waiting for him. "Follow me, Commissar Yakov."

The aide ran up a flight of granite steps up to a stone-flagged archway and Yakov followed. In a square below a battery of trucks and artillery was drawn up, and everywhere there were vigilant Red Army guards armed with rifles.

The aide came to a studded oak door, which he opened. "Inside, Commissar. Mind your step, the floor's slippery."

They entered a highly polished, ornate corridor. The parquet floors smelled of disinfectant and wax polish. The walls were painted duck-egg blue, and plush red, navy, and yellow rugs with the tsar's royal insignia still covered the floor.

Two guards with rifles slung over their shoulders kept watch either side of another door at the end of the hallway. Yakov said to the aide as they approached the door, "I presume you know why I'm here?"

His face was set in a blank expression. "You're asking the wrong man, Commissar. My task is simply to deliver you to your destination."

The two guards admitted them into a plush outer office draped with magnificent tsarist tapestries, a sparkling chandelier hanging overhead. Paintings adorned the walls, their frames covered in solid gold leaf, and in the center of the outer office was a pair of floor-to-ceiling double oak doors.

The aide held out a hand. "Your sidearm, please. No visitors are allowed to carry weapons past this point. But with luck, you shouldn't have long to wait."

Yakov removed his revolver and handed it across. The aide placed the revolver in a desk drawer.

Almost on cue the floor-to-ceiling doors burst open and an arrogant-looking man appeared.

He bristled with restless energy and was dressed in a black military uniform and polished knee-high boots. In one hand he carried his trademark officer's baton, in his other he held a stiff paper envelope. His full head of untamed, wavy hair, his black Vandyke beard, and wire-rimmed spectacles gave him the look of an eccentric academic.

Yakov recognized Leon Trotsky, the defense minister and Lenin's ruthless right-hand man. He had the glittering, dark eyes of a fanatic, and coldness emanated from him like a physical force. Yakov always found something slightly chilling about him.

He snapped to attention, clicked his heels. "Comrade Trotsky."

"Come."

The balcony overlooked Moscow. The tall French windows were already open and Trotsky stepped out. He fitted a cigarette into a long cigarette holder, lit it, and blew out smoke.

Yakov joined him. Farther along, he glimpsed another French-windowed room where a man with a balding head was hunched down over some paperwork. He recognized the unmistakable figure of Vladimir Lenin.

"You're proving very capable. Comrade Lenin is well pleased with you, Yakov. But I wonder if you're up to the task he has in mind for you."

"Comrade Minister?"

Trotsky delicately balanced the cigarette holder between slim, aristocratic fingers. He removed the envelope from under his arm, opened it, and handed Yakov a photograph. It was a picture of the tsar and his family, the kind of royal memento commonly sold in street kiosks and stores before the tsar's abdication.

Trotsky said, "Your wife was one of the first to be shot during the uprising, I believe. What do you feel when you look at that photograph, Yakov? Hatred? Fury? Bitterness? Answer honestly."

"For the children, the wife, I feel nothing. For her husband, hate is too mild a word. I despise him."

"I'm glad to hear that. Personally, I'd put the tsar on public trial and hang him, but Comrade Lenin has other plans."

Yakov went to hand back the snapshot.

Trotsky shook his head. "Keep it. Let it be a reminder of your hatred, never to allow your loathing to diminish, even for a second."

"Why?"

"Because we want you to administer the execution of the entire Romanov family."

31

It was easy to believe that the most brutal war in world history was happening a million miles away that evening.

The gala fund-raising concert in Albert Hall was attended by the usual dignitaries, the ladies in their finest silks, the gentlemen in formal evening wear.

The London Symphony was playing Sibelius and just before the interval the American ambassador, Walter Page, left his wife's side and stepped out of his box. He was guided by an usher to a private room at the end of a hall.

The lights were out and the curtains open, the room faintly illuminated by the amber streaks in London's evening sky. A figure stood in shadows.

Page lit a cigar and strolled over. Someone had placed a silver tray on a side table, champagne already poured for the interval into a half-dozen flute glasses, the bottle stuck in a silver bucket of crushed ice.

Page selected a glass and knocked back the champagne in one gulp. "I always find these things so terribly boring, don't you, Mack?"

The American ambassador's aide, John MacKenzie, appeared out of the shadows. He was tall, immaculately groomed, his hair well oiled, his Brooks Brothers suit crisply pressed. "What can I say, Mr. Ambassador? It's a diversion."

Page took a couple of pills from a bottle in his pocket and washed them down with another glass of champagne. "It's giving me the headache from hell. What are you doing here?"

"I wanted to talk with you about our agent in Russia, sir."

"Can't it wait until tomorrow?"

"I'm afraid not. What do you know about Philip Sorg, sir?"

"Only what our friends in State tell me. That he's kept a watch on the Romanovs since their imprisonment, following them from Tsarskoye Selo to Tobolsk, and on to Ekaterinburg. That his efforts are a vital part of our plans. Why?"

"What do you know about Sorg personally?"

"Very little, except he must have had his nerves surgically removed to do what he's doing."

Mack looked out at London's rooftops. "I met him once when I worked in Washington. He's a strange character. Thrives on danger. I heard whispers that he spied for us in Russia in 1913, when we were following the rise of the socialist groups, and that he was picked up by the Ochrana and tortured. He had a very rough time of it by all accounts, before he escaped and managed to flee the country."

"And they sent him back in? Why, for heaven's sake?"

"He volunteered, sir. But here's the thing—his nerves are shot to pieces. The only way he can cope is by using laudanum, apparently."

Page looked askew. "You're not serious. Can we rely on this fellow?"

"State says we can. But it brings me to our problem." Mack unfolded a typed page. "This came over the secure telegraph, sir. I've decoded the original."

Page put down his empty glass and took the typed sheet.

Mack added, "In Dimitri's last report he suspected that he was being hunted by the secret police. It seems he may have run out of luck."

Page looked worried as he finished reading the paper. "You're sure of this?"

"I'm afraid our man in Ekaterinburg may be finished before we even start."

PART THREE

PART THREE

32

Everything was going fine until Sorg had to stab the woman to death.

That morning he dragged a wooden handcart behind him, its wheels bouncing over the cobbled backstreets. He was dressed in a worker's cotton smock, a worn cap, coarse woolen trousers, and scuffed high boots. With his bushy beard and greasy hair he looked every inch a Russian peasant.

The handcart he found in a secondhand huckster shop in the markets. A wheel was damaged and one of the handles loose, but for eight rubles the man in the shop had thrown in a hammer and nails to cement the deal.

Sorg fixed up the cart and piled in some scraps of wood and a few red bricks, his frayed black overcoat draped over the handles. A man with a handcart was a man with a purpose, the kind of busy worker who thronged Ekaterinburg's streets. Under the pile of scrap Sorg had hidden the revolver he'd taken from the landlord, Ravich.

In the space of a year, Ekaterinburg had been occupied by the Whites, then overrun by the Reds, then seized by the Whites again, and now retaken by the Reds in fierce and bloody battles. The bustling Siberian city at the crossroads with Asia was in turmoil, the streets teeming with refugees, poor and wealthy alike, desperate to flee Moscow and St. Petersburg.

Everyone looked wretched. Electric streetcars were crowded, the backstreets narrow and noisy, and the gutters choked with filth and stinking to heaven. The population of over a hundred thousand was swelled by almost half that again, and an air of panic saturated the city.

The industrial heartland of Siberia, with the richest mines of platinum, gold, and valuable metals, was under constant siege. Each evening at eight the sirens signaled the commencement of curfew, which lasted until 5 a.m.

Sorg dragged his cart past the log houses of the working class and came to a warren of backstreets teeming with workers' tenements, where the stench of uncollected garbage hit his nostrils. Here and there along the city's three-mile-long Voznesensky Prospect, lined with linden trees, the stucco fronts of mansions, businesses, and churches were blistered by gunfire.

It was now illegal to sell maps in Russia—the Reds feared they could be of use to enemy spies. Simple possession was punishable by execution, so Sorg took mental note of streets, alleyways, and bridges.

He paid special attention to the hotels, lodging houses, and barracks that garrisoned restless gangs of Red Guard units. The idiots made it easy for him: everywhere they stayed, they hung fluttering red flags. After a couple of weeks, Sorg was familiar with every back alley.

In one side street he came across a grotesque sight: five bodies slumped against the wall of a merchant's grain store. What looked like an entire family, father, mother, and their three juvenile children, had been executed, their corpses riddled with bullets and left to rot. A message daubed in white paint on the grain store wall said, "These traitors tried to starve the revolution! All traitors will be executed!"

Nobody was safe from the Reds' paranoia and carnage. And yet despite it, every hotel and lodging house in Ekaterinburg was filled to bursting.

Arriving in late May, Sorg found a ruin of a lodging house on the edge of the markets area, laundry hanging from its upstairs balconies. But it had a huge rear garden that backed into thick woods, perfect if Sorg needed to escape in a hurry. He bought a sturdy lock and chain and fastened his handcart to a backyard drainpipe each night.

He shared a squalid room with three other men, a wooden bunk each and a filthy toilet and washroom down the hall with a chipped enamel bath and a cold water tap that didn't always work.

Two of the men were railway workers; the third was a twitchy young man with a wispy beard, whom he sometimes played cards with to pass the time. Sorg suspected that he was a White deserter.

What cash Sorg had left, he stashed in his boots and buried in an oilskin bag in the woods behind the lodging house. He kept his steel pen handy at all times.

That morning, as he dragged his cart toward the snaking Iset River and its broad lake, Sorg heard a church bell tower chime 10 a.m.

He hurried his pace.

With luck, today I'm going to contact Anastasia.

Sorg turned up a hill into a cobbled alleyway of dilapidated old warehouses, most of them boarded up. He halted outside one of the buildings, checked that the alleyway was empty, then lifted the latch on a pair of double doors and dragged the cart in after him.

The warehouse he entered was covered in rotted hay that smelled of excrement, the lime-washed walls daubed with revolutionary slogans: "Down with the rich." "Kill the bourgeoisie who bleed us."

Sorg lowered the door latch again and wedged a wooden plank lengthways against the door to prevent anyone from entering. The cart would act as an obstacle in case he needed to flee out the rear. From under the scrap wood he took the revolver and stuffed it in his pocket.

He climbed creaking wooden stairs to a huge loft, stacked with piles of old birch logs. Four glass panes sprayed frosty light into the room. The window looked down toward the Iset River. He had discovered the loft two weeks ago when scouring the city for an observation position.

Sorg crossed to a woodpile in a corner and removed some logs. Underneath was hidden the brass spyglass. He took it over to the window, wiped condensation from a fogged window pane with his sleeve, and saw in the distance the southern side of the Ipatiev House and its gardens.

Ekaterinburg's streets babbled with Chinese whispers. Within a day of arriving he heard about the "House of Special Purpose" near Voznesensky Prospect. The house once belonged to a wealthy local business before it was seized by the Reds to house the Romanovs.

He settled himself down on the grimy floor and peered through the spyglass. The two-story Ipatiev compound was guarded by a double wooden fence, parts of it over three meters high. Sorg spotted three bored-looking guards armed with rifles wandering the grounds. The view was so restricted by the high fence, he could only make out the heads or torsos of anyone strolling in the garden.

More guards patrolled a wide street outside. And in the soaring bell tower of nearby Voznesensky Cathedral was a Red Army machine-gun nest, the weapon trained on the Ipatiev House.

Sorg had no fear of the machine-gunner—every time he trained his spyglass on the tower, the gunner was either asleep or scratching himself.

Sorg checked his pocket watch: 10:20 a.m.

Anastasia and her family usually took their daily exercise twice in the gardens: at 11:30 a.m., and again about 3:30 p.m., on each occasion for half an hour. Sometimes it lasted longer, depending on the whim of the guards. It was over a year since he last communicated with her. It seemed an eternity. But today he hoped to change that and his heart soared with anticipation.

He settled down to wait, his nerves on edge.

In his pockets were stuffed a bottle of beer, a block of hard cheese wrapped in greaseproof paper, and the laudanum tincture. He removed the bottle, shook it, and twisted open the dropper cap.

He made his meager supply last by watering it down with vodka, until it became a weak, watery brown mixture. On occasions when his supply ran out, he chain-smoked cigarettes and drank vast amounts of tea and coffee.

But even coffee and cigarettes were getting scarce with rationing. He squeezed a few drops into his lower gums, screwed back on the stopper, and ran a forefinger around the inside of his mouth, vigorously rubbing the laudanum into his gums.

Within minutes he began to relax.

An image floated in front of him—Anastasia's face—and his mind drifted back to their last meeting.

33

Sorg could never forget that final day. It was seared into his mind like an open wound.

Every Wednesday afternoon for almost four months he would take the train to Tsarskoye Selo and just before 4 p.m. would present himself at the palace gate.

The sentries checked his papers—Sorg's special pass was stamped with the Romanov crest, along with a letter stating that he was a piano tutor by royal appointment. A palace aide would escort him across the courtyard and up some stone steps to the royal family quarters.

He and Anastasia would spend two hours together in a cold palace room with wooden floors, seated on two stools in front of the piano.

The family lived simply. Sorg learned the tsar was no believer in an easy life for his children; they slept on hard beds and were obliged to do daily chores.

Despite Anastasia's enthusiasm, it took only one lesson to discover that she was a terrible pupil—she preferred to distract him with mimicry, palace gossip, and news about her relatives and family, which helped Sorg fill his reports.

"I've decided," Anastasia announced after a month of lessons, "I don't have the talent to be a good musician. But can we keep it our secret, Philip? I enjoy your company so much. Life gets so boring here. My sisters say we children can never have a normal life. It's like living in a gilded cage—we almost never go out."

She laid the ground rules on their second meeting. "Please don't call me Princess or Grand Duchess. I hate formality. Just call me Anastasia and I'll call you Philip. How's that?"

She said, "Tell me more about America. Would I really like it there, do you think?" She laid her hand on Sorg's arm and the touch of her fingers felt like silk.

Her infectious spirit always lifted his mood, but that afternoon he knew something was wrong.

All week St. Petersburg was in chaos, the government in turmoil, troops everywhere. When Sorg approached the sentry post he noticed soldiers all over the palace grounds. His documents got him past the sentry, but there was no sign of the aide and Sorg strolled toward the courtyard that led up to the royal quarters.

An elderly palace officer with a monocle halted him. "What's your business here?" he demanded.

"I'm expected." Sorg showed his pass and letter.

The officer squinted through his monocle at the pieces of paper as if they were worthless currency. "No more lessons, all that's over now. Haven't you heard the news? The tsar's abdicated. He's under house arrest."

So that's it. Rumors flew for days in St. Petersburg that the tsar might abdicate. Sorg worried it might be his last opportunity to see Anastasia. "If you could summon a member of the royal household, I'm sure they'll—"

The officer went to reach for his revolver. "Are you deaf?"

"No, please! Don't harm him."

Anastasia hurried down the steps, carrying a brown leather pouch. She wore a simple white muslin dress, a pearl choker around her neck, black shoes, and white socks. Her blue eyes begged the officer as she said, "Please, sir, this gentleman's my tutor and I need to speak with him in private. I thank you for being so kind as to allow it."

Disarmed by her plea, the officer snapped off a salute. "As you wish, Grand Duchess, but please remain within the courtyard where I can see you."

"I knew you'd come; that's why I had to meet you. Papa's heard that we may eventually be moved east to the Urals, so I wanted to say good-bye."

Strolling in the distance of the gardens, Sorg caught sight of the tsar. He wore his trademark tunic and hat and pushed a wheelchair in which sat his invalid young son, the tsarevitch, Alexei. "Why the Urals?"

"They think we'll be safer there, whoever *they* are. Mama is worried that it's so far away we won't have a proper doctor for Alexei. He's often ill these days."

"I thought the officer said you weren't to leave his sight."

Anastasia smiled as she led him toward a private garden with a stone fountain, out of view of the officer. She swung the leather pouch she carried and plucked a flower as they walked, smelling its scent. Sorg realized that she had never once mentioned his lame pace.

"You mean old Squinty? He knows I break the rules, but he won't cause a rumpus. Anyway, I wanted us to talk."

They came to a bench and she gestured for him to sit. "I won't be able to see you again and I'm going to miss our friendship and our talks. I'm sorry for being such a terrible pupil, Philip."

"I've known worse but none as entertaining."

"Really? Your visits always help relieve the monotony." She giggled. "Maria says the formality here makes her want to set fire to the palace. What will you do? Will you stay in Russia?"

"That depends on how much worse things get."

"Do you think they'll get worse?"

"I'm afraid so. How are the guards treating your family?"

"Well enough. Why?"

"This government isn't going to last forever, Anastasia. Others may come to power, and some may be angry people who'll want to harm your father."

"I overheard my mother say that to Papa. But Papa said that won't happen. That the people would never allow it." She looked at Sorg intently. "Papa always puts his faith in God. He says he'll never leave Russia, not ever. He loves it too much. I just don't understand why anyone would hate Papa. He's such a kind and gentle man."

"Not everyone thinks that way. There are some who believe he did terrible wrongs in the past."

"I'm not stupid, Philip. I've overheard people talk about such things, especially the guards. They said sometimes Papa allowed very bad things to happen. Some people call him 'Bloody Nicholas.' What's your opinion?"

The question threw Sorg. Part of him wanted to protect her, but he couldn't hide the bitter truth. "May I be honest?"

"Of course."

Sorg told her. When he finished there was a silence. A shocked Anastasia put a hand to her mouth and looked close to tears. "I—I expect you must hate my father for what happened to your family."

"At times I have."

She considered. "I don't doubt you, but I still love my father. I know he tries to be a better person. We all do. My sister Maria says we all commit sins but that emperors can commit bigger sins than most. And my mama always tells us to be considerate of others. To think of ourselves last, to always show a loving heart. Do—do you secretly hate me?"

"How could I? It's not your fault. But some people may want revenge for the wrongs they believe your father did."

"Do you know what Rasputin said to my parents before he was killed?"

"What?"

"He prophesied that none of us Romanovs would live. That we'd be killed by the Russian people. I know some say Rasputin was insane, and Papa would probably agree, but he was always good to Alexei. The trouble is my mama's a superstitious woman and she fears his prophecy."

He feared the truth of her words but tried to comfort her. "I think perhaps your mother worries too much."

"I hope you're right." She brightened, then said earnestly, "I'm going to miss your company, Philip. May I tell you a secret? Maria also said that there may be more to you than I think."

"I don't understand."

"What's the expression she used? 'A dark horse.' She says you might even be a spy. You're not a spy, are you, Philip?"

The teasing question startled Sorg. *Is she just making fun or does she suspect me?*

Before Sorg could even speak, she fumbled in the leather pouch on her lap and produced a Kodak camera—the small vest pocket model that was all the rage. "Do you like boats?"

"Why?"

"No reason. There are a few things I really like. Messing about on boats is one. And taking photographs is another. May I take yours? I'd like to have a photograph of you to remember you by. I'll keep it among my albums."

"Of—of course."

"You're not smiling. Smile."

"I find it hard to, knowing I'll never see you again."

"Then imagine that we will."

A self-conscious Sorg looked into the lens, tried to smile, and barely managed it.

Anastasia said, "Try not to look like I'm going to shoot you, Philip. This isn't an execution, you know."

That made him smile.

Anastasia brightened. "Actually, I think I'd prefer it if I took one of us both. Would you mind?"

"No."

She shifted back on the bench and leaned close to him—so close he could smell her lavender scent—held one hand outstretched so that the camera was aimed at them, and pressed the shutter.

"Thank you," she said. "I feel better knowing I have this to remember you by."

Sorg saw the officer march toward them, adjusting his monocle.

Anastasia jumped to her feet and stuffed the Kodak in the pouch. "I better go. Mama will get worried. She always gets worried these days. Papa says she's a bag of nerves. May I say something very personal?"

"Of course."

"I don't know if we'll ever see each other again, but I want you to know that I enjoyed our meetings. In fact, Maria thinks I'm a little in love with you."

Anastasia blushed and offered him her hand. Sorg, speechless, accepted it. He felt his heart beat furiously as he held her soft fingers.

At that moment, she looked like the lost adolescent she truly was, trying to find her way in the harsh adult world. There seemed to be something incredibly naïve and touching about her, an almost childish honesty that again aroused in him the powerful feeling that he wanted to protect her.

Then, without warning, she leaned forward and kissed him on the cheek. "Good-bye, Philip. I'm sorry for what happened to your father, I truly am. Please forgive my family." She turned and raced past the officer through the garden and up a flight of stone steps.

Sorg, watching her go, put a hand up to feel the ghost of her lips on his cheek.

34

Sorg heard the harsh rattle of a motor engine and came alert.

A truck passed him in the alleyway outside the loft window. Seated in the back were at least ten Red Army soldiers. A couple were females, rough-looking peasant girls. The Reds recruited anyone able to carry a rifle.

The laudanum had worn off and now his adrenaline kicked in. He tensed and checked his pocket watch: 10:50 a.m. He had nodded off.

He glimpsed a movement in the Ipatiev House garden and settled his right eye into the spyglass. His heart skipped. The Romanovs had stepped out into the garden. Sorg recognized Anastasia walking next to her sisters, Maria and Tatiana, who pushed Alexei in a wheelchair.

The usual half dozen or so armed sentries patrolled the grounds, while two more washed down a truck parked near the fence.

Sorg swore. For some reason, the guards had allowed the family out early for their daily exercise. It could ruin his plans.

He shifted his attention back to the alleyway below. The truck drove slowly to the farthest end, turned, and disappeared.

Sorg wasted no time. He stashed the spyglass and tripod under the woodpile and clambered down the stairs.

Sorg dragged the handcart along the public road that ran along the eastern side of the Ipatiev House. As he walked he slipped on a red armband and tucked the revolver under the scrap in the handcart.

A few pedestrians passed him in the street, most of them gawking at the house. The Romanovs' prison was the worst-kept secret in town.

The building's whitewashed upstairs windows meant he could see nothing inside the house, nor could he make out anything beyond the double paling. In the Voznesensky Cathedral bell tower, Sorg couldn't even spot the Red Army soldier manning the machine gun. The man was probably asleep.

The day was hot, with a light breeze blowing. Sorg halted the cart. Two guards patrolling farther along the fence chatted and paid him no attention. From his handcart, Sorg grabbed a glass bottle filled with water and took a long drink.

From his observations, Anastasia and her sisters often lingered at this sunny part of the property on their walks. As he stood drinking he was convinced he heard the murmur of girlish voices beyond the fence.

His heart pounded. The guards were still chatting. He knew he had to act fast.

From his pocket he took a smooth, round stone. Tied to it was a piece of string to secure the note he'd written. Sorg tossed the stone over the fence. It landed with a dull *clunk*.

"Hey, you!"

Sorg froze. A small, aggressive guard with a thick mustache came hurrying toward him. "What's your business here? What are you up to?"

Sorg felt his blood drain. He prayed the man didn't see him toss the stone.

"I asked you a question," the guard barked as he walked around Sorg, shifting his rifle to waist level, studying him suspiciously. "What's your business here?"

Sorg gestured to the bottle in his hand, then to his red armband. "Can't a hardworking comrade take a drink of water to quench his thirst?"

The guard relaxed a touch, pointed his rifle down. "Be quick about it, citizen, and don't loiter here in the future, you hear? Or you're liable to get shot."

Sorg dragged the cart into a side street, scurrying away as fast as he could.

He felt lucky the guard didn't see him, or he could have been arrested and shot. It was getting even more difficult to get close to the

Ipatiev House. That worried him. It made carrying out his tasks almost impossible.

As Sorg pushed his handcart through the crowded alleyways, he glanced over his shoulder. He wasn't being followed. *Did Anastasia or one of her family find the stone? What if one of the guards found it?* His worried mind was assaulted by questions, and the frustration of not knowing the answers was killing him.

Fifteen minutes later he came out onto Yentov Street, across the road from his lodgings. Sorg stopped in his tracks.

A crowd of Red Army troops was gathered outside the lodging house, their truck parked on the pavement. A man was being led out in handcuffs. It was Sorg's fellow tenant, the card-playing young man with the wispy beard who he thought was a White deserter.

Sorg felt his stomach churn. Leading him out of the house was a fleshy man with a bald head and wearing a long black coat.

Kazan.

A stunned Sorg heard a voice behind him say, "Put your arms up high!"

Sorg snapped round. A female Red Guard stood behind him, brandishing a worn-looking rifle with a long bayonet. He hadn't heard her approach. She was skinny and too small for her weapon, but the look on her face was sheer determination. "I said put your arms high. Don't take a step or I'll kill you."

Sorg had no time to reach for the hidden revolver and tried to side-step. The woman squeezed the trigger of the old rifle.

There was a click. The round either misfired or she forgot to load the chamber. The woman came at him with the bayonet. It pierced Sorg's side and he felt a searing pain.

He staggered back as his left hand came up instinctively and grabbed the rifle, pulling the woman closer, just as his steel pen appeared in his other hand. In an instant he slipped the blade between her ribs. The woman gave a terrifying final croak and fell still. Sorg let her body slide to the ground.

He put a hand to his side. He was bleeding heavily, the pain excruciating.

"You! Halt!"

Kazan must have seen him and barked at him from across the road. The sound of his voice rattled Sorg.

Some instinct made him grab the woman's rifle. He snapped open the bolt—the chamber was empty but the magazine full, meaning the woman hadn't loaded a round.

He quickly loaded, aimed, and fired at Kazan. The rifle kicked painfully into his shoulder and as the round cracked the soldiers ducked behind a wall—all except Kazan, who stood staring defiantly like an enraged bull as he reached for the holstered gun on his belt.

Sorg quickly snapped home another round, caught Kazan directly in his sights, and squeezed the trigger.

The shot struck Kazan and he buckled, clasping both hands to his crotch.

Across the street, someone screamed an order and a rifle volley rang out, shots chipping the brickwork above Sorg's head, the ricochets whistling. The soldiers advanced, aiming their rifles.

Sorg abandoned his cart and ran into the backstreets, an explosion of gunfire raging behind him.

35

The bullet-scarred train with the red star on front thundered into Ekaterinburg's main station.

It ground to a halt with a squeal of brakes and a cloud of steam.

Yakov stepped down from his mud-stained carriage. The station was bedlam, passengers and troops milling in all directions.

A fleshy, bald-headed man approached from the platform. His face was bone white and he looked in pain, a finger of his right hand heavily bandaged. "Commissar Yakov. You had a pleasant trip?"

"What are you doing here, Kazan?" The turncoat former Ochrana agent always reminded Yakov of a snake.

"I wanted to pass on information that may interest you."

"And since when are the Romanovs your concern?"

"A case I'm working on, Commissar. It has the highest priority."

"That's news to me. What happened to your hand?"

"Someone tried to kill me." Kazan's face flushed with rage as he showed the flap of his holster, where a hole was drilled through. "My revolver was hit; I had to replace it. The bullet took off the tip of my finger. An inch lower and I could have lost my manhood."

Yakov raised an eyebrow. "That certainly made the day a little more interesting. What's your information?"

"There's been a disturbing development in regard to the Romanovs. Perhaps we might travel together and I can tell you on the way?"

An Austin-Putilov armored car was parked outside with its engine running, a Fiat truck behind it, and when they climbed aboard the truck Kazan snapped an order and the armored car hooted the horse-drawn traffic out of the way.

"I've taken the liberty of booking you a room in the city's best hotel, the Amerika, a favorite of the local Cheka."

"I've no need. I'll quarter aboard my train."

"As you wish. Do you know Ekaterinburg, Commissar?"

"Vaguely." As the convoy trundled through the streets, Yakov saw a skyline crowded with stunning golden-domed churches and spires, alongside ugly smokestacks of redbrick iron factories and smelting works. Some of the tough Siberian inhabitants looked like a product of the iron factories they served: stocky and muscular, with broad shoulders and fists like hammers.

Kazan went on, "There's a population of just over a hundred thousand, but that's grown since hostilities began. Wealthy mine owners and nobles have homes here, but we're rooting out these vermin. Many have been shot, others banished to camps."

"The kind of butcher's work you enjoy, no doubt. What about the Romanovs: are they behaving?"

"I believe so. The family take their meals with their guards, the same rations. They're allowed an hour's exercise daily, half in the morning, and half in the early evening."

"What's this disturbing development you wanted to discuss?"

Kazan took a creased sheet of paper from his pocket. "This morning one of the guards found this note near the Romanov daughter Anastasia. He observed her attempt to pick it up while she exercised in the garden."

Yakov examined the note. Oddly, the Cyrillic handwriting was in ink. It read: *Be strong. Help is near. Philip.* "Was she questioned?"

"She told us nothing. I doubt she had time to read the note. Still, it concerns me that whoever left the note may be trying to rescue the family."

"Tell me your suspicions."

"*Philip* may be a name or even a code word. It's impossible to tell without further interrogation. Ekaterinburg's full of spies, but I believe the message may have come from a foreign agent we've been hunting for well over a year. Perhaps you've heard?"

"The one they call 'the Phantom'? Lenin has taken a personal interest and wants him caught. But this Phantom has eluded you so far, I hear."

Kazan's mouth curled with displeasure. "He's been lucky to have stayed one step ahead of us. But his luck won't last forever."

"You sound confident, Kazan."

"I've been hunting him since he murdered the landlord of a property near the Alexander Palace. He made it look like an accident by burning down his apartment. I'm convinced he was observing the Romanovs and that we may be dealing with the same man."

"What makes you think that?"

"Thirty years' experience. And this." Kazan produced a small brown medicine bottle from his pocket. "I raided a lodging house in the markets' area this morning as part of a search for White deserters. One of my men found this empty bottle hidden under a bed in one of the rooms."

Yakov examined the bottle and smelled a faint but bitter whiff.

Kazan said, "It contained laudanum, commonly used to quell pain or anxiety. I found a similar bottle in Tsarskoye Selo. A lodger I arrested claimed it belonged to another occupant who went by the name Felix Zentov, but that's probably an alias. As I took the lodger into custody, Zentov showed up."

Yakov handed back the bottle. "And?"

"He was challenged by one of our female soldiers, there was a scuffle, and he stabbed the woman to death. Then he fired at me before he escaped. We found a revolver hidden in the handcart."

"He's got guts, I'll give him that. Did you get a good look at him?"

Kazan said, "It all happened too fast, but I have a detailed description from the landlady and the deserter. He matched a rough description of the Phantom: twenty-five to thirty, medium height, with a curious gait that may be the result of an old wound, which could be why he's taking the laudanum."

Yakov again studied the handwritten note. "Anything else?"

"With your permission, I'd like to interrogate Anastasia Romanov more forcefully. See if she knows more than she's telling."

"You mean torture her? No, I'll handle her myself." Yakov tucked the note inside his pocket. "I'll hold on to this for now."

Kazan's mouth narrowed with displeasure. "Be warned, she's a willful character, not easily intimidated or broken."

"What about the guard on the family?"

Kazan said, "Forty men in total, all of them handpicked and loyal to Lenin. Over a dozen are billeted in the Ipatiev House, others in a place we've commandeered as a guardroom across the street called the Popov House."

They rounded a snaking bend in the river and approached a large, imposing white-painted house with a pantiled roof. Tall wooden palings made of silver birch, at least fifteen feet high, were erected all around the garden. It created a fortified compound, sealing the property from the outside world. Yakov saw watchful guards patrol the grounds with rifles. "Can they be relied upon?"

"They're baying for Romanov blood, every one of them. They'd kill the entire family this minute given half the chance."

The gates swung open and the convoy drove into the compound.

36

The thirteen-year-old boy whose face was known by millions stared, fascinated, at two black beetles crawling across the garden's wooden table. "I bet mine is faster than yours and wins the race."

"Bet how much?" Anastasia asked her brother.

Alexei's brow furrowed. He fumbled in his pocket and withdrew a polished pebble. "How about this? It's my best stone."

"A *stone*? Don't you ever use your noggin, Alexei? What would I want with a *stone*, for heaven's sake?"

Innocent mischief sparkled in her brother's eyes, his head tilting to one side, offering an impish grin. "You never know when it might come in useful. To throw, and suchlike. David killed Goliath with a stone. Stones can be very useful things."

"That's a pebble, not a stone."

"Do you want it or not? I'll not offer it again, you know?"

"Of course you will. You're always offering to trade useless pieces of scrap." Anastasia shook her head, smiled, and ruffled Alexei's hair. "Mama's right to call you her baby. You're such a child, Alexei."

"I'm thirteen! And it's not useless. You're useless." Alexei playfully slapped his sister's arm.

Anastasia went to slap him back but stopped. Alexei wasn't wearing his usual khaki tunic but a patched gray shirt and sailor pants, sewn in many places, and grubby with mud. With his huge, sad blue eyes sunken into his finely chiseled face, he appeared even more gaunt than usual. Every day, he looked more like a skeleton. She felt such pity for him. Their mother—seated in the far end of the garden in her wheelchair and deep in conversation with Papa—complained that her "baby" now weighed less than eighty pounds. "You're lucky I'm not in the mood to hit you back."

Her brother's smile widened. "Lucky? You're getting *soft*, Anastasia!"

The two beetles dawdled together on the edge of the table, despite Alexei poking them with a finger.

"You may as well use snails," she said, bored.

Alexei picked up the beetles and placed them in a matchbox.

Patrolling guards passed them, flicking watchful looks. When they were out of earshot, Alexei whispered, "What do you think was in the note?"

"I told you, I didn't have time to read it."

"Maria thinks it has to be from groups loyal to Papa who want to rescue us. Do you really think they'll rescue us, sis?" Her brother's big, soulful eyes gazed up at her.

She said, "I expect they will—eventually."

She heard singing. Her sisters, Tatiana, Olga, and Maria, strolled at the far end of the garden, arm in arm, singing a lullaby. The guards always paid them extra attention, especially when they looked pretty.

But even Olga and Tatiana looked more and more gaunt of late, all of them worn down by their close confinement, poor diet, and the stress of not knowing what would happen to them next.

Alexei stuffed the matchbox in his pocket. He removed a handkerchief and unwrapped a piece of sweetbread that the cook had given him that morning. He bit off a morsel before returning it to the handkerchief and stuffing it in his pocket. "Still, they're taking an awful long time to rescue us, aren't they?"

"Is that a clean handkerchief?" Anastasia asked.

"Sort of. It's a few days old."

"Alexei! I saw you blowing your nose in it yesterday!"

"It was only a little blow! It's clean enough. Olga says the novices, Maria and Antonina, will bring us fresh bread and eggs and cheese today. What do you think?"

"If the guards don't take most of it."

Anastasia's attention was drawn to a window in the upstairs floor of the house. The single window in their first-floor quarters that the *komendant* allowed to remain open. She saw a figure stare down at her.

"What's the matter?" Alexei asked.

"There's someone watching us from *our* quarters."

"You mean the *komendant*?"

"No, not that idiot. It's a man I've never seen before. He's wearing a leather jacket."

37

In the upstairs living quarters, Yakov observed the family through an open lime-washed window. Their voices drifted up from the patchy garden.

Rising above the voices was singing. Three of the sisters sang a lullaby that he recognized. At one end of the garden, the frail-looking boy and the girl named Anastasia sat huddled over a garden bench. Nearby, the ex-tsar chatted with his wife, seated in a wheelchair. All of them looked a little shabby, their clothes worn.

"You know what I found strange, Commissar?" Yurovsky, the *komendant*, observed.

"What?"

"How Russia could believe the Romanovs were like gods. But they're not, are they? They're no more than educated peasants."

Yakov thought, *He's right.* What surprised him was that they seemed so ordinary.

On the way upstairs to the family quarters, Yakov passed a stuffed mother bear and its cubs on the landing. Down in the hallway he spotted a child's battered wheelchair.

The *komendant* said, "The boy's a cripple, really. His legs are weak, and the father carries him everywhere. A rare blood disease can cause him to bleed to death, and he's in a lot of pain because he bruises easily. We allow the mother some ice packs to alleviate his discomfort."

"And his sister Anastasia?"

"She's the passionate one. Lots of spirit. The survivor in the family, if you ask me."

The *komendant*, Yurovsky, was a tall, well-built man with dark wavy hair and a neatly trimmed beard. He was about forty, with a thin mouth and weasel eyes. Yakov sensed a man who was incredibly cunning.

"We confiscated a fortune in gold and jewels and precious gems from the family. It's all locked in strongboxes. I'm certain they have more hidden on their persons. We'll find it all, don't worry, Commissar."

Yakov didn't fail to notice the electric wires running through downstairs windows and connected to bells, part of the elaborate security system.

The Ipatiev House was smaller inside than it appeared, the narrow corridors crammed with guards coming and going. In the living quarters, someone had placed sachets of lavender scent to mask the smells of food and stale air.

The rooms were littered with the Romanovs' personal belongings.

On a table lay a sewing basket, with rolls of thread, a set of playing cards, and a chessboard; some toys belonging to the boy, including a bow and arrow; and the random trinkets children collect: a few coins, some smooth stones, and a few old buttons; bits of string.

Yakov's eyes were drawn to a bright object—a finely made religious travel icon—lying on a nearby side table. He took it in his hands and studied it. Made of dark mahogany, the lid was shrouded in filigree silver and covered in turquoise beads. He opened the lid and an icon of St. Michael popped up, in gilded paint. It was the kind of thing often given to children on birthdays.

"It belongs to the daughter Anastasia, if I'm not mistaken," the *komendant* offered.

Yakov couldn't fail to notice that the room was filled with religious objects: icons, Bibles, images of saints, prayer books.

"The fools spend half their day praying," the *komendant* observed. "They share their quarters with their doctor, Botkin, and the three servants who decided to remain loyal to their masters. Loyal idiots, they may as well not be here."

"Why?"

"We make the Romanovs do their own housework. It keeps them in their place. The father's days of being called Tsar Nicholas are long gone. Here he's addressed as Nicholai Romanov, citizen."

Yakov laid aside the travel icon and stared down at the muddy garden.

His hatred for the ex-tsar felt all-consuming; the sight of the man made his blood boil. For the tsar's German wife, he felt nothing. It was the children who drew his attention like a magnet. Tatiana, Olga, and Maria looked like remarkably graceful young women. Anastasia was pretty, too, but seemed a more robust character.

The *komendant* said, "One or two of the guards seemed infatuated by the girls, so I replaced them."

Yakov studied the boy, Alexei, and Anastasia. There was something otherworldly about all of the children, an innocence almost, as if they had been protected from the harshness of the world around them. A chill went through him.

Can I really execute such beautiful, innocent creatures?

And he knew the answer to that question immediately. He would follow orders.

He snapped shut the window, felt an icy stab in his heart. He slipped the piece of paper from his tunic and lay it on the table. "Kazan explained about this latest note."

Yurovsky nodded. "The truth is, hardly a week goes by without some note or other being thrown over the fence from Romanov supporters or their enemies. Some are insults and threats, others suggest that help is imminent. Some I've had written myself."

"What?"

Yurovsky grinned slyly. "Not this one, but it's a tactic of mine, to keep up their spirits until we have no further use for them. If they lose hope, they'll fall apart, and I can't have that. Besides, my guards are always vigilant. These rescue notes will never come to anything."

Yakov folded away the note. "That's reassuring. Nevertheless, I want to talk with the daughter Anastasia."

"She can be a stubborn one, so may I suggest that you talk with her father present? It might be easier to get the truth out of her. He'll exert some influence."

"Very well. Summon the family."

■   ■   ■

Yakov waited in the office and heard the clatter of footsteps on the stairs and then a door closed. The *komendant* returned. "Ready whenever you are."

When they reached the Romanov quarters, the *komendant* pressed an electric bell on the wall by the door.

It rang inside, then Yakov snatched open the door and led them into an L-shaped drawing room, the walls covered with yellow patterned wallpaper.

Five people were crowded into the room and Yakov recognized every face.

Gathered around a table were the former tsar and his wife, Alexandra, their son, and Olga and Tatiana. Alexei was seated in a chair. They all looked surprised to have a visitor.

All of the family rose, except the crippled boy.

The mother, her graying hair tied in a severe bun, looked like an anxious headmistress. Gone was any impression of the arrogance she was famous for; now her hands trembled, her eyes darted nervously.

Many Russians mistrusted the German-born former tsarina because of her relationship with Rasputin. Others considered her a spy. Yakov thought she looked like a woman close to a nervous breakdown.

Up close, the former tsar appeared frail and nervous. But his shoulders looked well developed from carrying the boy. In his plain gray tunic, patched uniform pants, and scuffed riding boots, it was hard to believe that this man once ruled a sixth of the world with an iron fist. Yakov thought, *So much tyranny is carried out by people with innocent faces.*

"I'm Commissar Leonid Yakov. The purpose of my visit is to assess your security. I should warn you that enemy spies are at work in Ekaterinburg. For this reason it may be necessary to move you all again at short notice."

"May I ask to where this time?" The ex-tsar's voice was a tired whisper, his watery blue eyes vacant.

"That will be for others to decide. For now, I wish only to have two people in the room: Anastasia Romanov and her father. Everyone else leave," he ordered.

The boy held on to his father's hand and pleaded, "Papa, I want to stay with you."

His father gently pried open the boy's grip. "No, please do as you're told, Alexei. Obey like a good soldier. That's my boy."

"But Papa . . ."

"No buts. You must do as I say."

The boy turned and gave Yakov a pleading look.

Yakov ignored him and said to his father, "Where's your daughter?"

"In the next room, with her sister Maria."

"Fetch her. The rest of you get out of my sight."

38

"May I ask why you wish to see my daughter?" A ticking clock echoed somewhere in the house as the former tsar fidgeted with his fingers, a worried father edgy with nervous energy.

"You'll find out soon enough." Footsteps sounded in the hallway and a knock came on the door. "Enter," said Yakov.

Anastasia Romanov stepped into the room. High cheekbones and a determined mouth gave her a confident, strong-willed look.

"I'm Commissar Yakov. Sit down."

"Actually, I'd prefer to stand." She went to join her father, resting her hand on his shoulder. He held it tightly as if to reassure her. But something about the young woman's demeanor told Yakov that she didn't need reassurance. He sensed defiance, a fighting spirit.

"So, you're Anastasia?"

"Who else would I be? You summoned me, didn't you?"

Yakov bristled. "Don't be insolent. Of all the prisoners in this house, you've proven the most difficult, do you know that?"

The girl stared back at him, not a shred of fear in her eyes, only rebellion. "I can't argue with your opinion, Commissar. It must be as you say."

"You'd do well to bite back that tongue of yours, or it might get you into trouble." He noticed an object in her right hand. "What are you holding?"

She held out a small box in her palm.

"What is it?" Yakov demanded.

"A travel icon."

He took the box from her and opened it. It was the one he saw earlier in the family quarters. The side and top were little flaps, and once opened revealed a propped-up little altar.

Anastasia said, "It's St. Michael. A favorite saint of mine."

Yakov impatiently snapped it shut and tossed in on the table. He took the page from his pocket, unfolded it, and laid it down. "Do you recognize this? 'Be strong. Help is near. Philip.' The guards found it near you in the garden. You were about to pick it up."

Anastasia gave a puzzled glance at the paper. "That . . . that doesn't mean it's mine."

"Don't play games with me. Whom do you know named Philip?"

"Commissar, if I may speak?"

Yakov fixed the ex-tsar with a scornful look. "Keep your mouth shut. Citizen Nicholai Romanov, I'm not talking to you." He returned his attention to the daughter. "I'm waiting for an answer."

"I don't know who you're talking about."

Yakov walked round the table and confronted her. He smelled the faint scent of her lavender soap. "It may interest you to know that the man who wrote this note may be a foreign spy we're hunting."

The girl looked genuinely stunned. "A spy?"

"You heard me. What does this note mean? What help is near? Who is Philip? A friend of your family?"

"I . . . I have absolutely no idea."

Yakov picked up the note, thrust it in front of her face, losing his patience. "It's obviously someone who's trying to help you."

"Is it?"

"What if I told you that we've found this Philip? That we arrested him near this very house and that he's being interrogated as we speak?"

Was it Yakov's imagination, or did the girl react? He was certain he saw a flicker in her eyes.

But then she stood her ground. "Why would that matter to me? I already told you, I don't know who you're talking about. If you've found him as you say you have, then you ought to know who he is."

In frustration, Yakov brought a fist crashing down on the table. "Listen to me. Either you tell the truth or your privileges will be withdrawn: your daily walks, your food ration. Everything will be taken away."

The girl said stubbornly, "Look around you, Commissar. Does it look as if we have much to take? Isn't it enough that you persecute us?"

Yakov persisted. "I ask again, who is this Philip?"

Her father intervened. "Commissar, may we speak alone, man to man?"

Anastasia protested. "No, Father, you don't have to—"

"Respect my wishes, Anastasia. I wish to speak with the commissar alone, if he will allow it."

Yakov considered, and nodded.

Nicholai Romanov said to his daughter, "Please leave us, Anastasia."

"But Father—"

"Leave," he said firmly.

Yakov jerked his head at the girl. "Go. Join the others. If I need you again I'll summon you."

Anastasia picked up the St. Michael icon, defiance blazing in her eyes. "Don't you dare hurt my father." She went out, banging the door.

"You must forgive my daughter. Sometimes the young have no fear."

Yakov noticed that Nicholai Romanov's right hand twitched in an uncontrollable spasm. "May I see this note you speak of?" he asked.

Yakov handed it over.

Nicholai Romanov examined the paper and looked up. "Ever since we've been held captive we've heard whispers that promise our liberation."

"From whom?"

"Notes are usually thrown over the palings, although of late they've stopped. I've no doubt some are meant to bolster our spirits, but I believe that others are meant to taunt us. They have only given my family false hope, especially the children."

"Your point?"

"No doubt the note was meant for me, but I have no idea who sent it. I know no one of that name. You have my word on that."

"Your word means nothing to me," Yakov snapped. "I think your daughter's lying. I think she's a good little actress who knows more than she lets on. Heed my warning. Any more notes, or if anyone tries to contact you in any way, you inform the guards at once."

"I know my daughter, Commissar. I believe she spoke the truth.

And I'm sorry if Anastasia offended you. But in many ways she's still a child. Surely you understand?"

Yakov let loose his venom. "A pity you weren't sorry when you trampled on your people. When you and your kind crushed their spirit with your army and secret police."

Nicholai Romanov fell silent, his face gray.

Yakov leaned in close and spat out his words. "Once I had a wife. But she was shot down like a dog by your army. Once, I had a sister and mother. But their lives were nothing except poverty and squalor while you mocked them with your riches. You condemned them and countless others to death by your stupid arrogance."

Beads of sweat broke out on Nicholai Romanov's brow. "I . . . I'm truly sorry."

"'Sorry'? Is that all you can say? Your daughter asked if it wasn't enough that her father is persecuted. No, it isn't. It will never be. I won't rest until you and all your kind are never a threat to Russia again, do you understand me?" Yakov raised a clenched hand to lash out but at the last moment he held his fist in the air.

Nicholai Romanov stared back at him blankly, his lips trembling. "I—I meant it. I am truly sorry."

Yakov struck him. The force of his blow sent Nicholai Romanov reeling against the table. As he stumbled to his feet, he clasped a hand to his cheek.

Yakov slapped a hand on his holstered gun, rage in his voice. "Go, join your daughter. Get out of here before I put a bullet in you."

39

Yakov stepped into the *komendant*'s room.

It was empty except for Kazan, who stood alone at the window, toying with a brass knuckle-duster. He slipped it into his pocket as Yakov entered. "Any luck?"

"No. The girl proved obstinate."

"She's an insolent creature. I can hardly say I'm surprised."

"Something tells me she knows more than she's saying. I want the family observed more closely, especially the girls. If anyone attempts to pass them any notes, I want to know about it. Where's the guard commander?"

Kazan said, "I asked him to leave us, Commissar. I have a private matter to discuss."

Yakov selected a cigarette from his metal cigarette case. "I can't imagine you and I having anything to talk about, Kazan. But out with it."

"It has to do with your brother's murder."

Yakov was about to light his cigarette but he stopped short, pain turning his face to stone. "What's that got to do with you?"

"Such a terrible misfortune. One you no doubt wish to avenge?"

"Don't pretend you have a bleeding heart, Kazan. Get to the point."

"I heard you hunted down his killer, Captain Uri Andrev, in St. Petersburg, where you confronted him. There was a shoot-out; he escaped."

"Where's this going? What kind of scheming are you up to, Kazan?"

"I'm merely trying to be of service. If I can help you find Andrev, all the better."

Yakov strolled over to the wall map of Ekaterinburg and looked back. "How? I've scoured half of Russia looking for him. He's disappeared, most likely left the country."

Kazan removed a bottle-green folder from his leather attaché case. "You're right about that. I have reason to believe that Andrev left for England."

Yakov crushed his unsmoked cigarette in an ashtray on the desk. "What are you talking about?"

"Certain of my Ochrana colleagues fled to Europe since the revolution. I make it my business to stay in touch with several who've proven valuable informants. Needless to say, their information doesn't come cheap. I provided them with Andrev's name, background, and his physical description."

"I'm listening."

"One of them living in London claims he met a former army officer named Uri Andrev at a Russian émigré club. It's all here, in the file, as much as I've learned." Kazan handed over the file.

Yakov took it eagerly and read the two typed pages inside. When he finished, he felt a surge of rage. "So, Andrev's escaped. I knew it."

"Fled, but not escaped. Justice has a long arm. For a price my contact can arrange to have Andrev abducted and brought back to Russia. Or have him killed, whatever you wish."

Yakov slapped the file on the desk. "I want to deal with Andrev personally."

Kazan grinned. "I thought you might. Leave it to me. In return all I ask is that you allow me to interrogate the girl alone."

Yakov considered, then nodded reluctantly. "I'll give you an hour."

"That doesn't give me much time."

"It's an hour more than I should, Kazan."

A horn hooted beyond the window. A car appeared at the barricaded entrance. The lone driver showed his papers, was waved through, and halted in front of the house before he scurried up the front steps. "One of my men." Kazan said, joining Yakov at the window. "I'll see what he wants."

Yakov waited as Kazan left to join the driver in the open hallway. The men held a whispered conversation before Kazan returned.

"Well?"

Triumph lit Kazan's face. "My interrogation will have to wait. Our troops spotted a man matching the Phantom's description in one of the districts. We've surrounded the area and we're stopping everyone going in and out."

"What's your plan?"

Kazan tapped the Ekaterinburg wall map with his knuckle-duster. "A thorough search. We'll comb street by street, building by building. Tear the place apart brick by brick if we have to." He turned back, intensity blazing in his eye. "I'll catch this Phantom if it's the last thing I do."

In her bedroom, Anastasia sat on her narrow cot.

Next to her sat her sister Maria. In one hand she held a pair of worn underwear. In her other she clutched a needle and darning thread. On a square piece of linen that lay between them was nestled a collection of small precious stones: diamonds, rubies, emeralds.

Her dog Jimmy asleep at her feet, Anastasia finished stitching a ruby into the corset: the thread roll was empty.

Maria's voice was filled with excitement. "Are you *sure* he said Philip? I mean, could it *really* be the same Philip?"

"I'm sure of it."

"But he was your *piano* teacher."

"Remember, you said yourself that you wondered if he might be a spy."

Maria gave a nervous laugh. "I . . . I was only joking, Anastasia. Really I was. What did you tell Papa?"

"Nothing yet. I don't know if I should tell him anything."

"Why?"

"He has enough on his mind. Besides, I'm not really sure. All I have is a suspicion. But it's a strong one. I always felt that there was more to Philip than met the eye. I suppose that's why I found him so interesting."

Maria giggled and covered her mouth with a hand. "Try to be sensible, Anastasia, and not just a silly romantic."

"What do you mean?"

"You can't really think that your *piano* teacher followed us all the way to Siberia and means to help rescue us. Do you know how ridiculous that sounds? I'm glad you didn't tell Papa; he'd think you've gone crazy. It has to be someone else with the same name."

Anastasia considered, then put down her needle and stood. "Perhaps you're right. I'm being silly."

"Where are you going? We still have work to do." Maria indicated the gems. "Mama said we have to finish sewing these into our underclothes."

"We need more thread. The novices will be arriving soon. I'll go and get some. Promise me you'll tell no one about this."

"About what?"

"What I told you. That I thought it might be the piano teacher."

Maria giggled again.

"I mean it, Maria. *No one*. Keep it our secret."

In the hallway, Anastasia encountered two young guards. They glared at her. She made a face. The guards laughed. They always seemed to get fun out of her. "Where are you going, Anastasia Romanov?"

"To get more sewing thread."

"Don't be long."

"I'll be as long as it takes, you pair of idiots," Anastasia whispered under her breath.

"*What* did you say?" One of the guards frowned.

"I said I won't be, and thank you for allowing me." Anastasia smiled charmingly and skipped downstairs.

Once in the hallway, she waited by the exit door—she was not allowed go outside except when the *komendant* ordered. She saw the novices arrive; Antonina and Maria approached the palisade entrance. They carried two wicker baskets containing food and supplies.

Sometimes the two young women carried secret messages for her father, hidden in the fresh loaves of bread or in the milk containers they brought, but that happened less and less of late.

The novices saw her, smiled, and waved as the guards checked their baskets.

Anastasia waved back.

As she waited there, she saw no one in the hallway.

Her heart was beating as she slipped a hand in her skirt pocket and removed the photograph.

It was the one of her and Philip she'd taken with the Kodak at Tsarskoye Selo, the two of them smiling for the lens.

It wasn't the best of photographs, their features a little blurry, but she treasured the image. She had taken it from her collection the moment her interview with Yakov was over.

"Be strong. Help is near. Philip."

She felt her face flush and her heart race as she stared at Philip's image.

Could he *really* have sent the note?

It made absolutely no sense. And yet some ridiculous instinct told her it was he.

She heard a door creak somewhere in the house and slipped the photograph back in her pocket.

Even though Maria didn't care to admit it, her younger sister was the boss in the relationship. She would do as she was told.

For now, any suspicion she had would remain a secret.

40

It was a glorious June day and Boyle drove the Ford T on the inland road, Lydia in the passenger seat. They passed rolling countryside, the road dipping steeply as they entered Collon village.

It was all quaint stone houses and whitewashed cottages, with a handful of grocery stores and pubs, the village dominated by a magnificent Presbyterian church built of red granite.

A cattle market was in progress and the streets thronged with farmers and stank of livestock. Boyle steered out of the village through the herds of cattle and drove for another twenty minutes, until they came to a pair of granite gate pillars, each topped with a carved stone lion.

The lions guarded an eighteenth-century estate with a handsome manor house, its vast lawns dotted with ancient oaks. Boyle drove through the open gates. They left the main gravel driveway for a dirt road. It led past thick woodland to a thatched white cottage, another Ford T parked outside.

A black-painted iron sign by the front door was inscribed Briar Cottage.

Fragrant roses and honeysuckle scented the air, the site protected from the winds by rolling hills of thick yellow gorse, and there was a commanding view of the distant sea. Boyle hooted the horn but no one appeared.

"The others ought to be around somewhere. Well, what do you think?"

Lydia glimpsed a white lighthouse in the distance and to the north saw the Mountains of Mourne. "It looks familiar. Isn't that Clougher Head way over there? Where exactly are we?"

Boyle grabbed her bag from the backseat. "It's called Briar Cottage. It belongs to the widow of an old friend of mine named Volkov."

"*Vasily* Volkov?"

"You've heard of him?"

"He used to do business with my father in St. Petersburg. He's a horse breeder and businessman. And a gambler and womanizer if I recall correctly."

Boyle tipped back his hat and laughed. "That sounds like poor Vasily all right. He was certainly a boyo for the women in his day, until his wife, Hanna, put manners in him. After he died she inherited the estate."

"What happened to him?"

Boyle's humor faded. "Murdered by Lenin's secret police, and a brutal end it was, too. Come on, let me introduce you to Hanna and to Uri Andrev."

At that same moment, three hundred yards away, Hanna Volkov was climbing up a rock-strewn slope covered in yellow gorse. She wore a long skirt and a waisted coat that emphasized her figure—unsuitable clothes for climbing, which was why she was struggling.

As she neared the top, scattered with boulders, Andrev climbed on ahead with ease and then turned to hold out his hand. "Here, get a grip of my arm."

Hanna did so, and he pulled her up. The cottage lay far below the ridge, hidden by some woods. On the other side the land sloped down to a river, crossed by an old stone bridge. From there the landscape was flat like a pancake, the river flowing all the way to the coast, the view superb.

Hanna said breathlessly, "Well, I promised you a spectacle, Mr. Andrev."

"It's certainly that." Andrev studied the scenery and pointed to a distant scattering of ancient-looking granite ruins. "What's that?"

"The remains of Mellifont Abbey. It dates from the sixth century, when Ireland had a reputation as an island of saints and scholars. Christian monks came to the rugged coast from as far away as Egypt and Syria. They claimed Ireland was the one place where they felt closest to God."

"And those mountains?"

"They're called the Mountains of Mourne. They say the Celts who settled this land buried their kings and queens near the peaks and that the ghosts still linger."

Andrev half-smiled and sat on a boulder. "That sounds like just the kind of romantic myth that appeals to sentimental Russians."

She joined him. "We're certainly alike in many ways, the Russians and the Celts. Tough yet sentimental, a strange combination."

"Do you know this country well?"

"My husband, Vasily, and I first came here six years ago when he bought the estate to breed horses. We traveled all over the country, from Rathlin Island and the Giant's Causeway, all the way down to the rugged Kerry coast. We had fond memories of our time here."

"You still miss him, don't you?"

"Terribly."

"I know why *I'm* doing this, but what about you?"

Hanna's face darkened. "Before the Cheka beasts finished him in the cellars of the Lubyanka Prison, he was trying to rally international help to rescue the tsar. I promised myself I'd finish his work."

"Why's Boyle involved?"

"He and Vasily were friends. Boyle hates the Reds and all they stand for."

"Tell me more about this woman I'm supposed to be traveling with."

"She's American-born, of Irish extraction. She speaks Russian like a native. In fact, her father ran a business in St. Petersburg."

"To be honest, I'm not exactly happy at the thought of a woman accompanying me."

"Why?"

"We both know that Lenin's secret police are capable of rape and torture if we're caught."

"She knows the challenges and the dangers. And you certainly won't have to worry about her abilities, Mr. Andrev."

"Then unless she's a complete fool, why did she volunteer?"

Hanna rose from the boulder and smoothed her skirt. "That's a question for another day. And now, we better get back. Boyle ought to be here. Are you coming?"

The sun beat down, the afternoon glorious, and the river below looked cool and inviting. Andrev said, "I'll catch up, if you don't mind. On a warm summer's day like this, I think I'll make the most of it and take a swim."

"Don't be fooled by that water. It's always icy cold."

"It couldn't be colder than in Russia. Can you make your own way back?"

"Of course."

Without another word Andrev turned and moved down the hill, like a boy off on an adventure.

Hanna watched him go. When he reached the river bank he tore off his shirt, his bare chest muscled, but she didn't fail to notice the angry red scars on his back.

To her surprise, he undressed completely and plunged naked into the icy water. He resurfaced after a few moments with a splash, sucking in air, then he started to swim against the current with strong, even strokes.

She shook her head, smiling to herself. "It ought to be interesting to see what Miss Ryan makes of you."

And then she turned and started down the hill to the cottage.

41

Boyle carried Lydia's bag inside the cottage.

She was surprised to find it quite large, with a beamed ceiling and an open fireplace. Coarse slabs of chocolate-brown turf were stacked by the unlit open fireplace, the air rich with the earthy smell of peat.

Boyle moved to the kitchen area, dominated by a black iron range. "Anybody home?" he called out.

When no one appeared, Boyle said, "The cottage was once used by the gamekeeper until Vasily had it rebuilt as a visitors' lodge, and often used it as a study." He walked her through, showing her the two bedrooms and bathroom at the back. "The gamekeeper won't bother us, by the way. He has the week off."

"Where are the others?"

Boyle put a hand over the cooking range. "They'll turn up. The stove's hot, so let's see if I can rustle up some tea."

As he pumped water from the sink into a kettle, Lydia studied the room. In front of the fireplace was a rocking chair next to a big old chaise longue, the lime-colored velvet material scuffed and worn. She noticed several silver-framed photographs arranged on a rolltop writing desk.

Most were of a striking young woman, some quite obviously posed. In one the woman was dressed in a flowing white robe, the photograph taken on a theater stage. Lydia picked it up, said to Boyle, "Hanna Volkov?"

"Yes. Chekhov said she was the only actress he trusted to play the lead in *Three Sisters*."

"She looks like she could be in love with herself, and a bit of a diva."

Boyle laughed. "Now there you'd be wrong. Hanna's the most sensible woman you could meet, with not an ounce of pretension. Onstage, of course, she's whatever persona she's playing. Are you a theater lover?"

Lydia put down the photograph. "In case you hadn't noticed, Boyle, there's enough drama in my own life."

Boyle smiled and put the kettle on the stove just as Hanna entered the room, her hair down around her shoulders, her face flushed.

Boyle said, "Speak of the devil."

"Forgive me for being late. I was helping Mr. Andrev get his bearings."

"Isn't he with you?"

"He decided to make the most of the afternoon, but he'll join us shortly." Hanna's gaze turned from Boyle to their visitor and she thrust out her hand. "You must be Lydia. I'm Hanna Volkov. It's good to meet you."

Lydia ignored the offered hand. "Boyle explained who you are. Whose idea was it to involve me? Yours or his?"

Hanna withdrew her hand, acutely aware of the tension in the air. "We can talk about that another time. Has Mr. Boyle gone over the sleeping arrangements?"

"He's gone over nothing."

"The two bedrooms in the back are for you and Mr. Andrev. I've left fresh towels and soap. Once you all get acquainted, you and I have important work to discuss, so come up to the manor house, Miss Ryan."

"What sort of work?"

Hanna didn't explain and moved to the door. "I'll be expecting you and Mr. Andrev to join us at dinner each night in the main house, eight o'clock sharp."

Hanna went out and Boyle raised an eyebrow at Lydia. "I'd say that went well, wouldn't you?"

"Are you trying to be funny, Boyle?"

"Aren't you the quick-tempered one?" He grabbed two mugs, slapped them on the table next to a sugar bowl and milk jug. "By the way, is that arm of yours on the mend?"

"Why?"

"I've left provisions in the kitchen cabinets, so it might do no harm for you to play the caring role and prepare a bit of lunch for Mr. Andrev. Get things off to a friendly start."

Lydia flushed. "Are you trying to goad me, Boyle? Because you're well on your way. I won't be ordered around like some kind of domestic servant, as you and your lady friend seem to think I am."

Boyle heaped two spoonfuls of tea from a greaseproof packet into an enamel teapot and poured in boiling water from the kettle before he put it down. "We have your best interests at heart. Being the actress that she is, Hanna thought it would be a good role-playing exercise for you and Uri to spend as much time together as possible, to get to know each other. A few cozy nights in, walks together, that sort of thing. I must say I agree."

"Do you now?"

Boyle moved closer and took a fistful of Lydia's thick hair in his hand, then let it fall and stepped back. "One other thing. Put your hair up, it'll look better. And wear a little face powder to get rid of that flushed look you've got on your complexion right now. It doesn't do you justice."

Lydia fumed, picked up a plate from the table, and flung it at Boyle. He ducked and the crockery smashed to pieces against the wall. Lydia picked up another plate, was about to throw it when a man's voice said, "I'd be careful or someone's liable to get hurt."

Lydia froze, the raised plate in her hand as she turned to the speaker.

Andrev stood in the doorway, leaning against the door frame, his hair dripping wet, his shirt drenched and clinging to his chest. As he came in he grabbed a towel from a kitchen rail and began to dry his hair.

Lydia felt something primitive stir inside her. It was a strange feeling, delicious and frightening almost at once, and she struggled to suppress it.

Boyle said, "You must be Uri."

Andrev's face illuminated with a smile of great natural charm. "I thought I'd take a swim, it was the perfect day for it. Only it seems I'm missing all the drama. You're Boyle?"

Boyle shook the offered hand, sizing up his visitor. "I've been looking forward to meeting you. Welcome on board. Say hello to Miss Ryan."

When Andrev offered her his hand, Lydia didn't hold out hers, if only because she was aware that it would have trembled. As she looked into his face her stomach felt hollow, her throat dry, and for once she was unable to speak. The attraction was instant, like a crack of thunder.

Boyle said to her, "Well, are you going to throw that plate or not? Make up your mind."

That seemed to be the last straw. Lydia let fly, and the plate smashed into pieces against the wall, barely missing Boyle. She stormed out, banging the door after her.

"I'm hoping that plate wasn't part of a set," Boyle said, unscrewing a pewter hip flask he took from his pocket and handing it to Andrev. "Don't worry about her. Here—try a real Irish welcome. Whiskey. *Uisce beatha* in Gaelic. That means 'the water of life.'" Boyle winked. "Keep the flask, in case of emergencies."

Andrev swallowed a mouthful, then moved to the window and watched Lydia hurry across the lawn. "She's got spirit, I'll give her that. Did I say something wrong?"

Boyle joined him. "I'd say that was me. She's a fiery lass. It's the Spanish blood in the Irish, I always say. They're the Latins of the north and thrive on a good argument."

"Is that so?"

"A lot like your own people."

Boyle smiled broadly, picked up the teapot, and began pouring tea into the two mugs. "Let's you and I have some tea and I'll tell you all about her."

"What's so amusing, Mr. Boyle?"

"Me? I'm just looking on the bright side, Uri."

"And what's that?"

"That it's you who's going into Russia with her and not me."

42

Lydia had no idea where she was going, her mind unable to focus after she left the cottage. Her brain was a fog, her heart racing. It was a long time since she felt that kind of instant reaction to a man, and she couldn't explain it in any rational way.

She felt flustered as she ran across the lawns to the manor house front steps. Ahead of her was a shiny black door with a brass knocker. Before she could reach the door it opened and Hanna Volkov appeared. "There you are. I take it you met Mr. Andrev?"

"Briefly."

"You'll be spending every waking hour together from now on, so you two better get used to each other's company. Come inside."

Hanna led them into a black-and-white tiled hallway, dominated by a sweeping staircase and huge chandelier. "Like many Irish manor houses, this one was built by the English aristocracy, an eighteenth-century earl no less. But I doubt you'll want a history lesson."

"I know enough about the English stealing Irish land, thank you."

A wry smile appeared on Hanna's face. "I had a feeling you might say something like that. This way."

They moved up the staircase and when they came to the top, Lydia said, "Boyle told me who you are. I saw you onstage when I was sixteen."

"Really?"

"Our headmistress took our class to see *The Three Sisters* at St. Petersburg's Imperial Theater. You played a lead role."

"And what did you think of the play?"

"I thought it was a lot of brooding old nonsense, seeing as you asked."

Hanna let out a hearty laugh as they moved along the hallway. "At least you're honest. Not exactly my best performance, but as an eager young actress of twenty-three I'd never have thought it back then."

"Where are you taking me?"

Hanna halted outside a door and reached for the handle. "I can only hope that you paid attention during your theater visit, Miss Ryan."

"Why?"

"Because you're going to need some acting skills for your journey. In fact, think of the next few days as rehearsals. We'll strictly speak in Russian from now on, if you don't mind. To do otherwise as a spy in Russia could cost you your life."

They stepped into a bedroom with a huge period fireplace. A mahogany four-poster bed was set in the middle, the drapes a rich burgundy.

On the bed lay a cheap suitcase with leather straps. It looked out of place in the imposing room. Hanna undid the straps.

Inside were ladies' garments: blouses and skirts, underwear, and a few plain headscarves, along with two pairs of sturdy-looking women's boots. "These are personal effects for the journey. All the clothes are Russian-made. I think they ought to fit you. Try them on for size."

"Now?" Lydia answered in Russian.

"No time like the present."

Lydia plucked out a few clothes. They looked the kind of coarse garments a peasant might wear. She undressed down to her underwear and tried on the garments.

Hanna checked them for fitting. "Not bad. Your Russian's excellent, by the way."

"What about identity documents?"

"I was coming to that." Hanna produced a set of papers and some items from the suitcase.

Lydia saw that they were travel documents and an identity card, a wad of Russian banknotes and some coins in a cloth purse, along with a fob watch.

Hanna handed them across. "The watch will come in useful. Later, Boyle will go over your background cover story. Familiarize yourself with it."

"Thanks to you and Boyle I don't have much choice, do I?"

Hanna said evenly, "You asked whose idea it was to involve you. It was mine. I heard about you through Vasily, my husband—he's the one who arranged for you to work as a governess for the Romanovs. Naturally, when we needed someone, I thought of you, even if it turned out that you'd made yourself a career smuggling guns."

"You have a problem with that?"

"No, quite the opposite—it showed courage. But the British certainly resented your work. You were on their wanted list. In fact, you and your brother would likely be dead by now if it weren't for Boyle. He managed to convince the right people of your usefulness. And permit me an observation: don't you think it's time you took off that suit of armor you wear?"

"What are you talking about?"

"I've been long enough an actress to know that we all hide our true selves. It's part of our natural defense mechanism. But with you, I think it goes even deeper. There's a wound buried inside you that you're hiding. It makes you angry with the world and it makes you defensive. The sooner you confront it, the better."

Lydia blushed. "You don't know what you're talking about."

"Don't I? Very well, have it your way. Just one more thing, Miss Ryan. And I gave Uri the same warning I'm about to give you."

"What's that?"

"Where you're going is a kind of hell. There's terror on the streets of Russia and police informers everywhere. Innocent victims are arrested at random. Men, women, children are thrown into prison cellars for the slightest reason, and some are even executed."

"What's your point?"

"Once you cross over that border, trust no one but yourself and Uri. Measure every word you speak. The smallest error on your part, the wrong answer to a Red soldier or a secret policeman, could have dire consequences."

"I'm no fool. I understand."

"Make sure you do. Your life and the lives of those you'll try to rescue could depend on it."

43

Sorg's wound felt on fire.

Stopping in an empty alleyway, he leaned against the wall. He wore his black overcoat to hide his blood-drenched shirt, and the heat was unbearable. He pulled up his shirt to examine his side.

Blood dribbled from a purple gash. He pressed his shirt to the wound, but it didn't stop the bleeding, just caused him a knifing pain that made him almost pass out.

He needed to find medical attention or he'd die. But almost every street he entered he saw armed Red Guards patrolling the sidewalks, and so he was forced to keep to the backstreets.

Sorg hurried on, sweat drenching his clothes. His legs began to hurt and his wound throbbed. Eventually he came to his destination and stopped to rest against a wall.

Across the street was a huge convent with whitewashed walls and enormous blue and gold minarets topped by the Russian cross. A Red Cross ambulance was parked on the street.

The Novo-Tikhvinsky Convent was famous—a vast complex staffed by over a thousand nuns who ran almshouses, an orphan asylum, workshops, a school, and a hospital. Their hospital was on another side of the square, but Sorg felt too exhausted to reach it.

He approached a wide archway with an oak door, the ancient wood split with cracks, a wrought-iron crucifix nailed above it.

Sorg summoned all his energy and yanked a bellpull on a rope. Tinkling sounded beyond the doors, mixed with the raucous sounds of noisy children.

He heard footsteps approach. A bolt scraped, a peephole opened in the door, and like a vision, there appeared the beautiful face of a young nun wearing a black wimple. "Yes?"

"I—I need your help, sister," Sorg said weakly.

"It's late," the nun answered. "We only tender alms to the needy before noon, not at this hour."

"I don't need charity, Sister—"

The peephole banged shut.

Sorg gritted his teeth as an agonizing pain blossomed in his side. He touched his shirt and his fingers felt drenched.

The whole thing was a disaster.

I'm afraid I'm going to die, he thought.

I want to see Anastasia again.

A second later his senses faded, his eyelids fluttered, and he was engulfed by a black tidal wave.

COLLON, IRELAND

The shooting range was in an old paddock at the back of the manor.

Boyle laid out a Nagant revolver and two boxes of ammunition on a trestle table. Fifteen yards out was a line of five tin cans, inches apart.

While Lydia and Andrev looked on, Boyle began to load rounds into the revolver. "No doubt you know it but this is a Nagant, the standard sidearm for the Russian army. It can be deadly enough up close but like most handguns, it's not very accurate beyond ten or fifteen yards unless you're a marksman."

Boyle cocked the Nagant. "You'll have one each for your journey. That said, if at any time you think the weapon's going to cause you trouble, get rid of it at once. Guns are everywhere in Russia these days. With a little ingenuity you'll get your hands on another."

Boyle aimed and fired in one fluid movement, snapping off seven shots and hitting four of the five cans. "I've done better."

He reloaded the revolver and handed it to Lydia. "The lady's turn."

"Do I have to, Boyle?"

"No, you don't, but practice makes perfect."

Lydia accepted the Nagant.

Boyle said, "You want to line those cans up again, Uri?"

Andrev walked out to the tin cans. He replaced four of the cans but before he could set down the last one, Lydia's right hand came up wielding the gun and she called out, "Stay exactly where you are. Don't move a hair."

She fired four shots in quick succession, sending the cans on the ground skittering across the grass. Then she called out to Andrev, "Toss the last one in the air, to your right, away from you."

"Are you joking? Hitting a moving target that size with a Nagant isn't easy."

"*Toss* it."

Andrev lobbed the can through the air. Lydia's Nagant cracked, sending the can skewing before it landed in the grass. The moment it did, Lydia fired another two rounds, each puncturing the metal.

Boyle said, astonished, "How the heck did you learn to shoot like that?"

Lydia ejected the spent cartridges and laid the weapon on the table. "A misspent childhood on a Kentucky farm, Boyle. My father believed that a woman should always be able to defend herself."

Boyle tipped back his hat. "I suppose you know that you just broke every safety rule on the range?"

"I know the rules, Mr. Boyle. And when to break them, don't you worry." And with that Lydia turned and strode back up to the manor.

Boyle looked on, speechless.

Andrev smiled. "Now there's a woman who knows how to look after herself."

44

Dinner was a simple affair in the manor's kitchen. Hanna served roasted chicken, potatoes, and cabbage, followed by dessert of stewed apples and custard. Boyle opened a bottle of Burgundy and when they finished their meal he stood and filled their glasses from a decanter of port. "I think the fact that we've managed to get this far calls for a special celebration. Drink up."

Andrev said, "Who are you, Boyle? Who are you working for? Isn't it time we knew?"

Boyle placed a foot on the chair and rested a hand on his knee. "I'm a businessman, an adventurer, a man of too many parts for my own good. I made my fortune in the Klondike gold rush in Canada and used part of it to invest in railways, about which I managed to acquire considerable expertise. That led to the Russian provisional government asking me to help organize their entire railway system, which was a badly run mess. Later, I did the same for the Bolsheviks."

Lydia said, puzzled, "You worked for the Reds?"

Boyle's jaw was set in an angry look. "Until I witnessed their brutality—entire towns destroyed, villages wiped out, their inhabitants executed. The low point came when I visited a town where a thirteen-year-old boy had the audacity to hang a royalist flag on the local square. A Red commissar had the child put up against a wall and shot him, then hung the body from a telegraph pole as a warning to others.

"After that, I swore to myself I'd do my utmost to see the Reds ripped from power in the same heartless way they grasped it. In the last year I've built up a spy network of over four hundred agents in Russia, gathering intelligence."

Lydia looked from Boyle to Hanna. "You still didn't say who you're working for."

It was Hanna who answered. "Let's just say we represent the tip of a rather complex iceberg. Have you ever heard of the Russian St. John?"

"He was a priest who liked to do good in secret."

"That's right." Boyle then took a pencil and notebook from his pocket and laid them on the table. "The Brotherhood of St. John of Tobolsk is a kind of legacy, a secret society if you like. Its members come from all walks of life."

He picked up the pencil. "Right now the Brotherhood has a single purpose: to save the Romanovs from being butchered. Hanna and I are willing accomplices. Let me show you something."

Boyle flipped open a fresh page in the notebook and penciled an odd shape on the page—a reverse swastika.

He went on: "The Brotherhood's mark is an ancient Tibetan symbol used for good luck, the reverse swastika. It's considered a symbol of faith, love, and hope. It's also a secret key that you'll encounter on your journey whenever you come into contact with our members."

Hanna put aside her glass. "Several rescue attempts were tried in Tobolsk, where the family was last held captive. Hence the Brotherhood's name. Two other secret attempts were made since the family was moved to Ekaterinburg. They also failed. But this time we believe we have a chance."

"What if we don't reach Ekaterinburg?" Lydia asked.

Boyle said, "Hanna and I will be coming with you. I'm hoping that at least one pair of us will make it and conclude the rescue. So we'll be taking exactly the same risks that you are. We'll travel with you into Russia but take different routes to Ekaterinburg, where hopefully we'll meet."

Lydia said, "Aren't you worried we might divulge all this to the Reds if we're caught?"

Boyle smiled tightly. "No, because I'm sure you're both sensible people."

"What's that supposed to mean?"

"The Reds are brutal in their dealings with foreign spies. If it's a woman, she'd most certainly be raped and tortured before being killed. Either way, if you're caught, you're corpses. But I'm going to help you avoid too much unpleasantness. Hanna?"

Hanna took two vials from her purse and placed them on the table. Each held dark brown liquid. "One each," she said.

Andrev picked up one of the vials and swirled the liquid. "What is it?"

"Potassium cyanide. It kills in seconds. If you're apprehended, I suggest you break the vial and immediately swallow the contents."

Andrev and Lydia regarded each other silently, then Andrev said, "On that cheerful note, is there anything else you'd care to tell us in case we're caught?"

Boyle stood, raised his glass. "All I can do is offer a suitable Irish toast. May you get to heaven long before the devil knows you're dead."

45

They cleared away the dishes from the table, then Boyle unfolded a map of Russia and stabbed it with a finger.

"St. Petersburg, which will roughly be your starting point when you arrive." He jabbed another point in the southern Urals. "Ekaterinburg, twelve hundred miles away, which you've got to reach as fast as you can. The quickest way is by train. Since Lenin took over he's made all public transport free. That includes trains and trolley cars, and they're all running. You can jump on and off any of them as you wish, and no need to buy a ticket. Free transport, Lenin's promise to the people. The only one he's kept so far."

"And the bad news?" Lydia asked.

"Half the freight and passenger trains in Russia are out of service due to lack of maintenance and general bedlam, so you can expect transport delays everywhere. Your best bet is to travel from St. Petersburg by train, overnight to Moscow.

"From there, the train journey to Ekaterinburg takes two and a half days or more, depending on delays on the line. But my advice is to move as quickly as you can. The swifter you move, the better your advantage. You'll find cheap lodging houses along the way if you need."

Andrev tapped his finger on the map. "What if we meet checkpoints en route?"

"Your papers will be in order and look genuine. We've used official Russian paper, so nobody can find fault with them."

"Assuming we make it to Ekaterinburg, what then?" Andrev asked.

"Novo-Tikhvinsky is a huge convent complex in the city run by Orthodox nuns. Over a thousand sisters in all. Once you arrive go there directly. There's a small church open to the public and on the back of the wooden entrance door, you'll chalk the Brotherhood's mark. That's the signal that you've arrived. Return to the church within two hours and you ought to see the same mark drawn beside yours. That means it's safe to meet. Wait in the church and you'll be approached by a nun. She'll ask, 'Are you lost? Do you need help?' You'll reply, 'I need to get to Market Street.'

"The words must be exact, so remember them. If there's no reply to your chalk mark, it may mean that it's unsafe to meet. You try again the next day at the same rendezvous. If there's still no reply, then it's dangerous to proceed."

"What happens then?"

Boyle said, "There's a local undertaker, one of our people, who'll step into the breach. Details later."

Lydia said, "What if we get separated en route?"

"You rendezvous in Ekaterinburg using the same drill. Go to the convent church and leave a mark." Boyle paused. "Obviously, I can't say how long it will take for you to reach Ekaterinburg. You could make it in two and a half days, or it may take longer. It depends on how lucky you get. We've had reports of trains being attacked by White battalions, so the schedule's likely to be erratic and you'll have to play the cards as they fall."

"Do we have a reason for traveling?" Andrev asked Boyle.

"You're bound for the Caspian Sea for a spot of convalescence with relatives. Conveniently, the train routes via Ekaterinburg."

"Convalescence?"

From his pocket, Boyle took an identity card and unfolded a sheet of paper. He laid them on the table. "Lydia's already got her papers in the name of Lydia Couris. You're her husband, a Red Army volunteer named Nicholai Couris. They're officially stamped with your invalidity discharge."

"What's my invalidity?"

"Shrapnel residue in your back, lungs, and skull, which you sustained fighting the Whites. The scars on your body will attest to that. You're prone to having epileptic fits on account of the head wound, which is why your wife is traveling with you.

"If anyone should ask why you're stopping in Ekaterinburg, it's because your health has taken a bad turn and you need to rest. The Reds are inclined to be sympathetic toward their wounded comrades."

Boyle paused and added, "Don't worry, we'll go over everything again in detail, including your backgrounds. Take the map with you and study it. The routes you choose will be entirely up to you, but I've penciled in the quickest."

He looked at his watch, then at the evening sky beyond the kitchen window. "Before the light starts to fade, I want you both to change into the clothes you'll be wearing for the journey."

Andrev said, "Any reason why?"

"We've got one last important thing to do."

46

It was still bright outside as Boyle and Hanna walked with them to the cottage. Boyle carried a box camera on a tripod, and a flash pan.

Lydia asked, "Why the camera?"

"You're supposed to be a married couple. Couples carry photographs of each other. So don those rags, and I'll do the necessary."

They dressed in their peasant clothing and came out to the front door, and Boyle took photographs of each of them from different angles, then of Lydia and Uri together in several casual poses.

When he finished he gathered up the camera tripod. "I'll have them developed tomorrow while you two are busy."

"Doing what?"

Hanna said to Lydia, "There's a village on the coast called Carlingford, about thirty miles away. It has a pleasant stretch of beach. Do you know it?"

"Yes."

"I'll have a picnic basket made up for you. Spend the afternoon getting to know one other. Can you drive, Miss Ryan?"

"If I have to."

"Good. You can take the Ford. You'll find bathing garments in your bedrooms."

As Boyle gathered up the rest of the equipment, Andrev said, "What's the plan for the morning?"

Boyle said, "Nothing too stressful. We'll all meet at the main house at eight for breakfast and go over your cover stories and identities. Then you can have your day at the beach, getting to know each other."

"And what will you two be doing?" Lydia asked.

Boyle smiled. "Hanna has some business to tend to in London, so she'll be leaving us tonight to take the mail boat. As for me, I'll be in Dublin trying not to enjoy myself."

Later that evening it turned chilly, a cold front that swept in across the Irish Sea.

Lydia lit the fire with some old newspaper and kindling, stacked on chunks of turf, and the smoky aroma wafted about the room.

Andrev made tea on the range, enamel mugs for each of them. He peered beyond the window at the howling wind tossing the branches, then let the curtain fall. "Today was a perfect summer's day, and now it's like a winter's night. Is it always this unpredictable?"

"That's why the Romans called Ireland *Hibernia*, meaning Winterland. I've known single days when I've experienced the four seasons."

Andrev smiled and took a packet of cigarettes from his pocket and offered her one. "Smoke?"

Lydia shook her head.

Andrev lit his cigarette with a taper he stuck in the fire, then examined the clutter of books on the shelves. "Do you know this place on the coast where we're driving to tomorrow?"

"Yes, I used to go there with my fiancé."

He removed a book from one of the shelves and flicked through it idly. "Where is he now?"

"Missing in action over three years. He served with the British army."

He looked up. "I'm sorry. There's no hope then?"

"There's always hope. I'll never give up on Sean, not ever. He was the kindest, warmest man I ever knew."

"He served with the British, yet you're an Irish republican. I don't understand."

"A story for another day. What did Boyle tell you about me?"

He put the book back on the shelf. "Enough to make me curious. Irish father, American mother, you lived in St. Petersburg for a time, as well as America. A governess to the tsar's children at eighteen, and later a wanted Irish rebel. You've certainly had a busy life for a woman of twenty-four. That's all I know, apart from your obvious weakness."

"What's that?"

Andrev smiled boyishly, with great charm. "Your Irish temper."

"Let me worry about my temper, Mr. Andrev." Lydia leaned over to warm her hands at the flames, the light illuminating her face. "Boyle said you have a wife and son?"

"Nina divorced me."

"What happened?"

Andrev didn't answer but stared away, toward the fire, his eyes dark, as if looking back across an unbridgeable gulf. "As you said, that's not a story meant for now."

"You must still love her. Why else would you be going back?"

He tossed his cigarette in the fire, crossed to his bedroom door, and looked back at her. "When was the last time you were in Russia, Miss Ryan?"

"Five years ago."

"Things have changed, so I hope you know what you're committing to. The odds of us making it to Ekaterinburg without encountering trouble are not in our favor. The country's in chaos and there are bandits and deserters everywhere. If we don't get caught by the Reds we'll probably get robbed or killed, or both."

"Are you trying to frighten me?"

"No, just make you aware of the truth."

"I'm well able to look after myself."

"No doubt. But if I were you I'd also try not be too cocky with that temper of yours. A sharp word to a Red guard at a checkpoint could be the end of us both."

"I've already had the lecture from Hanna Volkov, thank you. And I'm not stupid."

He gave a mock salute. "I'm glad to hear it. Good night, Miss Ryan."

Their eyes met, something passing between them again, of that Lydia was certain, and it brought the same rush of excitement. She felt it flow through her veins like a surge and she flushed, averting Andrev's stare.

And then he was gone, the door closing after him, the wind suddenly raging outside the cottage window, but the only sound Lydia was aware of was the ceaseless pounding of her own heart.

47

It was lunchtime the next day when Boyle strode into the Shelbourne Hotel on St. Stephen's Green.

In the lounge, decorated with green ferns and potted plants, a gramophone was playing a waltz, the dining room crowded with off-duty British officers and their ladies lunching.

Boyle found a free table by the window and ordered coffee and a couple of plates of mixed sandwiches. They came within five minutes and as he bit into a sandwich, the U.S. aide strolled into the lounge, dressed in a crisp flannel Brooks Brothers suit and carrying a Trilby.

"I see you've started without me," MacKenzie said as he settled into the easy chair opposite.

"I'm a man in need of sustenance, Mack. Help yourself to a sandwich. Rough crossing on the ferry?"

"Not that bad, considering. So how goes it?"

"They're settling in nicely. I got some photographs of the two of them developed and they certainly look the part. Take a gander."

Mack examined the photographs, his expression even more sober than usual. Boyle remarked, "You look like your horse came in last in the Derby."

Mack handed back the photographs and sighed. "There's a hitch, Joe."

"Big or small?"

"Big enough to worry me." Mack jerked his head toward St. Stephen's Green park. "Let's take a stroll."

Boyle finished his coffee and they left the hotel and walked over to the park. Mack said, "Our original plan was to send you all—Andrev,

Ryan, and you and Hanna—by cargo ship from Belfast to St. Petersburg. From there you'd take separate routes by train to Ekaterinburg, where you'd meet up. We estimated the journey would take three to four weeks."

"Why do I get a distinctly bad smell about this?"

"What do you know about our agent Dimitri?"

"Only what Ambassador Page told me. He's Russian-born with an American background, a man who's familiar with the tsar and his family, and his help is crucial."

As they strolled round the park's pond Mack kicked a pebble into the water and a half-dozen ducks went skittering after the splash, hoping it was food. "Dimitri's our best spy in Russia. The truth is, he'd be impossible to replace."

"Don't dance around it like a diplomat. Get to the nub, Mack."

Mack stopped walking. "We fear Dimitri may be compromised."

Boyle paled. "Don't tell me that, not at this late stage."

"We received news from Ekaterinburg that the Cheka raided his lodgings. Dimitri escaped by the skin of his teeth. But it's clear that he may be living on borrowed time."

"How much time?"

"Impossible to say. Our spy's a clever man who'll do his utmost to keep one step ahead of the enemy, but his luck can't last forever. If he's caught, our plans may be sunk. Just as worrying are the White allies, the Czech legions. They're fighting their way to Ekaterinburg faster than we reckoned."

Mack added, "We're trying to convince them to slow down, but they seem determined to seize Ekaterinburg. We fear any sudden advance may incite the Reds to execute the family."

"What do we do?"

"Hanna's in London to meet the ambassador. He'll propose to her that we speed things up. If we're lucky, we estimate we've got a couple more weeks to free the Romanovs. That means a faster route. Things really need to be under way a lot sooner."

"Spit it out, Mack. How much sooner?"

LONDON

That same evening, a Slavic-looking man with high cheekbones and wearing a shabby work suit sat in a black Ford delivery van parked near the Connaught Hotel.

The engine was running and he had his cap pulled well down over his face as he smoked a cigarette.

The van was borrowed, no markings on the side, and he watched as Hanna Volkov came down the hotel steps.

She carried a parasol and she looked across the road toward the busy tearooms.

The man smiled to himself and tossed away his cigarette.

Ten minutes earlier he left a note with the concierge, addressed to her. *Dear Hanna, please meet me in the tearooms across the street.* He signed it with an unreadable scrawl.

He watched as Hanna Volkov looked left and right before she started to cross the street.

The man released the handbrake and pressed the accelerator.

By the time she was halfway across the road he'd already covered the distance between them.

She heard the approaching engine because she looked up from under her parasol, her mouth open in horror as the Ford bore down on her at speed.

The van struck her with a terrible thud of flesh hitting metal, and the driver kept going.

Hanna Volkov was sent flying through the air in a swirl of skirts and limbs, her body bouncing off the sidewalk.

48

The coastal fishing village was once a busy Viking port. Dominated by the ruins of the twelfth-century King John's Castle, the inlet was peppered with sailboats that warm Sunday afternoon.

Children played along the strand; men in starched high collars and straw hats and women in bonnets and long dresses strolled the seafront.

Lydia and Andrev parked the Ford and found a picnic spot. They unrolled a blanket and looked inside the picnic basket: a bottle of Burgundy, chicken and cucumber sandwiches wrapped in greaseproof paper, crockery, and utensils.

Andrev opened the Burgundy with a corkscrew, poured two glasses, and handed one to Lydia. "Tell me about yourself. If we're to trust each other with our lives, we ought to know all we can about each other."

Lydia sipped from her glass. "My father traveled around a lot when my brother and I were young. We lived in St. Petersburg for eight years, where he ran a horse-breeding business. Luckily, my parents saw the writing on the wall and we got out of Russia well before the war started."

"And the governess job?"

"My father thought it might be an interesting way for me to spend a year."

"And was it?"

She considered. "I hated all the regal nonsense, if that's what you mean. But I liked the children. There's something very special about them, something especially sweet and unconventional. And surprisingly for royalty, they were quite unspoilt. They slept on hard beds and each had their chores."

"You became close?"

"I like to think so. They had their moments, like all children, but the family never seemed happier than when they were in their own company. Behind it all, they're simple, devoutly religious people."

Lydia put down her wine. "But no doubt you learned all that when you served in the royal guard. Alexei, of course, suffers from constant ill health. He's an invalid really, a terrible worry to his parents." She paused, then changed the subject. "What about you? What happened that caused your wife to seek a divorce?"

Andrev stared away, his eyes dark. "What always happens in such cases? People change."

"Is that what happened?"

"Would it surprise you if I said I don't know? All I'm certain of is that you can drive yourself insane trying to figure it out."

"You must still love her."

"I don't think I'm even sure what love is anymore, at least not the kind between a man and a woman."

"Why else would you be going back?"

Andrev said intently, "Because above all I want my son to grow up free and unafraid, and not to be used as part of some insane, blood-thirsty social experiment by a madman like Lenin." Raw pain etched Andrev's face and he changed the subject. "Tell me about your fiancé. How did you end up on different sides?"

"When hostilities began, everyone saw the Kaiser as a war-mongering tyrant bent on destroying Europe's liberty—at least that's how the British told it. So Sean joined up, like many Irishmen. Of course, after 1916 everything changed."

"Why?"

"That was the year of the Irish rebellion. When the British executed the republican leaders without a shred of mercy, there was no going back."

Andrev looked into her eyes, probing them. "Tell me the rest."

"What do you mean?

"I've had hell inside me, and I can see it in others. The moment we met I sensed you were devoured by hurt and anger. And I'm not just talking about what's happened to your country. I mean personally."

"What's that supposed to mean?"

"I've learned enough about human nature to know that behind anger or bitterness or hurt there's always a wound, or fear, or frustration. There's something you're hiding. Am I right?"

Lydia's neck flushed red, as if he'd struck a nerve. "I think I've told you enough already."

"Can I tell you what else I've learned? We never truly reveal ourselves. Like Salome and her dance. She hides herself from the world with seven veils. Most of us never remove our veils. It's our protection, a way to guard ourselves. That's just what you're doing now."

"Really? And you're an expert, are you?" Lydia yanked the blanket from the ground, scattering the food and plates, knocking over the wine bottle as she got to her feet. "I think it's time we stopped this nonsense and drove back."

A voice behind them said, "I'm glad to see you two getting along like a typical married couple."

They turned and saw Boyle standing there, smiling.

Lydia said, "What are you doing here?"

"I thought I'd drive out and give you the news. There's been a change of plan. We leave for Russia tomorrow."

49

Later that evening a heavy summer storm swept in suddenly, rain hammering on the cottage thatch and flailing against the glass.

Andrev was sitting up in his bed reading, a clutch of books on the nightstand, the oil lamp lit, one of the windows open a crack.

A knock came on his door and Lydia appeared.

She had on a worn Aran wool sweater a couple of sizes too big for her, and it made her look young and vulnerable. "May I come in? I wanted to apologize."

"For what?"

"Getting angry today."

"It's already forgotten. What's the book?"

She held up a slim volume in tan leather. "W. B. Yeats. He's an Irish poet I have a fondness for. I found it on the shelves outside. There's a poem in particular I've marked. It's a favorite of mine."

"May I?"

She sat on the end of the bed and handed him the book. Andrev opened the leaves on a silk marker and studied the page, his eyes drawn to several of the lines, which he read aloud:

> *How many loved your moments of glad grace,*
> *And loved your beauty with love false or true;*
> *But one man loved the pilgrim soul in you,*
> *And loved the sorrows of your changing face.*

When he finally looked up, he seemed touched. "I'm not sure I understand it, but it sounds very beautiful." He closed the book. "Are you afraid now that we're finally going into Russia?"

She brushed a strand of hair from her face. "To be honest, I don't know what I feel. I think I just want it all to be over, if that makes sense. But that wasn't why I wanted to talk."

"No?"

"Maybe you were right about the seven veils. That they're a way to protect ourselves. I think I've always felt like an outsider, ever since I was a child and my family moved around so much. Some people thought I was privileged, maybe even spoiled, but really I wasn't. I was just lonely, and never truly felt at home anywhere. Until I met Sean. For the first time in my life I felt connected to another human being."

She hesitated, emotion welling in her. "There's an old Irish saying: 'May I know you until the end of my days.' That was how I felt about him."

A powerful gust lashed the window, flickering the oil lamp, almost blowing it out. Andrev put down the book and said softly, "It's all right, Lydia. We're all entitled to our privacy. I shouldn't have been so inquisitive, and you don't have to explain."

Her eyes moistened. "No, I really think I need to tell someone. Sometimes, you see, it makes me feel so lost, so angry with the world because it can be so unjust. I haven't told it to another living soul, and it torments me."

"What does?"

"Before Sean left for the front we made love. It's a very human instinct when there's a war. Couples want to acknowledge their feelings, they fear they may never see each other again."

"Of course."

"Not long after Sean left I realized I was pregnant. It stunned me. I was all emotions—happy, lost, confused. I knew my parents would be shocked. In my family, daughters don't get pregnant before marriage. It's unheard-of."

She bit her lip. "I prayed for forgiveness and yet somehow I felt that God would understand what I'd done. I desperately wanted Sean's baby, you see. Maybe some instinct in me even knew he wouldn't ever come back and perhaps that was our only chance to have a child together."

"Did you tell your parents?"

"I never got the chance. A month later I received the telegram that Sean was missing in action. The news hit me hard. I—I lost our baby."

Rain lashed the window, the wind howled. She looked at Andrev, her eyes wet. "I've never told that to a soul, not even to Finn, my brother." She tugged at her sweater. "This old thing belonged to Sean. I wear it to remind me of him when I'm feeling lonely. Silly, isn't it?"

He saw torment in her face, and she seemed totally lost as she said, "I'm sorry, I think the reality of everything just hit me like a ton of bricks. I began to wonder what would happen to Finn if I don't make it back. He's still a child, really. I've looked after him since he was an infant. I—I worry about him."

Andrev saw that she was struggling with her emotions, and when she couldn't hold back any longer she started to cry, great convulsive sobs that shook her body. He reached out, pulled her toward him, gently stroked her hair. "You poor, tortured soul."

Another powerful gust pounded the cottage. It stormed into the room through the open window, rattling the bedroom door and the rafters, blowing out the oil lamp, tossing the tree branches wildly.

He cradled her head on his chest, holding her tightly in the raging darkness.

PART FOUR

50

Sorg came awake drenched in sweat.

His body felt seared by heat. He was lying on a metal bed in a cell with a barred metal door. It was deathly silent and the cell stank of damp air.

When he struggled to sit up he couldn't. His body was covered with a coarse gray blanket and he was tied down with leather straps. His clothes were gone and he felt naked under the blanket.

He moaned and slumped back on the bed. He remembered little after passing out. Just a vague memory of briefly coming awake while he was being dragged along a stone corridor. Now that he was fully conscious, he was certain he was in a prison. He heard footsteps and his heart hammered with alarm. A key rattled in the lock and the door clanged open.

A nun stood in the doorway. She was tall, middle-aged, with a gaunt but kindly face. Her bleached porcelain skin almost made her look sickly. Still, there was strength in her piercing blue eyes, no denying that, as she balanced a heavy tray in one hand.

It contained a towel, a basin, and a jug of steaming water. In her other hand she carried a lit oil lamp. "You're awake at last. How's the patient?"

"Where am I?"

The nun banged shut the door and hung the lamp on a wall hook. "In the basement of Novo-Tikhvinsky Convent. One of our nuns found you collapsed. I'm Sister Agnes, Mistress of Novices. Do you want to tell me who you are?"

Sorg didn't reply.

The nun saw caution on his face and said at once, "Forgive me, but

I'm not used to all this subterfuge. You were supposed to leave your mark inside the church door. I was to leave another just like it, then come and ask, 'Are you lost? Do you need help?' And you'd reply, 'I need to get to Market Street.' But I think we're past all that now, don't you?"

Sorg said, puzzled, "How did you know who I am?"

The nun smiled. "You were delirious because of your wound. You kept repeating that you needed to get to Market Street. I also found a ring on your finger."

"Where is it?"

"Stored safely with your clothes and belongings out in the hall."

The nun wore a plain silver band on her own finger. She removed it and handed it to Sorg. He saw the engraving inside the ring, next to the silversmith's mark, just like his own.

"Does that convince you?" the nun asked.

Sorg handed it back. "I came here the day I arrived in Ekaterinburg. I left my mark on the church door and there was no reply. I tried again every day for three days and there was still no answer. I wondered what happened to you. Finally, I asked for you by name at the hospital. They said you were gravely ill."

The nun slipped the ring back on her finger. "I fell victim to the typhus that's broken out all over the city. They moved me to a hospital in Perm. I was in a bad way so I left instructions with one of the nuns to make contact with you, but she herself fell ill and died. Still, I'm well now, and you've survived, that's all that matters. How are you feeling?"

"As if I've been trampled on by wild horses. This place looks like a prison."

The nun smiled. "Actually, it used to be. The convent was built on the ruins of a Mongol fort used by Genghis Khan, complete with dungeons. These days we run schools, a hospital, an orphanage, a bakery."

Sorg tried to raise himself. "Are you going to undo these straps?"

Sister Agnes pulled up a wooden stool and sat, placing the tray at her feet. She unbuckled the straps. "Your wound's turned septic and you were delirious for a time. We had to make sure you didn't fall out of bed."

Sorg massaged his wrists. "Where are the other patients?"

"In nearby wards. It's more private here. I didn't want to risk you saying something you shouldn't if you became delirious again." The nun unwrapped the cotton towel to reveal a handful of what looked like herbs, along with a thick slice of bread.

The pungent aromas of thyme and mint filled Sorg's nostrils. He saw that the tray contained cotton dressings and scissors.

Sister Agnes crushed a handful of the herbs, rolling them between her palms. The fragrances spiced the air. She placed the herbs in a bowl and then put a hand to Sorg's forehead. "You'll probably feel terrible for a few more days. You've lost blood. And you're still running a temperature. Here, drink this."

She offered Sorg a glass of cold water. Easing his head forward, he sipped the refreshing liquid. Sister Agnes lay the crushed herbs on the bread.

Sorg asked, "What are you doing?"

"Making a poultice. Proper medicines are in short supply so we have to make do with the old methods. The poultice will draw out any pus from your wound."

"Am I going to live?"

The nun unfolded the thick cotton cloth. She lay the bread in the middle and sprinkled on the herbs, moistening the concoction with steaming hot water. "With God's help. What happened?"

Sorg told her.

The nun said, "I don't think there's any internal damage, but time will tell. You'll definitely need to rest up and keep off the streets, in case the Reds are looking for you."

"That's impossible. I have work to do."

"I understand but I'm a qualified nurse. Move about too soon and your wound could open, become infected again, and you could die."

Sister Agnes pulled back the sheet and used the scissors to cut away Sorg's dressing. "Are you hungry?"

"Starving."

She dabbed the poultice in the steaming hot water. "Hunger's a good sign. I'll see that you're given some broth and freshly baked bread. We've been extraordinarily busy. Brutal skirmishes between the Whites and Reds in recent days have clogged the hospital with the sick and dying. Lean forward, please. This may hurt."

Sister Agnes gently but firmly pressed the hot poultice against Sorg's wound. Sorg gritted his teeth, feeling the heat sting his wound. Strangely, it seemed to ease the throbbing. "There's something I need," he said.

"What?"

"Laudanum."

The nun didn't flinch. "It's used by many who served in the trenches. Is that how you came to use it?"

"That's close enough."

"I'm afraid we have no laudanum here and it may be impossible to come by under present circumstances. The Reds raided our medicine supply last week. We have little of anything left. I may be able to manage some coffee and cigarettes, if they help?"

"Thank you."

The nun went to go.

Sorg gripped her arm. "Please, tell me about the family."

The nun gently pried his grip away and patted his hand. "Rest first. Sleep as long as you can. Then you and I have plans to discuss."

51

It was just after lunch that same afternoon as Boyle went up the steps to St. Andrew's Private Hospital. His clothes were crumpled and he looked as if he'd had a rough night.

He nodded to the uniformed policemen in the corridor who admitted him into the private room. A worried-looking Ambassador Walter Page stood by the hospital bed.

Boyle's heart stuttered when he saw Hanna.

She was unconscious, covered in bandages from head to toe, her legs and hips encased in some kind of metal contraption. Her face was heavily bruised, even her eyelids, which were purple, swollen, and closed.

Page said, "She's got internal injuries, broken bones, and she hemorrhaged badly. The doctors say she may not survive."

Boyle's eyes were burning, his face very pale. "Who did this, Walter?"

"The police haven't found the van or driver. But a witness said he looked Slavic and was actually grinning as he mowed her down. I'm convinced it's the long arm of our friends in Moscow."

Boyle gently touched Hanna's fingers, his voice hoarse. *"Why?"*

"The real question must surely be *why at this time*. I smell trouble. That they'd try to kill her now means they've been watching her. If they've been watching her, then what else have they seen, or surmised?"

Page saw Boyle struggle to keep his composure, his body trembling, as if finding it hard to keep his fury under control. When it seemed he couldn't bear to look at Hanna's injuries any longer, he turned away.

Page put a hand on his shoulder. "I think we should call it off, Joe. If we've been compromised, you could all be walking into a death trap."

"Forget it, Walter."

Boyle went down the hospital steps and climbed into a gray Packard parked on the curb, the engine kicking over. Lydia sat in the rear, Andrev in the passenger's seat. "How is she?" Lydia asked.

Boyle was grim, his eyes red. "Not the best, I'm afraid. But it changes nothing. We still go ahead." He shifted into gear and pulled out from the curb.

NEAR SOUTHEND-ON-SEA
4 P.M.

The wartime training aerodrome sixty miles from London had been abandoned since the early spring.

That afternoon Boyle drove them in the Packard down the muddy track. The aerodrome was once part of a derelict farmyard and Boyle halted the Packard outside a huge cowshed that was converted into an aircraft hangar. The green-painted corrugated doors were firmly shut, and several cars and a canvas open-top truck were parked outside.

A burly, energetic man in his late twenties with a toothbrush mustache stood outside the hangar, wearing glasses and a mustard-colored work coat. He clutched a pocket watch in one hand, a cup of steaming tea in the other, impatience braiding his voice as he said in Russian, "You're six hours late, Boyle. What the dickens kept you?"

Boyle climbed out. "Personal business in London. How are you, Igor? Well, I hope?"

The man put his pocket watch away. "I'd be even better if you kept to our schedule." He turned charmingly to Andrev and Lydia, and took her hand and kissed it as if she were an old friend. "My dear, you'll have to teach this man the good manners of keeping appointments on time. It's a virtue he's sometimes sadly lacking. So these are our guests?"

Boyle said, "Igor Sikorsky, meet Uri and Lydia."

Sikorsky shook Andrev's hand. "The pleasure is all mine."

Andrev said, astonished, "*The* Igor Sikorsky? The famous aircraft designer?"

"Guilty, I'm afraid."

"There's a rumor that the Reds shot you," Andrev said.

"I escaped by the skin of my teeth. If only some of my friends were so lucky. It seems anyone who questions Lenin is destined for the firing squads these days." He tossed the contents of his mug onto the grass. "I've got some fresh tea brewing inside. Then I'll show you the beast that's going to fly you into the jaws of hell."

Even at the tender age of twelve, when he designed a toy helicopter powered by a rubber band, Igor Sikorsky was already considered a genius.

Born in Kiev in 1889, Igor grew up with his father, a psychology professor, and his mother, a respected physician, and from childhood his parents instilled in their son a love of art, especially for the works of Michelangelo and Jules Verne. Not surprisingly the boy's passion for flight was ignited and he dedicated himself to a career in aviation. Barely ten years after the Wright Brothers flew at Kitty Hawk, by the age of twenty-three, Sikorsky had already designed the world's first long-range transport plane.

The four-engine Ilya Muromets, named after a Russian folk hero, was a sturdy transport aircraft capable of carrying up to sixteen passengers at a cruising speed of almost seventy miles an hour. When the war came, Sikorsky's beloved transport plane was converted into a bomber, adding nine machine guns and a heavy payload of bombs.

It seemed ironic that the Russians, while having a completely inferior air force during the war, possessed one of the most revolutionary, modern aircraft of its time.

As Sikorsky led Boyle and the others in through the hangar doors that afternoon, they witnessed an astonishing sight: parked in the middle of the floor was an enormous, pale green biplane with a long, cigar-shaped cabin and four massive engines. It bristled with at least eight strategically positioned Lewis machine guns.

Sikorsky said, "Say hello to the Ilya Muromets. Or the S-23V if you prefer. It's sixty feet long and has a wingspan of just over a hundred feet. You're looking at the future of air travel, my friends."

It was unlike any aircraft they had ever seen and as they marveled at the plane, Boyle said, "Good grief, Igor, so this is it? I've seen photographs in the press but they don't do it justice."

Inside the hangar, a half-dozen mechanics were working away in greasy overalls. Sikorsky led the way toward a small stepladder, beckoning Boyle and the others as he entered a spacious cabin.

"This model is a bastardized version, with many of the original passenger amenities, though with machine guns added. It was actually destined for the tsar, but he was a naval man and never enjoyed flying. It's got four Sunbeam Crusader V-8 engines, a specially built bedroom, internal heating, electrical lighting, a lounge, and the first airborne toilet. All the modern comforts, you might say."

"You're joking," Lydia said.

"I never joke about my inventions," Sikorsky said soberly. "I like to think of the Ilya as a hotel room on wings. Believe me, within the next twenty years everyone will be flying in a machine like this. We would have begun passenger flights in 1914 had the war not started. Watch your head."

They moved into a roomy cabin. The cockpit had space for several passengers to stand and observe the pilot at work, but the most impressive area was the lounge, complete with a wicker table and chairs. Toward the aircraft rear was a small bedroom cabin with two low, narrow cots, an electric light overhead. A door led to a washroom and toilet.

"Incredible," Boyle uttered. "I've never seen anything like it. It's straight out of a Jules Verne novel. And this thing actually *flies*?"

Sikorsky looked mildly offended and thrust his hands in his coat pockets. "Actually, it broke the world record for the longest recorded flight of over seventeen hundred miles in less than twenty-six hours, from St. Petersburg to Kiev and back, with two stops for refueling. That was in June 1914. We've made considerable improvements since then, increasing the range and engine performance."

"What about crew?"

"We usually carry a mechanic on board, along with the pilot and eight machine gunners—a total crew of ten. For your flight, we only need two pilots and a mechanic, so it'll save weight."

Boyle looked around the cabin, shaking his head. "It's unbelievable, Igor."

Sikorsky slapped a hand on the interior fuselage. "I built eighty of these beauties. We flew four out of Russia before the Reds could get their hands on them."

As they stood there, stunned, studying the cabin, Sikorsky said to Boyle, "I suppose you don't care to tell me exactly what it is you're all up to? Or do I simply follow instructions and provide the transport?"

"I'm afraid it'll have to remain our secret, Igor."

"Say no more." Sikorsky winked and gestured toward the stepladder. "Let's go to my office. We can discuss the flight plan for your journey and I'll give you the bad news—the risks you're going to face in flight."

52

They entered an office with glass windows at the back of the hangar. Sikorsky poured freshly brewed tea into mugs and handed them to his visitors, adding heaped spoonfuls of sugar into his own tea. "Help yourselves. Does anyone have any questions before I start?"

"Do you really think we can reach our destination, Igor?"

Before he addressed Boyle, Sikorsky crossed to a map of Europe and most of Russia on the wall, and slapped a big bony hand on it. "I don't see why not. With refueling the Ilya's capable of flying the distance, so that shouldn't be a problem." Sikorsky fingered his mustache. "The wild card will be the weather. It's forecast to be good with strong winds from west to east, but you never know, things can change. I'd be lying if I said it won't get rough up there at times, but if we're careful you ought to be able to avoid any really bad patches."

"Anything else we should know about?" Boyle asked, and sipped from his mug.

"The bad news is the Imperial German air service is still carrying out reconnaissance flights from their lines outside St. Petersburg. But if it's any comfort they usually avoid the Ilya. They call it 'the porcupine' because it's bristling with eight machine guns, which makes it a serious foe."

"Who's our pilot?" Lydia asked.

"Your captain is one of the best fliers I know, at least when he's sober." Sikorsky smiled, crossed to the office door, and yelled across the hangar, "Boris! Can you haul your backside in here right away?"

A small, dapper, bow-legged man with a wispy blond beard and bloodshot eyes crossed the hangar floor and entered the office. He was handsome in an odd sort of way, and wore a black mariner's cap set at a jaunty angle, a dark uniform suit, and grubby black boots, the laces undone.

Sikorsky made the introductions. "Meet the man who's going to fly you to Russia within twenty-four hours. This is Boris Pozner."

Pozner grinned, displaying a couple of gold teeth. "Charmed to meet you, ladies and gentlemen." He kissed Lydia's hand, then offered a handshake to Boyle and Andrev.

Sikorsky said, "Boris is ex-Imperial navy, like many of our Russian fliers."

Pozner shrugged. "Sea or air, it doesn't make much difference, does it? You'll get tossed about like a feather in a storm either way."

"Would you care to tell our passengers about their flight?"

Pozner moved to the wall map and tapped a fingertip at the southeast coast of England, then swung it in an arc until he touched St. Petersburg. "The plan is to fly across the North Sea for about six hours and land in northern Germany, near Kiel, and refuel."

"Surely we can't land on enemy territory?"

"I have news for you. All the aerodromes we'll be using to refuel are in German-held territory. But we'll be using abandoned civilian and military sites that I'm familiar with. I'm hoping we can land and depart before the Germans are any the wiser."

Pozner tapped the map. "Our next fuel stop will be across the Baltic at an airfield near the Gulf of Riga. With the winds on our side it should take about another eight hours, which is right at the limits of our range."

"It's also where we'll say our good-byes," Boyle added. "That's where I'll be getting off."

Pozner went on: "We'll quickly refuel and take off again. Another six hours or more should see us arrive outside St. Petersburg."

"Where do we get all the fuel?" Lydia asked Pozner.

Sikorsky said, "You'll be carrying extra fuel cans on board, enough for the complete outward journey, so if there are any smokers among you, I'd suggest you seriously think of giving up the habit right now. One spark and you risk causing a fireball."

Pozner addressed Uri and Lydia and pointed again at St. Petersburg.

"We've arranged a supply of fuel at your final destination, to cover the return leg. The airfield we'll put down in is over thirty miles from the city. There's a local train that'll take you to St. Petersburg in an hour."

Lydia looked back at the wood and metal Ilya through the office windows, then wrapped her arms around herself as if to keep out the hangar chill. "Are you certain that thing is safe?" she asked Pozner.

"Nothing in life is entirely safe, madame. But I assure you the Ilya's one of the safest aircraft around, tough as a jockey's hide."

Pozner looked back at the hangar, pride in his voice. "Only one has ever been lost in battle so far—shot down by four German Albatroses, three of which our crew managed to destroy with machine-gun fire. The aircraft has an excellent record."

"But won't it be dangerous flying and landing at night?"

"You forget, it's still white nights in the Baltic this time of year. The short nights hardly divide the evenings from the mornings, making it easier to land. We should be able to locate the airfields without too much bother, using our map-reading skills and compasses."

Andrev said, "You seriously believe we can reach Russia in less than twenty-four hours?"

"If the winds are with us I'm confident we can make it in less."

"That's astonishing," Lydia said.

"It's progress." Pozner pushed his greasy mariner's cap off his forehead, and rested his hands on his hips. "Right, I'll take a last look at our flight route, so if everyone gets their belongings on board we can get under way."

Lydia said, "You mean now?"

"Yes, madame, now. The weather's due to turn stormy this afternoon. If we want to avoid the worst of it we need to get off the ground."

53

EKATERINBURG

It was raining heavily that evening. Thunder rumbled in the darkened sky as the Fiat truck squealed to a halt outside the Imperial Hotel on Neva Street.

Yakov sat in the passenger seat beside the driver, rain lashing the windshield. Next to him, Kazan barked at two of his plainclothes Cheka huddled under the truck's drenched canvas. "Get going. You know what to do."

The men jumped down and ran through the rain into the hotel.

Kazan said in frustration, "Our spy's somewhere in the city, I'll bet my life on it, Commissar. His best bet for now is to remain hidden in Ekaterinburg."

Yakov stared out beyond the rain. The Imperial was the last hotel and lodging house on the list, and all had been checked twice in case their quarry had found housing there recently. The city was a warren of backstreets and tenements, but Yakov hadn't the manpower to search everywhere.

The two Cheka returned and climbed into the back of the truck, shaking rain from their coats, and one of them said, "No new guests have arrived, comrade. No one matching the man's description has tried to check in."

Kazan slammed a fist into his palm. "Where's he got to? He can't be sleeping rough, not while he's wounded and with a curfew. If he's not staying in a hotel or lodgings, then someone has to be helping him."

Yakov lit a cigarette and stared out past the rain, studying the city's distinctive skyline, dotted with church spires and cathedral domes. "Not short of religious orders this city, is it?"

"It's long been an Orthodox settlement. Monasteries and churches are everywhere."

"They're also known to offer sanctuary. Get me a complete list of church establishments."

NEAR SOUTHEND-ON-SEA
ENGLAND

"I think we've covered everything," Boyle said.

They were in the windowed office at the back of the hangar. Lydia carried a small suitcase and Andrev a well-worn Russian-army-issue kit bag.

Boyle added, "But no harm in checking all our papers. Let's have a look."

They all did as he suggested, then Boyle handed Andrev and Lydia each a Nagant revolver and a box of cartridges. "I'm hoping you won't need these. Remember, lose the weapons if ever you think they'll cause you trouble."

Boyle gave them each a small purse filled with rubles and kopeks, a *payok*—a booklet filled with ration stamps—and a single canvas bag of provisions containing cheese, butter, bread, jam, tinned sardines, and biscuits.

"The food's the kind that can be bought in Russia, and there's enough to last you both a week. The money will be enough to get you to your destination. You don't want to get caught with too much cash; it could only attract unwanted attention.

"I've given you ration booklets—the Reds have issued them because of severe shortages. I'll be carrying the same provisions and ration booklets. Once we land near Riga, I'll leave you, and make my way by train to Ekaterinburg. Is there anything you'd like me to go over again?"

Andrev glanced at Lydia, then shook his head.

"That's it, then. We're ready to go." Boyle tucked a hand inside his pocket and offered Lydia the small black Mauser with walnut grips, along with a spare magazine. "Yours, I believe. Maybe you'd like to hold on to it as extra insurance?"

Lydia accepted the pistol. "If I don't make it back, Boyle, promise me for Finn's sake your word will be kept?"

"You have my solemn pledge."

For a few moments no one spoke, and then they heard a rumbling sound as a pair of mechanics shoved open the hangar doors. The sky outside was turning charcoal as ominous clouds marched across the horizon.

Sikorsky strode into the office, all business, and holding a mug of tea. "Pozner's anxious to get under way, so whenever you're ready." He raised his mug in a toast. "Any enemy of the Reds is an ally of mine. So whatever it is you're up to, I hope you give them torment, my friends."

They moved outside the hangar as the Ilya Muromets was wheeled out onto a well-rutted meadow used as a landing strip.

One of the mechanics climbed on board along with Pozner's co-pilot, a boyish-faced young man barely out of his teens who helped push the aircraft out onto the field.

Pozner clutched a handful of weather and route charts and looked up worriedly at the gathering clouds. "We'll need to move things along, or the storm's going to hit. Climb aboard, please."

A mechanic placed a small stepladder at the aircraft door. They stepped on board to a strong smell of fuel, over a dozen metal drums stacked both sides of the long aircraft cabin.

Pozner said, "You can sit or stand up front and watch our takeoff—suit yourselves."

Boyle picked a passenger seat. Andrev and Lydia decided to stand in the front cabin behind Pozner and his young copilot, both perched on high chairs, Pozner operating the surface controls, the copilot the throttles.

Boyle waved a salute at Sikorsky, then Pozner closed the door and the aircraft was pushed farther out onto the field where the mechanics turned the props. One by one the four engines sputtered and ignited.

Pozner worked the controls. "Here we go; hold on tight."

Uri and Lydia held on to a couple of leather support straps overhead as Pozner increased the throttles. A powerful, noisy surge vibrated through the aircraft as the engines revved. Slowly the plane began to move, rattling and shaking as it bumped down the rutted airfield, building up power, faster and faster.

Then, just when the aircraft seemed about to disintegrate with the harsh vibration, it lifted gracefully into the air.

54

Andrev marveled as the coast of England disappeared below them.

Pozner was busily maneuvering the controls, trimming out the aircraft at a thousand feet before he began a steady climb up to five thousand as they flew out over the North Sea. Boyle was in the back, filling a cup from a flask of coffee.

Lydia gazed out at the sea, a look of dread unmistakable on her face.

"What's the matter?" Andrev asked. "Scared of flying?"

Suddenly the aircraft lurched violently in a rough pocket of air, throwing Lydia forward into his arms. He said, "Are you all right?"

She held on to him a few moments, until the turbulence passed and she eased herself from his grip. "Y—Yes. If you don't mind, I'll try and get some rest." She moved down the aisle to the cabin bedroom.

Andrev watched her go and when the cabin door closed, Pozner let the relief pilot take over at the controls and said, "It'll be a little bumpy until we clear the coast, but nothing to worry about. How's your lady friend? She seems a bit distracted. Flying for the first time can often be unsettling."

"It doesn't bother you?"

Pozner smiled. "We're all on borrowed time, my friend. What's the point in worrying? If you're feeling hungry there's a cupboard halfway down the aisle with sandwiches and water, tea, or coffee. Help yourself."

"Thanks."

Boyle appeared, carrying a cup of coffee, just as the captain produced a pack of cigarettes and said, "Smoke?"

"I thought that wasn't allowed on board."

Pozner grinned and slipped a cigarette between his lips. "Sikorsky's a born worrier. The fuel's safely stored, so you don't have to fret." He pointed to a sand-filled bucket by the cockpit. "Just be certain to remain up front and use the sand bin as an ashtray."

Andrev shook his head. "I'll remain on the side of caution if you don't mind."

Boyle sipped his coffee and said to Pozner, "Anything else you'd care to tell us about while you're in the mood?"

"Only that the weather may not be all that sweet for landing outside St. Petersburg."

"Why?" Andrev asked.

"Nasty Baltic storms can brew up pretty quickly. An old dog like me is used to the hard road but I didn't want to tell the woman. We don't want to frighten the life out of her, now do we?"

"We'll do our best not to vomit all over your cabin."

Pozner gave a cackling laugh. "Get some rest, all of you, we've a long haul ahead. Do either of you know how to operate a Lewis machine gun?"

"Yes, why?" Boyle answered.

"The German air patrols are a little more active than Sikorsky said. Igor tends to believe that his aircraft are invincible. Eight machine guns can solve a lot of problems but not every obstacle."

"What does that mean?" Andrev asked.

Pozner turned back to take the controls. "Odds are that we'll either get pounded by weather or attacked by the Germans, or maybe both."

Boyle said, "Give it to us straight. What are the real chances of us reaching Russia safely?"

"With luck, fifty-fifty."

Lydia lay on one of the cots, the harsh metallic rhythm of the engines droning on. She heard the knock on the cabin door and sat up. "Come in."

Andrev appeared, carrying a plate of food and an enamel mug. "I thought you might want something to eat. It's not much, just some bread and cheese and the tea's cold, but it's better than nothing."

Her hair was tousled and she looked strained. "Thank you."

"Can't you sleep?" He sat opposite and left the mug and plate by her bed.

"No. You?"

"I'll try later. Flying bothers you, doesn't it?"

"Sean was an observer with the Royal Flying Corps. He went missing over France. Every time I see an aircraft, it makes me shudder."

Andrev took the pewter hip flask from his pocket, unscrewed it, and poured a generous measure of amber liquid into Lydia's mug.

"What are you doing?"

"Some whiskey, thanks to Boyle. It might settle your nerves."

"In that case, I won't say no. How is he?"

"Angry, I'd say. What happened to Hanna has shaken him, but it's made him even more determined."

"Where does that leave us?"

"There's no going back now, I'm afraid. But the Reds can't know our exact plans, Boyle assured me of that."

Beyond the windows, Lydia saw only watery twilight. "Where are we?"

"Over the North Sea."

Lydia sipped from her mug. "May I ask you something?"

"Of course."

"Boyle said you broke out of a Bolshevik prison."

"My corporal and I managed to escape. There was a blizzard and we got delayed reaching Perm. By the time we made it to our lines our troops had retreated, and I was too late."

"For what?"

"To save my men." Andrev explained as best he could. "The Reds meant to force-march them to another camp. Most wouldn't have survived the weather. If I'd reached Perm in time maybe it could have made a difference."

"And that makes you feel guilty?"

"Something like that."

"And the youth's death, Stanislas?"

His face was bleak, and his shoulders slumped, as if he was carrying a terrible weight. "It haunts me every day. He was barely sixteen. Just a boy, and I loved him like family."

"What did Yakov do to your comrades?"

"I've no idea. I made it to Moscow with my corporal, where we parted company, and I managed to reach St. Petersburg. I was desperate to see Nina and my son. But Yakov was hunting me for a crime I didn't commit. I couldn't stay or I would have put their lives in danger."

"How did Nina seem?"

"Different. We'd been apart almost three years. She wasn't the woman I once knew, no more than I was the same man. The strain of war and separation made us like strangers."

"That must have been difficult, with a child involved."

"It tore my heart out. I don't know if I can convince her to leave Russia. But I have to try. If I lose Sergey, I don't know what I'll do."

Lydia saw the remorse in his face. It seemed to almost crush him.

"For your sake I hope they join you, Uri Andrev. I truly do."

She touched his hand. Their eyes met. Lydia was aware of her heart beating like a drum and the faint tremor in her voice. "Good night. I—I hope you sleep."

His gaze lingered on her face.

She saw it then, a look in his eyes that told her there was more to this, so much more.

"Good night." He held her stare a moment, then he left, closing the door softly after him.

She lay there, her breast still pounding, a warm feeling coursing through her body, and not from the alcohol. She emptied her mug and put it down. "Oh, you poor idiot, Lydia Ryan. Won't you ever learn? You're only asking to get your heart broken."

And with that she flicked out the small electric night-light and the cabin plunged into near darkness.

55

Andrev went up to the dimly lit cockpit where Pozner was at the controls, sipping cold tea from an enamel mug. Despite the rumbling engine noise the copilot was asleep on the cabin floor, under a coarse woolen blanket.

The faint electric light was just enough light to see by, and it was pleasantly warm. The sky was a silvery blue, the moon appearing from behind clouds. "What's the matter, can't sleep?" Pozner asked.

"I'm afraid not." Andrev rubbed his eyes.

"What about your lady friend? Did she manage to get some shut-eye?"

"She wasn't having much luck."

"Nerves?"

"I thought so, but you never can tell."

Pozner grinned. "That's women for you. One of life's great mysteries." He turned back to the controls, studied his charts, and pointed ahead. "See those lights in the far distance? That's northern Germany. About two hours from now we'll be attempting our landing to refuel."

"Attempting? That doesn't exactly sound reassuring."

"Flying isn't a business with absolute guarantees, my friend. Landing in twilight or darkness is always tricky."

The aircraft buffeted a little but otherwise the flight was going surprisingly smoothly, and Andrev said, "So where's this bad weather you predicted?"

Pozner sipped from his mug. "Not for a while yet. But weather forecasting is as much an art as a science, so hopefully I'll get it wrong for your sakes. Mind if I ask you a personal question?"

"That depends on the question."

"Do you like the woman?"

Andrev frowned. "What's it to you?"

"Back in the hangar, her eyes were on you like a searchlight the moment your back was turned."

"Do you usually make a habit of watching people?"

Pozner smiled. "It's a pastime of mine, observing human nature. Speaking of which, she might seem like the kind who's well able to take care of herself, but they're always the ones with the glass hearts, easily broken."

"You sound like an expert in such matters, Captain."

"Let's just say that after three marriages and a lady friend in every port I'm quick to recognize when a woman's attracted to a man. You mark my words, that lady's smitten with you."

Andrev came out of a doze. The aircraft cabin shuddered and the engines changed pitch and then came a sharp bump. He came awake and rubbed his eyes.

Lydia was fast asleep, curled up on her side, and he got up and left the cabin.

To his amazement the aircraft had already landed in a meadow, the first slivers of burnt orange tinting the dawn. The aircraft door was open, the crew outside along with Boyle, and Andrev went down the stepladder, the air smelling salty fresh mixed with the aroma of oil fumes from the engines.

By now they were shut down and the cold morning air fell eerily silent, his eardrums aching from the constant noise of the V-8s. Andrev heard seagulls overhead and guessed they were somewhere near a coast.

Pozner was busy supervising the copilot and the mechanics as they hooked up two hand pumps and began pumping fuel from the cans into the tanks. Boyle was helping unload the cans. "So, you're back in the land of the living. How'd you sleep?"

"Well enough. Where are we?"

"Near a place called Birken. We managed to find the landing field without too much difficulty. Smooth as glass as it turned out."

"Are we safe here?"

Pozner grinned. "Far from it. The locals are bound to have heard our engines. Give us a hand. The sooner we get refueled, the sooner we can get under way again before anyone comes to investigate."

They worked eagerly, transferring the fuel from the cans to the tanks, and ten minutes later when they finished Pozner tossed the fuel cans across the meadow. "Leave them. We've no more use for them."

They all helped maneuver the aircraft to face the direction they had landed. Pozner took a few deep breaths of salty air, then climbed back up the stepladder. Andrev followed. The copilot and mechanic restarted the engines, and then they all climbed back inside and pulled shut the door.

"No German air patrols in sight. So far, we're blessed."

Pozner wasted no time applying power, but the Ilya Muromets struggled to get traction on the dewy meadow before the propellers bit the air and the plane trundled down the field, building up speed. It ascended smoothly into the still air and Pozner climbed to five thousand feet, then gradually edged up to eight.

Below them in the slowly rising dawn a few stray sparkling lights betrayed German coastal villages and towns.

Pozner consulted his charts. "How's your lady friend?"

"Still asleep the last time I saw her. How much longer?"

"If these winds stay with us, maybe another six or seven hours. A new record, I'd say." Pozner winked, and put away the charts. "From here on, start saying your prayers that the Baltic weather doesn't turn nasty."

56

Sister Agnes dabbed Sorg's face with a cold, damp cloth. He was still in the basement room and felt groggy when he woke up.

"Did you rest well?" she asked.

He rubbed his eyes. "Well enough. How long was I asleep?"

"Twelve hours. You must have been exhausted." She dressed his wound with gray, tattered-looking bandages. "While you were out cold, I managed to stitch your wound."

Sorg stared at the frayed cotton and the nun said, "I'm sorry. There's a severe shortage of medical supplies, so we have to make do with boiling used bandages and sterilizing them. Lean forward if you can. I need to finish your dressing."

Sorg shifted, the movement an effort even with the nun's help. She wrapped the cotton around his stomach and finished tying it.

His side began to throb. He winced in agony and collapsed back on the bed. By the bed was a packet of cigarettes and a box of matches, and an empty coffee mug. The ashtray was stuffed with the ends of a half dozen cigarettes he'd smoked before falling asleep, and the room smelled of stale tobacco.

She said, "You need to make sure you don't open that wound again. To do so could be fatal. You wanted to know about the family?"

"Tell me everything you can. Leave nothing out."

The Fiat truck laden with Red Guards trundled to a halt outside the convent. It looked an impressive complex with gilded church cupolas, outbuildings, and a massive bell tower. Yakov observed the scene from the Fiat's front seat. "Where are we?"

Next to him, Kazan consulted a handwritten list. "The Convent of Novo-Tikhvinsky. Over a thousand nuns and there's a hospital in the grounds, as well as a bakery, a children's asylum, and workshops." He put down the list, eyes glinting. "I know of these nuns. They deliver fresh eggs and milk to the Romanovs most mornings."

Yakov climbed out, his gaze still fixed on the convent. "A hospital, you say. It could be just the place where our spy might seek medical help."

One of the troops went to move forward but Kazan grabbed his arm. "Where do you think you're going?"

"To yank the bell, comrade."

"And let them know we're coming? Don't be an idiot." Kazan withdrew his revolver. "We go in the back way and surprise them."

"The Ipatiev House is well guarded. Everyone who enters requires a special pass and they're thoroughly searched. Two of our young novices, Maria and Antonina, were given passes and are allowed to bring eggs, cream, butter, and fresh bread to the family every few days. They also bring thread."

"Thread?"

"To repair their worn clothes. The girls and their mother have also been sewing precious gems into their undergarments, should they need such valuables to aid their escape."

"How did you get passes for the novices?"

"From the guard commander. But a new one was appointed over a week ago. His name's Yurovsky. I don't know how much longer he'll allow us to continue to visit the family."

Sorg reached for his cigarettes and lit one. "Why?"

"The new commander trusts no one. He's tightened security and put in electric bells to warn of any trouble. He also replaced some of the guards with handpicked Latvian thugs. Ekaterinburg is a city of whispers, and the rumors I hear frighten me."

"What rumors?"

"The story going around is that one of Lenin's henchmen has arrived from Moscow. A Commissar Yakov. Even the dogs on the street know it's only a question of time before he orders the execution."

Sorg tapped the cigarette in the astray. "You say even the novices are thoroughly searched?"

"It depends on the guards. Some simply wave them in. Others seem to take delight in embarrassing them by searching under their habits. We passed the family messages not long after they arrived here, you see. One of our nuns had the clever idea of inscribing a message on some fresh radishes they delivered to the house. A guard noticed the inscriptions. Fortunately, he couldn't read and merely crushed the radishes with his boots. But the commander at the time heard about it. He threatened to shoot all of us if it happened again."

"Is it always the same two novices who deliver the milk and food?"

"Yes. Maria and Antonina."

Sorg considered. "Do you think they could draw me a diagram of the house from memory?"

"I don't see why not."

"I'll need to know where the entrances and exits are, which rooms are which, upstairs and downstairs. And where the guards are stationed. Detail like that is important. Better still if you could get hold of architectural drawings."

"That may be difficult, but I'll see what I can do."

"Tell me more about the family."

The nun shrugged. "What's there to tell? The tsar's a broken man and his wife is a frightened woman on the edge of madness. They're under enormous stress. Imagine the torment of knowing that your children may be murdered at any moment."

"What about the children?"

"Their health's reasonable. However, their doctor sometimes orders their hair to be cut short to battle head lice. They've also had to suffer the guards' taunts and abuse. And young Alexei is forever ill. They all know the fear of execution hangs over them."

"And Anastasia?"

"As well as could be expected." The nun frowned. "Why do you ask?"

Before Sorg could reply there was an echo of someone hammering on a door in the distance. He crushed out his cigarette.

Sister Agnes startled as a commotion erupted somewhere out in the hall and a terrorized young novice hurried into the cell. "You need to come quickly, Sister. The Reds are outside the rear door with their rifles. Their motor trucks have surrounded the convent."

Sorg pushed himself up from the bed in alarm. "You've betrayed me . . ."

Sister Agnes said, "No, never. Nobody here, I promise you. The Reds sometimes carry out a search just to strike fear into us, or to raid our medicine supplies."

She turned to the young novice. "Take him to the mortuary chambers; it ought to be safe there." Sister Agnes picked up the bandages and sponge, rolled them into a ball, and tucked them under her habit. She asked Sorg, "Can you walk?"

"I think so."

"This way." Sister Agnes emptied the water basin into a corner drain before placing it in a storage cabinet in the corridor, along with the tray. Then she briskly led the way along the hall, just as shouts sounded in the distance, followed by the clatter of heavy boots.

Fear braided her voice. "The Reds are not far away. Quickly now."

The young novice followed them, helping a struggling Sorg, who tried to drag on his clothes.

There was a sound of splintering wood and Sister Agnes said with alarm, "They're breaking down the door."

They came to a rusted iron trellis gate at the end of the hall. Sister Agnes took a key from a ring on her leather belt and inserted it in a rusting lock. The gate squeaked open, revealing a flight of metal steps leading down.

She grabbed a brass oil lamp hanging from a nail and lit the wick with a box of matches she took from a wall recess.

Sorg stared into the dark passageway, tinged by the faint yellow glow of the oil lamp. It looked forbidding, a stone-flagged floor, the slimy granite walls glistening with wet and tainted with green lichen. "Where's this?"

Sister Agnes pushed them inside the passageway, closing the trellis gate. "Explanations later. Follow Novice Maria. And just pray that I can delay these bloodthirsty thugs."

57

Sorg descended the stone stairway, the young novice leading the way and carrying the oil lamp. The slimy walls reeked of mold. "Where are we going?"

"To the torture chambers, part of the original Mongol fortress."

"Why there?"

"Some of the passageways once served as escape routes, if I can find them."

"What do you mean—if?"

The novice looked uncertain. "I—I've only been down here twice, after I joined the order. One of the nuns wanted to frighten me. Oh my—"

She put a hand over her mouth and staggered back into Sorg's arms, almost dropping the lamp as a huge black rat scurried across the floor in front of them. Its tail disappeared into a mound of rocks and the novice looked petrified.

Sorg grasped hold of the lamp. "Here, better give me that."

A split second later they both heard the sharp crack of a gunshot echo like an explosion from somewhere up above. Sorg looked back a moment, then gripped Maria's arm and dragged her after him. "Keep moving."

Sister Agnes was kneeling by the basement room when she heard the crash of wood and the door down the hallway splintered. Footsteps thundered down the corridor and Kazan rushed into the cell, brandishing a revolver. "Why didn't you open the door, you old witch?" he screamed.

The nun struggled to her feet. "I'm Sister Agnes, the Mistress of

Novices. And might I remind you that this is a place of God. Weapons are not—"

Kazan struck her savagely across the mouth with his knuckle-duster, and she stumbled back. "What are you doing here?" Kazan demanded.

The nun wiped blood from her lips. "The—the basement rooms are used as a place of prayer and contemplation."

Kazan sneered. "Is that a fact? Who else is with you?"

"No one."

"You better not be lying." Kazan turned to his men. "Search the place."

The guards fanned out and began searching. Kazan removed the oil lamp from the wall hook. He took his cigarette case from his pocket, removed the lamp's glass cowl, and touched the tip of his cigarette to the flame. The flickered shadows that lit his face gave him a truly wicked look. He replaced the lamp on the hook, a sly grin spreading on his lips. "So this is where you come to pray, is it?"

"Yes."

Kazan lashed out again, striking the nun across the jaw. She reeled back, slamming against the wall. As she struggled to keep her balance, Kazan moved in, smashing a fist into her face again, until it was a bloodied mess.

Sister Agnes stood swaying, her back to the wall.

A gloating Kazan sucked on his cigarette and said, "Well, what have you to say for yourself now?"

"That I forgive you, just as Christ would have."

Kazan's nostrils flared. "Don't mock me, you old witch. We'll see if you still feel that way when I've had more time to loosen your tongue."

Two of the guards came back in and one said, "There's not a sign of anyone down here."

Kazan snapped his fingers. "Drag her upstairs for now. If she still refuses to talk I'll put her against a wall and shoot her myself. And tell Commissar Yakov where we are—he's searching the main hospital. What are you waiting for? Take her away."

"Yes, comrade."

As the men hauled the nun along the corridor, Kazan followed. They passed a metal trellis and Kazan peered beyond the barred gate. "Wait," he called out to his men, then addressed the nun. "Where does this lead?"

When she didn't answer quickly enough, Kazan grabbed her threateningly.

"To—to a passageway of old torture chambers. The convent was once a Mongol fortress." Blood trickled from the nun's mouth and nose.

"We haven't checked there. Where's the gate key?"

"On—on my belt."

Kazan yanked the key chain from the nun's waist with such force that it almost knocked her off her feet. Malice twisted his face as he said to one of the men, "Take her upstairs. I'll deal with her later."

The man dragged the nun away. His comrade waited with Kazan, who tried several of the keys. He found the one that fit and inserted it in the lock. The gate yawned open with a screech of protest.

Kazan raised his revolver and barked at the other man, "Find a couple of lamps somewhere and come with me."

58

"I think we're lost." Sorg held up the lamp as he followed the nun along a darkened passageway. The air was chilled, the damp walls glistening.

The nun slowed to get her bearings. "No. The tunnels are a maze, but I know where we're going."

They came to a sturdy oak door with a heavily rusted lock. Another storm lamp hung next to it. The nun said, "Let me have that; we may need it."

Sorg lit the lamp and handed it over.

They passed the grim, rusted remains of medieval-looking torture implements, racks and chains. Sorg shivered in the icy air. "Where are we?"

"In part of the old torture chambers. This area of the convent was built on top of what was a peat bog. The peat is a perfect preservative, so the cellars are always cool, which makes it ideal to store the dead."

"What dead?" Sorg felt a biting cold below his feet, as if the floor he stood on was a block of ice.

"The overflow from the hospital."

Sorg watched as the novice swung the lantern toward a recess in a far wall, which revealed an iron-studded door. The bolt and hinges were smothered in grease and when she pulled back the metal door it opened silently.

Sorg's nostrils filled immediately with a horrid, sickly stench. It made him want to vomit. Stilettos of silver light knifed through a pair of narrow, iron-barred basement windows, revealing a huge chamber. It remained in near darkness until the novice raised her lamp, and then Sorg saw to his horror that they were in a makeshift mortuary.

The swollen blue corpses of at least three dozen men and women were stacked in mounds, two or three bodies high, their bloated limbs entangled. Most were uniformed soldiers, some with limbs hacked or blown off. Others were riddled with bullet holes or bayoneted. Some corpses were naked; others wore bloodied clothing.

Sorg's stomach heaved. "What in the name of . . . ?"

Maria blessed herself, then put a hand over her face to mask the stench. "Some are soldiers who died from their wounds. Others suffered from illness or disease. Some are executed civilians."

Sorg covered his mouth with his arm. The stench was so noxious he wanted to faint. "Why—why don't you bury them?"

"There's been so much death in the city that the undertakers haven't been able to get round to them all. Meanwhile, we've had to store the bodies here."

"Why are *we* here? What about my escape?"

Maria shook her head. "Escape's impossible with the convent surrounded. Your best hope is to hide among the corpses and pray the Reds won't find you. I'll come back when it's safe."

Sorg stood rigid, almost too shocked to speak, staring at the nearest mound of flesh in front of him. On top, in the yellow lamplight, he saw a dead soldier with bulging eyes, his chest spattered with dried blood. He stared back at Sorg with a ghoulish smile. The soldier was entangled with a woman's naked body, her blue flesh pockmarked with bullet holes.

"I—I can't do it."

"You must. Whatever you do, remain still. If they find you they'll kill us all. I'll return to the convent by another passageway. Stay here until I come back."

Maria stepped out and Sorg heard the door bolt being slid shut.

The stench was abominable. In the dim shafts of light filtering through the barred windows, Sorg stared at the obscene mounds of marbled corpses. Sweat drenched his face and terror paralyzed him. Noises echoed from the corridor, the sounds of boots scraping on stone.

The Reds are coming.

Sorg reluctantly stepped toward the nearest mound of bodies, aware of his heart pounding and his limbs trembling.

He felt knifing pains in his side. He put his hand under his shirt and touched the bandage. It felt damp. He was bleeding again from all his movement.

He turned back. The footsteps sounded closer.

He knelt on the chilled floor, facing a mound of bodies. Sick with revulsion, he lifted the rigid arm of the naked woman. It felt as cold as frozen marble. Then he raised the leg of the ghoul-faced soldier and tried to untangle the grim tapestry of limbs.

The sound of boots marched closer.

Sorg suppressed the bile rising in his throat, threatening to choke him.

Dread in his heart, he burrowed his way into the icy bodies.

59

Kazan marched down the corridor, his revolver held in midair. He halted and snapped his head.

"Did you hear that? A noise like a metal door banging."

The guard beside him frowned. "I heard something, I'm not sure what."

"Shut up. Don't make a noise." Kazan moved forward more cautiously, holding the lamp high, his chin jutting as if he was trying to detect a scent.

They passed an open chamber and saw the rusted remains of medieval torture implements. Kazan ran a hand over the racks and rattled the chains. "What's that stench?"

He sniffed the air and directed his lantern toward a recess in the wall. It revealed an iron-studded door, its heavy bolt greased. Kazan plucked at the remains of a flimsy web that hung limply from the door frame.

"What's wrong?" the guard asked.

"Someone's been here." Kazan leveled his gun and nodded. "Open it. Carefully, mind."

The guard slid the greased bolt and opened the door. He held up his lamp, revealing the chamber. "What in the name of—"

Yellow lamplight flickered over the mounds of corpses. Kazan recoiled at the stench but the sight of the bodies didn't seem to bother him. He strode into the chamber, his revolver at the ready. "Hold the lamp higher," he instructed.

The guard obeyed, the overpowering stench making him cover his nose.

Kazan studied the gruesome scene, but it was almost impossible to make out individual dead, the corpses twisted, limbs knotted with limbs.

The guard said, "They must be from the convent hospital."

"Why aren't they buried?"

"There you've got me, Comrade Inspector. Shall we carry on? This place gives me goose pimples."

But Kazan ignored him and strode along the mounds of dead. He halted, kicked at a bloated leg, only to discover that it was severed at the knee, tendons and flesh revealed, the cracked bone white as birch.

"Comrade Inspector?" the guard persisted.

Kazan took no notice, his animal instinct roused. He leveled his revolver at the nearest mound of corpses and cocked the hammer. The puzzled guard frowned.

"What—what are you doing?"

Kazan fired into the tangled mass of flesh, again and again.

Sister Agnes was seated at her desk. Her jaw was stained with a huge purple bruise and on the desk in front of her was a bowl of steaming hot water and a white cotton facecloth. She winced as she dabbed her cut lip with iodine.

The door crashed open and a young nun hurried in. "We heard shots down in the cellars where some of the Reds went, Sister Agnes. What if they've found—"

"Be quiet, someone's coming," Sister Agnes snapped.

They all heard the clatter of boots on the wooden stairs and moments later Kazan burst into the room, impatiently slapping his palm against his leg as he addressed the younger nun. "You, get out!"

The trembling woman left.

A smile curled on Kazan's lips as he crossed to a fearful Sister Agnes. He lifted her chin with a pincer-like grip of his hand and made a point of roughly examining her cut. "It'll heal. A mere scratch."

"Do you enjoy hurting people, Inspector?"

Kazan grinned.

Yakov strode into the room. "What do you think you're doing, Kazan?"

Kazan let go of the nun, his mouth fixed in a sneer. "Actually, I'm here to seek forgiveness." He turned to Sister Agnes. "You must excuse the behavior of me and my men. We're searching for a wanted spy and our zealousness got the better of us. It seems we owe you an apology."

The nun stared back at him, open-mouthed.

Kazan addressed Yakov: "We searched the entire convent and found no sign of the man we're looking for."

The nun said, "My sisters heard shooting."

Kazan said, "A little overenthusiasm on my part in the cellar morgue. I wanted to make sure the bodies were really dead."

Yakov asked the nun, "Why haven't the corpses been buried?"

"It's the same in every hospital in the city: the morgues are full. The undertakers can't keep up with all the butchery."

Yakov warned, "Understand something, sister. Harboring a spy is an offense punishable by death. If anyone suspicious shows up looking for medical help you're to contact the local Cheka at once, understand?"

The nun nodded.

"Finish up, Kazan, and let's get out of here." Yakov turned and left, his footsteps clattering down the hall.

Kazan glared at Sister Agnes. "Heed the warning. Ignore it and I'll kill you, nun."

He left, banging the door after him.

Sister Agnes crossed to the window, nursing her jaw. Minutes later she saw the cortege of trucks disappear down a side street. The young nun came back, opening the door, and said, "It's a miracle we're all safe."

"I wouldn't be so certain. Kazan's got cunning written all over him. Where's Maria?"

"Gone down to the cellars to find out what's happened to our visitor."

Sister Maria appeared within minutes, looking confused.

"Well, is he alive or dead?"

"I—I don't know. The man's gone, Sister Agnes."

"What do you mean, 'gone'? Where?"

"I've no idea. He wasn't in the mortuary chamber where I left him."

"Return to the cellars. Bring help, extra lanterns. Search everywhere."

"I already did. We found a blood trail leading to the hallway but no sign of him."

"Search again. He's weak; he's lost more blood. Worse, Kazan may have shot him and he's crawled into one of the passageways and died."

"What do we do then?"

Sister Agnes made a sign of the cross. "Summon the undertaker again."

60

Andrev felt a hand shake him and he came awake with a start.

It was the young copilot. "The captain asked me to wake you, sir."

"What time is it?"

"Just after eight a.m."

Bright sunlight poured in the windows and Uri looked over at Lydia's empty bed. "Where's the lady?"

The copilot smiled. "Up front with Captain Pozner. He's giving her a flying lesson."

Andrev sat up and ran a hand over his cropped hair. "How soon will we land?"

"In about an hour, sir." The copilot nodded to the washroom. "Just time for you to freshen up."

Andrev shaved and washed. The Ilya Muromets had landed near the Gulf of Kiev just after 4 a.m. in a white-night dawn, with just enough light to land by. It seemed as though the field was in the middle of nowhere, but Pozner had found it easily enough using his compass and map, and the coastline as a marker. After two passes he landed, the grass velvet-smooth, hardly a bump.

As he disembarked, Boyle said solemnly, "Good luck to you both. And remember everything I've told you."

He shook hands with Andrev and the crew, then disappeared across the field, vanishing like a ghost into the twilight.

Within fifteen minutes they refueled and took off again and Andrev finally managed to sleep for a few hours.

Now he dressed and went up to the cockpit. Pozner was seated at the controls, Lydia standing behind him.

She smiled over her shoulder and brushed a strand of hair from her face. "Good morning. Did you get enough rest?"

"More than enough, thanks. Have you tamed your dislike of aircraft?"

"I don't know about that, but take a look. It's astonishing." Lydia pointed beyond the cockpit window.

Seven thousand feet below Andrev saw the vast wheat fields of southwest Russia spread out before them, glorious in the morning sunshine. "No problems?" he asked Pozner.

"Apart from a slight murmur in engine number three that tells me it needs oil. But we'll sort that out when we land." Pozner craned his neck and studied the sky. "Luck must be on our side. The German air patrols are obviously keeping their wheels on the ground. We've about an hour to go. I was just showing the lady here the sights."

"I'll need to borrow her for a while if you don't mind."

When they moved back to the cabin, Andrev said, "We better go over our story one more time and make certain we've got all our papers and belongings."

When they rehearsed their cover story, he emptied his bag on the cot and checked through his things. Lydia did the same.

Andrev said finally, "It seems we're all in order. We ought to change clothes now, before we land."

They turned their backs on each other in the cramped cabin and dressed in their peasants' clothing, Lydia with her coarse woolen dress and cotton blouse and jacket, and Andrev pulling on his woolen trousers and riding boots.

He turned back in time to see Lydia wrap her headscarf around her neck, gypsy-style, and she let down her long hair, shook it.

Andrev finished dressing. "As soon as we land we'll heed Boyle's advice and walk to the nearest railway station. It'll be safer sticking to the fields and in these clothes we shouldn't attract attention. Any questions?"

"I don't think so."

"Good. I suppose we may as well go up front for the landing." Uri stuffed his cap into his trouser pocket and reached for his bag. "Are you afraid, Lydia?"

The question caught her by surprise and she looked away, beyond the cabin window. When she looked back her green eyes met his. "I don't know that I'm afraid of anything anymore. Once you experience war you can never be the same. You see the world differently."

"I know."

"It's not the safe place you thought it was when you were a child. It's cold and indifferent, and can be full of brutality. It makes you grateful for whatever morsel of love that comes your way. Maybe that's why I never give up on Sean."

"What if you never see him again? What if you meet someone else?"

"I think our hearts are big enough to love more than one person in a life, don't you?" She looked at him. "And you—are you afraid?"

He considered. "For Sergey and Nina, yes, but not for me. I just want you to know that whatever happens to us, I'll do my best to see that you make it back alive."

She seemed touched by his words and leaned over and kissed him on the cheek. "Thank you."

They were standing close in the tight cabin, their bodies almost touching. He reached out and took her in his arms.

She didn't protest and when he kissed her on the lips she responded, gently at first, then more hungrily, her arms going round his neck in a passion fiercer than she had ever known before.

As they embraced, the aircraft lurched and the engine noise changed in pitch.

"What the . . . ?" Andrev uttered.

The hoarse rattle of machine-gun fire sounded, seemed to go on forever, and in response the aircraft pitched and bucked violently. Andrev was thrown off his feet and landed against the bed, Lydia on top of him.

As they struggled to stand the cabin door was flung open and the ashen-faced copilot appeared. "Captain Pozner wants you up front— we've got big trouble."

61

When they moved to the front of the aircraft, Pozner was struggling to keep it under control.

Black smoke streamed from one of the port engines and the copilot was lying on his belly on the floor near the aircraft's nose, firing bursts from a Vickers machine gun. The young mechanic had one of the cabin doors open and was tossing out the heavy fuel cans as fast as he could.

A sustained volley of fire hit them and the plane shuddered violently as machine-gun rounds ripped into the wings and fuselage. Pozner pushed the stick forward and they nosed into a steep dive, the engines screaming. Andrev managed to grab hold of an overhead strap and gripped Lydia's waist to stop her from losing her balance.

A German aircraft roared past them, the black-and-white markings of an iron cross unmistakable on the wings and tail. It banked in a near-perfect arc, the pilot's goggled face craning to look back, his scarf streaming in the wind. He pitched his aircraft up sharply and powered ahead of them, maneuvering left and right to avoid being hit by frantic bursts from the Vickers machine gun.

Pozner shouted above the noise, "I spoke too soon. That Albatros appeared out of nowhere and hit one of our engines."

"Can we deal with the blaze?" Andrev stared back at the mechanic tossing out fuel cans. "What's he doing?"

Sweat drenched Pozner's face. "We can't risk the fuel igniting from a stray bullet, so we have to ditch it. Our other difficulty is we won't be able to extinguish the blaze unless we get rid of the Albatros."

"How do we do that?"

Pozner said grimly, "It won't be easy. The Albatros beats us hands down for speed. It's like a flying razor—the pilot can take his time cutting us to ribbons."

Pozner scanned the skies and they all saw the Albatros arc around, as if readying to attack them from behind.

Andrev went to help the mechanic, who continued to work feverishly, hurling out fuel cans.

Pozner shouted back at them, "If we can get the Albatros off our back one of us ought to be able to climb out on the wing and smother the engine with a fire blanket. If not the blaze is going to spread to the wings and we'll go down in flames."

Andrev continued to toss out the fuel and shouted desperately, "Tell me what you need me to do."

"The Albatros will probably attempt to shoot us down from the rear. If you and the lady can handle the machine guns at the back I'll try and maneuver to keep him from getting a straight shot at us."

"Then what?"

"If I can abruptly slow our speed he'll have to peel away to save himself from crashing into us. That's when he'll expose his underbelly and you can get your best shot."

"Can you do that?"

"I can try. You've got thirty seconds to get back there and get ready before I start to maneuver. Wait for my command before you shoot."

Andrev scrambled back to the rear, taking Lydia with him. As they reached the pair of Lewis machine guns the sound of an engine snarled past them again, frighteningly close, and another burst of fire from the Albatros ripped through the fuselage, tearing canvas to shreds and punching holes in the airframe.

Andrev forced Lydia down, covering her body with his until the shooting stopped, then he cocked both Lewis guns. "Do you know how to operate one of these things?" he asked her.

"I—I think so."

The Ilya began to lurch up and down as Pozner porpoised the aircraft. The plane rose and fell as if riding massive waves and they had to hold tight to the Lewis guns.

They glimpsed the Albatros turn in a tight circle and line up again for another rear attack. The pilot came in from below, narrowing the gap, and Lydia could make out his goggled face as he aimed his twin machine guns. "Uri, he's almost on top of us—"

She went to fire but he put his hand on her shoulder. "No, wait for Pozner's command."

Andrev calmly tried to fixed the Albatros in his sights.

Right on cue the Ilya slowed as Pozner pulled back on the throttles. The Albatros kept speeding toward them, but when its pilot saw the gap narrowing dangerously he pitched up sharply to avoid a collision, his engines snarling as he began to climb.

In the cockpit, Pozner glanced back over his shoulder and judged the moment. "Fire now!" he screamed.

Andrev squeezed the Lewis gun's trigger and a thunderous chatter of rounds stitched into the Albatros's vulnerable underbelly, ripping it to shreds, sending pieces of wood and canvas flying. Lydia joined in, firing a sustained burst into the stricken aircraft, which almost appeared suspended in midair.

Pozner applied thrust again to prevent the Ilya from stalling and then came a ferocious exploding ball of orange light as the Albatros burst into flames. It disintegrated, falling to earth in a cascade of debris and flames.

Lydia saw the pilot hurtled out into the air, his body turning cartwheels as he plummeted to his death.

Andrev smelled burning. "We're on fire."

Plumes of acrid smoke began to choke their lungs and sting their eyes. Andrev put a hand over his mouth and pulled Lydia toward the front of the cabin, where the smoke appeared less dense.

Pozner's right hand was clapped on his left shoulder, part of the bone shattered, blood pumping between his fingers, as his good hand tried to operate the controls.

Andrev saw a massive hole ripped in the fuselage, the copilot's body riddled with bullets. He went to see if he could help but Pozner said between gritted teeth, "Forget about him, he's dead. Help the mechanic try to put out the engine fire. It's our only hope if we're to land this thing."

The young mechanic lay huddled on the floor and was staring open-mouthed at the copilot's shredded body. He looked terrified, his eyes wide with dread. Clutched in his hands was a fire blanket. Andrev hauled him to his feet. The fear-stricken young man was unable to speak.

Pozner said, "He's in shock. Hit him and try to bring him to his senses. If he doesn't put that fire out soon we're doomed."

They heard the frightening sound of an engine splutter as another of the V-8s struggled to keep alight. The Ilya felt as if it was losing altitude fast. Andrev saw the fire spreading across the wing.

He grabbed the fire blanket from the petrified mechanic and went to climb out through the cabin door to try to contain the blaze, but the aircraft lurched violently and nosed down.

Andrev turned back and saw Pozner collapsed over the controls. He struggled to reach him and he and Lydia sat him in one of the chairs. He was barely conscious. Andrev said to Lydia, "Do you know how to stop this thing from dropping?"

"Pozner said if the stick's kept in the center it keeps the plane level." Lydia did so and the aircraft began to fly more evenly.

"Keep doing what you're doing," Andrev told her, hefting Pozner to his feet.

"I—I'm trying. We don't seem to have enough power."

The flames continued to rage out on the wing.

A vast expanse of golden wheat fields stretched below them and appeared to be slowing rising up to meet them. Andrev shook Pozner violently. "Wake up, man. Tell us what to do!"

Pozner became conscious again. He seemed to realize what was happening, his senses coming alert.

With Andrev's help he grabbed the controls from Lydia and applied power, forcing the throttles forward, but the aircraft nose hardly moved and Pozner was struggling. "It's hopeless. Get back to the cabin and brace yourselves. We're going to crash."

When they didn't move fast enough, he shouted, "Are you deaf? Get back to the cabin, it'll give you some protection."

With supreme effort Pozner managed to pull the aircraft out of the dive, the nose responding sluggishly, but they were still losing altitude as Andrev dragged Lydia back toward the rear cabin.

They reached the door and he thrust Lydia inside. He looked back and saw the terrified young mechanic, too shocked to move, still huddled on the floor. Andrev stumbled back, grabbed him by the collar, pushed him inside the cabin, and followed him in.

At that precise moment there was a terrifying grating sound of wood and metal disintegrating. The aircraft struck the ground with an almighty crash, hurtling them violently about the cabin.

Then it slid forward, hit something hard, and flipped on its side, bursting into flames.

Andrev awoke. He didn't know how long he had been unconscious but he was lying on his back in a wheat field. The sun felt hot on his face, the stench of acrid smoke in his nostrils, the airplane in flames, black, oily clouds rising into the turquoise sky.

His mouth felt dry and his eyes stung, his lungs choking from the smoke. He coughed, fought for breath.

He didn't recall being flung from the aircraft, but he could make out the shape of bodies inside the mangled fuselage. Smoke and flames billowed from the wreckage.

And then he saw Lydia, lying lifeless like a rag doll, her body draped across one of the shattered wings.

"No!" Andrev's heart sank and he staggered to his feet and lurched toward the wreckage.

PART FIVE

62

Drenching summer rain swept across the Kremlin's cobblestones that late afternoon, and as the clock in the twelfth-century watchtower chimed out five o'clock, the dark green truck bearing Leonid Yakov chugged to a halt outside the Armory courtyard.

He climbed out into the rain. His stomach tightened. The abrupt Kremlin summons he received by cable in Ekaterinburg made him wonder if he was in trouble.

A young army aide waited for him in the courtyard. "This way, Commissar."

As a door closed behind him Yakov found himself in a magnificent, high-ceilinged room. Tall windows overlooked a Kremlin courtyard and the spiced aroma of pipe tobacco scented the air.

Vladimir Lenin—a small man with a high forehead and goatee beard—was all charm as he put down his pipe and came round from behind the desk, his handshake firm. "Commissar Yakov, a pleasure to see you again. Sit down, sit down."

Chubby fingers gestured to a chair and Yakov sat. Lenin radiated energy. Behind him a sideboard contained a polished samovar and a basket filled with fresh fruit, fleshy peaches and plums, sweet Crimean oranges and apricots. Yakov hadn't seen such produce since Moscow's food shortages.

Leon Trotsky wandered in from another room, his dark eyes intimidating as he removed a silver cigarette case from his breast pocket, selected a cigarette, and lit it with a match, then blew a ring of smoke to the ceiling.

Lenin waved a telegram. "I read your cable about the Romanovs' security with interest. I'm also particularly intrigued by this enemy spy that Kazan's been hunting in Ekaterinburg. The one we call the Phantom."

"Is that why I was summoned here?"

"In a roundabout way, perhaps. The file, Leon."

Lenin snapped his fingers at Trotsky, who removed a folder from the desk. He handed it to Lenin, who tossed aside the cable and flicked the folder open.

A wrinkled smile appeared on Lenin's face. "I've been acquainting myself again with your personal history. A loyal party member. You're exactly the kind of man we need in this brave new future we're forging in Russia."

"I simply do my duty, Comrade Lenin."

The smile disappeared as Lenin tossed the file on his desk and rested his knuckled hands on his hips. "But I'm afraid that future may be under dire threat."

"I don't understand."

"British forces have landed in the north of our country and are intent on sabotaging our revolution. Now our intelligence tells us the Americans are about to invade in the east—they already have many of their best spies in our country. They want to strangle us by seizing our ports and disrupting our supplies. And now there's been an interesting twist. Tell him, Leon."

"Yesterday just before eight a.m. a Russian-made Ilya Muromets bomber crashed in a field just over our lines, almost forty miles south of St. Petersburg. Our area commander arrived at the location to investigate within an hour. The aircraft appeared to have been shot down. That's when it started to get really interesting, Yakov."

"In what way?"

Trotsky blew out cigarette smoke. "Of the three crew, only a young mechanic survived. He was badly burned but conscious enough to be interrogated. We managed to get out of him that the aircraft was transporting a man and woman to somewhere outside St. Petersburg. Before landing they dressed themselves in Russian peasant clothing."

Yakov said, "Do we know any more about them?"

Trotsky offered a razor smile. "We'll return to that important question in a moment. As of now, there's no sign of their bodies. They've disappeared."

Trotsky strode to the window. "It would be easy for them to vanish. Half the country is on the move because of this war. But the couple strikes me as especially interesting. Do you know why?"

"I'm at a loss."

"One of our spies in London has reliably learned that the Whites and their supporters intend to send a number of agents into Russia to attempt to rescue the Romanovs. We believe that the aircraft could be part of that attempt."

Yakov said, puzzled, "But the aircraft's Russian."

"Correct. Designed and built by Igor Sikorsky, a traitorous rebel who fled the motherland, taking a number of our aircraft with him. We've determined from the chassis number that the crashed plane was one of the aircraft he removed."

"And the crew?"

"All Russian, according to the mechanic. What's intriguing is that he claims they left England twenty hours previous. Shortly before they were to land they were attacked by a German fighter and crash-landed."

"Where was their final destination?"

Trotsky crushed his cigarette in an ashtray. "The mechanic didn't know. But the plan's clever, I'll give it that—using a Russian aircraft to land agents on our soil." He paused. "I learned a long time ago to suspect coincidence. I believe this is further evidence, along with these Allied landings, that they intend to challenge our revolution and rescue the Romanovs."

Lenin's fanatical gaze settled on Yakov. "I want you to hunt down these infiltrators. All enemy spies must be executed."

He handed over the files. "As of now you're in charge of this case. You'll find everything we have on the crash and the Allied plan. The man in particular should prove an interesting prey."

Trotsky's lips twisted in a mocking grin. "We believe it may be an old friend of yours. A Captain Uri Andrev."

Yakov's face drained.

Trotsky added, "According to Inspector Kazan, Andrev escaped from St. Petersburg on a vessel bound for England. His description matches the male passenger. Who his female companion is, we've no idea, but she speaks Russian."

Yakov was rigid.

Lenin said, "This rescue can't happen. I won't allow it. Very soon we'll finalize the Romanovs' fate. We must ensure that they can never rule Russia again."

Yakov asked quietly, "How can you be certain it's Andrev?"

It was Trotsky who answered. "An Orthodox priest recruited by one of our cells in London identified him as likely one of the conspirators."

Lenin placed a hand firmly on Yakov's shoulders. "You know Andrev better than most. Such knowledge can work to our advantage. You'll also have help from Inspector Kazan in Ekaterinburg. You'll have absolute authority in this case, but he'll act as your deputy."

"Why him?"

"The inspector has his uses, and two heads are always better than one. The letter, Leon," Lenin said.

Trotsky made a show of producing a sheet of paper from the desk. "If anyone doubts your authority, Comrade Lenin and I have signed an order. Study it."

Yakov accepted the letter, and read.

"Commissar Leonid Yakov of the Cheka is acting on a mission of special importance. Should he demand assistance from any quarter, be it military or civil, it must be given without question. Anyone who fails to obey this order will be shot." It was signed, "Vladimir Lenin and Leon Trotsky."

Lenin gestured at the wall clock; it read 5:30 p.m. "It's almost thirty-six hours since the crash. If a capable man like Andrev is involved, I imagine he's made swift progress. He could be anywhere by now. But his file says that his wife and son are in Moscow."

"Yes."

"After Andrev's escape you tracked him down to St. Petersburg. There was a confrontation, shots were fired, but he escaped."

"A mistake on my part. It won't happen again."

Lenin hooked his thumbs in his waistcoat pockets and the steel that was never far from the surface flashed, his eyes glinting dangerously. "I know it won't. I'm sure Inspector Kazan will make certain of that."

Lenin stepped over to the window, looked out. "Your wife was a brave and loyal party member. A true martyr. It's on her account I'm giving you another chance."

Yakov said nothing, simply stared ahead.

Lenin turned back to face him. "You've made more than one mistake. But so did I, seeing that I was stupid enough to be swayed into showing Andrev mercy. Then he makes a fool of us both and escapes. But this time, there will be no mercy, you understand? This time, you liquidate him."

63

The overnight train from St. Petersburg clattered into the station just after ten that morning with a belch of steam and a squeal of brakes.

Andrev stepped down from the train and scanned the crowded Moscow station. Imperial gilded eagles still adorned the vaulted walls, some with scarlet banners hanging high above them. The platforms were crowded with unhappy-looking, shabbily dressed peasants with bundles of their belongings.

He saw no sign of any Cheka security or checkpoints. He pulled his cap down over his eyes and hefted his bag on his shoulder. "So far, so good."

He clutched Lydia's arm and guided her out the station entrance doors and across the busy street, crowded with horse carriages and motorized taxis, to a grim-looking beer hall where they found a window table. The place was packed with railway workers and passengers and a handful of off-duty soldiers.

The only menu offering was a watery stew made of horse meat and cabbage with cuts of black bread, which Andrev ordered for them both, along with a beer for himself and tea for Lydia.

When the surly waiter finally returned with their food and drinks, Andrev sipped his beer and saw that Lydia looked distracted. "What's the matter?"

"It's a miracle we've made it this far without being stopped or having our papers checked."

"The crash won't go unnoticed. If the mechanic survived he's probably talked by now. That means they may be searching for us. At least he didn't know our plans, but the crash of a big aircraft like the Muromets is bound to arouse suspicion. How's your arm?"

"Bearable." Lydia touched her bandaged left forearm, where a six-inch strip of her flesh had been scorched by metal debris from the aircraft blaze. Otherwise she was unhurt. In St. Petersburg, Andrev cleaned and dressed the burn with some alcohol, iodine salts, and cotton gauze they bought at a pharmacy, but the pain was still a dull throb. She felt exhausted.

They'd slept fitfully in the previous thirty-six hours, almost half of it spent on the crowded overnight train from St. Petersburg—even the few stinking toilets were occupied by passengers who had to be begged to vacate them when the lavatory was required. All during the night Lydia feared the train would be halted by the Cheka and searched.

The beer hall food tasted terrible—Lydia couldn't even bring herself to eat the horse meat—and she pushed away her plate. She looked at the scene beyond the window. It was absurd. In the clutches of a brutal civil war, Moscow seemed so normal: the trams were running, cinemas were open, and on a nearby lamppost the Bolshoi Theater advertised an evening performance.

But the closer you looked you noticed the bullet-ridden buildings and the grim faces of passersby—everyone on the streets and in the beer hall seemed on edge, under duress. What few stores that were open had long lines, and most of the people were poorly dressed women with babies in their arms, others with children holding on to their skirts.

Andrev left his meal unfinished and stood. "There's a street full of lodging houses not far from here. We'll try to find a room and figure out our next step."

The sign in the window of the Odessa Boardinghouse said "Comfortable, well-appointed rooms and running water" but in truth it was a shabby affair, badly in need of a paint job and the ceilings yellow from cigarette smoke.

The elderly owner who greeted them was a bony woman with warts on her cheeks, and she smelled of vodka. She led them up stone steps along a grimy passageway into a filthy bedroom with two rickety chairs and a greasy cupboard. The unwashed window offered a distant, murky view of the gilded domes of St. Basil's and the Kremlin's red walls. "It's one ruble a night, clean sheets extra. Payment in advance."

Lydia recoiled. The bedstead had no blankets, the floorboards were bare, and peeling paper hung in damp strips from the walls. She saw a parade of insects on the floor below the grimy window. "Thank you. We'll take the sheets."

"The shared bathroom's down the hall. There's a curfew at ten, mind you, on Bolshevik orders. And the electricity goes off pretty frequently, so be prepared with a candle."

The woman showed them a ruin of a bathroom, then fetched a set of sheets before Andrev paid her and she left. He said to Lydia, "Not exactly home, but beggars can't be choosers. Here, let me take a look at your arm."

She sat on the bed and he removed the dressing and took the iodine, alcohol, and gauze from his bag and went to work. "You've really been through the wars, haven't you? Shot at and now this. No way for a young woman to live."

"Can I tell you a secret? When I volunteered for the republican movement, I was put to work as a courier, along with a handful of female volunteers. We used to smuggle ammunition and messages past British lines. I was never more terrified and death seemed a constant companion. But do you know the strangest thing? I never felt so alive. I loved every minute of it. I lived more in a day than I did in my entire life. Existence became real, and perilous and exciting. I couldn't get enough."

"Like a drug?"

"Yes. Sometimes when I was in danger, when I seemed to be staring death right in the face, I'd get the oddest feeling. It's as if I wanted to reach out and take his hand. Does that sound strange?"

Andrev shook his head and finished tying her dressing. "I remember my father telling me something he once read, that those who truly live are always on the edge of danger."

"Were you close to him?"

"More than that. He was called up in the first three months of the war because of a shortage of medical doctors at the front, even though he was far past conscription age. He was badly gassed and invalided home a month later. Nina and I were with him when he died."

She looked into his face, her emerald eyes dark, intense. "Tell me about you and your father."

The question caught Andrev by surprise. "I was six when my mother died. An influenza outbreak plagued St. Petersburg. Her death devastated my father. He adored her, you see. We both did. What made it so poignant was that he was a doctor. His business was saving lives, but he couldn't save my mother."

"That must have been dreadful for him."

"For a long time after her death I used to hear him crying in his room at night. He was desolate, inconsolable. Soon after he packed me off to relatives in Moscow for a time. I didn't realize it but he was only trying to protect me, didn't want me to see him so grief-stricken."

Andrev looked straight at her. "I can still remember him waving good-bye from the station platform, and the sound of the train whistle the night I left for my relatives'. It always haunts me, that sound, it seemed to echo how lonely we both felt. But that's life, isn't it? It's like a broken jigsaw puzzle. Somehow there's always a piece missing."

"And afterward? He didn't remarry?"

"He should have. He was the kind of man who needed a woman's love in his life. But instead he threw himself into his work. Sometimes he drank too much to forget his pain."

Andrev stood as if to shake off the memory and reached across for his jacket. "We need to figure out how to reach Ekaterinburg without attracting too much attention."

"How do we do that?"

He offered a smile. "I think it's time I introduced you to an old friend of mine."

64

The run-down street near the Trans-Siberian Railway station was home to some of Moscow's busiest pawnbrokers.

The universal sign of three golden balls that hung outside the storefront had seen better days, the gilt paintwork flaking, the windows protected by rusting metal bars, but the sign behind the front door said Open for Business.

Andrev pushed in the door, Lydia behind him, and a bell tinkled overhead. They entered a cramped store, racks of garments hanging on poles suspended from the ceiling—everything from velvet ball gowns to working clothes.

Glass display cases contained an array of personal belongings: eyeglasses and watches, jewelry and rings, even a wooden leg.

Seated behind a counter protected by a metal trellis was a man with wire-rimmed glasses. Two of the fingertips on one hand were missing, and the frostbitten stumps were blackened flesh. He wore a dark, shabby suit flecked with cigarette ash, and he was engrossed in examining a ring with a jeweler's eyepiece.

Andrev said, "How much for the typewriter in the front window?"

The man didn't look up. "Fifty rubles and not one less. We don't sell garbage here, you know. It's an American Remington, the best."

Andrev smiled. "You drive a hard bargain, Corporal Tarku."

The man's head came up and his jeweler's loupe fell from his fingers, his mouth open in shock. "Well, I'll be . . . ! Captain Andrev. What are you doing here?"

Andrev slipped shut the steel bolt that locked the front door and flipped over the Closed sign. "I need your help. Can we have a quiet word?"

Tarku came round from behind the counter and shook Andrev's hand vigorously. "I never thought I'd see you again, Captain. You came at the right time. I'm usually working in the back, out of sight, but my boss is gone on business."

Andrev gestured to Lydia. "A lady friend of mine, names are unimportant."

"Of course, whatever you say." Tarku inclined his head. "Enchanted, madame." He slapped Andrev's back. "This calls for a celebration. I've got a bottle of Ukrainian vodka that'll make your nose bleed. Have a drink? You will. You must."

A train whistled as it pulled out from the railway yard across the street, while Tarku rummaged for a vodka bottle in a desk drawer and wiped three small shot glasses with a handkerchief before he filled them to the brim. He handed out the glasses and raised his own. "A toast. May that power-hungry swine Lenin roast in hell. He promised bread and peace, and all we got was famine and civil war."

Andrev knocked back his vodka in one gulp, slapped down the glass, and looked around the cluttered store. "How is life treating you these days?"

"A lot better than we endured together, Captain. And it's safer here in a big city than in Kiev, easier to hide. I keep my head low."

"Busy?"

"As a one-handed jockey with an itch. Everyone needs cash for something or other these days." Tarku refilled his own glass. "What happened after we parted? Did you see your family?"

"Don't ask me to explain, it's complicated. Can you help me, Abraham?"

"Anything for an old comrade, especially you." Tarku looked at Lydia. "He's a true mensch, this one, to borrow from my Jewish friends. Always put his men first. Another drink, madame? A bear never walked on one paw."

Tarku went to pour but Lydia placed a hand on top of her glass. "If I do I'll be on the floor."

"At least it's clean, swept this morning. Captain?"

Andrev held out his glass. When it was refilled he wandered over to the window and peered at the railway yard, his mind ticking over.

A long line of cattle wagons were being loaded with supplies from trucks and horse-drawn carriages, the Red troops working busily. "Are the trains on time these days?"

"More or less. The Reds shot a few striking rail workers, which improved the service no end. Ironic, considering they once urged the same rail workers to strike to help Lenin seize power."

"What about the trains to the Urals?"

Tarku shrugged and joined Andrev at the window. "Depends. The Trans-Siberian passenger ones aren't always running on schedule. Troop reinforcements and carriages loaded with hospital supplies and ordnance seem to get priority these days. They run all night on Trotsky's orders on account of his troops having a hard time of it against the Whites in the east. Don't tell me you're headed there to help the cause."

"Maybe."

"You wouldn't be the only one. Ever since the tsar's imprisonment, volunteers have been heading to the Urals. Including little old ladies, nobility, and religious people who want to be close to their former emperor. Insane, I know. The tsar's finished."

Andrev swallowed his vodka. "When exactly do the troop trains leave?"

"Usually in the evening, after ten. Why?"

Andrev considered, finished his vodka, and slapped down the glass. "The less you know the better, Abraham."

"As you wish."

Andrev looked up at the clothes racks. "Is this everything you have in the line of clothing?"

"Are you joking? We could clothe half of Moscow with the stuff we've got in the back."

"I need a change. The lady, too. But first, I want to borrow that typewriter. Can you give me twenty minutes of privacy and some typing paper?"

"Paper, for what?"

"I have an important letter to type."

65

The warehouse at the back of the shop was bursting with garments, packing crates, and glass cases filled with more belongings.

Tarku hauled in the Remington typewriter, placed it on a writing table, and rummaged in a drawer filled with paper sheets and brown envelopes. "What about the lady?"

"See if you can find her some fresh clothes. She'll know what's suitable." Andrev placed a neat stack of rubles on the table. "For your trouble. These are hard times."

Tarku pushed away the money. "I couldn't take a kopek from you, and it's no trouble. I'll be back."

He left, and Andrev wound a sheet of paper onto the roller. His brow wrinkled in thought for a few minutes and then he pecked at the keyboard.

When he was done he unwound the typed page from the roller and slipped it in an envelope. As he stood, Tarku came back, carrying the vodka bottle. "All finished? How about another?"

"Not for me or I'll be on my knees. How are you two getting on with the clothes?"

"You know what women are like; they take their time in that department. She's trying to find her size. A friend of yours, you say?"

"Yes." Andrev didn't elaborate, tucked the envelope in his trouser pocket, and moved along a rack of men's clothes. He found a dark tan leather jacket and tried it on for size. "This feels about right. Have you a leather cap?"

Tarku found a black one among a pile of hats, dusted it with his sleeve, and handed it over. "Try this."

There was a mirror in the corner and Andrev slipped on the

leather jacket, tugged on the cap at a rakish angle, and studied his reflection.

The transformation was astonishing, a sudden chilling arrogance to his appearance that made Tarku step back to regard him. "If I didn't know any better, I'd say you'd pass for a Cheka."

"I'll try to take that as a compliment."

"They all have that look, you know. Sullen arrogance. A sideways glance almost gives you a heart attack."

Andrev's eye was drawn to one of the glass cases that contained a silver locket and chain. "May I?"

Tarku unlocked the glass case with a key and handed the locket across. "It's a handsome piece. Belonged to a lawyer's wife. She pawned it before fleeing the country."

Andrev smiled, tossed the locket in his palm. "How much do you want?"

"For the captain, I couldn't accept more than ten rubles."

"You're cheating yourself. I'll give you twenty, and I insist or you'll hurt my feelings."

"Very well. I'll even inscribe something on it if you wish. It won't take a minute."

"Perfect. Now, I need just one more thing. A bag of workman's tools."

They walked back to the lodging house, the trams too crowded, Uri wearing the leather jacket and cap, tipped back, and on his shoulder he carried a grubby canvas bag that contained workman's tools.

Lydia wore a fresh dark blue peasant skirt and cream blouse, her hair tied back under a headscarf. As they passed the Moscow River, they stopped under the trees and Andrev leaned on the stone bank. She said, "Do you trust Tarku?"

He lit a cigarette and looked out at the view. "More than most. I always found him loyal. Besides, he hates the Reds."

Lydia recognized a look of fear that ignited in the faces of anyone who passed, noticing Andrev's leather jacket and cap. "I'm not sure I like you wearing that outfit. People seem scared of the sight of you."

"You're not meant to. It's because I look like a Cheka. Do you know why they always wear leather?"

"It sets them apart. Emphasizes their power."

"Exactly. And it's a power we can use to our advantage. Wait here."

He stubbed out his cigarette and crossed the road to an elderly woman selling vegetables. Curiously, Andrev bought a handful of potatoes that the woman wrapped in dirty newspaper. On the stand were also single lilies wrapped in greaseproof paper and on impulse Andrev bought one. He strode back and presented Lydia with the flower.

She took it. "What's this for?"

"Something to remember me by."

She smiled, genuinely touched, and smelled the scent. "You're very kind. But it's the potatoes that have me puzzled."

"If you think I'm about to cook you a stew, you're sadly mistaken."

She laughed suddenly, for the first time he had known her, and for that moment it seemed as if she were a different person.

He said, "Let me show you what they're for. A trick that might come in useful someday."

They reached the lodging house and went up to their room. Uri took one of the potatoes and opened a penknife he slipped from his pocket. He laid both on the side table. "I've been thinking about what Tarku said about the troop and supply carriages running to the Urals all the time. We'll try and board one bound for Ekaterinburg."

"But we're not military."

Andrev took the envelope from his pocket, opened the typed page, and showed it to her. "With any luck, it won't be a worry. Read that."

Lydia read the page aloud, "To whom it may concern: The bearer of this letter, Nicholai Couris, is acting on the highest Cheka instructions. All military and civilian personnel, regardless of rank, will aid him in every way possible. Signed, Vladimir Lenin."

The letter was signed with a flourish.

Andrev said, "We'll bluff our way on board."

She looked at him, her face deadly serious a moment, and then an amused smile crossed her lips. "You're a devious man and it sounds impressive enough. But haven't you forgotten something? It's got no official stamp."

Andrev held up a single potato. "It's about to get one. Watch this."

He sliced the potato in half with the knife and, choosing one of the halves, he wiped away the excess moisture with the old bedsheet. From his pocket he took his discharge notice, the one with the red-inked War Ministry stamp on it.

He laid it flat on the table and placed the exposed inside part of the potato over the red stamp. He pressed it hard against the inked stamp for several minutes.

When he removed it, the exposed potato had absorbed the red-ink image. Andrev placed the potato over the lower right corner of his own typed page and held it there for at least a minute, until the image was transferred onto his typed page. "Voilà, as the French say. It'll look perfectly official when it dries. The starch in the potato absorbs the ink."

He waved the page in the air to dry the moist red stamp. "If there's one thing the Bolsheviks are masters at, it's inciting terror. This ought to strike the fear of the devil into anyone who reads it and get us on board a troop train."

"Do you really think it'll pass for an official document?"

"I saw my own death warrant signed by Lenin, and believe me this will do the job. Besides, it's all about attitude, as my old grandmother used to say."

"When do we leave for Ekaterinburg?"

"Tonight. After I see Nina and my son."

66

The tenement flat near the Arbat district was on the second floor. The two rooms were barely furnished but they had a homey feel, scrupulously clean, with earthenware flowerpots in the windows.

On top of the table were the remains of a small birthday cake, some cheap toy trinkets, and a couple of plates of sugary biscuits baked by Zoba's wife.

Yakov, his shirt collar open, a glass of vodka in his hand, studied his daughter with tender fascination as she played with a half dozen children milling around the kitchen, all of them wearing party hats made of old newspaper.

Katerina was no longer an infant. She was developing a mind all her own: going to school, talking, arguing. Yakov thought to himself, *Years in the trenches changed you, made you forget there was anything beautiful in the world.* But sitting by her bed sometimes, stroking her hair, gazing down at her sleeping face, he never ceased to be amazed by how much he loved her.

The loss of her mother had been hard on her. Had it not been for Zoba's wife he didn't know what he would have done: his daughter called her "Auntie," but the woman had become a substitute mother.

Katerina skipped over, clutching the rag doll he'd bought as her birthday present, her huge eyes devouring him. "Papa, will you stay tonight? Auntie says you can sleep by my bed and she'll make you supper. Will you?"

He swept her up in his arms, kissed her cheek. "Papa told you, sweetheart, I have work to do."

"But Auntie says you and Zoba never stop working for Comrade

Lenin. Can't you stay? He must be a very selfish man to want you to work all the time. Is he selfish, Papa?"

"No, he's going to change the world for the better, Katerina."

"Some children in my class say that he's a good man for getting rid of the tsar. But others say he's evil because he's killing so many people. Is he evil or good, Papa?"

Before Yakov could reply, Zoba, leaning by the window, glass in hand, beckoned with a wave of his palm. "You better take a look at this."

Yakov put Katerina down, her interest already drawn back to her companions. She gave him a puckered kiss and scampered off to rejoin her friends.

Yakov wandered over to the window. A chauffeured, open-topped black Mercedes pulled up in the street, its polished black paintwork gleaming. Two Fiat trucks loaded with troops rolled up behind. They jumped down, keeping watchful guard.

The familiar, wild-haired figure of Leon Trotsky stepped out of the Mercedes. He was wielding his officer's baton, wearing his Sam Brown leather belt and holster.

Zoba said, "Nothing but the best for Trotsky. He swans around Moscow in that Mercedes as if he's the tsar himself. Me, I have to make do with a filthy tram seat."

"You're beginning to sound disillusioned."

Zoba sipped his vodka, smiled. "Give me a car like that and I wouldn't be. Still, I never thought I'd see the day when the defense minister came calling. I thought you did all your business at the Kremlin. What does he want?"

Trotsky climbed the tenement steps, a pair of armed guards leading the way. Yakov buttoned his shirt collar, straightened his jacket. "We'll soon find out."

The clatter of footsteps halted out in the hall and a knock came on the door. Zoba's wife went to open it. She put a hand to her mouth and stepped back as she recognized Trotsky. He looked as arrogant as ever as he removed his hat, tucked it under his arm, and strode in to meet

Yakov. He gave Zoba a dismissive stare. The Georgian took the hint and moved away.

Trotsky observed the children. "Have I disturbed your afternoon, Yakov?"

Yakov indicated Katerina. "My daughter's birthday."

Trotsky stripped his leather gloves from his fingers. "I met your wife at party rallies. She was a good woman. Her death must have been a terrible loss for you both. You need to find another wife, Yakov. Children need parents."

"Katerina and I manage. To what do I owe the honor, Comrade Minister?"

Trotsky's tone suddenly bristled with annoyance. "To be honest, when I heard you were still in Moscow I was disappointed. I would have thought you'd be well on your way to St. Petersburg by now, hunting down Andrev."

"My train is ready to leave at a moment's notice, but I believe that would be pointless."

"Why?"

"Andrev's a shrewd and capable man, and he'll keep on the move. But he'll try to make contact with his family. Their apartment is being watched day and night."

Trotsky's dark eyes glinted. "So you're going to sit and wait, hoping he'll take the bait? But what if he doesn't?"

"I know the kind of man he is. He wouldn't return to Russia without trying to see his wife and child, especially after he failed the last time."

"I'll have to take your word for it. But to business. After you left, Comrade Lenin and I finalized an important matter—the Romanovs' execution goes ahead. The entire family will perish."

"When?"

"This very week in Ekaterinburg, and the bodies secretly disposed of. The guard *komendant* at the Ipatiev house, Yurovsky, will be charged with carrying out the order. Though at all times you will be in command. Once it's done, and you've witnessed the disposal of the bodies, you'll return to Moscow immediately. Comrade Lenin and I will be waiting for your final report."

Yakov fell silent.

"You're an ambitious man, Yakov. A senior post needs to be filled—Commander of the Moscow Regional Cheka. Foil this plot, direct the execution to Lenin's satisfaction, and the post is yours. Frankly, I'd hate to see a turncoat like Kazan best you in this matter."

"I'll do my duty, you can be sure of it."

Trotsky started to turn toward the door but hesitated. "One more thing. Once this is over, I want you to make the arrangements for Andrev's child and former wife to be deported to a Siberian camp, on Lenin's personal order. Understood?"

"Is it really necessary?"

Trotsky tapped his baton in his palm, and the evil threat that always lurked beneath his dark, intense eyes flared. "They're bad seed. And the only way to deal with bad seed is to destroy it."

Trotsky's baton reached out and its tip touched Yakov's chest. "You better do more than your duty, Yakov. I expect great things of you. I don't want to see a man of promise such as yourself fail, and end up keeping Andrev's family company in some cold and brutal corner of Siberia."

Trotsky removed his baton, gave a sideways glance at Katerina, playing with her friends, and a tiny, malicious grin twitched in the corners of his mouth. "I'll make sure your daughter is looked after in your absence. I'll have my men check on her while you're busy with your duties. I hope we understand each other?"

67

The hand-painted wooden sign on the redbrick courtyard building said Oleg Markov & Son, Undertakers.

Markov senior was busy in the mortuary that evening, applying his skills to the corpse of a young girl no more than fifteen. A tall man of sixty with a neatly trimmed black mustache, he wore an apron over his coarse dark suit, and had a well-practiced, mournful look.

On a wooden table next to him was a selection of mortician's implements: a rubber mallet, a jar of embalming fluid, and pots of makeup and brushes. The child's body lay on a metal trolley, a white sheet drawn up to her neck.

Such a terrible waste of youth and beauty, Markov reflected with a sigh, but then death was all too common these days, since the barbarous Reds came to power.

When he finished applying a touch of rouge to the young woman's cheeks, Markov tugged on a ceramic bell pull hanging by the door. Moments later a pale-faced young man wearing a dark suit a size too large for him appeared. Karl Markov was endowed with a dour look as practiced as his father's.

"We have two more corpses due shortly, Karl. A pair of White officers executed this morning. Be a good lad and finish the young lady while I see to the paperwork."

"Yes, father."

Markov senior removed his apron and turned to a washbasin. As he scrubbed his hands with warm soapy water, the echo of a bell tinkled from somewhere deep in the mortuary and he came alert.

Grabbing a towel, he arched an eyebrow at his son. "It seems Lazarus has come back to life. Take care of things while I attend to our guest."

This time when Sorg awoke he was lying on a mattress on the floor of a room that smelled of disinfectant, the walls covered in glazed white tiles.

As he tried to take in his surroundings he felt something tied to one of his big toes. He saw it was a piece of string that snaked across the room and entered a piece of metal tubing. A puzzled Sorg moved his toe and heard a distant bell tinkle.

The door snapped open and a dark-suited man with a mustache and desolate eyes entered. He carried a small glass bottle in his hand. "So, you're back with us. For a while there I was certain I had another coffin case on my hands."

Sorg said groggily, "Where am I? Who are you?"

"Oleg Markov, undertaker. You're in my mortuary." He knelt, put down the bottle, and untied the string from Sorg's toe.

"What's going on?" Sorg demanded.

"An interesting contraption this, used when medicine was less of an exact science and doctors sometimes wrongly diagnosed death. Should the corpse move the string pulls on a bell in the hall."

Sorg shook his head, as if to clear the fog in his brain. "You learn something new every day."

"In your case, I used it because I've been far too busy to keep watch on you. How do you feel?"

"Like I've been clubbed with rifle butts."

Markov smiled. "My son, Karl, and I brought you from the convent in our hearse, along with some bodies from the cellar. One of the nuns found you hiding in a nearby alcove. Sister Agnes didn't think you'd live. You were in a bad state—your wound had opened. Don't you remember?"

"I remember being shot at by a Cheka swine."

"Yes, Sister Agnes mentioned that. Fortunately for you, he missed. Here, sniff this. It'll help clear your head."

He removed a cork stopper from the bottle and thrust it under

Sorg's nose. The smelling salts hit Sorg's nostrils like a blow and he came sharply to his senses.

Markov put the cork back in the bottle. "Can you stand?"

Sorg's eyes watered as he swung his legs off the mattress and stood. The moment he did so he felt lightheaded.

"You look weak," Markov commented.

"I'll be fine." Sorg's lightheaded feeling passed, but then a twinge stabbed his side. A fresh dressing had been applied, and this time the bandages looked new. He felt well rested, better than he had in days.

Markov said, "Sister Agnes came and tended to you. You'll remain here for now. It's too dangerous to stay at the monastery in case the Reds return."

Sorg stared at the undertaker. "How do I know I can trust you?"

Markov held out his left hand. On his wedding finger he wore a silver ring, inset with the ancient Tibetan symbol.

"Does that answer your question? I'm here to help you in any way I can."

Sorg rubbed his jaw and felt stubble. "How long have I been here?"

"Almost three days. You slept most of it. Thankfully your wound's healing nicely."

Markov offered a cigarette from a silver case.

Sorg accepted. "What have I missed?"

Markov tapped a cigarette, lit both, and exhaled smoke. "White forces and Czech troops are less than twenty miles from the city now, maybe a week away from liberating us. Even less, if the rumors are to be believed, so time is precious.

"We're certain the Reds won't go to the trouble of moving the family again. It's too much of a risk. Instead, they intend to execute them here in Ekaterinburg and dispose of the bodies, before the city falls."

"Says who?"

"The Brotherhood has its sources, even among the Reds. Extra Cheka have arrived from Moscow. The new *komendant*, Yurovsky, is making trips into the woods outside the city. Especially to an area of old, unused mine shafts called the Four Brothers. We believe he's looking for a suitable burial spot."

A piercing siren suddenly shrieked like a banshee, startling Sorg.

Markov said, "The eight o'clock curfew. You must be starving. I'll have my son bring you some food. By the way, Sister Agnes said you'd need these."

He slipped a hand inside his coat pocket and handed Sorg some folded sheets of paper. "Detailed drawings of the Ipatiev House."

Sorg took them eagerly as the siren ended.

Markov shook his head. "But I'm afraid they won't help us. Only Vilim Ivanovitch de Gennin can do that."

"Who?"

Markov blew out smoke, crossed to a cupboard, and removed what looked like some rolled-up parchments, stained amber with age.

"One of Ekaterinburg's original founders. This city goes back to 1723, when de Gennin oversaw its design as a fortress. He was a military man and a fortification engineer, who insisted on a number of secret tunnels being built to serve as escape routes in case of siege."

"Enlighten me."

Markov came back and handed the parchments to Sorg. "The tunnels are still there. Some bore deep under the bowels of the streets, or crisscross beneath cathedrals and churches and go down to the river. Some are dangerous places where the walls have collapsed or are flooded with water, or are bricked up, but others are still passable.

"The Reds know some of the passageways exist but they can't know them all. The Brotherhood has a full set of the original fortress plans. It's important you see for yourself the more important of these tunnels as soon as you're well enough to walk. Especially the ones I've marked."

Sorg's heart twinged as he unrolled what looked like a set of intricate ink-and-pencil architectural drawings that appeared centuries old. "Spit it out."

"We know a route to get the family safely from their prison."

"Explain."

"One wing of the lower part of the Ipatiev House is built into a solid granite hillside. I've marked a passageway on the drawings that tunnels through the rock and leads directly to a basement storage room, used to store furniture."

"You're sure about this?"

"As you're my judge. I've been in the passageway. It runs from the east and can be entered through Voznesensky Cathedral, or from under an archway east of the Iset's City Pond. The passageway under the house was shored up but I helped demolish the brickwork to make it passable."

Sorg was electrified. "I want to see it."

"When?"

"Tonight."

"You're crazy. You're still healing."

"I'm capable of walking. There's no time to waste."

Markov looked hesitant. "What about the curfew? Anyone who ventures out without a permit risks being shot."

"You're an undertaker. Don't you have a permit?"

"Well, yes. The Reds need me to remove the typhoid victims day and night for public health reasons. But we'd be taking a big risk. All of Ekaterinburg's garrison will be on the lookout for you."

"Get your hearse ready. I've got an idea."

68

The trolley squealed to a halt at the end of Kolinsky Prospect and Andrev and Lydia climbed down. After a short walk they reached the tenement building, a shabby-looking affair.

Trolley cars trundled past on the crowded street, electric flashes sparking from the overhead cables, tired-looking pedestrians strolling by, many of them returning home after a day's hard labor.

Andrev carried his duffel on his back, the canvas bag of workman's tools by his side, and as they came near the building, he said, "Slip your arm through mine, like we're walking home after work."

They ambled by a busy tobacco kiosk, past a swarthy-looking Georgian or Armenian shoe shiner sitting on some steps. Like most of the shoe shiners in Moscow—they could be found at any street corner—he didn't have polish but would spit on his customer's shoes and rub them hard with a rag until they shone.

As they strolled on, Lydia said, "Do you really think the Cheka will be keeping watch on Nina?"

"After the last time, it's more than likely. Don't look back, but the shoe shiner is probably Cheka, or at least in their pay, keeping an eye on the comings and goings from the building. The man working in the tobacco kiosk, too—and they won't be the only ones."

A little farther on they came to a park, far enough away from the tenement building but still within viewing distance. They sat on a bench. A handful of children played at scattering the scrawny pigeons, while tired-looking workmen cycled or walked past on their way home. Lydia said, "What are you going to do?"

Andrev opened the duffel bag, took off his leather jacket, and stuffed it inside. He wore his peasant's work shirt and cap, and with his tool bag he looked like a tradesman. "Try to find the building's rear entrance and see if I can locate Nina. It may take a while."

"What if the Cheka are waiting inside the building?"

Andrev slipped the Nagant revolver from his pocket and tucked it into the tool bag. "I'll have to cross that bridge if I come to it. If anyone asks, I'm there to repair the plumbing. If that doesn't work, I'll have to fall back on my other plan."

"What's that?"

"Shoot my way out."

"Won't that endanger Nina and your son?"

"That's what worries me."

"Do you want me to go with you?"

"No, it's best I go alone. If you hear gunfire, get back to our lodgings as fast as you can and wait there until I show up."

Lydia put a hand on his, concern in her eyes. "Be careful, Uri. Please."

He stood, smiled down at her, but there was no hiding the strain in his face. "Remember, any sign of trouble, get away fast."

By five o'clock that evening Abraham Tarku was drunk. He swallowed a glass of vodka and sat staring at the Remington typewriter with glazed eyes.

"Why in the name of all that's good did you have to come back, Uri? *Why?*" he asked the question aloud, then flung the glass against the wall, shattering it to pieces.

He stumbled to his feet, went out the front door of the pawnbroker's shop, locked it after him, and staggered out into the street.

Minutes later he spotted an empty droshky coming toward him, and he waved down the carriage driver.

"Where to, citizen?"

"Cheka headquarters, and be quick about it."

69

A lane led all along the back of the tenements and Andrev counted off the buildings.

When he neared Nina's building he noticed a thin, weaselly-looking man with a pencil mustache sitting on a low wall, reading a newspaper.

The man was Cheka, he had no doubt, and was watching the rear entrance. Andrev stepped into a door recess to avoid being seen. The rotted door hung open on its hinges and he squeezed past it into a back garden.

He made his way across the overgrown weeds and peered over the wall into the next back garden. If he climbed over the back walls he might be able to reach Nina's building without the man noticing him.

Andrev hefted his tool bag over his shoulder, pulled himself up over the wall, and slid down the other side. He crossed the ragged garden and peered over the next wall into Nina's backyard.

Lines of laundry ran along the narrow garden, a couple of storage sheds on one side. A green-painted rear entrance door into the tenement was wide open. He slid over the wall and let himself down silently.

Moving cautiously between the rows of hanging clothes, he came to the first storage shed and ducked inside. Metal garbage bins stank to high heaven. As he stood peering between a crack in the door, wondering what to do next, a waif of a child came out of the tenement rear, carrying a wooden bucket.

She sloshed the contents down a water drain, then moved back inside the darkened hallway and disappeared into darkness.

After a few more minutes Andrev saw a door open on the right side of the hallway and a woman stepped out into the backyard, carrying an empty wicker basket.

She wore a work apron and she looked tired and drawn.

It was Nina.

A small, pale-looking child with curly blond hair followed her out, sobbing tiredly as he rubbed his eyes.

Andrev's chest tightened the instant he saw his son.

Sergey began tugging at his mother's apron, as if wanting to be comforted.

Every tug Sergey made at the apron tore at Andrev's heart.

As Nina moved along the clothesline, retrieving her laundry, she tried to soothe Sergey with soft words. He sounded cranky with tiredness, holding out his hands to her, wanting to be picked up.

Finally, when Nina finished, she lifted him up, balancing Sergey on her hip before she carried him back inside with her clothes basket. She moved into the hallway and reentered her room.

Andrev wanted to call out after her but he dared not. What if the Cheka were lurking inside the building?

His stomach churned.

Minutes passed, then several more.

Finally, after another fifteen minutes, his heart beating wildly, his stomach knotted with apprehension, and when he could bear it no longer he slipped the loaded Nagant from the tool bag.

He moved between the washing lines and came to the dim hallway.

It was empty and stank of boiled cabbage and greasy mutton.

Distant noises drifted from inside the building; a baby's shrill cry and the abrasive singsong of adults arguing. Andrev moved deeper into the hall. He came to the door Nina entered and rapped on the wood. Footsteps sounded on bare floorboards and then the door opened.

When Nina saw him her hand went to her mouth in disbelief and she gave a gasp.

Before she could speak Andrev pushed his way into the room and kicked shut the door.

70

The door burst open and Yakov strode into the office. "You smell like a backstreet drunk. What do you want?" he demanded.

Abraham Tarku looked up with blurry eyes, then fell silent and nervously licked his lips.

Yakov's eyes sparked. "It's about Andrev, isn't it? It's got to be."

"After you hunted me down in Moscow, you let me go again. You said you wanted to use me as bait in case Andrev showed up. You said that was the only reason I didn't get a bullet in the neck. I told the commissar that the captain didn't kill his brother."

Yakov's mouth twisted. "A lie for a start. You claimed you were unconscious. Sergeant Mersk confirmed that. You're half-blind, and your glasses were cracked. So how could you have seen *anything* clearly, let alone know what happened?"

"I know the captain."

"And I know that desperate men will do desperate things. Now out with it, and no harm will come to you or your family."

"He contacted me."

"When?"

"Earlier this afternoon. He wanted help, fresh clothes, and to borrow a typewriter. He was interested in the trains going east to the Urals and Ekaterinburg."

"Did he have a woman with him?"

"As a matter of fact he did."

■ ■ ■

They sat at the table, the silence broken only by the labored sound of Sergey's breathing as he slept.

Nina whispered fearfully, "Please, put away the gun, Uri."

Only when Andrev knew the room was safe did he do as Nina asked, stuffing the Nagant into his pocket.

He looked at Nina, unease between them as if they were strangers, and then he went to stand over the bed and stare down at his son. He noticed the medicine bottle by the bed. "How is he?"

"His chest is congested. The winter was bad on him. The doctor says to keep him warm and let him rest. Please don't wake him, I only just got him to sleep, Uri."

As his hand lingered over Sergey's forehead, Andrev seemed to be having difficulty holding himself together, worry tightening his face, then he leaned over and gently kissed his son's damp forehead.

Nina said quietly, "Please, don't disturb him. I've even had to hide your photograph, so don't let him see you. I beg you, Uri. It would only distress him. He'll get confused and upset, and when you've gone he'll be heartbroken."

Andrev's eyes were moist as he looked down at his son, then Nina whispered, "Please, sit at the table. Keep your voice down."

He joined her, and Nina said, "You can't stay. It's not safe. You've taken a great risk coming here. It endangers us all."

"I know. I won't stay long. But I had to see you both again."

There was no mistaking the signs of stress: Nina looked washed out and tired, her figure even more slender. He reached out, touched her hand. "How have you been?"

"Surviving."

"And your parents?"

"They were arrested months ago. The Reds threw them into a cell in Lefortovo."

"For what reason?"

"Does there have to be a reason anymore? My father was a businessman, he owned property. That's reason enough."

He squeezed her hand. "I'm truly sorry, Nina."

She pulled her hand away, took a handkerchief from her apron, and wiped her eyes, then stood anxiously and went to peer out the rear window. "If the Cheka find you here we're all finished. You really can't stay, Uri."

"Nina, there's a reason why I came, not just to see you both. I escaped to England."

"Leonid Yakov came here the other day. He thought you had gone there. He said if you ever appeared I was to tell him."

Andrev said bitterly, "I thought he might show up."

"They're watching me, Uri, surely you know that."

"I know." He moved again to the curtain and peered out. "I've been careful. I don't believe I've been spotted. I had to leave Russia, Nina, but I've returned for a reason. I want you and Sergey to leave Moscow and come with me."

She stared back at him, almost a look of panic on her face. "Leave Moscow? For where?"

He came back to the table. "England. We can start a new life there, all of us together."

"We're divorced, Uri. I thought I made that clear."

"Nina, whatever our differences are, I ask you to put them aside and think of Sergey. Even if we were never again to be man and wife, I ask you to put our son first. He needs us both. Especially now."

He heard the bitter edge in her voice. "And what kind of life has this been? Living in poverty, with no husband? With the constant fear of being imprisoned?"

"Nina—"

"For the last four years you've been either a soldier or a prisoner, not a husband and father. I know there's the war, I know that you're a victim of it as much as we are, but I couldn't go on like that. I couldn't live with the uncertainty, the wondering if you'd ever come home alive, if Sergey would always have a father . . . can't you see? Can't you see why I had to end it?"

Suddenly she broke down, racked by sobbing, her shoulders heaving as she leaned over the table, burying her face in her hands.

She sounded close to the breaking point, and he realized then the enormous strain she was under. Sergey stirred in his sleep. Nina heard him, and put a hand to her mouth to stifle her cries.

"Nina, please . . ." Andrev pulled her close, held her.

She clung to him and they remained like that a while, as he rocked her back and forth, until she pulled away from him, wiped her eyes, and managed to compose herself.

"This isn't getting us anywhere, Uri. I'll always care about you. Always. But you must understand that I have to think of our son. There's something else you should know. Yakov said if I didn't inform on you Lenin would exile Sergey and me to a camp in Siberia."

The color left Andrev's face. "Then you can't stay: you have to leave with me at once."

"No, it's you who have to leave, Uri. Quietly and quickly, so no one will know you were here."

"Nina—"

"To do otherwise will only endanger Sergey's life. By remaining in Moscow, he and I stand some chance. Trying to escape, we'd risk death."

Andrev felt overcome, his face distraught. "There's no hope, then? I can never see you both again?"

She looked at him, her eyes welling. "I can't risk sacrificing our son's life by putting him in jeopardy. I can't do it, Uri. Don't you see? Please, just go. Don't put us in any more danger. *Please.*"

He understood the brutal logic to it, the awful truth at its core, but before Andrev could reply, Sergey stirred from sleep as a fit of hoarse coughing rattled his lungs.

He rubbed his eyes and whimpered as he sat up in bed. The moment he recognized his father his eyes snapped open in disbelief. He looked to his mother, as if for confirmation, then his lips began to tremble uncertainly.

Nina said unhappily, "Uri, go now, I beg you, just go . . ."

Andrev moved over to the bed and lifted his son in his arms. Sergey was confused and stared at him, but then nature kicked in and the child clung to his father's chest like an animal cub, unwilling to let go. "Papa . . . Papa!"

"Sergey . . . Papa's here, it's fine."

"Mama . . . Mama said you were gone."

"I was, but I'm here now. It's all right."

Andrev embraced his son, feeling so choked with emotion that all he could do was stand there, kissing him, rocking him in his arms.

A second later came the rumble of engines out in the street, followed by the squeal of brakes.

His heart pounded as he peered out the window and saw several trucks pull up at the curb. Plainclothes men and troops jumped out.

Nina said palely, "What's wrong?"

Andrev was ashen. "Soldiers, lots of them." He saw the familiar figure of Leonid Yakov striding out of one of the trucks and barking orders at the men. "Yakov's among them."

He kissed a confused Sergey, handed him to Nina, and reached for his gun.

Nina put a hand on his arm that held the weapon. "No, you must go, Uri, out the back way, disappear *now*! For pity's sake, you can't be found here."

71

Lydia heard the squeal of brakes as the three trucks rounded the corner. Her stomach churned with unease, her hand tightening on the Nagant in her pocket.

Suddenly there were soldiers everywhere, climbing out of the trucks and rushing toward the tenement. She had a terrible feeling of doom.

She could simply walk away as Andrev had told her, but some instinct wouldn't allow it. She crossed the street and turned into the back lane that ran along the tenements. A British-made Douglas motorcycle with two Red Army soldiers roared up behind her, one of them riding in a sidecar.

The man climbed out, and as he aimed his rifle at her his comrade tore off his goggles, hung them on the handlebars, and dismounted.

"And where do you think you're going, woman?"

"I—I live here," Lydia said. The man with the rifle had her in his sights.

"Really? We'll soon find out if that's true." The driver had a sharp, cunning face and as he came forward he tore out his revolver. "Get your hands up where I can see them."

"I—I've done nothing wrong," Lydia protested.

The man pushed her roughly against the wall. His hand moved coarsely between her legs as he patted her down. He searched her pockets and found the Nagant, triumph on his face. "Not so innocent now, are we? What are you doing with a weapon?"

When Lydia didn't answer, he grinned and pushed her forward. "Don't worry, we'll get the answer out of you. Keep walking, straight ahead. There's a Commissar Yakov who'd like to have a word."

■ ■ ■

Yakov pushed through the tenement front door and moved cautiously along the hallway to Nina's apartment. He nodded to the two men accompanying him and they kicked in Nina's door, splintering wood, before they rushed in, rifles sweeping the room.

Nina was standing by the bed, clutching her son to her breast, the child in tears, his lips trembling.

"Where is he?" Yakov demanded, brandishing his gun.

She didn't answer.

Yakov crossed to her, the crying child clinging to his mother, his face a mask of confusion and terror.

"Don't make this any more difficult than it already is. And don't play games, Nina. You're in enough trouble."

When she still didn't reply one of the soldiers went to strike her with his rifle but Yakov caught the man by the arm and spun him round. "Get out. Both of you. Go the back way. Find him."

The men rushed out. Yakov stood staring at her with livid rage.

"You fool, what have you done, Nina? This can only end badly for you. Where is he? Tell me and I promise to ask for leniency for you and your son."

But she seemed rooted to the spot, unable even to speak, a growing terror in her eyes. The sobbing boy clung even more tightly to his mother and shot fearful glances at Yakov.

He was getting nowhere. "Stay here until I come back, and don't move. Uri can't escape, the area's completely surrounded."

Only when he went toward the door did she react, reaching out for him with a pitiful expression, the child still in her arms. "Please, don't harm him, Leonid, for Sergey's sake, I beg you."

"It's far too late for that."

72

Andrev hurried between the back garden clotheslines, just as the weaselly-looking man with the pencil mustache who was guarding the rear rushed in, brandishing a handgun and followed by a group of armed soldiers.

Andrev darted into the storage shed.

The soldiers stormed toward the tenement. Andrev vaulted the wall and slid down the other side. He mounted the next wall, and when he reached the ramshackle door that led to the lane he heard the clatter of boots. He froze and his stomach knotted.

In the lane, two armed soldiers went marching past, escorting Lydia.

He stepped out behind them, wielding the Nagant, no mistaking the menace in his voice. "Not a sound or you're both dead."

The men turned and saw Andrev aim his revolver at them.

"Put down your weapons and lie on the ground."

The terrified soldiers obeyed.

Andrev tossed away their rifles and picked up the revolver belonging to one of the men. He was about to toss it to Lydia when behind him he heard the soft click of a weapon being cocked.

A familiar voice said, "Toss the gun aside. Don't attempt to move."

He spun round as Yakov came through the ramshackle door, aiming his revolver, his face seething. "I said toss the gun. *Now*, or you'll die here this minute."

Andrev threw the gun on the ground. Yakov struck him across the head with the butt of his revolver, and he staggered back against the wall.

When Lydia rushed to help him, Yakov aimed at her and roared, "Don't take a step unless I tell you."

Lydia obeyed. The two soldiers scrambled to retrieve their rifles. Yakov replaced his pistol in his holster and stepped over to Andrev.

He struck him a savage blow that slammed him against the wall. "Consider that another small down payment on a debt I owe you."

Andrev tried to rise, unsteadily. "Leonid, you're wrong if you think I killed Stanislas."

But Yakov wasn't listening. He lashed out with his boot, kicking one of Andrev's legs from under him, and he hit the ground.

Yakov moved in fast, placing his boot on Andrev's throat, crushing his windpipe. "Don't try to lie to me."

"Take your foot off his neck."

Yakov's head snapped round. The woman's eyes had a steely look. "Who are you to demand anything?"

Lydia simply said, "Do as I say."

The guard nearest Yakov stepped forward, a grin spreading on his face. "Let me deal with her, Commissar. Maybe a good beating will teach this one some manners." He raised the butt of his rifle to strike out at her. "You stupid woman, answer with respect when the commissar asks you a question."

Lydia raised her hand and the Mauser appeared. It cracked once, hitting the guard in the forehead, and he collapsed like a sack of flour.

The second guard was already bringing up his rifle.

Lydia shot him once in the chest and again in the head and he was hammered back against the wall.

As Yakov reached frantically for his holstered Nagant, Lydia stepped in and touched the barrel to his forehead. "Hand away from the gun."

Yakov reluctantly did as he was told.

Andrev pushed himself up and removed the pistol from Yakov's holster. A stone-faced Yakov looked at the dead guards, then up at Lydia and said, "You've both signed your death warrants."

"Be grateful she didn't kill you, Leonid," Andrev told him.

All around them now they heard barked orders and shouts as troops reacted to the gunfire.

Andrev grabbed the motorcycle and said to Lydia, "Get in the sidecar."

She joined him, clutching the Mauser and grabbing the second Nagant, the sound of rushing feet and voices growing louder.

Yakov glared, filled with vehemence. "This isn't finished. Not by a long way."

Andrev said, "Something tells me that even if there was time, you still wouldn't listen to me, Leonid. Have it your way. But know one thing—this is between you and me, no one else. Harm Nina and my son and I swear I'll kill you. I'd do it right here and now only I know it would condemn them. So heed my warning. I'll hold you personally responsible."

He started the motorcycle, revving the engine just as a group of soldiers appeared and advanced uncertainly toward them from the far end of the lane. Lydia fired two quick shots and the troops darted for cover.

The last thing an enraged Yakov saw was Andrev speeding off, the woman in the sidecar firing both guns at the soldiers, and then the motorcycle skewed around a corner and roared away.

73

Markov eased back gently on the reins and the horses slowed. His heart skipped when he saw the barricade up ahead in the milky darkness.

Markov reached behind him, rapped his knuckles on the wooden coffin in the back of the carriage, and whispered, "There's a checkpoint ahead. How are you holding up?"

The lid was raised a little, enough for Sorg to breathe through. "Well enough. What do you want me to do?"

"Keep the lid on and remain still, especially if the guards check inside the coffin. Get ready, we're almost there."

Sorg slid the lid back on. Markov eased the horses to a halt at the checkpoint and two young armed soldiers came forward, each carrying a lantern, their rifles fixed with long bayonets. One said, "Don't you know there's a curfew, old man?"

Markov waved a sheet of paper. "Oleg Markov, undertaker, comrades. I have a special pass from the local commissars. I'm taking a corpse to my mortuary, and there'll be several more before the night's out."

"Let me see that." One of the soldiers grabbed the paper, studying it in the lamplight.

Markov said, "Check the coffin if you like. He's as dead as a doorpost. But be careful."

"What's that supposed to mean?"

"He had typhus. It's highly contagious."

The soldiers didn't look happy at the prospect of examining the coffin but one of them used his bayonet to pry open the lid, then held up his lamp.

Sorg lay inside, his face bone-white, his eyes closed, hands folded across his chest. He wore a black suit and on one sleeve was a red armband.

Markov tipped his cap respectfully and said, "A good Bolshevik, gone to meet his maker."

The guard recoiled in disgust and let the lid fall back into place. "There is no God, undertaker. Don't you listen to Comrade Lenin? Now get yourself out of here."

Five minutes later Markov jerked the reins to a halt. The horses snorted, their hooves fading on the cobble. "We're here. It's safe to come out now."

In the back, Sorg lifted the lid and eased himself from the coffin. He used a towel to wipe the flour Markov had applied to his face, and slipped off the red armband and thrust it in his pocket.

The undertaker grinned. "A nice touch, that armband."

Sorg saw the huge church spire looming way off in the lunar darkness and recognized Voznesensky Cathedral. In the distance shimmered the broad Iset City Pond. "Where exactly are we?"

"About three hundred yards from the Ipatiev House." Markov pointed into the darkness beneath a granite archway. "The tunnel entrance is under there, beyond a locked iron sewer door," he explained.

"It leads to a turret set in the brickwork. You'll see the Brotherhood's mark painted above it. Behind it is a passageway that eventually ends at a brick wall. Behind that lies the basement storage room."

"I think I've got it."

"The bricks in the wall are loosened, but whatever you do don't remove them, not until we're ready to proceed with the recue. We don't want to give the game away."

Markov handed over an unlit kerosene lamp, a box of matches, and a metal ring with a key. "You'll need the lamp. The key's for the iron door." He consulted his pocket watch, then snapped it shut. "Eleven-fifteen. I'll meet you back here in an hour. That ought to give you enough time. You recall the map details?"

Sorg nodded.

Markov touched his whip to the horses' flanks. "Remember, any hint of trouble and get away fast. The Reds around here are all trigger-happy. They'll shoot you dead at the slightest provocation."

74

Sorg moved under the bridge as the sound of Markov's horses faded.

The archway was poorly lit but he spotted the sturdy, rusted iron door set in the middle of the wall. He checked to make sure no one was watching him and slid the key in the lock. It opened easily and he moved into pitch darkness.

Closing the door behind him, he fumbled for a box of matches and lit the lamp. Yellow light flared all around him. He was in a passageway, a foul, sulfur-smelling channel with a gurgling sewer running down the middle, raised stone walkways on either side, the lamplight casting flickering shadows on damp walls.

A rat scurried past, squealing as it went, startling Sorg. He put up his sleeve to cover his nose and splashed his way along the puddled walkway, wearing the rubber-soled boots Markov gave him.

A little farther on he came to a rusty metal turret set in the walkway. Raising the lamp high he saw a reverse swastika etched in white paint, high above the brickwork. The turret had a simple latch and when he snapped it open, it squealed on its hinges.

Inside, an arched tunnel lay beyond, white glazed tiles lining the walls.

He heard a faint, echoing murmur of voices and cocked his ears. The murmur seemed to come from the end of the tunnel. Markov said to go no farther, but Sorg's mind was gripped by a powerful curiosity.

His heart thudding in his chest, he raised the lamp and crawled inside the tunnel.

■ ■ ■

In the Ipatiev House courtyard, Kazan's truck slid to a halt and he climbed out.

Yurovsky, the *komendant*, was leaning against the door frame smoking a cigarette, his tunic unbuttoned, exposing his vest underneath.

Kazan said, "Anastasia Romanov. I want to interrogate her now."

The *komendant* flicked away his cigarette. "It's late. Come back tomorrow."

"I have Yakov's permission. He may have something to say about that."

The *komendant*'s eyes flared. "I don't know who I despise more—the Romanovs, or turncoats like you."

"We're on the same side now. Get used to it. The girl, and quickly. I want to soften her up before I carry out a full interrogation tomorrow." Kazan grinned. "Don't fret, I won't leave a mark on her."

"The parents will be concerned. I don't want them panicking. My job is to keep them on an even keel until we're ready to carry out the execution."

"Tell them we just need to ask the girl some routine questions. Don't make a big fuss about it. Use all your charm. You're good at that, Yurovsky."

The *komendant* grunted, buttoned his tunic, and called out to one of the guards, "Fetch Anastasia Romanov."

The man hurried off.

Kazan followed the *komendant* into his office and strode over to the wall map. "Our spy's gone quiet but I'm convinced he's still out there. I'm having more checkpoints set up within a five-hundred-yard radius of here."

"Your problem, not mine. Where do you want to interrogate her?"

Kazan cracked his knuckles. "The basement will do. It's suitably dark and dingy. The perfect setting to frighten the life out of her."

"You can use one of the rooms I've cleared out. But you'll have your work cut out for you. She's a resourceful young woman, Kazan. Not the kind who scares easily."

"We'll see about that."

75

It started to rain heavily as Andrev came round a bend.

He saw the roadblock ahead in the distance and eased into the curb. He wore the driver's goggles and he pulled them up.

Lydia said, alarmed, "That's the second roadblock we've seen in the last ten minutes."

Andrev considered. "I doubt Yakov's had time to throw up checkpoints all over Moscow. My guess is they're just routine."

He smiled down at her, nodding to the Nagant and the Mauser lying at her feet in the sidecar. "That was quite a performance back there."

"You can thank my Kentucky upbringing." As the rain fell harder, Lydia rummaged around in the sidecar, found an olive-colored oilskin cape, unfolded it, and covered herself as best she could. "What now?"

"There's a turn a mile or so back that'll take us onto a minor road out of Moscow. We'll try our chances there."

He went to pull down the goggles but suddenly he looked ready to crumple, as if there were a terrible weight on his shoulders.

Lydia put a hand on his arm. "You want to go back, don't you? To make sure Nina and Sergey haven't come to any harm?"

He tried to keep his voice steady with some difficulty. "It's an agony not knowing."

"You can't do any more, Uri. Surely Yakov won't hurt them."

"If he does I'll kill him."

THE KREMLIN

Yakov entered the same impressive anterooms as before.

The guard took his firearm, then knocked on the floor-to-ceiling doors and gestured for him to enter.

Trotsky was standing by the window, immersed in his own thoughts, a glass of what looked like water in one hand as he stared out at the drenching rain. He turned, and his sullen dark eyes drilled into Yakov. "Step forward. Don't stand there like a fool."

Yakov obeyed. He noticed that the door at the other end of the room was open. In an adjoining office, Lenin was standing by his desk reading a letter. When he saw Yakov, he eyed him with a cold stare, walked over to the door, and kicked it shut.

As the door slammed, Trotsky sipped from his glass and began to slowly circle Yakov.

Without warning, he flung the contents of his glass in Yakov's face.

"I don't employ fools, Yakov. But it seems in your case I may have committed an error. You greatly disappointed me."

Yakov silently wiped a hand over his drenched face.

"Out with it. What happened? How did Andrev and the woman escape?"

Yakov explained.

Trotsky let out a deep sigh, his mouth tightening with extreme displeasure. "You've failed in your duty, Yakov. How will you rectify the situation?"

"I'm having checkpoints set up all over the city. All hotels in Moscow and every barracks will be given a description of Andrev and the woman."

Trotsky slammed his glass on the desk, strolled over to a wall map of Moscow, and studied it. "You seem to forget that if anyone can escape a dragnet, it's your shrewd friend Andrev. My gut feeling is you're wasting your time and stretching our troops thin trying to find him in Moscow."

"If we have no luck in the coming hours, I'll travel directly to Ekaterinburg. That has to be Andrev's destination."

"Good, we're thinking alike. What about his former wife and son?"

"I have them in custody."

Trotsky almost spat his reply. "They must pay the price of his folly. I want it done tonight. Have them transported to the harshest prison camp you can find. Take care of it, Yakov. Fail me again and I'll take it personally."

76

One of the guards led Anastasia down the stairs. She wore a cotton dressing gown over her nightdress, her hair around her shoulders.

The guards escorted her along the hallway until they entered a small, airless room with patterned yellow wallpaper. A single lightbulb was on overhead, casting a faint glow about the dim chamber, with only a small, round table and two bentwood chairs. Another pair of double doors was set in the far wall.

Suddenly the door behind her banged shut and the guard was gone.

"I'm Inspector Viktor Kazan of the Cheka. Sit down," a voice said hoarsely.

A bald-headed man stepped out of the shadows, causing her heart to skip.

He wore black clothes, a sinister air about him. Several fingers of his left hand were bandaged. He indicated one of two chairs next to the table. "I said sit."

"I prefer to stand."

He grabbed hold of her arm and pushed her into a chair with considerable force. "And I told you to sit. Your formal interrogation will take place tomorrow. But for now, I just want a chat."

"My . . . my parents are concerned that I'm being questioned."

"Too bad." He unfolded a page from his pocket and laid it on the table. "Tell me the truth about the note."

"What truth? What are you talking about?"

Suddenly Kazan's fist slammed down hard on the table, the noise booming about the room, his mouth twisting. "No games. I'm a harsher man than *komendant*. If I have to break bones to get the truth out of you, I will. Do we understand each other?"

Anastasia didn't reply but fear ignited in her eyes.

"I asked you a question."

Her lips quivered. She looked faintly overwhelmed, a nervous seventeen-year-old faced with the threatening presence of a brutish thug, but there was no mistaking the resolve in her voice. "You—you're a callous, cruel man."

Kazan struck her a blow across the side of her skull with his palm. The slap rang around the chamber. Her head jolted sideways but before she could cry out, Kazan slammed a hand over her mouth. "Call out or make another sound and I'll hit you even harder."

She struggled fiercely but Kazan kept his hand firmly in place and leaned in close. "Nod if you understand."

Anastasia stopped struggling. She nodded.

Kazan took his hand away.

She stared up at him in shocked disbelief, and for a moment she looked not like a young woman but a child in distress, and it took her to the brink of tears. "How . . . how dare you . . ."

Kazan grabbed her by the hair, thoroughly enjoying himself. "Listen to me, you little witch. I could beat you to within an inch of your life and not leave a scratch on you. Tell me the truth about the note, or there will be serious repercussions for all your family. Out with it, before I lose my temper and this turns nasty."

Sorg moved along the white-tiled passageway, holding the lamp high. Condensation dripped from the walls and he stepped over puddles. Twenty yards farther on he was faced with a dead end—a brick wall.

He knelt and felt the cement between the bricks pointing—as Markov said, it had been removed and the bricks loosened. He thought he heard faint voices.

They seemed to come from beyond the wall. He considered a moment, wondering if he should go any farther, then he carefully removed over a dozen bricks, revealing a hole big enough to crawl through.

He crawled past the hole and found himself in a dusty storeroom. Stacked around the bare walls were ancient wicker chairs and a broken display cabinet, its glass shattered. The far wall was covered with a crisscross of planks nailed into a wooden door frame. He crawled over, his nerves taut as piano wire.

Underneath the nailed planks was a pair of double doors. Muted sounds came from behind them. Sorg dimmed his lamp to the barest flicker, then stood and placed it on the ground behind him.

Light filtered through a crack between the doors. He peered through. A room lay beyond. He could hardly believe his eyes.

Anastasia.

For a moment he could barely breathe, his stomach knotting with excitement, and then his heart felt like ice.

She sat at a table, her face lit by the wash of an electric light. Kazan stood over her. On the table was a slip of paper.

Suddenly Kazan's fist slammed down hard on the table, the noise booming about the chamber.

"I asked you a question."

"You—you're a callous, cruel man."

Anastasia's voice was filled with confidence, but there was no mistaking the emotion. What happened next filled Sorg with fury. Kazan slapped Anastasia hard across the side of her head, and the noise rang around the chamber.

Her head jerked sideways and she nearly cried out, but Kazan forced a hand over her mouth, cutting off her scream. He seemed to be strangling her as she struggled fiercely.

Sorg felt helpless.

"Call out or make another sound and I'll hit you even harder."

Anastasia stopped struggling and Kazan slowly took his hand away.

She muttered something inaudible and the next thing Sorg knew, Kazan grabbed her savagely by the hair. His voice came in snatches.

"Listen to me, you little witch . . . I could beat you to within an inch of your life . . . Tell me the truth about the note . . . Out with it . . ."

Sorg's chest pounded. *The note.* So that was it—*What have I done?* It was his fault Kazan was interrogating Anastasia. Guilt devoured him, his frustrated rage like molten lava.

What can I do? Break down the door and kill Kazan? He felt for the

Toledo steel pen in his pocket. That was what he wanted to do. What he felt he *ought* to do.

But that would give the game away.

He saw Kazan twist her hair even tighter and heard Anastasia stifle a scream.

Sorg put an arm over his eyes and stepped back, unable to look, the image too painful.

As he did so he knocked over the lamp behind him.

Its light flared a second before it smashed on the ground, the glass shattering, and then the lamp rolled away. The metallic noise echoed loudly throughout the passageway. Sorg's nerves jangled like an electric bell.

A second later the lamplight extinguished and the storeroom plunged into total darkness.

Kazan heard the noise and his head jerked up, his senses alert.

It sounded as if someone had kicked a tin can and it rattled over cobblestone. The racket came from somewhere beyond the second pair of double doors in the far wall. Kazan stiffened. He saw from the look on the girl's face that she'd heard the noise, too. He let go of her hair and strode over to the doors.

Putting his ear to the wood, he thought he heard the noise wash away. He tried the door handles: they were locked. He pushed his shoulder to the wood but still they didn't budge.

He crossed back to the entrance doors, opened them, and called out, "Guards!"

Three men rushed in with rifles. Kazan pointed to the far wall. "Where do those doors lead?"

"Nowhere, Inspector. They're blocked up. There's some kind of storage room beyond, so I hear."

Kazan crossed the room in a fit of rage and kicked at the doors with his boot. "I heard a noise from behind. Get over here, help me. One of you get some lamps."

Two of the guards smashed at the doors with their rifle butts, and when that didn't work, they pried at them with their bayonets until the lock gave. The doors opened a few inches and Kazan saw criss-crossed planking beyond, nailed firmly in place. "Force your way in," he ordered.

The men obeyed, using their shoulders, and they crashed into a darkened storage room packed with old furniture.

A guard returned with three lit kerosene lamps. Kazan held up a lamp and saw that shards of glass littered the floor. A gaping hole yawned in the brickwork in the far wall. He strode over, his feet crunching on the glass.

He knelt, waved his lamp, and peered into an empty passageway patched with water puddles. "Take the girl back upstairs. Where's the *komendant?*"

"Asleep," one of the men said.

"Wake him. Tell everyone to be extra vigilant. We may have intruders."

The man dragged Anastasia away.

Kazan removed his revolver and crawled into the passageway, the other two guards following. He heard a noise—the clatter of fleeing feet, splashing through water puddles.

"Come with me," Kazan ordered the guards, and he plunged into the passageway.

77

Sorg hurried through the pitch-dark tunnel, feeling his way along the moist walls.

The lamp was still extinguished and he stumbled in compete darkness. The lamp's glass cowl was missing, and the wick felt drenched with kerosene from rolling on the ground. He heard the slosh of liquid—at least he still had fuel.

Behind him came the sound of crashing wood, and it echoed throughout the tunnels like gunshots. It sounded as if Kazan was breaking down the doors.

Sorg came to a halt as his head cracked into something solid—he felt a painful ringing sensation in his skull and staggered back, seeing stars.

He'd hit a wall.

He felt like vomiting and put a hand to his skull and massaged it. Gritting his teeth in agony, he closed his eyes and took slow, deep breaths. He knew he was panicking, but every instinct told him to get far away as fast as he could.

He fumbled desperately in his pockets for the box of matches, dropping them in the darkness.

No!

He knelt and frantically searched the ground for the matches.

His hand splashed in a puddle. He swore, fumbling until he found the box.

It felt wet.

He carefully placed the lamp on the ground to his right, still unable to see anything. Removing one of the matches, he struck it on the box.

Nothing happened. Sorg felt the coarse striker on the box's side—it was wet to the touch.

Behind him came the deafening crash of wood splintering, then muted shouts and orders.

Raw terror jolted Sorg's heart. He fumbled to find the lamp in the pitch darkness and then stumbled on.

Kazan plunged through the passageway, clutching his revolver, his lamp throwing shadows on the damp walls.

Moments later he halted. In front of him two archways led in different directions, one left, the other right.

The guards rushed up behind him, their boots splashing in puddles.

Kazan hissed, "Be quiet, both of you. Don't make a sound."

The guards fell silent.

Kazan listened, his ears cocked, but heard only silence.

He jerked a thumb at one of the guards.

"You go left."

The man obeyed, his rifle leveled as he held up his lamp.

Kazan nodded for the second man to follow him, and they plunged into the passageway on the right.

Sorg was beginning to panic. He halted and tried to strike three more matches but none worked.

He heard the echo of voices and footfalls behind him.

Kazan.

He knew he couldn't go on in complete darkness. He put down the lamp again and tried to light another match. Nothing—the striker still felt damp.

In frustration, he tried once more, this time striking a match on his trouser knee. He felt a slash of heat as the match ignited and illuminated the passageway.

Thank God.

Sorg knelt and touched the match to the saturated wick. It flared instantly, throwing shadows around the walls. He thought he recognized where he was. Another hundred or so yards and he'd come to the turret exit.

He stood, elated.

More noises echoed from behind: the sound of splashing, hurrying footsteps.

His heart thudding in his chest, Sorg shielded the lamp's naked flame with his hand and hurried on.

Kazan came to two more archways veining off in different directions.

He swung his lamp and spotted a scattering of spent matches on the ground. He knelt, felt the warm tips. A noise echoed down one of the passageways: footsteps, no question.

Kazan grinned.

Sorg was completely lost.

He couldn't find the metal turret. In his panic, he must have taken the wrong turn. The passageways were a maze. He felt utterly confused, his chest throbbing with stress pains.

A scraping noise sounded behind him, like a boot on concrete.

He spun round but saw no one—and heard only dripping water.

He turned and kept going, his feet drenched by deep puddles. When he rounded the next bend his spirits soared.

Somehow he had ended up in a main channel—a passageway that ran down to the pond or river, the distant water glinting with silver lunar light, a faint breeze wafting up, soothing on his face. *At last.*

Archways bled off from the passageway every twenty yards or so, feeding into the main tributary. As he went to move on, he heard a faint rush of feet and his heart stuttered.

A figure stepped out of an archway, five yards ahead.

Sorg felt a stab of fear and froze.

Kazan stood holding a lamp, a triumphant grin on his face.

"Going somewhere?" He stepped closer, his question echoing around the chamber.

Sorg grabbed wildly for the steel pen in his pocket.

Kazan's fist smashed into his jaw, he felt a lightning bolt of pain, and a second later he drowned in darkness.

PART SIX

78

The train rattled through the night.

Yakov sat at his desk, the table lamp on as he finished writing a letter. A knock came on the door and Zoba entered. "Don't you ever take a break?"

Yakov folded the written page, sealed it in an envelope, and tossed it on the desk. He stood, rubbed his eyes with thumb and forefinger. "Where are we?"

"Still a long way from Ekaterinburg. I ordered the driver to halt at the next major town. We can cable Moscow to find out if there's been any sighting of Andrev."

Yakov undid the top buttons of his tunic, then cracked open the carriage window and a rush of cool air blew in. "Pour me a drink. Help yourself."

Zoba went to the cabinet and poured vodka into a pair of tumblers. He handed one to Yakov and bleakly raised his own. "Here's to a quick death. If we're lucky, that's what we can expect, Leonid."

"How is she?"

"Confined in one of the carriages, as you instructed. The child's asleep. Why do it? Why take them with us? Why risk our necks by defying Trotsky's orders?"

Yakov nodded at the envelope on the desk. "I've put it in writing that my decision was mine alone. If anything goes wrong, you're covered."

"We will be when this is over. We'll be six feet under."

Yakov swallowed his drink and grimaced. "Bring Nina here."

■　■　■

Andrev drove into the outskirts of a desolate-looking village, the motorcycle engine throbbing in the darkness.

The place didn't look like much, an unpaved main road with some abandoned-looking buildings either side. The remains of a railway station were riddled with bullet holes.

"Where are we?"

Andrev halted and pulled up his goggles "It's a village near Kovrov, almost two hundred miles from Moscow. There's a minor rail track into the village to serve the local mines, but they've been closed since the war." He slapped the gas tank and heard a hollow echo. "If we don't find more gasoline soon we're in trouble."

"And you think we'll find it *here*?"

"There's a military depot around here somewhere, if I'm not mistaken. It used to serve the transports heading east." He nudged the motorcycle round a corner. "That's what we're looking for."

Across the street was a military garage dimly lit by the motorcycle headlight, a half-dozen trucks and private vehicles trucks parked outside. Two more trucks were inside a big workshop, the doors open wide. One truck had its wheels up on wooden blocks, half a dozen soldiers working away, the workshop lit by kerosene lamps.

Lydia said, "They're the first troops we've seen for the last two hours."

"The Red Army's stretched a bit thin once you leave Moscow. They're a ragged bunch. Take a look at their uniforms."

Lydia saw that some of the soldiers wore full field-gray uniforms and carried rifles and grenades on their belts. Others wore partial uniforms mixed with scruffy civilian garb. They were a tough-looking lot, in need of a wash.

"They look like bad luck. Is this really wise, Uri?"

He loosened his holster flap. "We need more fuel. Where else are we going to get it?"

He revved the engine and drove over toward the garage forecourt, halting by a village water pump. The soldiers stopped working, all eyes suddenly on their visitors. Andrev climbed off. "Who's in charge here, comrades?"

The men looked wary of Andrev's leather jacket. An older man said, "How can we help?"

Andrev produced his letter. "Commissar Couris. I'm acting as a special courier for the Kremlin. I'm heading east and need fuel."

The man shrugged. "There's not much of that here. We barely have enough for ourselves."

"I'd suggest you find some." Andrev handed the man the letter.

He studied it, scratching his jaw, then turned to address the others. "It looks official, signed by Lenin himself, no less. It says that the commissar's to be assisted in every way possible. Anyone who hinders him will be shot."

Andrev said, "I'd appreciate it if you could find that fuel, comrade."

"Not so fast."

Andrev turned as a giant of a man with thick eyebrows and a bushy beard appeared behind him. His beard was flecked with food, as if he'd been interrupted eating supper. "Let me see that letter."

Andrev handed it over.

He read the page, then regarded Lydia, before he said, "It seems to be in order, right enough. Better give the commissar the fuel he needs."

"Thank you, comrade." Andrev removed the gas tank cap.

One of the soldiers came forward with a gasoline can, and the man with the mustache said, "Do you need lodgings for the night, comrade?"

"No thanks, we'll press on."

"Who's the woman?"

"My wife."

He grinned, stroking his grubby beard. "Nice-looking wench, I'll give her that."

Andrev sensed trouble and reached for his gun but the man's hand came up grasping a pistol. "Fingers off the gun or you'll lose your head."

Lydia went to reach for a Nagant on the sidecar floor, but soldiers rushed forward and grabbed her arms, dragging her from the motorcycle, wrenching the weapon from her. She kicked and fought but it was useless.

Andrev said, "You're making a mistake interfering with a Cheka officer."

The bearded man took his revolver. "Does it look like I give a fiddler's curse? I spit on Lenin."

"You're not Red Army?"

The man sneered. "Deserters, all of us. The Reds know better than to bother us around here; they have enough on their plate." He stepped closer to Andrev. "And you're Captain Andrev, aren't you?"

Andrev stared back, astounded.

"Meet an old friend of yours."

Before Andrev could reply, a voice said, "It's certainly a small world, captain."

Andrev spun. The unmistakable figure of Sergeant Mersk—with his drooping mustache and wearing his grubby sheepskin hat—stepped out of a room at the back. His *nagaika* whip hung from the Ukrainian's greasy belt and he had a malicious grin on his face, as if he'd been watching the proceedings.

Andrev's heart sank like an anchor.

Mersk spat on the ground, then he grabbed Andrev's letter. "If you're a Cheka officer, then I'm a dancer with the Bolshoi. What are you up to with this, Andrev? The last I heard you were on the run."

Andrev didn't answer.

"I asked you a question, you scumbag." Mersk's fist came up and crashed into Andrev's jaw. He slammed against the truck and slid to the floor. Mersk moved in, lashing out viciously with his boot and stamping on Andrev's neck. "Every dog has its day. I'll teach you to have respect when I ask you a question."

Andrev was choking for breath.

"You and I have unfinished business, I think." He jerked his head at the soldiers and took his boot away. "Tie his hands and watch him closely; he's a slippery customer."

Two soldiers manhandled Andrev. They searched him before they tied his hands together with rope.

Two others grappled with a struggling Lydia, and one of them found the black Mauser.

He tossed it to Mersk, who weighed the gun in his palm.

"Plucky, aren't you? Let's see if I can turn you two into a profit. What do you think might happen if I cabled the nearest Red barracks with a message for Commissar Yakov, telling him I have you?"

He slipped the Mauser into his jacket pocket and grinned at Andrev. "Business first. I'll send the cable. Then I'm going to have some fun with this wench of yours before the Reds get their hands on her."

79

The carriage door opened and Zoba led in Nina. She wore a shawl about her shoulders, her hair tied back. Zoba slipped out, silently closing the door. She regarded Yakov silently.

"How is Sergey?" he asked.

"He's sleeping but his chest is worse. I'm worried his lungs might hemorrhage. It's happened before. He needs to see a doctor."

Yakov saw the heavy strain on her face. Tiredness mixed with anxiety and despair.

"I have a medic on board. He's a qualified doctor. He'll do his best for you, though our medicines are limited."

"What's happened to Uri?"

"He's escaped, that's all I'm certain of right now."

"Why did you take us from Moscow?"

Yakov sighed. "I told you there would be consequences to your actions. I wasn't lying. I was ordered by Lenin to put you on a train bound for a prison camp. Right now, we're headed toward Ekaterinburg. Your situation's quite hopeless."

He saw the pained horror in her eyes. "What kind of man can condemn an innocent child to death for his parents' sins? What kind of man would do that? Sergey's done no wrong. You've sold your soul, Leonid. Sold it, do you hear?"

Yakov fell silent. When he spoke again, he was resolute. "Listen to me, Nina. I didn't put you on the prison transport. I'm disobeying orders to buy time for you to reconsider. It could cost me my life, and my daughter's." He stared into her face. "I may be able to still save you. But do you want to be?" His voice lowered to almost a whisper. "Do you know why Uri came back? If you think it was to save you, you're greatly mistaken. He's here to try to rescue the Romanovs."

"What are you talking about?"

"It's true. Half the Red Army is on the lookout for him and the woman he's with."

"What woman?"

"We haven't identified her yet, but when we do, you don't want to share their fate. You don't want to condemn your son to death. You owe it to him to survive, Nina, not end your days in a frozen grave in some godforsaken Siberian wasteland."

He paused. "You have to help me to find Uri, convince him of the folly of his mission, and get him to betray his fellow conspirators. It won't save him, but it may save you and your son. This is your last chance. When we reach Ekaterinburg tomorrow you'll be transferred by train to the prison camp and there will be nothing more I can do for you."

For a long time Nina said nothing, simply stared at him. When she spoke, her voice was strangely distant. "Did you mean it when you said you loved me?"

"Of course."

She slowly unbuttoned the neck of her dress, exposing the soft rise of her breasts. There was a deadness in her voice. "Is this what you want, Leonid? Is this what you desire? Well, you can have me, anything to save Sergey. But don't ask me to betray the father he loves."

She held his stare. Yakov saw tears fill the corners of her eyes. She broke down sobbing. He pulled her close. This time she didn't resist, as if all the fight was gone out of her, and they stood there, both of them silent, until Nina finally pulled away, wiping her eyes.

Yakov reached out and gently buttoned her dress.

She looked up at him, her watery brown eyes meeting his.

He said, "You don't know how long I've waited for a moment like this. How I've ached for it. But this isn't the time."

"I'll do whatever it takes to save Sergey."

"Then I'll ask you one last time—help me."

80

Yakov splashed water on his face in his bedchamber.

He looked at himself in the mirror and saw the desolation in his eyes.

The door opened and Zoba stepped in to join him. "I took her back to her cabin. How did it go?"

Yakov dried his face with a towel and tossed it on the bed. "She hasn't agreed to anything yet. I'm working on it."

"I take it there's definitely no hope if she refuses?"

Yakov said bleakly, "Not a shred."

The carriage shuddered with a squeal of brakes as the train slowed. Yakov peered out the window and saw a station up ahead. "Why are we halting?"

"To take on more fuel."

"Find the cable office. See if there's any news from Moscow."

Yakov remained by the window, staring at his reflection, tension around his mouth.

Nina's accusation echoed in his mind. "What kind of man can condemn an innocent child to death for his parents' sins? What kind of man would do that?"

He stared back at his reflection in the window. "Well? What do you say?"

Was she right? Had he sold his soul? He *had* changed. The passing years and the revolution had hardened his heart. But the grim thought of Nina and her child dying in some freezing hellhole of a camp weighed heavily. And one thing remained constant—his love for her. Even if she spurned him, he couldn't ignore his feelings.

He gave a hopeless sigh and turned from the window. Some instinct made him open his desk drawer and he removed the framed photograph he'd once cherished, taken at the St. Petersburg fair: of him and his mother and Stanislas and Uri Andrev and his father.

Ever since Stanislas's death he couldn't bear to look at it. But now he stood the frame on his desk. His mouth grim, he studied the image. The sight of Andrev enraged him. He swept the photograph from the desk with an angry blow.

It crashed against the wall, the glass splintering, and then he knelt and tore the photograph from the shattered frame. He ripped Andrev's image from the snapshot, crushed it in a ball in his hands, and tossed it on the floor, grinding it with the heel of his boot. All control gone, he kicked at the remains of the frame and they smashed against the corner wall.

He strode into the cramped stationmaster's office, where a couple of signal clerks were busy with paperwork behind a desk. He found Zoba reading a cable.

"Well?" Yakov demanded.

"Good news mostly, just a touch of bad. More like an inconvenience."

"Out with it. I don't have the patience."

"It's all happening—Kazan's apprehended the Phantom."

"How? Where?"

"In a tunnel near the Ipatiev House. He's under guard at the Amerika Hotel. We'll find out more in Ekaterinburg. I'll bet Kazan will be Lenin's sweetheart after this."

"We *have* to find Andrev."

Zoba said, "There's more good news. He's been caught, along with the woman."

"What?"

"The cable just came through. The bad part is they were seized by a gang of brigands and deserters." Zoba slapped a palm on a rail map on the station wall. "They're here. A village near Kovrov. The brigands cabled our nearest garrison, forty miles away, and asked that the message be passed on to you personally as a matter of urgency."

"*Me?* Who are these people?"

"Bandits and cutthroats most of them. A law unto themselves who steal, rape, and terrorize."

"Why ask for me in particular?"

"One of them is our old friend Sergeant Mersk."

"Mersk?"

"A bad penny always turns up again. He deserted, remember?" Zoba tapped the map. "There's a minor rail line that passes through the village, if it hasn't been blown up or sabotaged."

"How far?"

"Less than two hours should do it. One other thing."

"What?"

"Mersk's cable says he'd consider it an honor to kill Andrev for you. But if you want to take custody of the prisoners, his comrades are demanding a ransom of ten thousand rubles."

"Whatever it is, we'll pay."

81

The Amerika Hotel was the jewel in the city's crown.

It boasted all modern conveniences—electricity, flushing toilets, bathrooms with hot running water—and not surprisingly was seized by the Bolsheviks for their headquarters.

The luxury first-floor suites were reserved for the Cheka, one flight up from the staff quarters in the basement. There a dozen rooms were transformed into detention cells.

Kazan looked pleased with himself as he hurried down the steps that early morning, rapping his knuckle-duster against his leg. He approached a heavily padlocked metal gate. Two guards snapped to attention, and one of them inserted a key in the lock.

"Well? Has the quack arrived?" Kazan demanded.

"He's with the prisoner now."

"Perfect. Remember, no one gets past the gate unless they're authorized by me. Disobey and you'll get a bullet."

The cell had once been a staff bedroom, but now the window was barred.

Sorg lay unconscious on a metal gurney, a tattered white sheet pulled up to his neck. His jaw was bruised and heavily swollen.

A thin, anxious man wearing a frayed dark suit flecked with cigarette ash stood over the prisoner, a black doctor's bag open by his side. Fear ignited in his face the moment Kazan appeared. The milky-eyed inspector chilled his blood.

"Has he come to yet?" Kazan demanded.

"Briefly, but he lapsed back into unconsciousness. His jaw doesn't appear to have been fractured or broken, but you must have hit him hard."

Kazan pulled back the sheet. Sorg was naked above the waist and strapped down with leather restraints. His wound was freshly bandaged. "Can't you force him to come round?"

"With strong ammonia salts, perhaps. I wouldn't recommend slapping him in case there's internal cranial bleeding."

The doctor felt Sorg's pulse.

Kazan pinched Sorg's forehead between his thumb and forefinger. "This swine almost cost me my life. Do whatever you must to get him conscious."

Outside, the sound of footsteps clattered down the stairs.

Kazan snapped his fingers at the doctor. "I'm expecting company. Get out. Wait for me in the lobby."

The terrified doctor scurried out and the Ipatiev House *komendant*, Yurovsky, appeared.

He regarded Sorg with interest. "So, this is the spy? You think he'll be fit to talk?"

"He better, or the doctor's life won't be worth living."

Yurovsky looked in high form as he lit a cigarette. "I have excellent news. The couple have been caught."

"What?"

"Commissar Yakov is on his way to take them into custody. You don't exactly look brimming with joy, Inspector. Do I detect a touch of rivalry between you two?"

Kazan snorted and looked down at Sorg. "Think what you want. One thing is clear: this wasn't a one-man operation. Our friend here must have had help. Which is why I'm having every guard on checkpoint duty last night questioned, in case they saw anyone."

"But hundreds of guards were on duty. Besides, most of them are being moved back and forth to the front all the time."

"We'll question who we can. You saw the tunnel?"

Yurovsky nodded. "This city's full of them, They're like spiderwebs, going back to when Ekaterinburg was designed as a fortress. I didn't know about the passageway you found. But we've thoroughly searched it and it's empty, as are all the others."

"And they better remain that way."

"We've locked the doors again and arranged for guards to be posted at every tunnel entrance."

Kazan smirked. "A word of advice. It might be wise not to mention the tunnel when you're making your report to Moscow. As *komendant*, it could seem like a failure of your duty."

Yurovsky flushed at the reprimand, crushed his cigarette, and went to go.

Kazan said, "Where are you off to?"

"To inspect the woods I've chosen for the disposal of the Romanovs' bodies."

Kazan grinned. "Why don't I join you? I could do with some fresh air. By the time we get back our spy ought to be ready for interrogation."

82

"*How?* How could you be so reckless?"

Sister Agnes's temper was in full flow as she faced the undertaker.

Markov anxiously wrung his hands, dark patches under his eyes as if he hadn't slept a wink all night. "It wasn't my fault! I warned him to be careful. I was on my way back to pick him up when I saw troops everywhere, so I cleared off as fast as I could. I waited until curfew ended before I even risked coming here."

They were in Sister Agnes's office, her mood sombre once she heard Markov's news.

His voice was shaky. "What if he squeals on us? The Reds could have him screaming for mercy. We're finished, I tell you. Me, I'm getting out while I can still walk."

As he turned to leave, the nun put a hand on his arm. "Where do you think you're going?"

"To hide with relatives in Perm. My son's already gone ahead—"

She struck him a stinging slap across the face. Markov reeled back, clasping a hand to his jaw, shocked by the nun's ferocity.

"What—what was that for?"

Pious strength bristled in Sister Agnes's voice. "To bring you to your senses. This is a time to put your faith in God, not to panic. Tell me again what you heard."

Markov massaged his jaw. "The Reds delivered the corpse of a curfew-breaker to the mortuary an hour ago. They scared the life out of me when they banged on my door. I almost passed out. I thought they'd come for me."

"Go on."

"They boasted that an enemy spy was caught in a tunnel under the city. A Cheka inspector named Kazan made the arrest. The prisoner was taken to the cells in the Amerika Hotel for interrogation. Apparently, he was knocked unconscious. They had to summon a doctor from the city hospital."

Sister Agnes paced the room in dismay. "I know it looks hopeless, but there must be something we can do."

"The plan's a mess now that we can't use the tunnels. Worse, we're in danger of being betrayed if he talks."

A knock came on the door, and a young novice hurried in.

"There's a man in a uniform waiting for you in the chapel, Sister. He banged on the church door, asking for you."

Sister Agnes was immediately on guard. "Who is he?"

"I don't know. But he has the look of the military about him. He demanded to speak with you personally."

Markov began trembling. "I told you we were finished. What's the betting that the Reds have the place surrounded?"

Sister Agnes addressed the novice. "Did you see any army vehicles out in the street? Any troops?"

"I didn't look, Sister. Should I?"

"No, don't do it now, that might draw attention." Sister Agnes made the sign of the cross, then pushed Markov toward the door, her voice firm as she instructed the novice, "Take him down to the basement and keep him there. I'll try to deal with the military."

Sister Agnes bustled into the chapel, her black habit flapping about her legs.

Slim, ruby-red candles flickered in the dimness, and a powerful sense of peace suffused the chapel. In contrast, her heart was beating wildly.

The moment she saw the man standing near the entrance door she feared for her life. He was about fifty, a tough-looking specimen, his face unshaven, and he wore a dark uniform jacket and polished knee boots.

Sister Agnes approached him, her anxiety mounting with every step. "I . . . I'm Sister Agnes. I believe you wish to see me?"

The man's piercing eyes studied her, then he turned and rapped a knuckle on the back of the door, indicating a reverse swastika chalk mark. He stared back at her silently.

Sister Agnes's heart stuttered. She felt racked by terror, her mind completely addled. *Has the spy talked?* Was the man challenging her, trying to find out what she knew?

"You didn't answer my mark. It's been there since yesterday evening."

The man spoke in perfect English.

She stared back at him, realization dawning, and she felt a surge of relief.

He said, "You're supposed to ask: 'Are you lost? Do you need help?' Then I'm to say, 'I need to get to Market Street.'"

"Forgive me, my son. I . . . I've been distracted. It's been a difficult morning."

The man held out his hand. He wore a silver ring on his finger, and it bore a reverse swastika. He smiled with considerable charm. "I believe you're expecting me. The name's Joe Boyle."

83

The open-topped Opel bumped over the forest road. The Siberian night sky was an aching blue, stars bright, the light almost as pale as day.

Kazan wiped his nose with a handkerchief, his nostrils assaulted by the scent of pine sap drenching the air. "Where exactly are we?"

The *komendant* sat next to him in the backseat. "A disused ore-mining area called the Four Brothers. Countless abandoned mine shafts dot this part of the forest."

The Opel turned onto a muddy track, and when the driver finally halted, the *komendant* climbed out and marched deeper into the woods.

Kazan followed, the driver and another guard moving ahead of him, each carrying a lit lantern.

"Any reason you picked this place?" Kazan asked.

The *komendant* plunged ahead, deadwood crackling under their feet. "It's remote, so no one ought to bother us. Once we dispose of the bodies in one of the mine shafts, they won't easily be found."

"And the execution?"

"I'll pick a squad of eleven men, one to kill each victim—the entire family, the cook and two servants, and Dr. Bodkin. We'll liquidate them at the Ipatiev House. Then transport the bodies here by truck."

"So, the children, too?"

The *komendant* nodded. "All except the kitchen boy. He's a child, and it's been decided we'll send him out of the city and spare his life.

It's a grisly business but I don't want it descending into a disorganized bloodbath and the girls being raped. I've heard whispers that some of the guards may be tempted."

Kazan seemed amused. "Does it really matter at this stage?"

"I won't stand for any disobedience."

"Where will it happen?"

"We'll use the room where you interrogated the girl. It's small but the walls on one side are solid rock, part of the natural hillside. They're covered in plaster so they'll mask the noise of the shooting, and ought to absorb any ricochets. I'll also have a truck engine running to conceal the gunfire."

Kazan grunted. "It seems you've thought of everything."

They came to a clearing in the woods.

The *komendant* held up a lamp. Yards away in the middle of the clearing yawned the gaping mouth of an abandoned mine shaft, timber logs lining the sides. "This is where we'll bury the bloodsucking royalty."

Kazan stared down into the shaft, the bottom filled with brown, peaty water. The *komendant* said, "We'll light a funeral pyre and burn them after they've been stripped, and remove any valuables hidden in their clothing. We've got quantities of gasoline, sulfuric acid, and firewood organized, which ought to speed up the process. We'll leave no remains."

"And once it's done?"

"We'll shovel the ashes down the shaft."

Kazan turned slowly in a circle, examining the site. He dabbed his nose with his handkerchief, the pine scent still overpowering. "When?"

"After midnight tonight."

84

Boyle slumped into a chair, his expression sober. "It's not looking good, is it?"

Sister Agnes paced her office.

Markov, in his crumpled undertaker's suit, nervously cracked his knuckles. "That's what I told the sister," he fretted. "If it was up to me, I'd be getting my backside out of town fast. It's only a matter of time before the Reds come knocking, and then there'll be murder to pay."

The nun stopped pacing and regarded Boyle. "Is it really as hopeless as it seems?"

"Honest? It sounds like a complete mess."

"We expected you days ago."

Boyle rose, full of nervous energy. "The trains were delayed everywhere. I had to travel via the Ukraine, which didn't help."

"Can I get you anything? Food, refreshment?"

Boyle nodded to the samovar in the corner. "I wouldn't say no to some tea. And a hot bath wouldn't go amiss."

As Sister Agnes poured steaming hot tea from the samovar, Boyle ran a hand over his face and said to Markov, "Why? Why did the bloody fool have to go exploring the tunnel and put us all in jeopardy?"

Markov shook his head. "Only he can answer that question."

The nun said, "He seemed most interested to know about Princess Anastasia."

"Why her?"

"Heaven knows. But I found out which doctor Kazan's using—I know him, he's worked at our hospital—and called his home. His wife said her husband's still at the hotel."

Markov said, "What about the other couple we were expecting?"

Boyle said, "I wish I knew. For now our concern is if the Cheka makes our man talk. It may not be safe for any of us."

The nun said, "That's why I thought it better if you don't stay in the convent."

"Where else have you got in mind?"

"Markov has premises about a mile from here—you can stay there for now, but you both may have to move elsewhere. Go bring your carriage round."

Markov tipped his forehead as he left. "Yes, Sister."

She said to Boyle, "I'll find a dark suit for you, and Markov can take some more bodies from the basement while he's here. At least it'll look as if you'll be going about your rightful business if you're stopped."

"Bodies?"

"Our hospital's full of them. I'm afraid the Reds are killing all round them these days. Now, let me see about that suit."

It was very still in the chapel when Boyle went in. The gilded icon of Our Lady and Child seemed to float above the candles, the beautiful Byzantine faces eternally peaceful. His footsteps echoed on the cool flagstones between the pillars as he walked down to the entrance door.

He rubbed out the chalked swastika with his coat sleeve.

As he turned back toward the altar, he felt a heaviness in his chest, a kind of despair that was almost crushing, and he did something he hadn't done in years: he knelt in one of the pews, his hands joined, his head bowed, not praying, but trying to dissipate his frustration in the peace all around him.

As he knelt there, after a while he heard footsteps and saw Sister Agnes approach. "One of the nuns is fetching you clothes; she won't be long. Did I disturb your praying?"

Boyle looked miles away and shook his head, as if to stir himself from a trance. "I've heard it said that prayer is sometimes listening to yourself. If that's the case, then maybe mine have been answered."

"Pardon?"

"I have an idea. It's risky, and desperate, but if it works we may still be able to liberate our man before he talks."

"I'm listening."

"Markov and I bluff our way into the hotel with some false papers and claim custody of the prisoner." He saw the nun looked horrified. "Not impressed?"

"The hotel's swarming with Cheka; it's their headquarters. And trying to get their prize prisoner out would be impossible. Who knows what state he's in."

Boyle removed a Colt .45 pistol from his pocket, slid out the magazine, and made sure it was fully loaded. He slammed it home again. "Then we may have only one other option if we're to keep his lips sealed."

"And what's that?"

"We kill him."

85

Mersk dragged Lydia by the arm across a yard.

The stinking cluster of outbuildings at the back of the garage looked as if they had once been part of a farm, complete with a barn and milking sheds.

Mersk laughed. "Now it's time to have a little fun. Don't think your friend Andrev will avoid his due. Yakov can have him, but not before I have my pound of flesh."

Two armed guards followed closely. Lydia tried to struggle free but Mersk wrenched her back, grinning. "You've got spark, I'll give you that. Which ought to make this all the more interesting."

His fingers groped at the hem of her skirt and Lydia struggled to keep him away. "You animal!"

Mersk laughed, grabbing her savagely by the hair. "We can do this the hard way or the easy way. But either way, you're going to give me what I want."

Lydia continued to struggle, Mersk's grip tightening like a vise. She cried out.

He seemed to take delight in her pain. "After I've taken my pleasure, the men here will want to have theirs. So I hope you're fit, woman."

He opened the door to one of the barns. A Fiat truck was parked off to one side, and on the back was mounted a Maxim gun with an armor-plated surround.

A stench of cow dung wafted out of the barn, a couple of ladders rising to lofts on either side, hay stacked all around. Lying on one of the hay bales was a pair of scruffy boots and some filthy-looking clothes.

"My quarters," Mersk announced, and with his free hand he went to unbuckle his trousers. "I'm going to enjoy this."

Lydia wrenched free and ran across the barn, past the Fiat truck. One of the guards went to raise his rifle but Mersk pushed the man away. "Leave her. Get out, both of you. I'll call you when it's your turn."

The men left and Mersk watched, amused, as Lydia tried desperately to climb one of the loft ladders. She was halfway up when he walked over, grabbed the ladder, and yanked it. Lydia fell through the air and landed in the hay with a groan. Mersk grabbed a handful of her hair.

Lydia kicked furiously. "Let go of me!"

"You don't know when to stop, do you?" Mersk dragged her to her feet, pulling her close. "Keep this up and you might get hurt badly."

His stale breath stank of alcohol, and he began groping again at her skirt.

This time Lydia leaned down and bit his wrist savagely. He screamed in pain, releasing his grip, but grabbed at her with his other hand as she turned, her skirt ripping, revealing her underwear and bare legs. She ran for the other loft ladder.

Mersk gave a cry of rage and ran after her.

Yakov swayed as he moved through the carriages, the engine powering through the night. When he reached Nina's carriage, Zoba was outside, smoking a cigarette.

"How is she?"

"Sleeping. The child, too." Zoba tossed his finished cigarette with his boot.

Yakov peered in through the bare glass of the sleeper cabin, the blinds up. Nina and her son lay asleep on the lower cot; she had one hand under her head, the other protectively around her son.

Zoba said, "We're making good time. We'll be there soon. Do you think it's wise to trust these bandits, Leonid?"

"We'll scout the town first, on horseback, to make sure we're not walking into a trap. Have the horses made ready."

"How do you want to handle it?"

From his pocket, Yakov took a Trans-Siberian Railway route map and held it under the flickering carriage light. "We'll halt here, about half a mile from the village. Take a dozen men and enter on horseback. I'll wait for your signal that it's safe to proceed."

"What's the routine?"

Yakov handed over a green canvas pouch containing a British Verey flare gun and flares. "Just like the trenches. A green flare means we're to come as fast as we can. A red signals danger and we're to advance with caution. Two reds and we retreat. Prepare the men."

"What about the ransom? We haven't got ten thousand rubles to pay."

"No, but we've got supplies. I'm betting these bandits will negotiate."

Zoba went to go.

Yakov gripped his arm, held him with a stare. "Andrev is mine. Make sure the men know that."

86

Andrev was shoved across a barnyard toward a cluster of wooden out-buildings crammed with milking stalls. The place stank of manure. The guards forced him inside one of the stalls and locked the half door with a slide bolt.

One of them laughed as he stoked the charcoal embers of a samo-var. It lay on top of a tin drum in a corner rest area, a couple of coarse gray blankets tossed on top of some loose straw. "I'd start saying your prayers if I was you. There's nowhere to run in that stall once Mersk goes to work on you."

The second guard pulled up a three-legged wooden stool and sat, his rifle trained on the half door to Andrev's stall. He plucked a vodka bottle from his pocket, swallowed a mouthful, and wiped his mouth with his sleeve. "You were an officer, I hear?"

Andrev nodded. "How about a drink, comrade? Help deaden the pain to come?"

The man put down the bottle and crossed to a zinc bucket. He lifted out a wooden ladle filled with water, and flung the liquid at Andrev, drenching him.

"That's the only drink you'll get from me, you tsarist-commissioned muck," he snorted and tossed the ladle back in the bucket.

Andrev wiped water from his face.

A second later came a woman's scream. He felt a surge of rage.

The guard sat down again and cradled his rifle. "Knowing Mersk he'll take his time, so it'll be a while before we get our share. Likes the ladies, he does. And the bigger the fight in them the more he likes it."

Andrev rattled the stall gate helplessly, his hands bound, his face very white.

The guard smirked. "I'd forget about your lady friend, if I were you. Worry about your own skin. Once Mersk gets done with her and starts on you, you're going to wish he'd put a bullet in you."

In the barn, Lydia reached a few steps up the ladder before Mersk came after her. This time he jerked her ankle and she rolled into the hay.

For a big man, Mersk moved fast and in seconds he was scrambling on top of her. She struggled, but the Ukrainian was stronger, and as he knelt he pinned her arms. He went to kiss her and Lydia screamed.

Mersk laughed madly, then suddenly her face rose up to meet him and she bit him again, this time on the cheek, drawing blood.

Mersk roared with pain, blood streaming from his face, and then he seemed to lose all control, pummeling her head with his fists until she passed out.

Rabid now, like a wild animal, he tore at her clothes.

In the stall, Andrev heard another scream from Lydia, followed by a roar from Mersk. Then everything went terribly silent. His face was deathly, the skin stretched tight over his cheekbones.

He said aloud to the guards, "In my right boot there are three hundred rubles. They're yours for that vodka."

The two guards looked at each other, greedy but still wary.

The one at the samovar finished drawing boiling water into a small kettle he filled with tea and stirred it with a spoon. "Is that a fact? What do you take us for, fools?"

"It's the truth. If Mersk's going to beat me half to death, I may as well be drunk as sober."

The man licked his lips, then put down his tea and picked up his rifle. He said to the other guard. "Get him out here where I can see him. If he tries anything, shoot him."

The guard opened the stall. He kept his rifle trained on Andrev.

"Step out here and remove your right boot."

Andrev stepped out, leaned his back against the stall, and pulled off his leather boot.

"Toss the boot here."

Andrev did so. The first guard rummaged inside and found the wad of money at the bottom. Greed lit his face. "He's telling the bloody truth . . ."

Andrev punched him in the throat and the guard let out a gasp and went down, his face contorted with pain, eyes bulging as he fought for air through his shattered windpipe.

The second guard raised his rifle, but Andrev was already narrowing the distance between them. There was a moment of indecision as the guard panicked, not knowing whether to shoot or use his bayonet.

He thrust with the bayonet.

Andrev sidestepped and grabbed the boiling samovar by the handle. He swung it through the air, the metal smashing into the guard's face, lit charcoal and boiling water spraying his flesh, and he screamed.

Andrev stepped in, one hand going over the man's mouth to kill his scream and the other on his throat.

He twisted. There was a cracking sound as the man's neck snapped. He let go and the body slumped.

The smell of burning filled the air—charcoal from the samovar speckled the hay, and flames started to lick the stable floor.

The other guard was still bent double, gasping for breath. Andrev ignored him, grabbed the dead guard's rifle, and used the bayonet to sever the rope tying his hands. Then he pocketed a grenade tucked into the man's belt and raced out into the yard.

87

When he reached the barn, Lydia appeared unconscious as Mersk knelt over her in the hay, clawing at her underclothes like a frenzied animal.

He turned his head back and stared as Andrev burst in.

"Move away from her before I take your head off."

His voice sounded dangerously calm as he shouldered the rifle.

Mersk's eyes burned with hate. He rose to his feet, dragging Lydia up with him, one arm around her throat, using her as a shield. "Throw down the rifle or I'll snap her neck."

Andrev hesitated, and in an instant the *nagaika* appeared in Mersk's free hand. The whip flicked through the air like a serpent's tongue and coiled around Andrev's neck. Mersk jerked the whip, Andrev lost his balance, and the rifle exploded, kicking up dirt.

Mersk reeled him in, Andrev's eyes wide as he struggled to breathe, the whip choking him.

At the last moment Mersk flung Lydia away and his free hand palmed his Cossack dagger. "It's time you got what that stupid brother of Yakov's got."

His face beamed as he raised the dagger. A distinct *click* sounded.

He didn't see Lydia get to her feet, but he felt her hand slip into his jacket pocket. When he jerked round she was pointing the Mauser at his face, and he knew he had just made the worst mistake of his life.

She said calmly, "If you had even an ounce of human decency, I'd give you time to say your prayers. But an animal like you doesn't deserve that. You can go to the devil."

Mersk twisted his head sharply away just as Lydia squeezed the trigger.

His head snapped back, and the bullet rutted the right side of his skull, scouring flesh, blood everywhere. He reeled back, dazed, letting go of the whip and dagger.

But the moment he regained his balance he was like an angry bear and he moved in for the kill, all reason gone now, his fury seething.

As Andrev tried to struggle free of the whip, fighting for lungfuls of air, Mersk went after Lydia, not giving her a chance to aim the Mauser, his huge hands grabbing at her wildly.

She stumbled, losing her balance, and as the Ukrainian lunged at her Andrev picked up the dagger. "Mersk!"

The Ukrainian turned and Andrev crossed the distance between them fast, using the dagger like a sword, thrusting it deep into Mersk's chest.

The Ukrainian's eyes snapped wide open as he stared down at the blade embedded in his chest. He staggered back against a wooden post and slid to the ground, the life going out of him.

Andrev helped Lydia to her feet. He looked down at Mersk's body. "So much for my only witness."

"It couldn't have ended any other way. Mersk's the kind of wild animal you have to put down." Lydia examined her ripped clothes.

"Did he . . . ?"

"Rape me? No, and I can't even bear thinking about it."

Andrev grabbed a gray blanket lying on the hay and draped it around her shoulders. "That'll have to do until we find you some clothes."

They heard raised voices, Mersk's men roused by the gunshot. "I counted at least nine more men. Any second now they're going to be swarming in here like angry bees."

Sweat beading his face, Andrev tore off Mersk's pistol and ammunition belt. He jumped into the Fiat truck parked on the far side of the barn and checked the Maxim machine gun. He loaded a belt of ammunition and yanked the cocking handle. "Can you drive one of these trucks, assuming it's working?"

"Yes."

He jumped down and grabbed the Fiat's starting handle. "Get in the front. Be ready to back through those wooden gates when I tell you."

"But they're closed."

"They won't be for long."

Andrev moved to the front of the Fiat, grabbed the starting handle, and gave it a couple of turns. The engine ignited just as one the gates leading to the garage tore open and the remainder of Mersk's men appeared.

They opened fire as Andrev ducked for cover behind the Maxim's armor plate. He fired off a sustained burst, the stuttering machine gun cutting down the men and shredding the wooden doors.

Two of the soldiers managed to duck behind the doors and one lobbed a grenade toward the truck.

It erupted like thunder, and in reply Andrev tossed the grenade from his pocket, lobbing it just past the gates. It exploded seconds later, wounding both men. As they staggered out, still firing, he finished them with the Maxim.

He shouted, "Back up now, out through the gates, keep going until I tell you to stop!"

She put the truck in reverse and revved the engine, the Fiat picking up speed. It burst through the shattered wood, out into the garage forecourt and onto the deserted street, where it smashed into a wall.

Andrev remained with the machine gun as he tried to take stock. The blaze was getting worse, spreading everywhere, as ammunition exploded like firecrackers. The timbers in the back of the crashed Fiat were smoldering from the grenade blast and he jumped down. "Time we got away."

They crossed the forecourt and came to the motorcycle and sidecar where they left it, by the water pump.

When he climbed onto the saddle and tried to start the engine, it gave a sputtering cough and died. He tried again but this time the engine didn't even splutter. He dismounted and said in despair, "I'm wasting my time. There's the problem. Probably a ricochet." He indicated a bullet hole drilled into the engine block.

Tight-lipped, he moved out into the middle of the street.

The neighing of a horse carried on the night air. Andrev's gaze settled on the opposite end of the village, near the railway station. "It goes from bad to worse. See what's coming?"

Lydia followed his finger. A hundred yards away she saw shadowy horsemen advance like specters.

Andrev said stone-faced, "Yakov's surrounding the village." He strode back toward the bodies of Mersk's men, sprawled where they had fallen.

All the corpses were bloody, some of the uniforms stained worse than others. He began to remove one of the men's tunics. "Try and cobble together a complete uniform, one in reasonable shape that's near your size. Nothing we can do about the bloodstains, just pick the best you can. And tie back that hair of yours and keep it hidden under a uniform cap."

"Why?"

"We're about to join Yakov's army."

88

As the train idled half a mile from the village, Yakov's instinct told him that something was terribly wrong.

Flames erupted into the night sky as buildings were consumed by fire, the crack of ammunition exploding. Then a green flare exploded, the signal bursting into the sky.

He shouted to one of his men watching from the carriage steps, "Tell the driver to get moving. Everyone remain alert."

The train gathered momentum, and in no time it chugged into the village station, a dismal-looking place pockmarked with bullet holes, every window shattered.

Even before the engine halted, Yakov snapped open the carriage door and jumped down, followed by dozens of troops from the other carriages.

A sober-looking Zoba appeared on the platform, his pistol drawn.

Yakov said, "It looks like bedlam here. Any sign of Andrev?"

"You better see for yourself."

Andrev held on to Lydia's hand as they moved toward the rail track, careful to remain in the shadows.

Half a dozen of Yakov's guards were posted on the platform and along the tracks, but they seemed preoccupied by the village blaze. Andrev moved toward the front of the train and hauled himself aboard a carriage. He gave Lydia the all-clear, she ran to join him, and he held out his hand and pulled her up.

"Are you sure this is wise?" she whispered anxiously.

"We'll soon find out." He turned and softly clicked open the carriage door.

■ ■ ■

As watchful as hunters, Yakov and his men advanced through the village.

It was eerily deserted, and as they approached the military garage, they saw bodies strewn everywhere. "They're all dead," Zoba announced.

The entire village looked ablaze, and on the garage forecourt Yakov saw the shells of burning, fire-damaged trucks, empty gasoline cans strewn about, the heat almost unbearable. They passed a crashed Fiat truck with a Maxim machine gun mounted in the back, spent cartridges everywhere.

A British-made Douglas motorcycle and sidecar was left abandoned near a village water pump, and Zoba kicked at the rear wheel. "Andrev and the woman escaped from Moscow on something similar."

"Have you searched the entire village?"

"We're still checking, building by building. He isn't among the dead. If you ask me, he's been and gone." Zoba jerked his head at the flaming wrecks. "Most likely in a stolen vehicle."

A couple of ammunition rounds cracked like whips, sending ricochets flying, and they ducked instinctively.

"Show me what else you found."

Zoba led him to a barn.

Mersk's body lay slumped against a wooden post. He'd been shot once in the side of the skull and a dagger was planted deep in his chest.

Zoba said, "We counted over ten dead, not a single survivor. Andrev's on form, I'll give him that."

Yakov looked enraged as he tipped Mersk's body with the toe of his boot. "He probably killed Mersk, too. That knife looks personal."

Zoba grunted. "Renegades like these are the scum of the earth. Mersk was hunting with the wrong hounds."

Yakov kicked at a mound of hay, sending straw flying, his face crimson with frustration. Then he turned and strode out of the barn, flames beginning to lick at the timbers, the heat becoming unbearable.

"Where do we go from here?" Zoba asked.

Yakov strode out into the street toward the stationmaster's office. He saw wooden telegraph poles, the cables in place. "Check if the telegraph's still working. I'll need to use it."

"Anything else?"

Yakov said bitterly, "If you've no luck finding Andrev in the village, assemble the men. We're leaving."

"Where to?"

"Ekaterinburg." Yakov angrily punched his balled fist into his open palm. "That's where Andrev will head. That's where we'll find him."

Andrev stepped into a luxurious private carriage.

A samovar bubbled in a corner, charcoal scenting the air, a bottle of vodka and some glasses on a nearby side table. He crossed the polished walnut floor. "Leonid's done well for himself. This thing looks like a fortress on wheels."

"This is *his*?"

Andrev slapped a palm against one of the window's steel-hinged plates, complete with gun ports. "It probably belonged to some duke or prince, but with a few unsociable modifications by the Bolsheviks."

On a walnut desk lay a Trans-Siberian Railway route map, open on a page. Andrev picked it up and studied it.

"What is it?" Lydia asked.

Andrev smiled. "I think we could be in luck."

"I'd love to know exactly what's going through your mind."

"When I'm sure, I'll let you know."

Lydia noticed a crumpled photograph frame discarded in a corner, the glass completely shattered. A curled-up ball of photographic paper lay nearby. She opened it, studied the faces, Andrev easily recognizable as a child. "Does this bring back memories?"

He took the photograph, his mouth tightening. "It certainly does."

"I have the distinct impression Yakov isn't a happy man. What have you got in mind, Uri?"

He crumpled the photograph and replaced it exactly where Lydia found it, and a sudden spark in his eyes seemed to enliven him. "I'm working on it."

"You know what frightens me? The worse the danger, the more you come alive."

He offered her a smile. "I know. Troubling, isn't it?"

"Are you going to tell me what you intend?"

"We wait."

"For what?"

"Yakov."

"Are you insane?"

Andrev crossed to a door, opened it warily. A bedchamber lay beyond, furnished with a simple soldier's cot, gray blankets folded neatly on top. "We'll wait in here for now."

"And when Yakov appears?"

"A difficult thing for you Irish, but leave the talking to me."

89

AMERIKA HOTEL
EKATERINBURG

Kazan's footsteps clattered down the basement steps. The guards admitted him through the iron gate, and when he entered the cell a bitter stench of ammonia drenched the air.

The doctor was busy with the smelling salts, sweat on his brow as he wafted the open bottle under the prisoner's nose. He stopped what he was doing and looked up, distinctly uncomfortable once he saw Kazan.

"Well?" The Inspector's mouth was tight with impatience.

"He's stirred a few times. But I have to be careful not to overdo the ammonia. Too much could damage his lungs."

"How long before I can start work on him?"

"Difficult to say. But I'll need a little time to get him stable once he awakens."

Kazan grunted. "I'll be back."

As Yakov's train thundered through the night, the carriage rocking side to side, he poured vodka into a glass.

As he replaced the cork in the bottle, he stared at his reflection in the carriage window. He looked haggard, his eyes dark, tiredness wearing him down.

Seething with frustration, he went to take a drink. As it touched his lips he changed his mind and flung the glass against the wall. It shattered just as Zoba knocked and entered.

"Well for some, throwing it away. You don't look happy."

"Should I be? We lost him again. Lenin's wrath will be unforgiving."

"We can still finish this thing, Leonid. You sent the cable?"

Yakov nodded and rubbed his eyes. "Every stationmaster from here to Ekaterinburg will know to keep the rail lines open, or risk being shot. With any luck, we ought to get there by this afternoon. Check on our prisoners. Make sure they're all right."

Zoba paused at the door, then stared back at an exhausted Yakov. "Can I give you some well-meaning advice? You've hardly slept in two days. Try to get some rest or you'll collapse."

As the door closed, Yakov unbuttoned the top of his tunic and wandered into his bedchamber, overcome by fatigue.

As he entered he heard the soft click of a firearm being cocked.

His heart chilled.

"Don't move or make a sound, Leonid."

Andrev stepped out from behind the door, a gun in his hand. "Take his weapon and tie him up."

The woman appeared and removed the pistol from Yakov's holster. She tied his hands behind his back with a leather belt, then pushed him into the chair by the bed. Andrev took the bedsheet and used it to tie him to the chair.

Yakov said vehemently, "You're dead. You must know that?"

"It comes to us all. But a little gratitude might be in order, considering that I didn't kill you just now."

"Like you killed Mersk?"

"He deserved it. Mersk killed Stanislas in cold blood. He's paid the price."

"Why don't I believe you?"

"Because that's always been your problem, Leonid. You'll only believe what you want to believe."

"I know what you intend. But it won't work. You haven't a chance. The odds are stacked against you."

Andrev arched his eyebrows. "Don't dismiss me just yet. Where are Nina and Sergey?"

"Safe and unharmed. Whether they stay that way depends on you."

Andrev's expression darkened, in fury. "Like that, is it? My threat stands. Harm them and I'll tear your heart out."

"It's Lenin, he gives the orders."

"And you follow blindly, even if it means harming women and children?"

"I'd never willingly harm Nina or Sergey."

"Why do I suddenly find that hard to believe?" Grim-faced, Andrev checked the Trans-Siberian Railway map. "This is quite a machine you've got. But machines can always go wrong, can't they?"

Yakov said in frustration, "What are you scheming? You're playing with fire. The train's full of my men."

Andrev slipped the map in his pocket and opened the door at the far end of the bedroom. "You'll know soon enough. I'll be back. You and I aren't finished yet."

A ferocious clatter of metal wheels screamed into the room from the unseen engine. A coal wagon lay beyond, a rush of white steam flurrying overhead the train, the air thick with the smell and heat of burning coal.

Andrev moved toward the tender and said to Lydia, "If he tries to escape, shoot him." He fixed Yakov with a stare. "She's an excellent shot. Do yourself a favor and behave, Leonid."

Seven carriages away, Zoba halted outside the compartment.

Two guards stepped away, giving him privacy. Zoba stared in through the glass, the compartment lit by an oil lamp.

Nina sat on the lower sleeping bunk next to the window, holding her son as the medic examined Sergey's chest with a stethoscope.

Every now and then the child gave a wheezing cough and his mother looked fraught with worry.

When the medic finished his examination he spoke briefly with her, then he stepped out into the carriage hallway while Nina remained, rocking her child in her arms.

Zoba put a hand on the medic's arm as he slid shut the door. "Any change?"

The medic was a rake-thin, twitchy man with a nervous blink. He stuffed his stethoscope in his pocket and guided Zoba farther along the corridor.

"For the worst, I'm afraid. His temperature's raging. His lungs are severely congested. If you ask me, it's TB. I'm certain he's had it awhile."

"Is there anything we can do?"

"A trip to a decent Swiss sanatorium would help."

"Don't be smart."

"I wasn't. The boy needs to be in the hospital." The medic took a packet of cigarettes from his pocket, lit one, and blew smoke. "As I'm forever telling Yakov, I'd give my right arm to leave this country. There's nothing but sickness and despair."

Zoba craned his neck to see Nina by the light of the oil lamp, as she patted her son's brow with a damp cloth.

The medic shook his head. "Pitiful, isn't it? How long before we reach Ekaterinburg?"

"Why?"

"If we're delayed, I fear for the child's life."

90

Andrev scrambled over the fuel tender toward the engine cabin, trying to avoid the plume of hot smoke overhead.

The engine driver and his young boiler man had their backs to him, busy shoveling fuel into the raging furnace.

"Shut that furnace, gentlemen, and drop those shovels." Andrev eased himself down to join them, raising his voice above the clatter of the engine wheels. "Do anything more than that and you risk a bullet."

Terror lit the men's faces when they saw the gun. They shut the furnace door with their shovels before tossing them on the floor pan.

"Good. Stay sensible and everyone ought to come out of this still breathing."

Andrev gestured with the gun to the engine's array of steam indicators and valves. "First, you're going to show me how this thing works. Then you're going to do exactly as I tell you."

In the bedchamber, Yakov looked close to having a fit, his face crimson as he stared at Lydia.

"Who are you?"

"Why don't we keep you in suspense?"

"Listen to me: this can have only one outcome—your deaths. Why not save yourself? You have my word you'll be spared."

"If you want to keep your kneecaps, I'd keep my mouth shut if I were you."

The door near the coal tender burst open and Andrev came back. In his blackened hands he carried a sledgehammer and a long, thick steel rod. With him was the boiler man, a nervous beanpole of a young man with a coal-dirt face and soot-blackened clothes.

"Meet Pavel, the train driver's son. He's going to be my helper."

Pavel was quaking as he wrung his cap in his hands. "He threatened to kill me and my father, Commissar. We . . . we had no choice."

"What are you up to, Andrev?" Yakov raged.

Andrev held up the Trans-Siberian Railway map. "Have you any idea where we are? About three miles from the Menski Tunnel. It seems there's a station crossing just before the tunnel, and it has a siding—a parallel track that veers off to a mining depot after a mile or so. The perfect opportunity for us to part company."

Yakov's face stiffened as he suddenly realized what was happening.

The train began to slow a little, and Andrev nodded to the boiler man. "You may as well tell him, Pavel."

The young man anxiously licked his lips and nodded past the bedchamber door, toward the far end of the carriage. "He wants me to separate the rest of the train from the engine and your carriage."

Andrev explained: "We'll shunt the other carriages onto the track that runs alongside. It has a downward slope so they ought to keep moving for a distance. With any luck you'll be stranded there while we travel on."

Yakov was beside himself with frustration, struggling desperately to get out of the chair. "No . . . you can't! You don't know what you're doing."

Andrev grabbed a towel from the washbasin, put a hand on Yakov's shoulder, and pushed him back down. "Don't I?"

"No, you don't understand—"

Andrev gagged Yakov's mouth, tying the towel around it, as he continued to struggle, muttering behind the gag. "I understand all I need to, Leonid. And now I've heard enough."

He nodded to Lydia. "The same rule applies. Shoot him if he tries to escape."

The engine's air brakes hissed, and the engine slowed almost to a trot.

Andrev jerked his gun at Pavel. "All right, let's get this over with. Take the sledgehammer and the steel bar."

Pavel hefted them both and moved to the door. Andrev readied his weapon as Pavel opened the door to the passageway beyond the carriage. It was deserted. "Get to work," Andrev ordered.

Pavel used the steel bar as a jimmy, unhooking the safety linkage, then he went at it with the hammer, knocking out the iron tie that bound the wagons together. The tie separated and clattered away under the tracks, hanging on a metal chain, as the engine and Yakov's wagon started pulling ahead of the other carriages.

Pavel peered out. "The points are coming up."

Andrev grabbed the bar from him and indicated the carriage steps leading down. "Off you go, I'm right behind you."

Pavel jumped down, running ahead of the slow-moving train, the engine hissing. Andrev followed and they reached a set of points.

With Pavel's help he inserted the bar into the points switch. When the engine and carriage passed them, they changed over the points.

Andrev removed the bar and they raced after Yakov's carriage and struggled aboard.

They watched as the remaining carriages shunted onto the parallel line, then began picking up momentum on the downward slope.

Troops began to stare from their carriage windows. A few scratched their heads, wondering what was going on, seeing the engine and carriage on the other line.

Andrev said to Lydia, "Any moment now someone's going to realize what's happening and start shooting. Close the shutters just in case."

Lydia began to slam them shut.

Yakov was still struggling in the chair, eyes bulging and face crimson, as if he were having a seizure.

"Time for us to part company, Leonid."

In her compartment, Nina watched Sergey with growing dread. His breathing was shallow, his voice rasping, his coughing harsher with every passing minute.

Fraught with worry, she dabbed his sweat-beaded face with a cloth.

"Mama, it hurts . . ."

"I know, my love. We're trying to get you to a hospital soon."

"But it hurts *really* bad, Mama—" Sergey began coughing again, a terrible hacking sound that shook his entire body.

Her distress was beyond agony. One hand clutched Sergey's fingers; her other wrung the cloth in the basin of cold water by her side, as she tried to cool his fevered brow. "It'll be all right, my love. Mama's here. Try to rest, Sergey. Try to—"

Her attention was caught briefly by a surprise movement beyond the window—another train slid slowly past her carriage on an adjoining track.

She paid it only the briefest attention because at that moment Sergey began to cough violently, and then to her horror she saw he was coughing up blood, crimson spewing onto his chest.

She stifled her scream with her hand so as not to frighten him, but then she jumped to her feet. As she yanked open the door in wild panic, the guards came alert, stared back at her. "Find the medic— please—my son needs help urgently . . ."

With Yakov still seated, Andrev yanked round the chair. He dragged it out through the bedchamber and into the carriage office. He halted by the exit door. "This is where we say our good-byes."

Yakov resisted, muttering incoherently behind the gag, the veins on his neck bulging.

Andrev released the sheet that bound him to the chair but he left the gag in place and his hands tied. He yanked out his pistol, hauled Yakov to his feet, spun him toward the door, and opened it. A flight of metal steps descended, the tracks rushing away beneath.

"The tunnel's coming up soon. Get moving." Andrev yanked him by the scruff of his neck. "Ease yourself backward down the steps, unless you want to lose a leg in the fall."

Yakov didn't budge. The carriages with his men were already slowing to a walking pace, troops peering from the windows in curiosity, others coming out onto carriage steps, fingering their rifles, unsure what to do as they stared in utter confusion at the sight of the engine, coal tender, and Yakov's carriage chugging away separately.

Andrev said, "Get off now, before I change my mind."

The engine shuddered, then began to pick up speed.

Andrev forced Yakov at gunpoint to back down the steps, the tracks speeding away beneath him. "Now jump, before it's too late."

Andrev went to kick him away with his boot but even with his bound hands Yakov managed to cling on desperately, his protests mute behind the gag.

The train picked up more speed and the engine thrust forward with a powerful surge. Yakov lost his balance. He fell backward, tumbling away onto the darkened tracks.

Almost at once a ferocious volley of gunfire erupted as Yakov's troops realized what was happening.

Andrev was forced to retreat into the carriage.

"Stay down!" he screamed at Lydia and Pavel, as a withering hail of bullets struck the carriage. The engine roared into the tunnel and was swallowed by the pitch darkness.

Yakov rolled along the tracks until he slammed into a hard wooden railway sleeper and grunted, the breath knocked out of him.

He struggled to his feet but immediately he bent double, coughing up bile. A clatter of feet sounded behind him as a handful of his men rushed up, carrying storm lamps, Zoba leading the way. One of them tore off Yakov's gag and untied his hands.

Yakov was furious. "Andrev's duped us again. He's stranded us. The fool, what about his child?"

Zoba raised his lamp, his face grim. "It's too late, Leonid."

PART SEVEN

PART SEVEN

91

"You're mad, I tell you. You'll get us both shot." Markov snapped the reins. The horses trotted in the direction of Vonskaya Street. "Are you listening to anything I'm saying?"

Boyle sat beside him in the hearse, wearing a dark suit, collar, and tie. "Every word. Not mad, desperate. The next turn, you said?"

Markov sighed unhappily and swung the carriage left and they came down by the lake. As they trotted under a bridge, three Red guards patrolled beside a solid-looking iron door.

Markov was sober-faced after they passed the guards. "You see, it's just as I told you. Every tunnel entrance is guarded."

Minutes later, they saw more troops pacing outside an immaculately kept, stucco-fronted house with a fluttering Union Jack mounted on an upper-story flagpole. Markov said, "The British consulate's office. There's a tunnel entrance in the garden."

Boyle said, tight-lipped, "I've seen enough. Head to the hotel."

Five minutes later they clip-clopped past the Amerika. Boyle observed soldiers outside, four with bayoneted rifles, while another manned a Vickers machine gun protected by a mound of sandbags. On the street corners at each end of the hotel was a patrolling soldier. Several cars and trucks were pulled in front of the hotel.

An open-topped Opel car suddenly overtook them and slammed on its brakes near the front entrance. A couple of thugs in leather jackets dragged a terrified-looking young man from the back of the car and hauled him up the entrance steps. Markov said, "The poor devil is destined for the cells, no doubt."

He turned to Boyle. "You must be insane to enter that lions' den. I wouldn't have the nerve."

"Drive round the corner. I want to take a look at the rear."

Markov obeyed, nudging the horses with his whip. Boyle saw that the hotel's entire lower-floor basement had thick bars on the windows.

"The cells?" Boyle asked.

"Yes," Markov answered.

"Head toward the river."

Markov steered the horses and minutes later halted by the water. "Well?"

Boyle took out a notepad and pencil. He jotted down some notes and a few rough drawings. When he finished he massaged his forehead with his thumb and forefinger.

"Impossible?" Markov asked.

"Every suit of armor has a chink. However, there's one serious problem I can foresee if I try to enter the hotel."

"Which is?"

Boyle offered a crooked smile. "I can understand some Russian, but I can't speak it very well."

Markov tossed down the reins in dismay. "Wonderful. What now?"

92

The train thundered through the night.

Lydia yanked open one of the metal windows to let in some air, vast forests lurking in the moonlit darkness. When she turned back she said, "I know it's killing you, but you mustn't feel guilty."

Andrev sat behind Yakov's desk, his head in his hands, and then he looked up, tormented. "That's not the point. It's still my fault. Coming back here, all of this, it was a mistake, I see that now. If I'd left well enough alone at least Nina and Sergey wouldn't be harmed. I should have protected them."

She came over and put both hands on his shoulders. "You can't blame yourself, Uri. Yakov said he wouldn't deliberately harm them."

"I'm not sure what he's capable of anymore. But it stands to reason he'll try to use Nina and Sergey as pawns in all this."

She saw his anguish and he seemed to slump, racked by worry and exhaustion. "We haven't slept in over two days. You need to rest, Uri."

He got to his feet and grabbed the route map. "I can't, not now. Fetch Pavel."

"Then will you promise to try to rest?"

"In a while. Let me deal with Pavel first."

She went into the bedchamber and came back with the young rail worker. Andrev said bluntly, "Are you and your father Bolsheviks?"

The young man said nervously, "No, sir. We were employed by the railroad. Commissar Yakov had us seconded to his train."

Andrev crooked a finger. "Come with me." He said to Lydia. "Wait here, I'll be back."

She gripped his arm. "What are you going to do?"

He picked up Mersk's *nagaika* whip. "Yakov ordered the line to be kept open all the way to Ekaterinburg. I'm making sure he doesn't try to cancel the order and stop us."

Andrev moved over the wagon, following Pavel. They reached the engine, where the young man's father was busy shoveling coal. He looked relieved to see his son.

"Listen here," Andrev told him. "You both have my word that you won't be harmed so long as you do as I say. I want you to keep this train going until we're near Ekaterinburg. Can you do that?"

The driver nodded. "We've got enough fuel, that's not a problem. It just depends on the line staying open."

"If it does, how much longer would our journey take?"

"Eight hours, or thereabouts."

Andrev pointed to the route map. "I'll let you both off at a town fifty miles from Ekaterinburg, right here. You can say I threw you off, and no one will be the wiser." He stared out at the telegraph poles flashing past in the dusk. "Now, be a good fellow and halt the train for a few minutes."

"Why?"

"I've got work to do."

The driver slipped on a thick leather gauntlet and adjusted a couple of valves and knobs on the engine panel, then carefully applied the air brakes. Steam hissed and the train slowed, eventually shrieking to a halt in a cloud of hot vapor.

Andrev immediately climbed up high on the coal tender, until he was near the telegraph pole that ran alongside the rail line. He uncoiled the *nagaika* and flicked the whip at the pole. He pulled hard, then tied the whip's butt around a metal grip bar on the coal tender and told the driver, "Release the brakes and start moving, nice and slowly."

The driver obeyed and the engine inched forward.

The *nagaika* began to stretch tight, pulling on the telegraph cable, and then came a *zinging* sound as the cable finally snapped. It snaked wildly until one end of it came to rest on the coal wagon. Andrev grabbed the cable and anchored it to an engine handrail.

"Get moving, faster," he ordered the driver.

The train began to pick up speed.

Andrev watched as the telegraph cable was ripped from pole after pole . . .

Lydia poured some water from a jug into the washbasin in the bedchamber.

Andrev stood bare-chested, soaping clean his blackened hands and face. "Yakov won't repair the damage in a hurry."

"Where's Pavel?"

"With his father. I told them not to disturb us unless it's an emergency. We can take turns to rest, but keep the gun near you."

She handed him a towel as the train picked up speed. "Do you trust them to keep the engine going?"

He dried himself. "We're in the middle of nowhere—where can they go? Unless they want to take their chances in the forests with bandits and wolves, they'll be safer with us, at least until we're near Ekaterinburg."

She looked into his face, his eyes dark and sunken, his face drawn. She said, "Promise me you'll try to sleep. Two hours each. You rest first, I'll keep watch."

"If you think you can hold out."

"I'll be fine. You're on the verge of exhaustion, Uri."

Andrev collapsed onto the cot and removed his boots and breeches. He laid his head on the pillow and tried to force himself to relax. "Wake me if you need me."

"No more talking." Lydia sat on the chair by the bed and pressed a finger to his lips. "Just rest, Uri."

He turned away toward the wall, one hand under his head. She laid a hand on his back, kneading his shoulders, feeling his stress, the muscles knotted as hard as wood. "Sometimes when I was a little girl and frightened of the dark, my mother used to come to my room and rub my back. She always said that we need to feel a human touch to relax. What are you thinking?"

"That right this minute I wish I could close my eyes and everything would just go away and I could sleep for a week."

"I know the feeling," she said. "You want to shut out the world and wait for the darkness to pass. But then when you open your eyes again you find nothing's changed. It never does."

She noticed him clasping and unclasping his hand, as if still consumed by worry. "What else are you thinking?"

"Nina and Sergey. And the last time I saw them. Nina was hanging some washing, and Sergey was tugging at her skirt. It broke my heart that there was nothing I could do to comfort my son. It made me feel so helpless."

She stopped kneading his shoulders. He turned to face her. The look in his eyes said it all—his grief and anguish were still there, she saw that—but something else, too, a kind of longing that she understood all too well.

Not sexual, but something far more urgent: a heartbreaking need to simply connect with another human being.

There seemed no need to speak, no need to say a word, for she knew that he was as vulnerable as she.

She pulled him toward her, embracing him, her arms going around his neck as she kissed him, gently at first, then more fiercely as he clung desperately to her.

93

Andrev came awake with a kind of convulsion, a cry on his lips.

"Are you all right?" Lydia lay beside him, her head in the crook of his neck.

"Just a bad dream, that's all." He rubbed his eyes and checked his pocket watch in his jacket by the bed. Almost four hours had passed. He'd been exhausted. It was bright outside, shafts of sunlight filtering through the shutters.

She asked sleepily, "Did I make a terrible fool of myself?"

"If you did, that makes two of us." He touched her face gently with his hand. "How are you feeling?"

She sat up and smoothed her skirt, her face suddenly flushed. "I'm not sure. What . . . what happened between us, it's made me think."

"About what?"

"How would it have been if we met before now?"

Andrev looked into her eyes. "Before we did? I think we should go mad thinking about that."

Lydia changed the subject. "Do you think Yakov might have some tea for that samovar of his?"

"Let me look." He climbed out of bed and immediately sensed something was wrong, but he couldn't quite work out what it was.

Lydia said, alarmed, "What's the matter?"

And then Andrev realized: almost imperceptibly, the train's speed was decreasing.

"The engine's slowing. Get your clothes on quickly. There might be trouble." He dragged on his clothes and grabbed his revolver.

Lydia dressed, and he moved to the door leading to the engine. "No, wait, I'm coming with you."

He clambered over the coal wagon, Lydia following.

Thick forest lay all around, as far as the eye could see, the Urals towering above them, snowcapped in places. Behind them he thought he glimpsed wooden buildings, the outline of a scattered village.

They reached the engine. The driver and his son were gone.

He slapped his hand against the cabin wall in frustration. "Just what we need. The fools must have slowed and jumped ship." He examined the steam indicator. "The pressure's running low. Who knows how long we've been abandoned? If this keeps up we'll come to a grinding halt."

He grabbed the driver's thick leather gauntlet left discarded on the floor, slipped it on, and yanked open the furnace door. A wave of heat blasted out, the furnace a sea of yellow and bloodred coals.

"It's down to sheer, brutal donkey work, I'm afraid." He grabbed a pair of shovels from a rack behind him, handed one to Lydia, and dug the other into a coal pan behind them. "Start shoveling as fast as you can."

Sweat dripped from Andrev's face as he adjusted the valves, and the engine speed began to pick up. He wiped a patina of sweat from his brow. After thirty solid minutes of shoveling the steam pressure was constant.

Lydia felt fatigued. "Have you any idea where we are?"

"Absolutely none." He peered out at the snowcapped Urals, then studied the route map he took from his pocket. "I'll make a guess we're at least three or four hours from Ekaterinburg."

An hour later they chugged past a small town, a few gaunt-looking peasants lining the tracks, scrawny children waving at them from an abandoned station hut. Andrev checked the station name on the route map.

"We're making better time than I thought. If this keeps up, we ought to be nearing Ekaterinburg in another couple of hours."

"Then what? We can't just arrive in the city station. It'll be crawling with Reds."

"According to the map there should be a siding about five miles from Ekaterinburg. We'll shunt the train there and make our way in on foot." He put the map away. "We better take turns cleaning ourselves up. You first, I'll keep the furnace stoked. And try and gather any food and spare clothes you can find in the carriage. We may need them."

Two hours later the train entered a broad valley. In the far distance, they could make out a dramatic collection of domes and spires, mingled with the tall brick chimneys of factories and smelting works, the telltale signs of Ekaterinburg, in the shadow of the snow-topped Urals.

Andrev reduced their speed and when they approached the siding, he slowed to a snail's pace before stopping. He jumped down, taking with him the point-change bar, and when they shunted the train onto the siding, he went back and repositioned the points, then climbed aboard again, joining Lydia.

They drove the train for a quarter mile along the siding, coming to a halt in a cloud of steam. Andrev shoveled more coal into the furnace.

"We've stopped—why more fuel?"

"In case Yakov has a welcoming committee waiting for us in Ekaterinburg and we have to beat a hasty retreat."

When he finished shoveling they gathered their belongings and climbed down from the engine.

Andrev stared back at the vast Ural forests they'd left behind them, a shadow crossing his face.

"You don't look happy." Lydia touched his arm.

"That bad dream I had. It gave me this awful feeling something terrible happened to Nina and Sergey."

"You know you Russians. You're always quick to make a drama out of nothing."

"I hope that's all it is."

94

"It's done, Leonid. We felled a dozen trees and blockaded the rail line."

Yakov checked his pocket watch—2 a.m.—then snapped it shut. "And the guards?"

Zoba said, "They're stationed on the main track at five hundred paces. If a train appears, they'll wave it down with lanterns. The blockade will make sure it halts."

"It better, or we'll both be facing a firing squad." Yakov looked dismal as he peered out the open window, the Siberian night air balmy, fragrant with pine. His men were huddled in groups along the tracks, fires lit, brewing tea and eating their rations—hard biscuits and the tins of corned beef. "What about the scouts?"

"Half a dozen men are on their way along each end of the track. We'll try to reach the nearest town and find a telegraph. How is she?"

"Desolate. The medic's going to give her a little ether to sedate her. I had the child's body moved to the next compartment. We had to pry it from her embrace. She clung to the boy as if her life depended on it."

"You're going to talk to her?"

Yakov looked sober as he opened the door. "For what it's worth. But I have a feeling I'm the last person in the world she wants to talk with."

Yakov let himself into the compartment, where a guard patrolled the passageway.

The child's body lay on the bottom bunk, covered with a worn cotton sheet. Yakov knelt and grimly lifted the sheet.

Sergey's eyes were closed, the lids almost translucent.

He so often witnessed death in the trenches that he was almost immune to it. But the loss of a child still wrenched his heart. His stomach churned, as he imagined Katerina lying there.

A heavy sigh passed his lips as he replaced the sheet. Then he stood and left the compartment, silently closing the door.

He knocked before he went in.

Her eyes looked scalded from crying. She was seated by the window, a handkerchief held over her mouth, and she was weeping, deep, uncontrollable sobs that shook her body.

A lamp was lit, and in its sulfur-yellow glow Nina looked inconsolable. She didn't speak when he stepped in, just stared out at the darkness beyond the glass.

Yakov cleared his throat. "Nina . . . I don't know what to say."

"Get out of my sight."

He touched her arm. "No, please, hear me out—"

"Leave me." She stood, her tears welling. "I don't want you here. I don't want you near me."

Yakov sighed and went to sit on the lower bunk, his hands clasped together. "Nina, you must listen to what I say. It's important."

"Nothing's important. Nothing, not anymore. I want you to go." She spoke with such ferocity, her eyes blazing, and then she turned away, putting her handkerchief to her mouth.

Yakov closed his eyes tightly, opened them again, touched his clasped fingers to his lips. "I promise I will. Once I say what must."

She didn't turn back, or speak.

Yakov said quietly, "First, you have to understand something. It's not just about Stanislas. The reason I have to hunt Uri down—it's him or me. His life or mine, and Katerina's. That's what I'm faced with."

She turned and looked at him through wet eyes.

Yakov said, "It's that bleak. Do you understand? I can't allow him to succeed. Those above me won't allow me to fail."

"Why does that not surprise me? The kind of people you consort with, they're a ruthless pack of animals."

"Had Uri never come back, had he never involved himself in this, you and your son would still be in Moscow, and Sergey might still be alive."

She stared at him accusingly, and her tone was savage. "You say that. You—the man who intends to take us to a camp? I pity you, Leonid Yakov. I pity you and your kind."

"What are you talking about?"

"No one killed Sergey but you and your Bolshevik friends. You've drenched this country in blood."

Yakov said nothing, simply stared back at her.

She turned on him now, force in her voice. "Don't look at me like that. I'm not afraid to speak the truth anymore. I'm not afraid of you. How could I be, after losing Sergey? How can I ever live without him? *How?*"

Her voice sounded like a strangled, pitiful whisper. She broke down again, harsh sobs racking her body, and she sagged as if she was going to collapse.

Yakov took hold of her arms, pulled her to him, and she allowed herself to cling to him, if only because she needed to cling to someone, but the moment she regained control she pushed herself away and wiped her eyes.

"Do you know what else is pitiful? Your hatred of Uri. It has little to do with justice, but everything to do with envy."

"What are you talking about?"

It all came flowing out of her in a sudden burst. "You envied him all your life, but you'd never admit it. Envied everything he ever represented: the respect he earned, the kind of honorable man he is that others look up to, the kind of father he had. He had everything you craved, even the woman you couldn't have. That's the real source of your hatred, isn't it, Leonid? *Isn't it?* You called him a brother yet part of you always despised him."

He didn't reply.

Nina met his gaze. "I see now what it was I sensed in you the first moment we met, all those years ago—sensed but didn't understand until now. Always in your heart there's a sense of injustice and outrage. That you've been wrongly done by, and mostly by people like Uri and his class."

Yakov was pale, his voice hoarse. "You don't know what you're talking about."

"Don't I? You blamed Uri because in your heart you wanted to blame him, you wanted to destroy him."

Yakov answered bitterly, "You'll never convince me he isn't guilty."

Hostility braided her words. "Let me tell you something. He didn't kill Stanislas, no more than you did."

Outside the carriage, Yakov glimpsed a bustle of activity.

His men were running up and down the track, calling out to one another, waving storm lamps. He thought he heard a train whistle.

He ignored the distraction and said fiercely, "You don't know what you're talking about. You weren't there. How could you know? He was on the run, a desperate man, capable of anything."

"But not that. Not to kill a boy like that. Will I tell you why? Because they're two sides of the same coin."

"What's that supposed to mean?"

"When Uri's father died, we sat with him until the end. Uri and I, we heard his confession, his sad little secret, and he made us both promise him we'd never divulge it to anyone. Especially to you, because it might dishonor the memory of your mother, but I'll divulge it to you now. I know he'd understand. Because someone needs to tell you. Someone needs to put you to rights."

"What are you talking about?"

"It's time you knew, Leonid. It's time you knew the whole pitiful truth."

95

When Boyle entered the convent church that afternoon from the annex, he saw Novice Maria get up from one of the benches.

She wore a scarf around her head, and with her deeply sunken eyes she seemed absurdly young.

Boyle said, "I was told to meet you here."

"Sister Agnes could not come herself; she's busy in the hospital surgery. But she said there's something you must see."

Boyle said, "You speak excellent English."

"My father's a merchant. I had an English governess." The novice's footsteps echoed hollowly as she led him down the aisle to the entrance.

She pulled back one of the oak doors and pointed.

Boyle saw the chalk mark of a reverse swastika. "How long has it been there?"

"No more than an hour. Sister said to be careful, that it could be a trap. And to give you this."

She handed him a piece of chalk, which he took, a spark in his eyes now as if he seemed to come alive. "*Spasibo.* Run along, I'll take care of it from here."

He waited until the novice's footsteps faded, and then Boyle chalked another reverse swastika beside the first before he went to sit on one of the benches, one hand inside his jacket pocket, ready on the butt of his Colt pistol.

It didn't take long until he heard the footsteps.

A figure stepped into the doorway, followed by another. Strong sunlight filtered through the stained glass, and for a moment Boyle couldn't make out their faces, but then he saw one of the figures pull back the doors.

He recognized Andrev and Lydia, looking the worse for wear, their clothes shabby and blackened.

He stood and approached them. "So, you made it at last."

"We'll dispense with the formalities if you don't mind, Boyle," Andrev said. "We're here, and lucky to be alive."

"You weren't followed?"

"No, I made certain."

Boyle kept his hand on the Colt as he looked past the door, making sure. Satisfied, he relaxed. "You two look like you've been through the wars."

"You don't know the half of it, Boyle," said Lydia.

He smiled. "Does anything in life ever run smoothly? Let's get you cleaned up and you can tell me everything."

Sorg drifted awake, a stench of ammonia smelling salts filling his nostrils.

A terrible feeling of nausea swept over him, the vapors so powerful that they hurt his lungs. To make matters worse, his jaw felt as if it had been struck by a hammer.

He remembered being hit in the jaw by Kazan, a powerful blow that caused him to black out.

He blinked, looked around him.

A single light blazed overhead, the white intensity forcing him to shield his brow with his hand. He was lying on a table of some sort in a small airless room, the windows barred, rain beating against the glass.

There was no sign of Kazan. Instead, a small man with an unshaven face and his breath reeking of cigarette smoke stood over him, the elbows of his jacket crudely patched. He held a brown medicine bottle in his hand.

Sorg tried to sit up. He immediately felt dizzy. "Where—where am I?"

The man put a hand on his chest, gently pushed him back down. "Relax. For now just take slow, deep breaths."

96

"He's being held here, in the Amerika Hotel." Boyle used a pencil to mark a circle on the city map that was spread out on a wooden table.

"It's being used as the local Cheka headquarters, and sister here thinks we'd be insane to try to gain entry. But time's running out fast and we're desperate. With the Czech divisions so close, the city's in disarray. Rumor says the Reds will evacuate within days."

They were in Markov's huge, white-tiled mortuary. The air was pungent with the chemical smell of embalming fluid. Several corpses lay on the floor in a corner, wrapped in white cotton sheets. Adult and adolescent forms alike, at least a dozen bodies in all.

Around the table with Boyle were Sister Agnes and Markov, and Andrev and Lydia, who had washed and changed into fresh clothes.

Andrev said, "Is that why you think the executions will happen soon?"

Boyle tossed down his pencil and said to a solemn-looking Agnes, "Tell him, Sister."

"My two novices were turned away from the Ipatiev House this morning. They went to deliver fresh milk, bread, and dozens of eggs—more than usual—and extra rolls of sewing thread."

"Why thread?"

The nun explained, "The girls sew gems into their clothes, to be used in case of their escape. The *komendant* seized most of their jewelry but he strongly suspects more are hidden. He's fanatical about finding any remaining valuables."

"Go on, Sister."

"When the novices arrived, the *komendant* took the provisions but wouldn't allow them to see the family."

"Has that happened before?"

"Seldom. The guards are always happy to take their cut of the food we bring. So I called there myself to see what I could find out. The *komendant* refused to talk to me. As I left, one of the guards sniggered, 'We won't be having any more visits from you nuns soon enough.'"

Markov offered, "I heard that the *komendant's* ordered a truck and rolls of canvas from the central garage for midnight. And a quantity of sulfuric acid from one of the foundries. Such acid can be used to dissolve human flesh. It seems the only reason the Reds would want it."

Sister Agnes recoiled and blessed herself. "I wouldn't put any cruelty past them."

Boyle paced the room. "We'll have to forget about the tunnels, as they're all under heavy guard, but I'm open to suggestions. The same applies to getting our man out of the hotel."

Andrev unfolded the forged letter from his pocket. "Would this help?"

Boyle studied the page and frowned. "Where did you get it?"

Andrev explained.

Boyle said, "It could be worth a try. What do you two think?"

He handed the page to Sister Agnes and Markov, who studied it.

The undertaker rubbed his cheek. "It certainly looks official enough."

The nun shook her head. "Some of the Cheka may be peasants, but they're nobody's fool. I can't see them being easily duped."

Lydia wandered over to the white-sheeted bodies. "Who are these poor creatures?"

Markov said, "Some died of natural causes, others were executed. There's been a shortage of wood for coffins, so we have to bury them in simple sheets."

Boyle asked, "Are they dead long?"

"Mostly since this morning."

Boyle stared at the corpses and looked deep in thought.

Andrev said impatiently, "I hate to push you, Boyle, but time's running out."

Boyle crossed to the window, peered out into the yard where Markov kept his horses. "Sister, do you think you could find me a Red Army uniform?"

"We've got plenty, taken from dead soldiers."

Boyle looked invigorated at the prospect of action and said to Andrev, "We'll use the same plan I outlined to Markov, except it'll be you and me who enter the hotel. You can keep up the Cheka role. And don't forget that letter."

Boyle addressed the undertaker. "Have you anything faster than that hearse of yours?"

Sister Agnes said, "The convent has a motorized ambulance. The Reds only let us keep it because we've been transporting their wounded from the front."

"Perfect." Boyle pointed to the city map. "I'll want you waiting here, a street from the hotel, so we can beat a hasty retreat."

Lydia said, "What if the letter doesn't work?"

Boyle nodded to the corpses. "That's simple. We end up like these poor devils. But fortune belongs to the brave. Three months ago I bluffed my way into the Kremlin vaults, removed the Romanian crown jewels, and walked out again without a shot fired.

"All I had was a couple of men and an officious-looking letter. It's all about having the right attitude, as they say. Right, time to test the water, so let's be going."

As they left the room, Boyle caught Andrev by the arm. "Yakov taking your family hostage changes everything, you realize that? I'm afraid it'll be impossible to keep my end of the bargain and get them out. We have no way of knowing what Yakov may have hidden up his sleeve."

Andrev nodded bleakly. "One thing. If he shows up, he's mine."

97

The train kissed the buffers and the air brakes hissed.

Yakov slid open a carriage window. The station platforms were bedlam, crowded with peasants pushing handcarts and carrying belongings.

Zoba jumped down, spoke with a military official, and came back. "He said we can order transport from the local military garage. How long it'll take is another matter; the town's being evacuated. It might be quicker if we walked."

Yakov buttoned his tunic. "Stay here, I'll find the garage. Don't allow anyone to move the train. I've commandeered it. And see that the men are looked after—they'll need food and to bathe. There ought to be hotels near the station. Requisition as many rooms as you need."

"What about Nina?"

"Stay with her, she's fragile. Have the medic give her some more ether to calm her."

"Ether?"

"It'll make her sleep. When reality hits her again she'll be hysterical. Then take care of the child's body. Make sure it's treated with respect." Yakov turned to go.

"Can I ask you a personal question, Leonid?"

"What?"

"I know longing when I see it. You love her, don't you?"

Yakov didn't reply, his mouth tight with exhaustion. "All that matters right now is that I stay alive, and not make my daughter an orphan."

"Even if that means killing Uri, after what Nina told you?"

"Do I have a choice?"

Zoba put a hand on Yakov's arm. "I'm suddenly beginning to wonder if all this war is worth it. Will you be all right, Leonid?"

"That's another question I don't know the answer to."

Yakov climbed the front steps to the Amerika Hotel. He stepped into the bar. It was half-empty, a handful of leather-jacketed Cheka and local Bolshevik officials drowning their sorrows amid clouds of cigarette smoke.

He approached a nervous-looking bartender who was wiping some glasses. "Give me a vodka. Better still, make it a bottle."

The bartender placed a vodka bottle and a single glass on the bar. Yakov slapped down a handful of coins, uncorked the bottle, and filled his glass to the brim. He emptied it in one swallow and poured another, then stared into space, the corners of his eyes moist.

He still felt shocked, and angry, and . . .

He didn't know what he felt—he hadn't slept in almost three days, exhaustion grinding him.

But he felt angry at his mother for not telling him the truth. Yet another part of him understood. She was a good woman, but a lonely human being with a desolate life. Didn't she deserve affection?

Whenever we're offered love, we should accept it . . . wherever we encounter tenderness, we should embrace it.

He swallowed more vodka, the raw alcohol a flame in his throat.

His vision began to blur with tiredness. Drinking only worsened his exhaustion. He told himself, *No more—I need my wits about me.*

He still had bloody work to do.

Find and destroy Andrev. Execute the Romanovs.

He couldn't fail in his duty. Katerina's life depended on it. Bile rose in his throat at the very thought of his daughter being harmed.

"Drowning your sorrows, Commissar?"

Yakov turned. Kazan stood wearing his broad-rimmed hat, his face smug. "You look like you've had a shock."

"What's it to you?"

"I heard about your drama." Kazan nodded to the bartender, who poured him a whiskey.

"Who told you?"

Kazan removed his hat, placed it on the counter, and ran a hand over his bald head. "You've only arrived, but it seems that tongues are already wagging. Your men can't stop talking about how yet again you were made a fool of by Andrev."

Yakov's mouth was a slash as he fought to control his anger.

Malice glinted in Kazan's face. "I can only hope for your sake Moscow doesn't hear about your latest mistake. It won't look good, Andrev besting you at every turn. Tell me, is it true you have a soft spot for Andrev's ex-wife? I'm sure she'll be glad of the company now that her brat's dead."

Yakov hit Kazan across the jaw. He reeled back, slammed against the counter, and slid to the floor, a crimson gash on his mouth.

Kazan put a hand on his lip, looked at the blood on his fingers, and grinned. "Temper, Commissar. We need each other. More than ever."

"Don't flatter yourself, Kazan."

Kazan pushed himself up. "My prisoner's the only conspirator we have in custody, and therefore our only hope of finding the others."

"He's not *your* prisoner, he's the state's. And let's not forget who's in charge. Has he talked?"

Kazan smiled tightly. "Not unless you count his screams. He's proving obstinate. But that's about to change. I have a couple of tricks up my sleeve that will loosen his tongue."

Yakov emptied his glass and hammered it on the counter. "Where is he?"

"In the cells."

Markov gently snapped the horses' reins as the hearse clattered toward the Amerika Hotel.

It looked busy with Cheka types coming and going, some of them carrying packed bags and loading belongings onto hand carts and droshkies.

The occasional crack of artillery fire erupted in the distance; the Czech divisions were less than twenty miles away.

"The rats are deserting the sinking ship while they can," Markov commented.

Boyle wore a Red Army uniform and regulation hat, the tunic a little tight around the neck.

Andrev was dressed in the Cheka-style leather jacket and cap, a holstered Nagant on the leather belt around his waist.

Boyle said, "All right, once more round the block to make sure Sister Agnes is in place with the ambulance, then we go in, gentlemen. Remember, if we can't get our man out, we kill him."

98

Yakov followed Kazan down the steps past the guards and stepped into the cell.

Sorg was strapped down onto a metal trolley. His jaw was a bruised mess, and alarm lit in his eyes as he stared up at his visitors.

Kazan regarded him with scorn. "Meet Commissar Yakov, from Moscow. I hope you're not going to disappoint us."

Kazan leaned in closer until Sorg could smell the sour breath on his face. His heart sank. He felt overcome by fear, expecting Kazan to lash out.

But instead, he removed a small brown medicine bottle from his pocket and unscrewed the glass-and-rubber stopper. He said to Yakov, "Laudanum. I believe our prisoner has a weakness for it."

Kazan grinned down at Sorg. "Don't you?"

Markov eased the hearse toward the curb, making a clicking sound with his tongue. "Whoa! Settle down now."

The horses reared to a halt a hundred yards past the hotel. Boyle and Andrev climbed down.

Boyle told Markov, "Wait here. If anyone asks, you're picking up a typhus victim. That ought to dull their interest."

Markov made a sign of the cross. "What if you don't return?"

"I've yet to meet an undertaker who's an optimist. We'll be back; don't go anywhere."

Sorg's eyes widened at the sight of the brown bottle. His craving felt like a wild beast gnawing inside his head.

Kazan dunked the stopper into the bottle, squeezed, and removed the rubber. A single watery drop of laudanum dangled from the end of the stopper. The bitter infusion of opiate and alcohol stained the air. Kazan leaned in closer, dangling the dropper above Sorg's mouth.

"You'd like some, wouldn't you? Put your tongue out. Have a drop for now, more if you talk."

Sorg's eyes bulged. He tightened his lips until they hurt. Every fiber of his being longed for the peace the drug promised. But he resisted, willing himself not to be seduced by the glistening dewdrop on the end of the stopper.

Kazan dangled his bait closer to Sorg's lips. "You want it, don't you? Go ahead, lick it. Enjoy."

Sorg felt as if he was having a fit. His face turned crimson; his breathing came in shallow spurts.

"What's the matter?" Kazan said. "Wouldn't you like a little pleasure to ease the pain?"

Sorg's bruised jaw was set like granite.

"I said take it." Kazan's temper flared.

Sorg's entire body shook as he fought the temptation.

Yakov said, "I thought you said he'd talk! We haven't time for these stupid games."

An angry Kazan screwed the stopper back on and slammed the laudanum down on the nearby table. "I'll make him confess, don't you worry."

He grabbed a dirty cotton towel and twisted it. Grabbing Sorg's mouth, he stuffed the towel between his lips until he almost gagged. "Keep biting on that, unless you want to chew off your tongue."

Sorg's eyes widened with panic as Kazan picked up two insulated black wires that snaked across the floor to an electric outlet.

"Electricity can light up a room," Kazan remarked to Yakov. "But I prefer its other uses—the painful kind that can loosen a man's tongue." He growled at Sorg, "Resistance is futile. I want the names of your co-conspirators. I want every detail of your foolish plans."

He tore open Sorg's shirt, exposing his bare chest. Without another word he touched the two wires together, producing a bright blue spark, and then promptly pressed both wires against Sorg's bare chest.

His body convulsed in an uncontrollable spasm, his eyes bulging as he bit down hard on the towel.

Kazan removed the wires and Sorg's body relaxed, but only for an instant. With a sadistic grin, Kazan again touched the wires to Sorg's chest.

He bucked wildly, like a deranged puppet, crying out behind the gag.

Kazan stopped. "Now the real pain begins. His private parts next."

Yakov said bluntly, "Enough."

But Kazan was barely listening, a look of perverted pleasure in his face as he lay down the wires and began to loosen Sorg's trousers.

Yakov crossed to the wall and tore out the cable.

Kazan stared at him. "What do you think you're doing?"

"I said enough. Get out of here."

Kazan turned livid. "This man is my prisoner. I insist—"

Yakov tore the gag from Sorg's mouth, yanked his Nagant from his holster, and cocked the hammer. "You can insist all you want. Now get out. I'll take over from here."

AMERIKA HOTEL

Boyle led the way toward the entrance steps. "I'll leave all the talking to you."

Four sentries with rifles guarded the doors. Off to the right was a sand-bagged machine-gun emplacement, manned by another two sentries.

"Halt," one of the guards challenged. "What's your business here?"

Andrev produced his letter. "Commissar Couris, from Moscow. We need a room for the night."

A crack of artillery fire sounded, but it didn't seem to bother the guards. Andrev remarked, "The enemy's getting close."

"They'll be even closer before the night's out, Commissar."

The guard waved them through, and Andrev led the way into a huge lobby, busy with a sea of uniforms. A vast staircase led up, potted plants on either side, an immense sparkling chandelier high above them.

Rooms led off in every direction, the lavish hotel a hive of activity.

Andrev whispered, "Where to now? Our man could be anywhere."

"Let's find the bar," Boyle said optimistically, "and see if we can get some information."

Yakov said, "Who do you work for?"

Silence.

Yakov raised his Nagant and pressed the tip of the barrel against Sorg's head. "One last time. I want the names of your fellow conspirators. Help me and you go free."

Sorg remained steadfast.

Yakov slowly squeezed his finger on the trigger.

Sorg tensed, closing his eyes, fearing the bullet to come.

"Last chance," Yakov said.

Sorg closed his eyes tighter.

Yakov squeezed harder.

A metallic click sounded.

Sorg snapped his eyes open.

Yakov opened the Nagant to reveal empty chambers. "You're either a very brave man, or a very foolish one."

He took a handful of cartridges from his pocket and loaded the gun. "Whichever it is, you'll never talk, I know that much. But you or your friends can't win. The family's fate is sealed. Once midnight passes, they'll all be dead. No one can save them."

Yakov replaced the Nagant in his holster. "Can you walk?"

Sorg stared back in silence.

"You heard me. Can you walk? Try to." Yakov undid the leather straps.

Sorg pushed himself up, groaning.

He looked fit to collapse, but with great effort he managed to sit on the edge of the trolley. He placed his feet on the floor and tried to walk, his legs unsteady.

Yakov supported him. "Do you think you could you muster the strength to walk out of here if I released you?"

Sorg stared back at him as if he were mad. "Is this your idea of a joke?" He touched his swollen jaw.

"Answer me. Could you walk out of here?"

"I think so."

"There's an exit door at the end of the hall, past the guards. Go that way."

Sorg's face clouded. "I don't understand."

"You don't have to. Just take the exit door and keep walking. I'll take care of the guards. I promise no one will follow. You have my solemn word."

Sorg was incredulous. "You're trying to trick me, aren't you?"

"No trick. Leave now. There'll be no curfew tonight. But be careful. The enemy is close and the city's in disarray and being evacuated."

Sorg's stare fixed on the laudanum bottle on the table.

Yakov noticed, picked up the bottle, and said, "You want it? Take it."

He tossed the bottle at Sorg, who caught it and said, "This is insane. Kazan hunts me down like a dog, yet you release me. Why?"

Yakov held out a small manila envelope. "There's a man named Andrev among your fellow conspirators. Give him this."

"What is it?"

"A note from me. As well as a map and directions to an abandoned grain warehouse, a half mile north of the Ipatiev House. Tell him to meet me at eleven tonight. He's to come alone. I'll do the same. Emphasize *alone*. Tell him Nina's life may depend on it."

"Nina?"

"He'll know. Will you remember all that?"

A stunned Sorg nodded, his expression a question mark.

"Go, before Kazan returns or I change my mind."

99

Despite the crowded lobby, the bar was almost empty when Boyle and Andrev entered.

In a far corner sat a group of dismal-looking men in leather jackets, shrouded in a haze of tobacco smoke and with bottles of vodka in front of them.

A bartender was huddled talking with a colleague. He broke away, nervously wiping the countertop with a damp cloth. "What can I get you, gentlemen?"

"Not too busy, are you?" Andrev remarked.

"The city's being evacuated, or haven't you heard, comrades?"

"All the more reason for a drink. We'll have vodka."

As the man went to fetch their drinks, Boyle glanced round the near-empty room and whispered, "Maybe this wasn't such a good idea after all."

The double doors into the bar suddenly burst open and a bullish, bald-headed man stormed in. He looked in a foul mood, banging his fist on the counter. "You! Whiskey. Give me a bottle."

The frightened bartender looked as if he couldn't move fast enough, scurrying to fetch a whiskey bottle and glass for the customer, before he served Andrev and Boyle their drinks.

Kazan filled his glass and knocked it back in one swallow. He splashed more whiskey into his glass, refilling it to the brim.

"Bad day, comrade?" Andrev asked.

Kazan's cold, dark glare swiveled toward him with contempt, one of his eyes milky white. "What's it to you?"

"We all have them now and then." Andrev raised his glass. "Your health."

Kazan emptied his glass, slammed it down, and stepped threateningly closer. "My health's none of your business. That's what's wrong with this country. Too many people sticking their noses in where they're not wanted." A strange, twisted grin appeared on Kazan's face. "But that's all about to change . . ."

"My apologies, comrade, I didn't mean to offend."

"Then shut your mouth before I shut it for you." Kazan gave a final growl, grabbed the bottle, and left, the doors swinging after him.

Andrev pushed some coins across to the bartender. "Is he always in such a good mood?"

"That's Kazan, from the Moscow Cheka. Don't you know him?"

"We're just passing through. Should we?"

"Kazan's got a savage reputation. Maybe I shouldn't say this, but . . ."

Andrev winked good-humoredly and slid the bartender a generous tip. "There's nothing like a bit of gossip. It'll go no further."

"It's been all over the hotel like wildfire. A Moscow commissar named Yakov released a spy Kazan caught. When he found out he went crazy. He and the commissar just had a blazing row in the lobby that almost came to blows."

"Really? Over what?"

"Kazan's been ranting that Yakov released the prisoner so he could tail him to his comrades and grab all the glory. Kazan's fit to burst. There'll be trouble, I tell you. Kazan's not one to cross."

"So where's the commissar now?"

"He left the hotel five minutes ago."

100

EKATERINBURG

Sorg made his way through the backstreets.

Sweat drenched his body. He checked his dressing—his wound wasn't bleeding but he felt fatigued, and his jaw throbbed. He touched his mouth with his fingers; it was crusted with blood. After ten minutes walking he left the backstreets and came out by the river.

A few solitary barges floated past. He saw a public water pump and he greedily stuck his mouth under the faucet and pumped.

His thirst quenched, he dabbed his lips and glanced over his shoulder to see if he was being pursued. *I promise no one will follow. You have my solemn word.*

He didn't trust Yakov. But he saw no one following him.

He sat on one of the promenade benches. After leaving the hotel he stopped a passing stranger for a cigarette. The man looked so bewildered by Sorg's bruised state that he gave him two cigarettes and some matches, before hurrying away.

Sorg smoked the cigarettes one after the other. He wished he had more, and some coffee. Coffee would be good. The laudanum bottle felt like a lead weight in his pocket. Fighting his desperation to use it, he had ceased feeling its contours, its tempting shape.

I need a clear head, not a mind fogged by narcotic.

His hands shook. Reason told him to toss the bottle into the river but he couldn't.

The evening light was fading but the sky was still pale. He tried to judge the time. He guessed it was somewhere close to ten.

He recalled Yakov's words. The family's fate is sealed. Once midnight passes, they'll all be dead. No one can save them.

Was Yakov telling the truth? For some reason, he didn't doubt him.

His heart began to race, anxiety overtaking him. He hadn't much time but he knew he had to be careful not to fall into a trap.

And he felt certain it *was* a trap.

A couple of scrawny pigeons landed nearby, scavenging for food.

The city appeared deserted already, not a soldier in sight. It was well past curfew but Sorg hadn't seen any roadblocks or checkpoints. Only droves of worried-looking peasant families pushing handcarts loaded with their belongings, heading in the direction of the city's main railway station. He heard the thump of artillery fire in the distance.

In his pocket, he fingered Yakov's envelope. He felt tempted to tear it open and see what was inside. It was all so baffling.

He looked around him yet again. He still saw no one observe him.

What if Yakov told the truth and this wasn't a trap? His mind refused to contemplate that. It made no sense.

He hurried on, past boarded-up huckster shops, and entered a maze of foul-smelling alleyways strewn with abandoned garbage.

He began to relax. For the first time he questioned if he really was being followed. But almost immediately his anxiety returned.

He heard shallow footsteps behind him.

He looked over his shoulder.

No one.

It's only fear, he told himself.

But still he fretted.

Please, God, don't let her be harmed.

His thoughts raced, panic driving him deeper into the backstreets, determined to reach his destination.

I have to save Anastasia.

As he rounded the next corner, rough hands reached out of the shadows and grabbed him.

Then something smelling and feeling of coarse sackcloth was pulled over his head and his vision plunged into darkness.

101

The room at the back of the mortuary was windowless.

A single lightbulb dazzled the lime-washed walls and when the sackcloth was ripped from Sorg's head he blinked. The room was bare except for a pine table and chairs. A smell of embalming fluid filled his nostrils.

He recognized Markov, but the two other men and the woman present were strangers. A well-built, military-looking fellow stepped forward. He removed a ring from his finger, indicated the ancient symbol inscribed inside the band, and said in a North American accent, "Recognize this?"

Sorg felt a swell of relief.

"The name's Boyle. Forgive the dramatics, but we couldn't be certain if you were being followed. Or if you'd talked."

"I told them nothing. Not a word."

Boyle slipped back on the ring. "Knowing the Reds' interrogation methods, I find that hard to believe."

"I swear. All I know is when I wouldn't talk, Yakov released me."

Boyle nodded. "With the intention of following you, apparently. But he must have made a bad job of it; we got to you first. Sit."

Sorg sat.

Boyle said angrily, "So you're Sorg. If you weren't in such a poor state, I'd horsewhip you to within an inch of your life. How the heck did you get yourself caught?"

"I made a stupid mistake," Sorg answered and then explained.

Boyle was grim-faced. "And now the Reds are guarding every tunnel entrance. Why the dickens were you so desperate to overhear Kazan's conversation?"

"Wouldn't *you* have wanted to?"

Boyle's jaw tightened hard as a knot, and he stood, scraping back his chair. "I wouldn't have ignored Markov's warning. The wall wasn't to be breached until we were ready to use it. Now all our plans are ruined."

Sorg said desperately, "Yakov claimed the family's to be executed soon after midnight."

Markov offered, "It's definite, so. That's why the truck was ordered."

Boyle flicked open his pocket watch. "It's after ten now."

Sorg clutched his arm. "We *have* to do something."

Boyle looked under pressure. He began to pace the room like a wild animal and asked Markov, "Is your telephone working?"

"If the local exchange workers have been drinking, probably not."

"Then I'll need a volunteer wearing one of the Red Army uniforms to run over to the central garage as fast as their legs can carry them. I'm betting the *komendant* will want the truck in place before he carries out the executions. If we can divert it elsewhere, that may delay things and give me time to think."

He said to Markov, "Can you lay your hands on any explosive material?"

"I'm an undertaker, not a bomb maker. Why?"

"We may need to create a diversion. This is a mining town. Dynamite can't be in short supply."

Markov shrugged. "If I had time perhaps, but we're cutting it a bit close."

"Do your best."

Sorg massaged his jaw and said to Boyle, "One other thing. Kazan."

"What about him?"

"He and I have unfinished business."

"Forget it. Focus on what's important. What else can you tell us?"

"Who's Andrev?"

Andrev frowned. "Me, why?"

"Yakov told me to pass you on a message. And to give you this."

Sorg pulled out the envelope. "He said there's a map and note with directions how to get to an abandoned grain warehouse a half mile north of the Ipatiev House. Yakov wants you to meet him there at eleven tonight. He said Nina's life may depend on it."

Stone-faced, Andrev took the envelope.

"He wants you to come alone."

Lydia stepped into the mortuary annex.

Andrev was standing over a table, checking his Nagant pistol, before he emptied a boxful of cartridges into his pockets.

She said, "Do you really think it's safe to go alone?"

"Probably not. That's why I'm taking some insurance."

As he slipped the revolver into his pocket, she put a hand on his arm. "I have a bad feeling about this, Uri. I really do."

"How else do I find out what's happened to Nina and Sergey? How else do I know if I can still save them?"

"What do you think Yakov wants?"

"To stop us, you can be sure that hasn't changed. Whatever else he's up to."

"What will you do? How will you handle it?"

"Honestly? I really don't know. I can only see how the cards fall."

"Let me go with you, please?"

He pulled on his jacket. "No, it's best you go back to the convent with the sister. Please, Lydia."

She met his stare, then on impulse she kissed him, her arms going around his neck. They embraced until at last he said, "I must go."

Yakov's envelope lay on the table unopened and he picked it up.

As he moved to the door, he turned up his jacket collar and looked back at her, a curious expression on his face. "Can I tell you something? I think you're right: our hearts are big enough to love more than one person in a life. I just wish we'd met another time, another place."

Her expression was very pale, and there was a heartrending look in her eyes. She touched her fingers to his lips, concern in her voice. "Be careful. Are you certain you can find the warehouse?"

Andrev tore open the envelope. "I've got Yakov's map."

From inside, he plucked two pieces of folded paper and opened them. Lydia saw that one was a rough map. The other was a handwritten letter.

Andrev read the letter.

As he did so his face drained of color, and he fell very still, his mouth open with a look of mute horror.

She saw his eyes become wet and he looked ready to crumple. "What . . . what's the matter?"

"It's Sergey." In a daze, Andrev handed her the letter.

102

IPATIEV HOUSE

Yakov drove the Fiat truck up to the barrier.

The guards waved him through and he marched up the steps and into Yurovsky's office. The *komendant* looked exhausted as he jumped to his feet, his eyes puffy.

"Commissar. I expected you sooner. You apprehended the enemy agents?"

A brooding Yakov helped himself to a samovar bubbling in a corner, heaping three spoonfuls of sugar into his glass of tea. "No. They evaded capture again. That's what delayed me."

"They won't cause us trouble, will they?"

Yakov said, tight-lipped, "Not if I can help it. Don't worry, we'll find them."

"The telegraph line to Moscow is still down. I assume you still have authority to confirm the execution order?"

"That's why I'm here. Is everything ready?"

"The basement room has been emptied in preparation. I have the truck ordered from the military garage for midnight, along with rolls of canvas to wrap the bodies. We'll keep the engine running so it'll help drown out the shooting."

Yakov said, "Don't begin until you have the truck in place. I don't want things getting messy. What about weapons?"

"We'll use handguns. They're easier to conceal from the family until the last moment."

"Tell me what you intend."

When the *komendant* explained, Yakov said, "You look uncertain."

The *komendant* shrugged. "It's the children. I sensed some of my men would have difficulty killing them. So I've changed several of the guards. After the executions are carried out, we'll take the corpses to the woods for disposal. I have stores of sulfuric acid and gasoline put by in case they're needed."

"What about you? Are you up to it, Yurovsky?"

The *komendant* smiled crookedly, as if he relished his task. "Have no doubt about that."

"You'll feel different afterward, I promise you that, so try not to look too happy about it. It'll be a bloody business, so make sure everyone clearly understands their orders."

"I was once a photographer. I intend arranging our victims in a particular order before we enter the room for the execution. It'll make things easier."

"Very well. Fetch the men you've chosen."

The *komendant* left and reappeared, ten of his troops trailing in, some in uniform, others wearing civilian clothes with red armbands. Yakov closed the door. "I've had all the weapons we need gathered from the other guards."

One of the men carried a wooden box containing handguns and ammunition, which he placed on the table. He began removing the firearms one by one. Nagants, a couple of Mausers, a pair of Colts, a Smith & Wesson. Assorted spare clips and boxes of ammunition.

Yakov held up one of the Colts. "You all know what's expected. If any one of you has *any* hesitation about using these weapons on women and children, step forward now. There's no shame. I won't criticize you."

The men shuffled, but nobody moved out of line.

Yakov said, "Questions?"

A thin, young man with narrow eyes and a wispy mustache said, "We shoot them *all together*?"

"The *komendant* thinks it'll be quicker that way."

Yakov's gaze swept round the half circle of men, meeting each of their stares in turn. "Let me make something perfectly clear. There's to be no stealing from the corpses. Any jewelry or personal items you find are to be left untouched and the *komendant* notified. If anyone disobeys, or the corpses are defiled in any way, I'll shoot the culprit personally. Understood?"

Heads nodded.

Yakov said, "You'll assemble here again once the truck arrives at midnight. Then the *komendant* will press the electric bell to summon the Romanovs from their quarters. They'll be told to gather downstairs in the basement room."

Yakov barely paused. "The *komendant* will inform the Romanovs that there are doubts about their safety, because the enemy is near the city, and they're to have their photograph taken to prove that they're alive and well. They'll be left alone to await the photographer. Explain your strategy, Komendant."

Yurovsky grinned. "There'll be no photographer. It's a ploy to put them at their ease. There are eleven of us, and eleven of them. I'll assign each of you a victim. Once we enter the room, I'll read out the execution order and immediately shoot Nicholai Romanov. Each of you will execute your chosen victim. Aim for the heart, so there'll be less blood."

The room fell as still as a grave.

Yakov could almost *feel* the silence. "Any more questions?"

No one answered.

Yakov checked his pocket watch and snapped it shut.

"Until our task begins, you're all dismissed. But remain in the house."

The men filed out of the room. Only the *komendant* remained and said to Yakov, "You'll stay?"

"No, I'll be back around midnight. I'll need to witness the disposal of the bodies before I return to Moscow with my report. Meantime, I have work to finish."

"Finding the enemy agents?"

Yakov nodded, his face solemn, and then he moved to the door and was gone.

103

Lydia opened the chapel door.

It creaked as she closed it again and then the chapel fell still.

Beeswax candles flickered, and she was aware of being enveloped by an immense calm, like being plunged into warm water.

She knelt beside one of benches, in front of an icon of the Virgin and child.

She lost any sense of time until she heard the patter of feet on the flagstones. Sister Agnes came toward her, her habit rustling.

The nun genuflected toward the altar, making a sign of the cross. "There you are. Forgive me for interrupting your prayers." She observed Lydia keenly. "You look troubled. Are you worried that your friend won't make it back?"

"Does it show?"

"I'm worried, too. But with you, it seems personal. Do you love him, my child?"

"He's the first man I've cared deeply about in a long time."

"And this troubles you?"

Lydia glanced up at the Virgin and child. "It's always a question of the human heart, isn't it? How do we live? What do we do? How do we know what's right or wrong? I came here to pray for guidance, I suppose. I feel a little lost, and maybe more than a little afraid."

The nun faced the altar. "For me, there is the simple joy of being here, in this place, that soothes me. Here, I'm always utterly aware of my human faults and weaknesses, and how imperfect I am in God's presence. Yet I'm aware of his infinite compassion and love."

Sister Agnes looked back at her. "Do you know what most people don't grasp? That God has already forgiven us our sins before we even commit them." She reached out, gently took Lydia's hands in hers. "I recognize anguish when I see it. Whatever's troubling you, don't be afraid to unburden yourself."

It all came out in a torrent as Lydia struggled to hold back her emotion.

Sister Agnes said gently, "It hasn't been easy, has it? Losing your child, and your fiancé, and now all this." The nun made the sign of the cross. "I'll pray for your friend, and for the soul of his child."

"Uri's an honorable man. I think he feels caught between duty to his son's mother and whatever he might feel for me."

"I understand."

Lydia put her hand on her stomach. "No, you don't, Sister. He and I, we . . . we've been close. Perhaps in my heart I wanted it to happen, wanted another chance to create life. I'm sure that sounds foolish. None of us knows if we'll come out of this alive. But people often act irrationally in wartime, don't they? We're driven by our most primitive instincts to survive."

"Whatever wrong you may have done, I'm sure God forgives you already, my child."

"But do love and emotion always have to be so complex?"

The nun rose. "What happens in the heart, simply happens. But sometimes real love calls us to a higher duty. We have to do what's right, and not always what we desire."

Sister Agnes's face was a study in pious strength as she looked down at Lydia. "It's the eternal question, isn't it? That's what you really asked. How should I live? By my own way, or the right way? Yet the answer is simple. In our hearts we know what's the right thing. We always do."

She laid a hand gently on Lydia's shoulder. "And now, we really have to go. Time's running out."

104

The abandoned grain warehouse had long ago been let go to wrack and ruin. The roof was caved in, the plaster walls crumbling and overgrown.

Yakov halted the Fiat at the entrance, lit a cigarette, and strode down to the ramshackle wooden boardwalk overlooking the lake. The moon shimmered on the water, the light good enough to see by.

He could just make out the white outline of the Ipatiev House farther along the shore, pale as a ghostly apparition. He felt in turmoil as he stood there, smoking furiously, one foot propped on an uprooted tree stump.

"You came alone?"

He spun round as Andrev stepped out from the ruins of the abandoned warehouse. He clutched a Nagant in his hand.

Yakov tossed away his cigarette. It cartwheeled into the water, vanishing with a tiny hiss. "Yes. We need to talk, Uri."

Andrev stepped closer. His eyes were wild and he looked desolate, his face grimmer than Yakov had ever seen.

Without a word he lashed out with the revolver and struck Yakov a blow across the head. Yakov reeled, clapping a hand to his skull as he fell against the uprooted tree.

"I ought to kill you here and now." Andrev spat the words.

Yakov stumbled to his feet. "Nothing I did would have made a difference. *Nothing.* You have to believe that, Uri."

Andrev's tone was savage. "My son had a chance to live if he'd remained in Moscow. You took that chance away."

"No, Uri, nothing could have saved him. My medic did his best but Sergey was past help, believe me."

Andrev let out an anguished cry. He stifled it, put his sleeve to his mouth.

Yakov said, "The truth is, Trotsky ordered me to transport Nina and your son to a prison camp. I disobeyed the order. I took them from Moscow to try to save them. How, I wasn't sure, but I knew I had to get them away."

"How can I ever believe you?"

"Because I know now that you didn't kill Stanislas. I was wrong. I had my reasons, selfish and foolish ones. Now, I accept your word, just as I ask you to accept mine."

Andrev struggled to compose himself. He looked lost, devastated. "How is Nina taking it?"

"She's broken. Disconsolate. She needs you. Whatever your differences, I'm not sure she's ever truly stopped loving you."

Andrev's mouth tightened. "Where is she?"

"On board my train at Ekaterinburg station. Zoba's taking care of her."

"If she's been harmed . . ."

"She hasn't. I care too much for her. Can I tell you something? All those years ago, when we first met, I think I fell in love with her."

Andrev frowned.

"Don't look at me like that, Uri. It was something pure. I was a street urchin from the Black Quarter. I'd never seen such beauty. To me, Nina was something rare and exotic. I'll admit there were times when just to be able to think about her helped keep me sane in the grimness all around me. Does that make sense? I'd never deliberately harm her. You have to accept that."

Andrev took the envelope from his pocket, held it up. "So, she told you everything?"

Yakov nodded. "A man loses a wife, a woman loses a husband; they find comfort in each other's company. That's what happened to our parents. A simple story; they did nothing wrong. In truth, only good came of it. I found a brother."

"Did Nina tell you why they kept their secret?"

Yakov said, "Having a relationship with a female patient was bad enough. Having a child by her would have destroyed your father if it became public."

"You're not bitter?"

"I've no reason. Your father was an honorable man. He cared for us, he did his duty. You know, there's something he once said to me. I didn't understand it then, but I do now. He said that whenever we're offered love, we should accept it. Wherever we encounter tenderness, we should embrace it. I know now what he meant. Just as I know now that you could never have harmed our own brother. I only hope that Mersk went screaming to his death."

Andrev looked as if a terrible weight still pressed down on him, and he said, "There were times when I wanted to tell you the truth. Times after my father died when I felt I should break my promise to him. You see, he never wanted their secret to hurt you. But they both should have told us, I realize that now."

Yakov put a hand on his shoulder. "That was then, this is now. *We* know, and that's enough."

"You never told me what happened to my men after I escaped."

"I did what I could. No one walked, no one perished."

There seemed a timelessness to everything. The moon on the still water, the dim outline of the Ipatiev House in the far distance. The only sound was their own breathing until finally Yakov said, "I know it looks hopeless. But maybe there's a way out of this for all of us."

"How?"

"You leave, tonight, with Nina. Just go. You and your friends. You can take the train I seized. Leave the city and don't come back."

"And the tsar and his family?"

Yakov shook his head. "That's out of my hands, Uri. It's bigger than both of us. I can't change their fate, even if I wanted to. I don't care a whit for Nicholai Romanov or his wife. The children I can feel for, but their parents dug their own grave."

"Yet you'd bury the children in it, too?"

"It's Lenin's wish, not mine. I'm a soldier. I obey orders, just like you."

"And what happens to you and Katerina if you let us go?"

"That's my worry."

"How will you explain Nina's disappearance?"

"This isn't a city short of bodies. Who's to say if she lived or died?"

Andrev considered. "Your train's at the station?"

"In a siding next to platform three."

"What about your men?"

"They're billeted in nearby hotels, but Zoba's on board with Nina and my medic. Zoba will follow my orders and have the train ready for you. The driver's been told to keep the boiler stoked. What do you say?"

Andrev fell silent. His mouth was set tightly, as if he was struggling with his conscience, then his hand went down and the Nagant came up again. He leveled it at Yakov. "You can come out now."

There was a rustle of bushes and Boyle stepped out of the shadows, carrying a Colt and clutching a coarse sack and some rope.

Yakov said angrily, "I said to come alone, Uri."

"I didn't know if I could trust you. I'm sorry, but it has to be this way."

"What are you talking about?"

"I'm not one to break my word, but in war, all's fair." He jerked his head at Boyle. "Take his weapon. Make sure he doesn't have more than one."

Boyle removed Yakov's firearm and patted down his body.

Andrev said, "We intend to finish the job we came to do." He nodded to Boyle. "Put the sack over his head and lead him to the truck."

"Where are you taking me?" Yakov demanded.

"After a short detour, the Ipatiev House."

Yakov erupted. "You're insane. You'll never get near the house."

"You're right, Leonid. But *you* will."

105

As he replaced the telephone earpiece in its cradle, Yurovsky heard the rattle of an engine. He stepped over to the open doorway.

He saw an open-topped Opel car halt outside the courtyard. Four men were seated inside, wearing Chekist leather jackets, Kazan in the driver's seat.

The guards leveled their rifles. "No vehicles are allowed past the barricade. Order of the *komendant*."

"Let me through, you idiot." Kazan stumbled drunkenly from the car, but one of guards cocked his rifle. "Another step and I'll shoot."

Yurovsky strode out to the barrier. The other three men in the Opel looked as intoxicated as their driver. "What do you want, Kazan?"

"We have to talk." The Inspector stank of alcohol, a bottle protruding from his left pocket, and his eyes had a disturbed look.

"No, we don't. You ought to know the compound's out of bounds tonight." The *komendant* jerked his head. "Get yourself some coffee in the guardhouse across the street and sober up. You're in no fit state to drive."

Kazan wiped his mouth with the back of his hand and lowered his voice to a whisper. "Believe me, Yurovsky, you'll want to hear what I have to say. Have you commenced your bloody work yet?"

"No, but what's it to you?"

"Yakov released the spy I caught. *Released* him, would you believe?"

"For what reason?"

"I asked myself the same question. I thought he was trying to grab all the glory but now, I'm not so sure. He and one of the plotters are old friends."

"What the blazes are you muttering about?"

"Let me put it simply. I've been a policeman long enough to know when I smell a rat. I'm convinced Yakov's in league with the enemy and up to no good."

"Have you lost your mind? Whatever's in that bottle you're drinking, I'd get rid of it now."

"There's something sinister afoot, I tell you. How do you explain Yakov releasing the spy? Answer me that."

The *komendant* said gruffly, "I don't have to. It's not my business. But when I last saw him a few hours ago he was sober and clearheaded, unlike you."

"Where did he go?"

"I've no idea, but he's quartered in his train. Now get out of here, I have a job to finish."

"You're being an idiot! We'll see who's right before the night's out."

The *komendant* turned to go but Kazan clutched his arm. "Wait— I've only three men. I need more."

"For what?"

"I'm going to find that accursed spy if I have to tear Ekaterinburg apart."

The *komendant* jerked his arm away. "Forget it. I need every man I've got." He turned to the guards and said, "Throw this drunken madman out."

The *komendant* lit a cigarette in the doorway and watched Kazan back up the Opel and drive away, the car weaving erratically.

"Trouble, *komendant*?" one of the guards asked.

"Kazan thinks Commissar Yakov is in league with enemy agents."

The guard laughed. "I wish I could find alcohol like that. The really good stuff. No sign of the truck?"

"I just made a call. The idiots said they got an order to send it to the Amerika Hotel by mistake."

Just then twin headlights swept up the street. The driver was grinding the gears as he drove the Fiat open-topped truck toward the Ipatiev courtyard.

"About time," said Yurovsky, checking his pocket watch. It read 1:30 a.m. exactly. He said to the guard, "Alert the men. Tell them we're ready."

Yurovsky climbed the stairs to the Romanovs' quarters. At their door he raised his right index finger, and let it hover over the electric doorbell.

Then he pressed it.

Anastasia heard the shrill sound of the electric bell echo throughout the family quarters and it woke her with a start.

It was dark outside, pale moonlight filtering though the white-washed windows. Next to her, Maria came awake groggily, rubbing her tousled hair. "Was that the bell? What's happening?"

"I don't know. I thought I heard a car engine," Anastasia replied.

Footsteps sounded from their parents' room. A knock came on wood, then more footsteps and voices, until moments later someone approached their door. Maria said, "Papa's coming."

The door opened and their father stood tired and disheveled, buttoning his shirt. "It seems the *komendant* wants us to assemble downstairs."

"Why, Papa?"

"He says the enemy is encircling the city and that battle is imminent. He's afraid that artillery may fall on the house and he wants to move us for our own safety."

Maria said innocently, "*Our* artillery?"

"Yes, my sweet."

Anastasia perked up. "Do you think they'll finally rescue us?"

Her father smiled briefly and fondly touched her face. "We can only pray, my darlings. Now, get yourselves washed and dressed. The others are already up."

A nervous Yurovsky felt sweat rise on the back of his neck, his impatience mounting. Standing in the hallway, smoking another cigarette, his stomach a knot of tension, he heard the family pace their rooms as they washed and got ready. He wanted to hurry them up.

One of his guards came up the stairs and said, "Any sign of Commissar Yakov?"

"Not yet. But that won't delay us. Everything goes ahead."

But Yurovsky was becoming more worried by the minute. He again checked his pocket watch. It was 2:10 a.m. Forty minutes had passed since he rang the bell. He swore softly.

He was tempted to ring the bell again to hurry things along when the door snapped open. One by one the Romanovs appeared on the landing, all dressed and tidy. Nicholai Romanov was the first to lead out his family, holding his crippled son in his arms.

The girls came next, wearing their simple white blouses and dark skirts, carrying pillows, bags, and other personal items. The former tsarina appeared behind them, gaunt and tense as ever, plainly dressed in a dark skirt and blouse, her gray hair untidy. Last, Dr. Botkin and the three servants crowded the landing.

"All ready, I see," the *komendant* remarked to Nicholai Romanov.

"At least we're going to leave this place, *komendant*. But what about our personal belongings?"

"That's not necessary right now. We'll fetch them later. This way." Yurovsky offered a reassuring smile, then escorted them down the stairs.

As they passed the stuffed mother bear and its cubs on the landing, the family paused and devoutly blessed themselves: a familiar sign of respect for the dead, believing that they were about to leave the house for the last time.

Yurovsky heard familiar yelping above on the landing as their three dogs barked and scampered, trying to follow them. The guards grabbed their collars and held them back but one of the dogs managed to squirm free and scurried into Anastasia's arms.

She said, "What about the other animals, *komendant*?"

A distant *crump* of artillery fire sounded, startling them all.

Yurovsky shook his head. "Please, don't worry. They'll be brought to you later. For now it's important that we hurry . . ."

106

Yurovsky led the family down to the basement. He opened the double doors and ushered them inside a room with a single lightbulb dangling from the vaulted ceiling. Along one wall, a grime-covered window was protected with metal bars. The bare floorboards echoed, and there were no chairs.

"You'll wait here for now."

Alexandra indicated her husband, struggling under the weight of their son. "Aren't we allowed to sit? My husband has to carry our child."

The *komendant* jerked his head at one of the three-guard escort. "Fetch two chairs."

The guard returned carrying a pair of bentwood chairs, which he placed near the doors by the far wall. Nicholai Romanov gently lowered his son onto one. His wife eased into the other. Their daughters gathered beside their mother, while Dr. Botkin and the others stood nearby.

As the boy watched him with wide, curious eyes, Yurovsky began to arrange his victims in a particular order, behind the chairs. "There have been rumors that your health is not good," he told them, "and that you are being poorly treated. So before we leave, I will need a photograph to prove otherwise. Please stand as I ask."

The family obeyed as the *komendant* posed them: Maria, Tatiana, and Olga standing close behind their mother, who remained seated; the family doctor and the three domestic servants in front of Anastasia, who stood defiantly alone. Nicholai Romanov stood next to his son, sitting in the second chair.

The *komendant* once again checked his watch. "The photographer is delayed but will be here presently. I'll be back once he arrives."

His men retreated from the room. Yurovsky was the last to leave. He paused at the door. Did he see a faint hint of uncertainty, a glimmer of terror on their faces?

His said reassuringly, "Once we've finished taking the photograph, you will board the truck in an orderly fashion. You'll be driven to a safer location, away from any shelling."

He took a final look at his victims, making sure they were still in the same pose, and then he nodded, pulling the doors shut after him with a soft click.

In the room at the back of the mortuary, lit by a bare lightbulb, Boyle donned dark breeches and leather knee boots and pulled on a Chekist leather jacket.

He studied the de Gennin map, the parchment laid out on the table, then looked up. "How are they getting on with the bodies?"

Andrev peered out into the courtyard and saw Markov and Sorg finish loading a dozen of the white-sheeted corpses onto the back of the hearse. "It looks like they're done."

They returned, Markov closing the door after them, carrying a sledgehammer and a pick. "Once I hitch up the horses we're ready to go. Here are the tools you wanted."

Boyle examined them. "Perfect. What about explosives?"

"I'm afraid all I have are some cans of kerosene and a supply of embalming fluid. I'm no chemist, but I'd bet that if you ignite both you'll make quite a bang."

"I'll have to take your word for it. Load everything on board the hearse before we leave. And I'll need clear directions for the tunnels."

Markov nodded and left.

Andrev said to Boyle, "You mind telling me now what exactly you have in mind?"

"First, you better bring Yakov in and see what kind of mood he's in."

Andrev returned, escorting Yakov, still blindfolded by the sackcloth and with his hands tied. Boyle stood in front of him and tore the sack from his head.

Yakov blinked and took in the scene. Facing him, next to Andrev, was a big, solidly built man. He looked formidable, all business, his hands on his hips. Yakov's eyes darted around the windowless chamber. "Where are we? What goes here?"

Boyle said bluntly, "Tell the commissar we'll need his full cooperation. If he gives it, he'll live to see his daughter."

Andrev translated. Yakov was silent, stern-faced.

Boyle went on: "Tell him that in return for his help he can accompany us when we leave Ekaterinburg once we've finished our business. I solemnly promise we'll get him and his daughter out of Russia. I have people in Moscow who can do that, just as soon as I can arrange it. Tell him."

Andrev translated.

Yakov uttered a terse reply.

Boyle asked, "What did he say?"

"You're insane, and haven't a hope."

Boyle's mouth tightened in an almost chilling grimace. He stepped up to Yakov, grabbed him by both lapels as he stared into his face. "You could be right about both. But you'll do exactly as you're told, whether you like it or not."

Andrev translated.

Boyle added, "Tell him if he doesn't, I'll make sure he's keeping the devil company before the night's out."

Andrev interpreted; Yakov remained tight-lipped.

Boyle stepped back and Lydia asked, "What happens now?"

"Markov, you and I will travel in the hearse. Yakov will lead us in the truck, Uri with him, to get us past any checkpoints."

"I hope you have a solid plan, Boyle," Andrev said.

Boyle jabbed a finger at the parchment. "It's bluntly simple. We'll haul the bodies into the tunnel entrance, along with the kerosene and embalming fluid. Later, when we exit the tunnel, we ignite both fluids. In an enclosed space, it should cause an impressive blast."

"What about the guards on the tunnel?"

"I'll deal with that," Boyle said. "But first, you and Yakov have to gain entry to the house. I need you to convince the *komendant* that the executions will go ahead, but that you're to conduct a last-minute interrogation of the family, on Moscow's orders."

"Interrogate them about what?"

"The missing jewels are as good a reason as any. Make it clear that Lenin wants all the Romanov valuables accounted for. Tell the *komendant* you have information that precious stones have been withheld and that you intend to find them. You'll need to get the family into the basement room and keep the guards out. Only then can we attempt to evacuate them through the tunnel."

"That's asking an awful lot, Boyle."

He smiled and slapped a hand on Andrev's shoulder. "Of course it is, but I have every confidence in a man of your abilities."

"What will *we* be doing?" Lydia asked.

"You and I will make our way to the basement, to guide the family out through the storeroom. Once everyone's safely aboard the ambulance, I'll blow the tunnel." Boyle hefted up the sledgehammer and the pickaxe. "I want to be prepared in case we need to open up the wall some more or breach the basement doors."

Lydia said, "Troops will be swarming all over the area after the blast. What happens when they find the bodies?"

"If the blast does its job, there won't be much left to identify, which ought to distract them while we're quitting town."

"How?" asked Sorg.

"I want you and Markov to get down to the railway station. Make sure that Yakov's train is stoked and ready to depart."

"And how do we do that?"

"You'll have a written order from Yakov here. We'll join you just as soon as we can."

Sorg shook his head stubbornly. "No, I'm going into the tunnel with you."

Boyle snapped, "We've all got a job to do for this to stand a chance, and I've given you yours. It's vital the train's ready. Now can I depend on you or not?"

Sorg didn't look happy but answered, "Yes."

Andrev said, "What if by some miracle we all manage to make it to the station, then what?"

"We'll head south, toward the White lines. Beyond that, I'm hoping we'll have a clear run all the way to Bucharest."

"Aren't you forgetting about the machine-gun nest in the church tower? And the other two at the house?"

"We'll be out of their line of fire and in darkness, so they shouldn't bother us."

Andrev considered. "I still don't like it. Everything's too rushed."

Boyle replied, "It could either go as smoothly as silk, or we could all wind up dead. But do you have you a better idea at this stage?"

"No."

"Then we're stuck with it." Boyle tore his Colt pistol from its holster. He slapped his notebook and a fountain pen on the table. "Now, tell Yakov here I want him to write a note, and he's to be quick about it."

107

In the guardroom, Yurovsky nervously rechecked his two firearms, a Colt and a Mauser. The final moment was approaching. His men sat hunched together, chain-smoking cigarettes, clutching their weapons, a few with bayonets stuck inside their belts. Adrenaline coursed through their veins; every one of them was on edge, their tempers frayed, Yurovsky could see that.

One of them, a swaggering drunk named Ermakov, looked eager for action with three revolvers. He clutched two near-empty bottles of vodka, one in each hand, and splashed generous measures into the men's enamel mugs. "Get that into you, you're going to need it, comrades. But make sure you shoot straight." Ermakov grinned drunkenly. "Send them all to hell, every last one of them; there'll be no sparing women or children."

Yurovsky swallowed a mouthful of vodka from a bottle on the table and wiped his lips. He allowed the alcohol because he knew his men needed it for the grim task ahead. He already felt a little drunk himself, but not so much that he didn't realize the men were getting out of control. Their fast and furious drinking was giving them Dutch courage, but if it kept up they would be in no fit state.

He slapped down his mug and grabbed the bottles from Ermakov. "Enough! We all need clear heads."

"When are we going to do it? When?" Ermakov snarled.

Yurovsky again consulted his watch: 2:15 a.m. From his tunic, he took the piece of paper that contained the execution order he would read to the family. He beckoned one of the younger guards. "Have the driver start the truck. The rest of you, prepare your weapons."

■   ■   ■

The Fiat drove toward the lake and slowed as it approached the arch-way. They were over three hundred yards from the Ipatiev House.

A pair of Reds with bayoneted rifles guarded the iron door. They stepped out from under the archway, one of them waving a lantern. The second guard held up his hand for the truck to halt. The guards looked young, barely in their teens, but alert and cautious. They stud-ied the men wearing leather jackets seated in the truck. A female in the back wore a Red Army uniform and carried a lantern. One of the guards said, "We have orders not to let anyone pass here."

Andrev left the engine running and climbed down, leaving Boyle on the other side of the front seat, holding an unseen Colt pistol to Yakov's side.

"I'm Commissar Couris. This is Commissar Yakov, from Moscow."

The guard nodded, recognizing Yakov from the compound, and respectfully tipped his forehead. "Yes, Commissar."

Andrev snapped, "This area is under control of the Cheka for now. We'll take over here. You two keep watch down by the lake."

"But we have orders—"

"And now you have mine."

As the guards disappeared in the lake's direction, Andrev jumped back into the Fiat.

Boyle said, "You did the wise thing, Commissar." He offered Yakov a cigarette, and he accepted it. Boyle tossed him a box of matches. "Tell him what I said, Uri."

Andrev translated.

Yakov lit a cigarette, blew out smoke, and seemed strangely calm. "You're walking to your deaths, all of you. There are more guards around the Ipatiev House than there are flies on a jam pot on a sum-mer's day."

Andrev interpreted, and Boyle smiled. "Typically Russian, always the pessimist. But it's not over yet." He nodded to Lydia. "Give the signal."

Lydia waved her lantern.

Within minutes there came the sound of horses' hooves, clip-clopping through the darkness. Markov appeared driving the hearse, Sorg beside him, the carriage laden down with white-sheeted corpses. The undertaker jerked the reins and the hearse settled to a halt.

Boyle wasted no time inserting the key in the gate lock. The door yawned open, revealing the tunnel. He gestured to Sorg. "Fetch some lamps and we'll get these bodies unloaded."

Sorg climbed down and grabbed two more lamps from the back of the carriage and lit them. They worked quickly, moving the corpses into the tunnel. Markov removed the white sheets, the sickly smell of death already on the air.

When they were finished, Markov folded the sheets and tossed them on the hearse. He handed Boyle a single written sheet of paper containing a diagram. "My directions are simple enough to follow, and I've drawn a map so you won't get lost. You'll see our symbol marked in paint above the metal turret."

Boyle took the page. "With any luck, we'll meet you at the station. Give us no more than an hour."

Markov climbed up on the hearse and took the reins. Sorg joined him and said, "Mind telling me what happens if you don't appear by then?"

Boyle slapped one of the horse's flanks. "It's a case of every man for himself. Go!"

As the sound of the horses' hooves faded, Boyle checked his watch. The rattle of a vehicle sounded on cobblestone and he said to Andrev, "Right on time."

The motorized ambulance appeared out of the gloom, its head-lights off, Sister Agnes driving. She halted under the archway, the engine running.

Boyle went to speak with her and when he came back he said to Andrev, "We're all set. Here's hoping we'll meet you in the basement."

Lydia said, "Good luck, Uri."

"You be careful."

Boyle hurried them, and they barely had a moment to embrace

before he handed Lydia a lantern and ushered her inside the iron door. He grabbed a lantern for himself, and the sledgehammer and pickaxe, and went to join her.

He paused at the doorway. Fixing Yakov with a threatening stare, he addressed Andrev. "Make certain Yakov understands. If he gives us the slightest hint of trouble, he gets a bullet."

Somewhere outside the house, Anastasia heard a truck start up. Then came a harsh crunch of gears and the engine noise grew louder. The vibration rattled the grimy, barred window.

She realized she was in the same room where her interrogation took place. The table was gone, but the chairs the guard had brought looked like the same ones.

Everyone appeared tense and expectant, even her papa. No one spoke, apart from a few whispers from her mother, and little Alexei. Beyond the double doors, they all heard raised, muffled noises that sounded like the guards getting drunk.

"Where's the photographer, Papa?" Alexei asked for the third time.

"Heaven knows. But I'm sure he'll be here soon."

"They told us to hurry but they're leaving us to wait."

"I'm sure they have their reasons, Anastasia. They can't be long."

Anastasia clutched her dog in her arms. Jimmy had settled down, the little spaniel content to be stroked. She looked over at her papa again. Why did he keep giving Dr. Botkin odd glances? Her father smiled back at her reassuringly. But she had a strange feeling in the pit of her stomach—a feeling she couldn't explain—and it wouldn't go away. "Maybe they've got drunk and forgotten about us, Papa?" she said, looking for an answer—any answer.

"I hope not, my love."

Anxiety was growing in everyone, she sensed that. Alexei, wide-eyed as always, shifted uneasily in his chair, clutching his crippled leg. Olga, emaciated with worry this last year, was wringing her hands and hovering by their mother, tight-lipped and nervous. Tatiana, as ever of late, looked pale and sickly as death. Maria, with her baby face and her lush hair down about her shoulders, somehow still managed to look the picture of health, but she offered her sister a fleeting, anxious smile.

Anastasia winked back. *How I love them all.*

And at that moment, for some strange reason, she felt the intensity of that love all the more. Perhaps because they were all here, huddled expectantly as prisoners in this small room, ignorant of what would happen to them next. She felt vulnerable, and sensed that vulnerability in each member of her family, though not a word was spoken now.

Of the others, Dr. Botkin looked the most apprehensive. He fidgeted, clasping and unclasping his hands, sweat beading his forehead.

The small room felt warm and claustrophobic.

But Anastasia felt that their discomfort was more than that: it was as if everyone in the room sensed *something* was about to happen, and yet no one knew what. *Or is it simply my imagination?*

A second later, they all heard it: a rumbling, jarring noise. Not the vehicle engine—that was still humming in the background. This sound was different.

Heavy footsteps. Lots of them, marching toward the doors.

Her dog's ears pricked up and his tiny body fidgeted in her arms. For some reason she glanced at her brother's face: Alexei's skin was even more bone-white than usual. He looked petrified with fear.

The floorboards trembled and shook like thunder. A split second later, the doors burst open . . .

108

Andrev sat in front next to Yakov, who drove the Fiat up a deserted Voznesensky Prospect. As the wheels bumped over cobble, Yakov said, "Why sacrifice your life and Nina's? Why dare so much, and for what? We can still turn back. I beg you. This stands no hope."

Andrev kept one hand in his jacket pocket on the Nagant. "In spite of that I must try."

"The family could already be dead for all we know."

"We delayed the truck from the garage. Nothing's going to happen without transport to remove the bodies."

"And even if you make it inside the house, then what?"

Andrev said, "You tell the *komendant* we have a special directive from Lenin. The execution order's to be delayed just long enough for us to search the family for the missing gems."

"And how do you convince him you have the authority?"

Andrev removed the forged letter from his pocket. "This ought to confuse him for long enough. All I need is five minutes alone with the family to get them into the tunnel."

"I tell you it's doomed, Uri."

"We'll see. No tricks, Leonid. I don't want to kill you, but if I have to, so help me I will."

They approached the Ipatiev House compound. The guards on the barrier looked tense but they relaxed a little when they saw Yakov. "Raise the barrier," he ordered. The guards studied Andrev. Yakov said, "This is Commissar Couris, on a special mission from Moscow."

Andrev produced his letter but the guards, probably illiterate, didn't examine it, and instead looked to Yakov for reassurance. "The *komendant* gave orders for no one to enter."

"I gave him those orders. Now raise the barrier. We have urgent business."

Anastasia almost jumped as the door burst open and the *komendant* reappeared.

Behind him were more of his men. She got a strong smell of alcohol. She felt a catch in her heart: something about this was not right. She looked at her sisters, and all of them appeared frightened.

Her mother stiffened, her father bravely stepped forward, but there was an anxious note in his voice. "Well, here we all are. What are you going to do now?"

The tiny room seemed even smaller, crowded to extreme, and whether it was the enclosed space or her nervous reaction to all the men suddenly storming into the room, she found it harder to breathe.

Yurovsky held a piece of paper in his left hand, his other hand stuck in his pocket. Anastasia noticed tiny beads of sweat on his forehead.

"Will you please all stand?"

Anastasia saw her mother struggle to her feet. Only Alexei remained seated, unable to raise himself.

The *komendant* took a step forward, his voice raised as he read from the note. "In view of the fact that your relatives and supporters, and enemy agents, continue to try to rescue you, you have been sentenced to be shot."

Nicholai Romanov stared at the *komendant* blankly before he turned to his family, incomprehension on his face. "What . . . what?" He turned back, deathly white. "I don't understand. Read it again."

Yurovsky repeated his words and added, "The revolution has decreed that the former tsar, Nicholai Romanov, is guilty of countless bloody crimes against his people and is to be shot."

Anastasia saw her sisters cross themselves, fear in all their faces now, for it all seemed to happen so fast as the *komendant* drew a pistol from his right pocket. He shot her father point-blank in the chest.

Anastasia shrieked in horror.

And then sheer madness broke loose as the room erupted in a torrent of gunfire and screams . . .

109

Yakov drove into the courtyard. Another truck was already parked there, its engine running, a driver at the wheel, smoking a cigarette. He acknowledged them with a nod.

"Get out, leave the engine running," Andrev whispered to Yakov.

Yakov obeyed. Andrev joined him.

With both truck engines running, it took a moment to register but then they heard an explosion of gunfire from somewhere inside the house.

Andrev's face drained of color and he felt his heart sink. "No . . ."

"I told you, Uri."

Andrev was rooted to the spot as the gunfire raged inside the house, a savage volley, followed by sporadic shots and hysterical screams, then came complete silence.

Yakov said, "Turn back *now* and no one will be the wiser. It's not too late."

But Andrev kept his hand on his revolver and grimly urged Yakov toward the entrance. "Inside, quickly."

Boyle stumbled through the tunnel. He carried the sledgehammer and pickaxe on one shoulder, the lamp held high in his hand, shadows flickering on the walls.

Beside him, Lydia consulted Markov's directions.

Boyle said, "Well?"

"The storeroom can't be much farther."

They heard a ferocious crack, like thunder. Lydia recognized a gunshot and at the same instant Boyle stiffened and their eyes locked. His face looked deathly as an eruption of gunfire echoed like an avalanche in the passageway.

"Dear God, no . . ." Lydia put a hand to her mouth.

Boyle's face was desolate as he wrenched the pistol from his pocket and they hurried on.

The house seemed in chaos as Andrev followed Yakov through several rooms toward the basement.

A stench of gunpowder choked the air and there was mayhem as about a dozen guards appeared from one of the basement rooms, all of them armed and gasping for breath. Most carried pistols, but a few grasped long bayonets dripping blood. They covered their mouths and noses with their jacket sleeves and coughed and spluttered. There was no mistaking the stink of alcohol as the men staggered toward the guardroom.

The *komendant* looked badly shaken, his face bleached. He stuffed a handkerchief over his mouth, his eyes streaming red from the choking smoke, and he barely recognized Yakov and his comrade.

"What's wrong?" An ashen Yakov gripped his arm.

Yurovsky gave a hacking cough and glanced over his shoulder toward the basement double doors, one of them half open, the view inside obscured by a gray cloud of fog.

"We couldn't see for gunsmoke . . . there were ricochets everywhere. We had to stop shooting . . . it's like hell in there. There's blood everywhere."

"Are they dead?"

Yurovsky looked ill as he fought to breathe, his lungs rasping. "As far as I could tell—I checked pulses. It was brutal—our shots didn't seem to penetrate the children. It got very bloody toward the end, we had to use bayonets." Just then the *komendant* threw up into the handkerchief, vomit spewing onto the floor and Yakov's boots. The *komendant* wiped his mouth. "I—I'm sorry, Commissar."

"Go to the guardroom and remain there with your men," Yakov ordered. He pushed past, Andrev following stone-faced as they both strode toward the basement's double doors.

EKATERINBURG RAILWAY STATION

Markov halted the hearse with a jerk of the reins. A couple of carriages were parked outside the station, the drivers curled up in the back, asleep, sheepskin blankets pulled over them.

Past the entrance archway, the platforms looked crowded, mostly with peasants hugging their belongings, some awake, some sleeping, all of them waiting for trains. A stench of stale food and sweaty bodies wafted out on the night air.

Sorg climbed down. "Wait here."

A jittery Markov tied the reins to a tethering post. "Forget it. I can't leave this town fast enough. I'm coming with you."

Sorg moved through the crowded station and found the train parked in a siding by platform number three.

Markov said worriedly, "It looks deserted."

They approached the carriage nearest the locomotive, and its blinds were down. Sorg tried the door. It was locked. He rapped on the glass. No response. He rapped again.

Finally, the carriage door snapped open. A short, stocky man stared warily at his visitors.

"I'm looking for Zoba."

"I'm Zoba. What do you want?"

Sorg said, "I have a written order from Commissar Yakov. He wants the train made ready immediately for departure."

The man named Zoba glanced over his shoulder, as if he had company, then finally said, "You better come aboard." He stepped back, admitting them into a spacious private lounge with a bedchamber leading off. A woman lay on a cot at the far end of the carriage. Her eyes looked red from crying, a deadness in her, as if her senses had lost their sharpness.

A medic was kneeling over her, a black doctor's bag beside him. He had an anesthetic gauze mask in his hand and he was holding it over the woman's face, pouring drops of clear liquid from a bottle onto the gauze, the sickly smell of ether cutting the air. The woman's eyes flickered and closed.

Sorg offered Zoba the written note. "You'll want to see this."

A voice from somewhere said, "Everything comes to him who waits."

A door was slammed.

Sorg spun round. His heart chilled.

An armed, leather-jacketed man appeared out of nowhere to cover Zoba and the woman. Two others stepped from the carriage annex, and they roughly grabbed a frightened Markov.

Kazan followed, holding a pistol, a sly grin on his face. "Well, well. Will you look at what the cat's dragged in?"

110

The room looked like a slaughterhouse.

Through a fog and stench of gunsmoke, Andrev entered behind Yakov and closed the doors. Andrev's voice choked with despair, "Dear God..."

It was a scene to shock the hardest of hearts. Eleven bodies lay in a twisted, pitiful sprawl—the family, their doctor, and their servants. A sea of blood covered the wooden floors. Bullet holes gouged the walls, which were spattered with crimson splashes and flecks of brain matter.

Two of the sisters, Olga and Tatiana, lay almost entwined together, as if in a last, pitiful embrace. Both had been shot and bayoneted, their white blouses drenched in blood still flowing from gaping head and body wounds.

The boy, Alexei, lay slumped on the floor beneath an upturned chair, his crippled legs twisted beneath him, the back of his skull shattered by bullets. Crumpled on the floor, the ex-tsar and his wife were covered in blood. Nearby were the family doctor and the maids, their eyes open in death, their agonized expressions testament to their brutal death.

Anastasia lay slumped against the wall on the right, near her sister Maria. Both had their arms outstretched, as if they had tried to fend off their killers until the very end. Anastasia's head was bleeding, her skull slashed by cuts.

Yakov stared blankly at the spectacle until he was forced to cover his mouth with his sleeve.

As Andrev stood clutching his revolver, the fog of gunsmoke catching in his lungs, he felt completely revolted. The grisly scene was almost too much to take in.

A scraping noise sounded from behind the storeroom. He waded between the corpses, slipping on the blood-soaked floor until he managed to reach the doors. He gave three sharp raps and almost instantly the doors seemed to cave in.

Boyle appeared in the doorway, Lydia behind him. They gaped at the hideous scene. Lydia already had tears in her eyes.

Boyle dropped the pick he carried. Enraged, he stumbled through the carnage toward Yakov, as if to strike him. "I ought to shoot you here and now. You and your kind are nothing but butchers."

An almost eerie groan sounded from the mass of bodies.

Boyle froze, they all did, nobody uttering a word.

And then another groan shattered the silence . . .

EKATERINBURG RAILWAY STATION

"You two showing up here may be the perfect end to my night." Kazan had a sadistic look on his face. He nodded to one of his men, who wore a gray slouch hat. "Tie him. He's a slippery customer, this one."

Kazan's man produced a length of rope from his pocket and tied Sorg's hands together.

The medic, still kneeling beside an unconscious Nina, screwed the top back on the ether bottle and stood, ashen-faced. "Please—this is not my business. I'm only here to treat the woman. She lost her child—"

"Shut up," Kazan said and strode over to Sorg. He held up Yakov's note. "Where did you get this? Is it real or a forgery?"

Sorg was tight-lipped, his hands tied in front of him, unable to grasp the steel-bladed pen in his pocket.

Kazan leaned into his face. "Yakov's one of you, isn't he? A traitor."

Zoba interrupted. "You're out of your mind, Kazan. He's no turncoat, not like you."

Kazan's mouth tightened and he aimed his gun at him. "If I want your opinion, I'll ask for it. Speak another word unless you're told to, and it'll be your last."

Zoba fell silent.

Kazan addressed Sorg. "I'm waiting for an answer."

This time, Sorg actually replied. "I've got no idea what you're talking about."

Kazan's expression was a cross between a sneer and a grimace. "Is that a fact? Violence may be wasted on you. But your friend here might be different." He crossed to Markov, trembling as the two men held him up by the arms.

Kazan aimed his pistol at Markov's left knee. "Tell me the truth. If you do, I promise to let you go."

Markov stood rigid with fear, too petrified to even speak.

Kazan fired.

The round shattered Markov's kneecap and he let out a terrifying scream. He jerked violently as he was held up by Kazan's men, blood spewing from his wound onto the floor.

Kazan aimed his pistol at Markov's other knee. "It seems you're determined to become a cripple."

"No, please," Markov begged, agony beading his face with sweat. "I'll tell you—"

"Everything. Or it's your brains on the floor."

III

"Check all their pulses—be absolutely certain," Boyle ordered.

The fog of gunpowder lifted as Andrev and Lydia negotiated their way through the bodies, trying not to slip on the blood. They checked for pulses, feeling necks or wrists or both.

Boyle's anger was like a fast-burning fuse, and he brandished his Colt at Yakov. "What kind of men could do this? Look at your dirty work. Look at it!"

"The boy's still alive," Andrev cried, carefully moving the chair from under Alexei. "His pulse is weak, but it's there."

The announcement sent a jolt through them all. Just as Lydia went to feel Anastasia's left wrist the girl emitted a tiny shriek, her body jerking as if she'd received an electric shock. Crimson spewed from her mouth in an obscene gush and then her body fell still again.

Lydia recoiled.

"Feel her pulse—feel it, for heaven's sake," Boyle said desperately.

Lydia dropped to her knees and gripped Anastasia's left wrist while her other hand felt her neck. Blood flowed from an obscene purple wound in her side. "She—she's still alive."

Hope sparked in Boyle's eyes. He knelt over Nicholai Romanov's body, feeling for a heartbeat. "Hurry, check them all again. And try and stem that wound . . ."

EKATERINBURG RAILWAY STATION

"You better not be lying." When Markov finished talking, Kazan pointed his pistol at the undertaker's head while the men held him up. "Are you, Markov?"

"I swear. Every word's the truth." Markov looked in agony, blood running down his leg and spreading in a pool on the floor.

Victory lit Kazan's face. He stepped back, his brow furrowed, his mind working feverishly.

Markov looked close to fainting. "You—you said you'd let me go."

Kazan grinned, "So I did. But I didn't say it was to hell," and his pistol came up and he shot Markov point-blank in the heart.

His body slumped, and the men let him go.

Kazan turned his attention to Sorg, saying with a smirk, "So, now I know. You've caused me a lot of trouble, you know that?"

Sorg stood silent and pale as one of Kazan's men, the one wearing the gray slouch hat, asked, "What do you want to do with them?"

"I'm thinking about it." Kazan turned to look at an unconscious Nina, then at the medic who trembled with fear. "Tie these two up. Give the medic some of his own ether. That ought to keep him quiet. Find somewhere to lock them both up. The woman may come in handy to bait Andrev."

"There's a sleeper wagon four carriages back."

"Do it."

Zoba moved protectively in front of Nina. "I wouldn't lay a finger on her if I were you, or you'll have Yakov to answer to."

Kazan's smile was forced. "Yakov's for the firing squad. And I thought I told you not to speak unless spoken to." Kazan shot Zoba in the head and he reeled back, collapsing against the wall.

The medic screamed. The two men who had been holding Markov now grabbed the medic by the arms.

Kazan told them, "Leave the bodies. Do as I say, then bring the car round."

He turned to Sorg. "You're coming with us to the tunnels. I'd hate to miss the final tragic act of this stupid farce. What a waste of time—the Romanovs are dead by now. Including the little witch whose interrogation you interrupted. What do you have to say to that?"

Sorg went cold, but then rage consumed him. He spat in Kazan's face.

Kazan actually grinned and wiped away the spittle. "We'll see how spirited you are when I get you back to the hotel basement." He nodded to his man. "Take him out to the car. I'll join you in a minute."

Kazan strode along the platform. He came to the engine, a lazy wisp of smoke rising from its funnel. Kazan dragged himself up some metal steps to the driver's cabin.

A grimy-looking man badly in need of a shave was seated on a three-legged wooden stool. He was smoking a cigarette and wore soot-stained clothes, a shovel resting across his knees. He rose when Kazan appeared and tossed away his cigarette. "Can I help you, comrade?"

"You certainly can." Kazan studied the maze of pressure dials, glass water-level indicators, and brass and copper pipes that crisscrossed the locomotive's panel. "You must be Yakov's driver."

The man nodded. "That's right. What can I do for you?"

Kazan produced a pistol and held out his free hand. "You can start by giving me the shovel."

The shocked driver wasn't arguing with the gun. He handed over the shovel.

Kazan held it sideways, like a machete, bringing the blade down hard, slicing into several narrow pipes, a spray of steam escaping. He pounded the glass dials and indicators, smashing them with the shovel's butt until they were a shattered mess. "This train's going nowhere," he spat, tossing the shovel aside.

The driver looked distraught. "You fool! Yakov will have your life."

Kazan callously shot him twice in the chest, and he crumpled.

Kazan nudged the man's body with the tip of his boot. "You got that wrong. It's the other way round," he said, and he climbed down the cabin steps.

112

"Alexei and Anastasia are barely alive. The others are dead," Andrev announced.

Lydia crouched beside Anastasia, holding her wrist. "Her pulse is still there, but it's weak."

"And the boy?" Boyle demanded. "Will he make it?

Andrev shook his head. "I don't know. His heartbeat's faint."

Yakov stared speechless at the family's corpses.

Andrev said angrily, "Well, what are you gaping at? This is what you wanted, isn't it?"

"Not the children," Yakov said hoarsely.

"It's a bit late now," Andrev answered bitterly, and brandished his gun. "Help with the girl. Go easy with her."

Yakov helped Lydia gingerly raise Anastasia from the floor.

Boyle told Andrev, "Cover Yakov, and I'll take the boy." Boyle knelt, gently lifting him. As he did so, a mournful cry escaped from the child's lips, the sound of his last breath leaving his body, and he shuddered and fell still.

"No . . ." Boyle said hoarsely. He gently lay the child down and felt his pulse. Finally he looked up in despair and shook his head. "He's gone for good. God have mercy on his soul." Boyle used his thumb and forefinger to close Alexei's eyes. An overpowering sense of grief seemed to smother them all, but it barely lasted, Boyle already hustling them toward the storage room. "What are you all waiting for? Uri, take the girl from Lydia, she'll lead the way with the lamp. I'll cover our back." He jerked his gun at Yakov. "Get going."

As they withdrew, Boyle was the last to leave. He took one last look around the execution room, barely able to fathom the awful carnage, and then he pulled the doors shut after him.

Kazan turned the Opel into Voznesensky Prospect, the car's suspension bouncing on the stones.

Sorg was cramped between two of Kazan's comrades, his hands still tied.

Kazan approached the compound and halted, a truck parked near the doorway, its engine running. The barrier was down, and the guards looked even more jittery as Kazan clambered out of the car. "Is the grisly business done yet?" he demanded.

One of the older guards said, "What's it to you? I thought we threw you out!"

"I want to know, are they *dead*?"

The man grinned. "No one could have lived through that hail of gunfire."

"When?"

"Less than ten minutes ago. Now get out of here before I'm tempted to shoot you."

Kazan raged, "You're the one who'll be shot, you imbecile. I'll see that you face a firing squad for your contempt. Where's Komendant Yurovsky?"

The guard balked at the threat. "Inside. Why?"

"Lead me to him. It's a matter of the utmost urgency."

They moved through the tunnel. When they finally came toward the exit, Boyle passed Markov's pile of dead bodies, the fuel cans and containers of embalming fluid stacked next to them. "Everyone be quiet."

They fell still, not a sound from anyone, and Boyle listened intently behind them, cupping an ear, but he heard nothing. He nodded to Lydia. "Signal to the sister. Then come back here."

She opened the iron door and moved outside, carrying her lamp. They all heard an engine move closer, there was a wash of headlights, and Lydia stepped back in. "She's here."

Andrev reached across and felt Anastasia's wrist, blood still flowing from her wounds, then he put a finger to her neck. "She's still got a heartbeat, but I wonder for how much longer."

Lydia said, "What about igniting the fuel?"

"There's not much point now, is there?" Boyle replied, and ushered them toward the iron door.

In the guardroom, now that the killing was over, Yurovsky experienced a strange kind of relief and it made him feel lightheaded. He raised a vodka bottle to his lips and took another long swig, the alcohol helping numb his mind.

All around the room his men were doing the same, collapsed on cots and chairs, chain-smoking cigarettes and getting drunker by the minute, trying to settle their frayed nerves after the savage, close-quarter butchery.

A guard appeared. Yurovsky said, "What do you want?"

"It's Kazan, he's turned up again."

"Tell the fool to go away."

"Now who's been drinking too much?"

He looked up to see Kazan standing over him, accompanied by a man wearing a gray slouch hat.

Kazan stared at the drunken guards through clouds of cigarette smoke, a stash of handguns and bloodied bayonets discarded on the table, cluttered with overflowing ashtrays and vodka bottles.

"What do you want?" the *komendant* demanded, his eyes blurred from drink.

"You're certain the family's all dead?" Kazan demanded.

With a frenzied look, the *komendant* took another swig from the bottle and waved a blood-soaked bayonet from the table. "Of course I'm sure. We had to use these to finish them off. Yakov's in there now, checking our work, before we move them to the truck and clean up. See for yourself if you don't believe me."

"*Yakov?*" A chill rippled through Kazan.

"Hurl your accusations against him now, Kazan, and see where they get you." The *komendant* sneered. "He'll have you up against a wall to face a firing squad."

"You drunken fool," Kazan spat, and stormed from the room, already reaching for his pistol.

He burst open the basement doors and stalked into the grisly scene, ignoring the stench of death and gunpowder. Unmoved, he took in the knot of bullet-ridden corpses and the walls, splashed with crimson.

His comrade recoiled, putting a hand over his mouth. "They really slaughtered them, didn't they? No mistake."

"Shut up. Don't make a sound." Like the eyes of a preying animal, Kazan's gaze flicked between the bodies and the storage room doors. Clutching his pistol, he moved toward the doors, trampling on the victims, wading in their blood. It was impossible to tell how many dead there were, the corpses were such a tangle, but Kazan said to his comrade, "Count the bodies."

Kazan halted by the doors and listened. When he heard nothing he gripped the handles and pushed. The doors gave easily. Darkness lay beyond.

"How many bodies?" Kazan demanded.

"Ten, I think."

"You *think*?"

The man counted again. Kazan did, too, to be absolutely certain.

"Yes, ten."

"One's missing." Kazan was livid. He searched the dead faces and saw no sign of Anastasia Romanov. "The conniving little witch is gone."

"Will I get a lamp to enter the tunnel?"

"Forget it, we're too late."

"What will I tell the *komendant*?"

Kazan said viciously, "That drunken moron? Nothing. Let him earn himself a hangman's noose. Get back to the car; we'll head them off at the station."

"What if they try to leave?"

"They can't. I sabotaged their engine and ordered the stationmaster to block all trains leaving the city. The vermin aren't going anywhere, I'll make sure of that."

They reached the Opel, clambered in, and Kazan backed the car like a madman out past the barrier. He sped down Voznesensky Prospect, then slammed on the brakes. Across the street was the city's main Red Army barracks. He swung round in the seat, the engine still running, and fixed Sorg with a triumphant grin.

"I was right—the family's been executed. They're all dead, except perhaps that little witch whose interrogation you interrupted. It appears your friends have taken her out through the tunnel. But they'll not get far."

Sorg slumped, torn between hope and dismay.

Kazan nodded to his comrade in the passenger seat and jerked a thumb toward the barracks. "Alert the commander. Tell him we've cornered enemy agents. We'll need every man from the barracks he can spare. I want the railway station sealed as tight as a drum."

113

Andrev turned the ambulance down a littered backstreet. A wispy, early morning fog began to descend as they arrived behind the railway, near the cargo bays.

A tired-looking elderly railway employee smoking a clay pipe manned a barrier, and Andrev shouted, "Get that barrier up, we've got wounded to transport!"

The man snapped to life when he saw the leather jacket and Andrev drove through and down by a platform. He halted as close as he could to Yakov's train, sixty yards away. He climbed out and ordered Yakov to do likewise.

Boyle said, "See if the engine's steamed up and ready to go. Take Yakov with you. We'll join you."

Andrev trained his gun at Yakov. "You heard him, Leonid. Let's go chat with the driver."

They marched away and Boyle went round the back of the ambulance and opened the doors. By the light of a lamp, Sister Agnes and Lydia tended to Anastasia, removing blood-soaked clothes with a scissors and placing fresh cotton on her wounds. The nun covered her with a coarse blanket.

"How is she?"

Sister Agnes shook her head and held up a bloodied corset. "I've managed to stem the bleeding but I don't know what's happening internally. Cup your hands and hold them out."

Boyle did as he was told.

The nun turned the corset inside out. With scissors, she cut jagged lines crisscrossing the material. A spray of sapphires, diamonds, and emeralds filled Boyle's hands, cascading from the corset.

He palmed the gems into one hand. Even in the poor light, they glinted brilliantly. "It seems to me not all the bullets penetrated her body where the gems were sewn into her clothing."

The nun nodded. "They saved her from being killed instantly." She indicated tight columns of gems woven inside the corset lining. "It's probably why Alexei didn't die at first. No doubt they were sewn into his clothing, too."

Boyle took the corset and examined the fabric. "Will she make it?"

"Impossible to say. But she'll need proper medical attention, a hospital really."

"Too risky. But Yakov has a medic. The sooner we get her on board and depart, the better."

Andrev came back, looking despondent as he escorted Yakov, who didn't look much better.

Boyle weighed the gems in his palm and held up the corset. "This is what saved her—precious stones sewn into her underclothes." He handed them back to the nun, who took a leather coin pouch from under her habit, filling it with the gems for safekeeping. Boyle said to Andrev, "What's wrong? You both look like death."

"Zoba, Markov, and the engine driver have been shot dead."

Boyle sighed and ran a hand over his face. "Any more bad news?"

"Nina's unconscious four carriages down the back. She was with the medic; they were both tied up. He was out cold, too, but I managed to wake him. They're alive at least. The medic's gone to see to Anastasia."

"Did he say what happened?"

"It was Kazan. The medic thinks he went back to the Ipatiev House, determined to find us. He took Sorg."

Boyle's broad shoulders appeared to slump. "Can it get any worse?"

"The locomotive's been sabotaged. We're going nowhere, Boyle."

114

The fog seemed to be getting worse as they marched to the engine and climbed up the boarding steps. When Boyle saw the engineer's body, he fixed Yakov with an iron stare. "A nasty piece of work, Kazan."

Andrev said, "It seems he learned his craft in the tsar's secret police."

Boyle examined the shattered dials and the severed pipes. "They obviously didn't teach him anything about steam power."

"What do you mean?" Andrev asked.

Boyle examined a metal pipe where it had been sliced through, then he fiddled with a couple of valves. "I know something about locomotive engines. None of the main pipes have been cut. Just the ones to the indicators."

"Meaning?" Andrev inquired.

"I think the train will still operate, but we've no way of knowing if the steam pressure or water level are right. Where exactly did you leave Yakov's engine and tender?"

"About five miles from here."

He considered and sighed. "We might not make it that far. We'll have to be careful how we stoke; I'd hate to risk blowing up the boiler." Boyle slipped on a heavy padded glove and opened the furnace door. A blast of heat greeted them. "Grab a shovel and start working as fast as you can," he told Yakov.

Andrev translated.

"This is all a waste of time," Yakov said, tight-lipped.

"Let me be the judge of that."

Yakov began shoveling coal into the furnace.

Boyle told Andrev, "Get the others on board. Use the carriage closest to the engine. And see how the medic's doing with the girl."

Andrev hurried down the engine's steps.

Boyle fiddled with the shattered instruments and pipes, seeing if he could repair them, but it was useless. He checked the water tank, making sure it was filled. "Come on, Yakov, keep that shovel working." After a time, Boyle made a gesture for Yakov to stop. "Okay, that's enough coal for now. We ought to be ready to give it a go."

Yakov tossed down the shovel and wiped his brow.

Boyle smiled at him. "I'll bet you're asking yourself if it's insane to risk driving this thing. What if it blows up in our faces?"

Yakov stared back at him, not comprehending, his eyebrows raised.

Boyle said, "Well, you better pray it doesn't explode, Yakov. Because it's you who'll be doing all the shoveling." He gestured with the Colt. "Now get yourself down those steps; our job's not done yet."

Boyle hustled Yakov back to the carriage and they climbed aboard. The floor was congealed with blood. Two bodies lay sprawled on the floor, Zoba's and Markov's, his bloodied left leg shattered at the knee.

"Butcher's work," Boyle remarked angrily.

Yakov stared down bitterly at Zoba's corpse. "He was a good man."

Boyle understood that much in Russian, and he offered a reply. "Then he kept the wrong company." He gestured to the bodies and added, "Move them over there, against the wall."

Boyle turned his attention to Anastasia. She lay on a soldier's metal cot at the far end of the carriage, her head now swathed in bandages.

She moaned once or twice in pain, but didn't stir. Her eyes were closed, her breathing shallow. Lydia and Sister Agnes knelt on one side of her while the medic dabbed his stethoscope on her neck and chest, then felt her pulse.

"How is she?" Boyle asked.

The medic looked doubtful. "The wounds to her skull appear to have been caused by bayonets and have probably concussed her. The good news is the bleeding from her abdomen has stopped. The bad news is she could be bleeding internally. But it's impossible for me to know exactly at this stage if any of her major organs are damaged. Only time will tell."

"Can you operate, if necessary?"

The medic scratched his jaw. "If it comes down to it. But there's no guarantee she'd live through it, not in her state. It's all in the lap of the gods, I'm afraid."

Boyle sighed with frustration. "Where's Uri?"

Lydia replied, "Gone to check on Nina."

"Go fetch him. Tell him we're ready to leave."

Lydia moved along the corridors. She noticed a sweet, pungent smell of some kind of narcotic as she came to a sleeper compartment. A pretty, blond-haired woman lay unconscious on the lower bunk.

Even in repose she looked distraught, her eyes blotched from crying. She stirred and cried out, her sleep troubled, and then fell still again.

Concern in her eyes, Lydia stood watching her from the doorway.

And then came a mournful cry, a noise almost more animal than human, from the next compartment . . .

As she entered, Andrev was kneeling by a lower bunk, next to Sergey's body. The boy was wrapped in a sheet. His eyes were closed, his body stiff, the lips slightly parted.

Andrev rocked his son back and forth in his arms. He looked crushed, his face stricken, and his dark, tormented eyes hinted at a soul in hell.

Lydia could do nothing but watch him suffer.

He turned and their eyes met. He gently laid his son's body down, kissed his cheek, and stood.

For a moment she thought his misery would choke him and then he lurched past her, out into the corridor, drawing the back of his hand over his mouth to stifle his tears.

She had no words to console him, and so she did the only thing she could, her arms going around him, binding him to her, sharing his grief.

He clung to her for a long time until finally he drew away.

"I—I don't know what to say, Uri. How to comfort you."

"You can't."

"I—I saw Nina. Is she going to be all right?"

He wiped his eyes, and they moved into the compartment where Nina lay unconscious. He stared down at her sleeping face, touched it with the back of his hand. "The medic gave her ether to help her sleep. She was distraught. She lived for Sergey. We both did."

They heard a sudden noise in the corridor behind them.

Sister Agnes came rushing up, her habit flapping. "Boyle wants you both back in the carriage. It's more bad news."

They followed the nun back to the carriage, just as the sound of a car engine roared onto the fogged platform.

Boyle was peering out the window. "It seems you can't get rid of a bad thing."

Andrev and Lydia joined him.

An open-topped Opel halted nearby. Kazan was in the driver's seat. With him were two of his men, one in front, one in the back, guarding Sorg. Kazan jumped out and spoke to Sorg.

"What the devil is he up to?" Boyle remarked.

Almost immediately at least six trucks laden with armed troops rumbled onto the far end of the platform. Dozens of soldiers jumped down and began taking up positions, a uniformed commander shouting orders. At least a hundred more stormed into the station, appearing out of the thin veil of fog, their boots echoing like thunder.

Boyle's face crumpled, Andrev's, too, knowing that all was lost.

Yakov wandered over to join them. "I warned you. The same old roads all lead to hell in the end."

115

Kazan climbed out of the Opel. He said to Sorg, "Let's see if I can talk sense into these friends of yours. Unless they want a bloodbath." He jerked a thumb at his men. "One of you come with me."

One man joined Kazan, while the second man slipped into the driver's seat, covering Sorg with his gun.

A ferocious rumble of trucks drove onto the far end of the platform, near the ticket kiosks. Dozens of troops jumped down. Hundreds more marched into the station. They took up positions seventy yards from the train.

Sorg's heart sank like a lead weight.

A smug Kazan reached over and gripped his cheek in a painful vise. "See? Your friends have no hope. If they think they can escape with that Romanov witch they're sadly mistaken. She's going to die tonight after all, make no mistake." He turned to the driver. "Shoot him if he misbehaves. But try not to kill him. I want that pleasure myself."

Kazan strode back the seventy yards along the platform to the troop commander, an energetic, muscular-looking man who clutched his revolver by his side, ready for action.

"So, you're Kazan? This better not be a waste of my time." He indicated Kazan's comrade, standing nearby. "He tells me you've apprehended dangerous enemy agents."

"Wanted by Lenin himself."

"They're on board?"

Kazan nodded and beckoned for his man to rejoin him. "I'll attempt to get them to surrender. But if they try to make a run for it, mow them down, kill all of them."

"How many are there?" the commander asked.

Kazan took a white handkerchief from his pocket. "A handful. But be vigilant, they're as cunning as foxes. No one leaves the station until I say so."

And with that Kazan turned with his men and marched back toward the train, holding the white handkerchief aloft.

Boyle watched as Kazan, holding the handkerchief, approached the carriage with his two comrades. They halted and Kazan rapped on the door.

Boyle said grimly to Andrev, "We may as well see what he has to say."

Andrev opened the door, wielding his gun. "I take it this isn't a social visit?"

Kazan offered a tortured smile. "I'm afraid not. Unless you want the men on the platform to start firing, I'd suggest you let me in and listen to what I have to say."

Boyle nodded to Andrev, who said, "Come aboard. But keep your hands where I can see them."

Kazan and his men entered. "I'm Inspector Kazan."

Andrev said, "We know who you are. What do you want?"

Kazan's gaze shifted past Lydia and the nun to Anastasia, still unconscious as she was tended by the medic. "I would have thought that was obvious. Her for a start."

"Are you trying to negotiate, Kazan?"

"There's no negotiation. The station's surrounded. The rail lines are blocked. Make a run for it and you'll be cut down like dogs. Surrender is your only option."

Andrev said calmly, "That's it?"

Kazan managed a ghastly smile. "I'll make one concession, if only to bring this to an end. I'll spare the women a bullet, except for that Romanov witch. And that's it. Unless you have any last requests?"

Andrev translated for Boyle, who said drily, "I suppose a first-class ticket to Paris for all of us is out of the question?"

Yakov said, "I'll take over from here, Kazan."

Kazan skewered him with a look of contempt. "You? You're no lon-ger in charge. Keep your nose out of this, Yakov."

"On whose orders?"

"Mine. You're a traitor. You released a wanted spy. Worse, you helped the enemy rescue one of the Romanovs."

"Don't be an idiot. You're losing the run of yourself, Kazan."

"Am I? We'll see what Lenin thinks when he hears what I have to say."

In the corner, Anastasia gave a pained groan, the medic swabbing away sweat and blood, taking out a needle and thread as if to sew more of her wounds.

Kazan said, "All very noble, but a sheer waste." He took out his pocket watch. "I'll give you thirty seconds to think about it. Then it's over."

In the Opel, Sorg watched Kazan step into the carriage, holding the white handkerchief. He felt a hatred so powerful that it almost over-whelmed him. He looked down at his bound hands. He tried to loosen the rope but it was useless. The pen was in his right pocket, but he couldn't reach it from a sitting position, the rope too tight.

If Anastasia wasn't already dead, she soon would be—the troops would make sure of that. He accepted his failure. It was all a disaster. But if they were both going to die, he wanted to be with her. Something else he wanted: to kill Kazan.

If I could get on board the train . . . He shifted his body weight to the right and struggled to grasp the pen.

The driver in the front seat was still busy watching the carriage.

Sorg felt the nub of the pen through his pocket. But he couldn't stretch his fingers far enough to reach. He twisted his body more, felt an intense stab of pain in his wounded side, and grunted.

The driver snapped his head round, waving his gun. "What are you up to?" he demanded.

Sorg groaned. "My—my wound's bleeding."

The man grinned. "Tough." He turned back to watch the carriage.

Sorg twisted his body until the pain in his side became so intense he could hardly breathe. He felt himself passing out. His fingers grasped the pen. He tried to inch it out of his pocket.

The pen slipped onto the floor.

The man in the front turned round again. "What was that?"

"My . . . wound . . . the bleeding's getting worse."

"Let me see."

Sorg lurched forward, groaning as if in pain. He felt for the pen on the floor, grasped it between his fingers, and managed to unscrew the top with his thumbs and forefingers.

The guard twisted to look into the backseat. "I said let me see! What are you up to—"

Sorg's hands came up and skewered the blade into the man's wind-pipe. Blood gushed, cutting off the cry in his throat. He slumped forward, gave a tiny grunt, and fell still.

Sorg, drenched in sweat, managed to cut the rope with the blade, freeing his hands. They were covered in blood. He wiped them on the dead man's clothes and grasped the pistol. Looking behind him, he saw that most of the troops on the platform were watching the train, but several observed him. He saw an officer stare back at him. He hoped the man was too far away to see what had happened.

Sorg gave him a nod.

The officer nodded in reply.

It occurred to Sorg that the troops might not know if he was held prisoner, or if he was one of Kazan's men. He'd have to take the risk.

Sorg slipped the pistol into his pocket. Two thoughts seared his mind. *Find Anastasia. Kill Kazan.* His rage boiled, but there was a strange calmness in him, too, as if he had already embraced death.

He stepped out of the Opel and strode toward the train. Three wagons back from the lead carriage, he opened the door and climbed aboard.

"Time's up. What's it to be?" Kazan said.

Boyle looked at Andrev and their demeanor said it all, total defeat on their faces. Andrev said, "Why don't I trust you to keep your word?"

Kazan drew his pistol. "You have no choice. Be sensible. Place all your weapons on the table and move to the end of the carriage."

Boyle placed his Colt on the table, and Andrev his Nagant.

Kazan said, "The woman, too."

Lydia produced the Mauser and tossed it with the others.

Kazan gestured with his gun at Yakov. "Move to the end of the carriage and join them."

"Kazan, you'll die for this."

"The only one who's going to die is you."

In a rage, Yakov lunged. Kazan stepped back. His weapon came up and he clubbed Yakov across the head, who stumbled back against the wall. Kazan said through gritted teeth, "Get over there and join the others. I want the pleasure of seeing you face a firing squad."

Yakov lurched to his feet.

Kazan said to his men, "Search them all. Make sure they have no more weapons."

One of Kazan's comrades, standing near the open window, spotted their prisoner stepping out of the Opel and calmly striding to the train. Curious, he leaned his head out the window and saw the prisoner step aboard, about three carriages back.

In disbelief, the man said to Kazan, "Inspector . . ."

"What is it?"

"The prisoner just boarded the train."

116

Sorg moved through the carriage corridor. He clutched the pistol in one hand, the pen in the other. He listened, every sense alert, but heard nothing, not even voices, and that made him suspicious. His heart raced. *Where's Anastasia?*

He came to the end of the deserted aisle. A door led to a short footbridge that crossed to the next carriage. He opened it, moved across, and slowly turned the handle on the next door.

It opened with a squeak. He stepped inside the next carriage, closed the door softly behind him, and made his way along the corridor. He never checked the lavatory he passed, which was his mistake, because just then he heard a distinct click behind him and felt a cold gun barrel pressed into his neck. A man's voice said, "Throw it down, or I'll drop you."

Sorg tossed down his gun.

Ahead of him another of Kazan's men, the one wearing the gray slouch hat, stepped out of a compartment and grinned. "We meet again. Who's a glutton for punishment?" He knelt, picked up Sorg's gun, and slipped it into his pocket. "Make sure he has no more weapons."

As the man behind him patted him down with one hand, Sorg glanced at him over his shoulder.

"Look straight ahead," the man ordered.

Sorg chose the nearest target first. His hand came up, gripping the blade, swinging it over his shoulder with a tremendous force. He stabbed the man just below the left eye.

He screamed and fell back, clapping a hand to his face.

The man in front of him was already reacting, leveling his pistol as Sorg arced his arm again, this time lunging forward to plunge the blade into the man's heart.

His victim gasped aloud, the force of the blow causing him to stagger backward before he slumped to the floor.

Sorg turned back to the first man. He was still screaming, a hand over his bloodied face, his other hand blindly waving his gun. Sorg stabbed him in the chest, finishing him off, and the man pitched forward.

Sorg knelt, retrieved the gun, and picked up the dead man's gray slouch hat.

He tugged it onto his head and strode toward the front carriage.

They all heard the scream and a look of panic spread on Kazan's face. "Stay still, all of you. Nobody utter a sound."

He tried to cover his prisoners with his gun as he inched toward the door leading to the next carriage. He peered through the glass but saw no one.

The screaming had died abruptly. He looked uncertain.

Kazan licked his dry lips nervously. "I warn you, if anyone attempts to leave the train, the troops on the platform have orders to kill every one of you. Remain here." He carefully opened the door and moved out into the aisle.

He had gone barely five yards when he hesitated. Ahead of Kazan was a deserted corridor. The silence in the carriage was ominous. Fearful, he drew back to the carriage door again and called out, "Federov! Sakovitch!"

His men didn't answer.

Kazan kept his pistol at the ready, beads of sweat rising on his face. "Federov! Sakovitch!" he called again.

A figure rounded the corner, head down. Kazan startled, about to shoot, but then he recognized Federov's gray hat. Kazan said, "What kept you? Where is he?"

Kazan relaxed for a split second, but it was too long because the face that looked up wasn't Federov's.

A hammer clicked and the pistol in Sorg's hand pointed straight in the middle of Kazan's forehead. The rage in Sorg's eyes was like a living thing. "Let it drop."

Kazan dropped his pistol with a clatter on the floor.

"Where are the others?" Sorg demanded, his gun barrel still pointed to Kazan's head.

Sweat formed on Kazan's upper lip. "In—in the carriage behind me. Don't make the mistake of shooting me, or the guards on the platform will come running. It will only make things worse for you and your friends."

"Worse? I don't think it can get any worse, Kazan. Do you? But don't worry, I'm not going to shoot you."

Kazan relaxed, swallowing hard. "That's very wise. Surrender now, and I promise your death will at least be quick."

"Where's Anastasia?"

"In the carriage behind me."

"Is she alive?"

A savage look of victory lit Kazan's face. "Yes. But who's to say if it will be for long?"

Sorg felt his heart beat faster. "Tell me, Kazan, have you killed many people?"

Kazan's eyebrows knit. "What's that got to do with anything?"

"You've been a secret policeman a long time, and no doubt you have. Do you remember a man named Jacob Sorg?"

"No."

"I didn't think you would. But I want you to remember his name."

"Why?"

"He was my father, and it's the last name you'll ever hear."

Sorg's hand came up, clasping the pen. He embedded the blade deep in Kazan's neck, striking bone.

Kazan staggered back, a look of utter disbelief on his face, and then he reeled like a wounded bear, grabbing the air with outstretched hands and crashing back the way he had come, through the carriage door.

A sense of physical release surged through Sorg. He followed

Kazan's path into the carriage and watched him collapse on the floor with a thud. His eyes bulged in death. The others in the carriage stared at him, then at Sorg.

Anastasia was in the far corner, her eyes closed, and she was half-covered with a blanket but she appeared to be still breathing. A man with a black bag attended her. Sorg's heart thudded with elation but it was short-lived.

Boyle stepped over and tipped Kazan's body with the toe of his boot, then said with an edge of bitterness, "That may be the second bad mistake you've made tonight. Did you have to kill him?"

"You don't understand. It was personal."

Andrev said in Russian, "What about his men?"

Sorg flashed the steel pen. "Dead, a few carriages back."

Boyle understood, and raised his eyes. "They say it's the quiet ones you want to watch."

Sorg knelt beside Anastasia, clasping her hand. "How is she?"

"Still breathing, but I'm betting it won't be for long," Boyle said. "Not with half the Red Army encircling us and a train that's going nowhere."

Andrev looked at Yakov and said hopelessly, "Well? What now? Will you at least let the women live and honor Kazan's pledge?"

A sound of marching boots erupted outside.

Andrev looked beyond the window. Dozens of soldiers tramped toward the carriage, led by their commander, his pistol drawn.

Yakov moved over to the table and picked up Boyle's Colt automatic. "I'm afraid I can promise nothing."

117

A fist rapped on the carriage door.

Yakov ordered Lydia, "Cover the girl's face with the blanket."

"Why?"

"Just do as I say."

She pulled the blanket over Anastasia.

Yakov held out his hand to Sister Agnes. "Give me the gems."

The nun handed him the leather pouch.

Another harsh rap came on the door and Yakov opened it. He beckoned the barrack commander and his men inside.

They stepped in warily. The commander took one look at Kazan's body, and the bodies of Markov and Zoba, and his hand tightened on his weapon. "What's happened here?" he demanded.

Yakov handed over his letter. "I'm Commissar Yakov. On a mission of special purpose for Comrade Lenin."

The barrack commander examined the letter, studying its official stamp and signature. Then his gaze swept over everyone in the carriage, and at the figure lying on the cot, covered by a blanket.

He turned to Yakov uncertainly. "Do you mind telling me what's going on?"

Yakov jerked his head toward the floor. "Remove Inspector Kazan's body from the train, and the other two. You'll also find the bodies of a couple of his men farther along the train."

"Two more dead? I don't understand—"

"You don't have to. All you have to do is obey my orders. But if you must know, Kazan was a traitor and criminal. He and his men got their just reward for their crime."

"What crime?"

Yakov opened the pouch, spilling out a handful of glittering gems. "Attempting to steal Romanov jewels from their rightful owners, the Russian people. Now, unless you want to be associated with Kazan's crime I'd suggest you do as I say at once."

"Of—of course, Commissar."

"I want this locomotive replaced immediately. Any delay, and I'll have whoever's responsible shot."

The barrack commander paled, and Yakov snapped, "What's keeping you? Let me know the moment the train is ready to depart."

"Yes, Commissar." The commander barked at his men and when they had removed the corpses and gone, Yakov refilled the pouch and handed it back to the nun. The others stared at him in disbelief.

Boyle said, "Will someone slap me in case I'm dreaming?"

Yakov said to the medic attending Anastasia, "Well?"

"She seems stable enough, but whether she stays that way is another matter. I could do with an explanation, too."

Yakov laid a hand on the man's shoulder. "If I was you, I'd stay with the train, and pray you make it over the border. Look on the bright side: maybe finally you'll get out of this godforsaken country."

Sorg said, "I don't understand you, Yakov."

"No one's asking you to. Just get yourselves out of Russia. I presume you have a strategy?"

"Boyle does. He's an expert on the railway routes."

Andrev stepped over. "I hate to be a pessimist, Leonid, but as soon as the *komendant* sobers up he may notice there's a body missing."

"Leave the *komendant* to me. Once I find out what he does or doesn't know, I'll deal with it then. There's no shortage of corpses in the tunnel, if need be."

Yakov removed his cigarette case from his breast pocket and held up a box of matches. "A spark to the fuel ought to take care of any loose ends."

"That's not going to explain Kazan's death."

"Kazan was despised. I caught him stealing. He paid the price, end of story. That's my version of events and I'll stick to it."

He turned to address Sister Agnes. "I'd suggest you get out of here immediately. Whether the girl lives or dies is beyond any one of us right now, but my medic will do his best."

Sister Agnes made a sign of the cross, took the back of Yakov's hand, and kissed it. "Thank you, my son. Thank you for what you've done."

"A word of advice. I'd get your nuns out of this city if I were you. I have a feeling that when all this is done, I'll have no say in what comes afterward. Leave now. Don't delay."

Sister Agnes patted Anastasia's hand, hugged Lydia, and bid good-bye to the others.

When she'd left the carriage Yakov pulled down the blinds. "I'd leave these down if I were you, at least until you're well clear of the station."

Andrev said, "Why the change of heart, Leonid?"

"You're right. There's been enough death, enough killing. Let it end here."

"Come with us?"

"Not possible right now. I'm expected at the Kremlin to make my report. Besides, how could I abandon Katerina?"

"Boyle wasn't lying when he said he could get her out of Moscow."

"And I intend to accept his offer. Explanations later. First, do something for me?"

"Anything."

"Go make sure Nina's all right. But hurry. This fog's only going to get worse. I want you out of here while there's still time."

Yakov opened his cigarette case and offered a cigarette to Boyle, who accepted. Yakov lit them both and said to Lydia, "Your friend here doesn't speak much Russian, so I'll ask you to translate. I want my daughter taken out of Moscow."

"And you?"

"That's not important right now. I no longer trust Trotsky or Lenin. If I can, I'll arrange the release of Nina's parents. Can he do it? Can he get them all out?"

Lydia translated, and when Boyle answered, she replied, "He says it can be done."

"How soon?"

"Within weeks. You have his word."

Yakov considered. "I'll need more than that. After what's happened tonight, I've no idea if I'll be alive for much longer. That's why I have a condition in return for my help. One of you must come with me to Moscow and keep Katerina safe until you take her out. I'll arrange for you to both stay somewhere secure. Anything less may only jeopardize her life."

"What about you?"

"If I'm still alive, we can all leave together." Yakov took a notebook from his pocket and scribbled an address. "That's the apartment where your people can make contact."

When Lydia explained to Boyle, there was a sound behind them. Andrev returned and was leaning against the doorway, listening.

Yakov said, "You heard?"

Andrev stepped away from the doorway. "Enough of it. I'll stay, Leonid."

Yakov shook his head. "No. Nina's going to need her son's father close to her for now. Be good to her. Her heart's broken. Otherwise, I fear she'll go over the edge. Besides, you're a wanted man; your presence would be risky." Yakov gestured to Sorg. "He needs medical attention. And Boyle's your ticket out of here." He turned to Lydia. "I'm afraid it's down to you."

She said, "I'll stay."

Boyle said, "Would someone care to explain?"

Lydia did so, and when Andrev went to protest, she said, "I've made up my mind, Uri. It won't be long, weeks at most."

A look passed between them, something close to distress.

A locomotive engine whistled, the carriage jerked a little, and then came the brittle, metallic noise of buffers shunting.

A sharp rap came on the door, and the barrack commander poked his head round. "We've shunted another engine in place. Whenever you're ready, the train can depart, Commissar." The man snapped off a salute and disappeared.

Boyle said, "Lydia's right, Uri. It won't be long. I really hate to rush this, but we need to move."

Yakov peered out at the thickening fog, descending rapidly like a gauze veil.

Off in the distance, cathedral bells rang out 3 a.m.

Yakov turned back, put a hand on Uri's shoulder. "There's nothing more to say. Go, before it's too late. With any luck, we'll meet again."

On the platform, the fog was thickening. It shrouded everything in a gray steam.

Andrev, Lydia, and Yakov waited as Boyle checked the dials in the engine cabin, then he scurried down the steps. "The steam pressure's good, we're all set. You've said your good-byes?"

Andrev nodded grimly. "As best we could under the circumstances."

Boyle offered Yakov his hand. "Here's to our reunion, and with any luck cracking open a bottle in London."

Andrev translated, and Yakov told Boyle, "I may hold you to that."

Boyle took Lydia's hand, kissed it, and winked at her. "As for you, young lady, keep your head down, watch that Irish temper of yours, and try not to get in any trouble. Do what Yakov tells you, and I'm sure you'll be fine."

"Good-bye, Boyle. I hope you make it."

Boyle smiled tightly. "One interesting aspect of life is that whenever we endure a terrible experience, everything that comes after seems like a bonus. Until we meet again." He turned to Andrev. "We leave now, before this fog gets any worse."

Boyle climbed up on the engine again. As the locomotive started to move, he gestured to Andrev. "Don't delay. Time waits for no man, Uri."

The carriages jerked forward.

Andrev produced a silver locket and pressed it into Lydia's palm. "I meant to give you this in Moscow. But then everything got muddled and there never seemed to be the right moment." He closed her fingers around the locket, then kissed her on the cheek. "A small memento. Look after her, Leonid."

Yakov nodded. They shook hands.

The train picked up speed. Andrev jumped on board. He stood

on the carriage footplate, staring back at them as the engine drew away.

As Lydia watched it go, she touched a hand to her cheek, let it linger and fall, then looked at Yakov. "Why? Why let them go?"

He lit a cigarette. "Life is always one thing on the surface, but something else beneath, don't you think? Perhaps sometimes we never know how deep feelings run until they're tested. And you and Uri, I sensed something, if I'm not mistaken."

She didn't speak but unclenched her hand and looked down at the silver locket. On the front were the double-headed Imperial eagles, inlaid in gold. She turned it over in her palm. There was an inscription. She studied it.

Yakov said, "It means something to you?"

She nodded and looked up. Yakov thought he saw tears at the corners of her eyes. "Yes, it means something," she said hoarsely. "And you and Nina?"

The question caught him by surprise. She said, "Don't look so shocked. Women sense these things."

He took another drag on his cigarette. "There are many kinds of love, I think. There's passionate love, and there's dutiful love, though often we don't realize that really they're just different sides of the same coin." He pulled up his collar. "And then there's another kind of love. The kind we can only show by setting someone free."

Lydia shivered in the early morning chill. "Is that why you did it?"

"Who knows? Who knows anything, anyhow? Except what our hearts tell us." Yakov removed his coat and placed it around her shoulders to ward off the cold. "Allow me."

They heard the fading rumble of the train, and then a haunting, sad whistle as it was swallowed up by the fog.

They both stood staring into the cold gray veil of nothingness, until finally Yakov offered his arm and Lydia took it, and let him lead her back toward the platform.

THE PRESENT

118

The rain had stopped. Yakov threw another log on the dying fire and a volcano of sparks erupted. "Now you know how it ended. It certainly ended brutally, and with bloody and violent death, but not exactly as history records.

"Not that we've ever had a watertight account of the Romanov executions. The story's always been murky. We had the bones that were eventually discovered, minus two of the family. We had the executioners' confessions, which varied over the years. And we had lots of speculation about the events of that night—some of it insane, some credible. It's often been hard to know where truth began and falsehood ended."

He looked at me. "But I can tell you this with certainty. It ended with Anastasia and the boy not dying at once. Even the written evidence offered by the executioners tells us that. And it ended with Anastasia not being buried with the rest of her family." Yakov paused. "The DNA experts can speculate all they want, but they still can't say with *absolute* certainty that any of the bones later found belonged to her. I doubt they ever will."

I felt dazed. "How can I know that your version of events is true?"

Yakov stood, resting a hand on his hip, looking frail. "The truth is out there if you care to look. Every one of my claims can be proven."

I heard the conviction in his voice. "How?"

"Uri Andrev, Joe Boyle, Hanna Volkov, Lydia Ryan, Leonid Yakov, Philip Sorg—they're all *real* people. And there are so many clues that the truth screams out at you. You simply have to look and find them."

"Where do I begin?"

Yakov took a notebook from the shelves and tore out a written page. "Start with these people. They can validate the strands of my

story. I'm sure you know that the Ipatiev House was demolished in
a single night in 1977. Uri Andropov, the head of the KGB, and later
Russia's president, gave the order.

"All of which was really quite baffling, seeing as the house was
attracting no great attention. But within two years of the demolition
the first of the Romanov bodies were unearthed. Quite a coincidence,
I've always thought, considering that in the previous sixty years they
could never be found."

He handed me the page. I saw what looked like a list of names and
international phone numbers and addresses. I recognized Russian,
American, and British prefixes among them.

Yakov half-smiled. "It's all about finding strands, doctor. Irrefutable
strands that weave a different story from the one we're led to believe.
It will mean some plane-hopping. But I think you'll find the air miles
well worth it."

I asked the questions that burned on the end of my tongue. "And
Anna Anderson, the woman rescued from a Berlin canal whom many
people believed to be Anastasia. You said you'd explain about her."

"Her truth is out there, too—not the fabricated one we've all come
to know."

"The body I discovered. It's Lydia's, isn't it?"

"Yes, it is. She died in Russia."

"How? What *happened* to her?"

I had so many more questions, but before I could ask, he indicated
the page. "Talk to these people. Many are experts in their field. They
won't know the bigger picture, although some may have their suspicions. But they'll know individual pieces of the puzzle—the secrets and
lies I spoke about. Track them down. Listen to what they have to say."

"Then what?"

"Come back and see me. This story's not over yet."

All during my eighty-mile drive from Toronto's Pearson International
Airport to the pretty Victorian town of Woodstock, I thought about
Joe Boyle.

His remains were repatriated to his hometown in Canada in 1983 from the graveyard in Hampton Hill, London, where he was buried in April 1923. Woodstock is still home to some of Boyle's descendants, but Frank Evans isn't one of them.

A slim, academic-looking man with a furrowed, high forehead, Evans is a former history teacher who has long been fascinated by Boyle's exploits.

It was sunny as he walked me to the Presbyterian cemetery on Vansittart Avenue. Boyle's burial site is marked by a new granite headstone in the family plot, a stone that replaced the original ancient urn and slab—donated by Queen Marie, of Romania, a cousin of the Romanovs and a friend of Boyle's—which now reside in a local museum.

"They called him 'Klondike Joe Boyle,'" Evans told me, "and he was a swashbuckling character, straight out of an adventure novel. The term 'larger than life' doesn't do him justice. Boyle was a remarkable figure, a man who experienced enough escapades in his life to fill several books."

Evans knelt and brushed away some gravel from the tombstone. "But he's been largely forgotten by history. All those stories about him—running a spy network with hundreds of secret agents in Russia and helping to rescue royals—they're all factual. The spy ring was secretly financed by the U.S., French, and British governments."

"What about the rumor that he took part in a rescue of the Romanovs in Ekaterinburg?"

Evans smiled. "I believe it's true. Boyle was familiar with several figures in the Tobolsk Brotherhood. He also kept detailed lists of his expenses. His private papers show that in early July 1918, he spent considerable sums on travel, photography, hotels, and clothes for more than one person.

"They also record that he was involved in a mammoth amount of flying and train travel. His daughter Flora always maintained her father led a last-ditch Romanov rescue, and while she didn't know the outcome, her father claimed that he was one of the last people to see the tsar on the night he died."

"You accept that?"

"Yes I do. It's just the kind of audacious adventure that Boyle relished.

He was really the only man for the job. He also had an intimate knowledge of the Russian rail system, and had spies all along its main routes."

"Tell me more."

"He'd already proved his mettle by helping retrieve the Romanian royal jewels from the Kremlin, using not much more than his Irish blarney and fleeing by train over a two-thousand-mile journey. On another occasion, he liberated kidnapped Romanian royals from under the Bolsheviks' noses. Later, he took part in the rescue of the tsar's empress mother."

"You *really* believe he was in Ekaterinburg the night of the massacre?"

"I've absolutely no doubt. And that he fled to Bucharest by train. But his part in it all was kept completely secret."

"*Why?* And how can you know that for certain?"

"Several reasons. For one, Boyle's fortune was on the wane and he had several business investments in Russia he didn't want to lose. He also feared retaliation by the Reds, especially Trotsky, whom he met and distrusted. So his involvement was covered up neatly."

"How do you know that?" I asked.

"It's said that Boyle suffered a stroke in June 1918 and recovered in a Bucharest hospital. That's certainly true, but the timeline was a lie."

"What do you mean?"

"He definitely suffered a stroke but it was in late July 1918, after his mammoth flight to Russia and the drama of the rescue attempt. Boyle was a sturdy character, but he wasn't a young man anymore. His body couldn't take all the stress, and after he made it to Bucharest by train on July 23, 1918, he was immediately hospitalized."

"And afterward?"

"The brutality he witnessed affected him greatly. He was never quite right. It's remarkable, really. Look at any photographs that exist of Boyle taken soon after Ekaterinburg, and you can see it in his face. He has the look of someone who's witnessed an unspeakable horror. He died less than five years later, a broken man."

"If what you say is true, why weren't his incredible efforts recognized?"

Evans smiled knowingly. "They were. Joe Boyle was awarded the DSO—the Distinguished Service Order. It was conferred on him by none other than King George—Tsar Nicholas's cousin—at a private ceremony at Buckingham Palace in November 1919.

"The order was only given at that time to officers who served under fire in battle. The Ekaterinburg episode was the only incident in Boyle's life that really qualifies in that regard. It's recorded that he was given the award 'for services rendered.' It was an extraordinary honor, but it's a mystery, because no one ever explained what 'for services rendered' really meant."

"So nobody knows what he did to earn the king's respect?"

Evans gave the granite stone a gentle pat and looked me straight in the eye. "Me, I'm convinced it was for Boyle's brave efforts that bloody night in Ekaterinburg."

It was raining three days later in Riga, Latvia, when I met Maxim Petrovsky. A graduate of Moscow State University, Petrovsky is a quiet, pleasant civil engineer with a wispy gray beard. He once worked as one of the senior demolition engineers on the Ipatiev House destruction.

Now retired, he lives with his wife in their small apartment on Riga's outskirts, and it was chilly that afternoon when he invited me in. Reluctant to talk at first, he grudgingly agreed when I told him over the phone that I was researching the Ipatiev House.

Once the Bushmills whisky I'd brought as a gift was opened and our glasses poured, Petrovsky soon warmed. In particular, I wanted to talk about the rumors of tunnels under the house.

"The tunnels existed, for sure," he told me. "It's no secret that there were many passageways that crisscrossed old Ekaterinburg. One we discovered during the demolition ran underneath the house, coming from the east, and led down near the River Iset's City Pond. There were natural caves in the rock that had been expanded upon, you see."

"From when de Gennin originally designed the city as a fortress?"

Petrovsky smiled. "You know your history."

I encouraged him, pouring another drink. "Tell me more."

"The entire demolition was carried out using a wrecking ball and bulldozers and with mysterious haste on the night of July 27, 1977, on the orders of Uri Andropov, at the time still head of the KGB. I remember clearly when we breached a basement tunnel. Part of it had those white glazed tiles you often see in late-nineteenth-century buildings. That's when the men from Moscow appeared."

"Men from Moscow?"

Petrovsky swirled his whiskey. "The KGB. Suddenly their senior people were swarming all over the site like flies. Even Boris Yeltsin, the future Russian president, came to have a look."

"Really?"

"I was ordered to give him a private tour of the underground passageways. The demolition was halted for a time that night. We donned our safety helmets, armed ourselves with electric flashlights, and I led Yeltsin and the KGB people down into the bowels.

"Actually, the tunnel ran directly from a breached wall in the bricked-up storeroom next to the infamous execution chamber—which was pretty small. Less than four yards by five. I found it incredible that up to twenty-two people were crowded into it for the shootings, half of them with guns blazing. I'm surprised many of the executioners weren't killed by ricochets. Yet none of them were, if we're to believe the official accounts."

Petrovsky rolled his glass between his hands. "I especially recall the excitement as we went down. Yeltsin seemed extremely interested in the tunnel. The KGB told me not to discuss it with anyone, and later I never saw it mentioned in any accounts of the demolition, which seemed to me strange."

Petrovsky looked at me uncertainly. "I suppose it's okay to mention it now. I mean, it's all such a long time ago. Anyway, I'm over eighty now. What can those swine do to me?"

"Is there anything else you remember?"

"Only that I noticed one of the senior KGB men consult some notes as we explored the tunnels—they actually looked like photocopies of old papers—and I distinctly overheard him using the words 'escape route' to Yeltsin. I remember my ears pricked up at that. That was it, basically. When the tour was over, Yeltsin shook my hand and everyone went back to work, and I was ordered to fill in the tunnels with rubble. Eventually, a church would be built on the site, called the Church on the Blood."

By the time we finished talking the whiskey bottle was half-empty. Petrovsky rose, a little unsteady, his face flushed.

I said, "Is there anything else you recollect, anything at all that you think important? And I do mean *anything*. Even the slightest memory that may stand out in your mind could be important to my research."

Petrovsky scratched his chin. "Only how surprised I was at the intensity of the KGB's curiosity. It's as if they wanted to examine every inch of the tunnels, like it was a history lesson."

"Why do you think that was?"

He shrugged. "Heaven knows."

I thanked him for his time and he led me to the door. We said our good-byes, but as I was about to descend the stairs, Petrovsky called out, "There is one other thing. It's probably unimportant. But you said if I remembered *anything*."

"Yes?"

"There was a metal turret in part of the tunnel. When I examined it with my flashlight I noticed a faded white paint mark scrawled on the wall above it. The KGB men seemed most interested in that and took pictures."

His words sent a chill through me. "What did the scrawl look like?"

"A swastika. Actually, a reverse swastika to be precise."

Vadim Fomenko was once an official KGB historian. He resigned and became an outspoken critic of the communist regime, a treachery for which he was sentenced to five years in a gulag. But that was over forty years ago, and now, in his late seventies, this gaunt, eccentric man is one of the most knowledgeable people alive on the subject of the Romanov assassination. He seemed happy to meet me for coffee in Stockholm, where he lives with his daughter.

Without much prompting, I steered Fomenko onto the subject of Yurovsky, the Ipatiev House *komendant,* and the "official" account he gave of the Romanov executions, in which he claimed all of the family had been killed.

"His account of that night has to be treated with a certain amount of suspicion," Fomenko began. "Yurovsky was a very devious character. The way he lulled the Romanovs into suspecting nothing was amiss speaks volumes. He was a natural liar who changed his account of the bloody events on several occasions. In 1918, he gave one version in a report to Moscow. In 1920, he gave a different version, in which he even got the number of victims wrong. In 1922 and in 1934, two more accounts were offered."

"Why do you think that was?"

Fomenko laughed. "Because liars need to have good memories and Yurovsky didn't have one. Even the official version offered by Moscow in 1921 was different from his." He met my gaze. "Frankly, it amazes me that in all of sixty years Moscow never *once* attempted to verify Yurovsky's version of the graves' location, or finally dispose of any buried remains. I find that truly amazing, don't you?"

"Why do you think they didn't?"

"Heaven knows." Fomenko shrugged. "But five different accounts— if you include the official 1921 Moscow version—smacks to me of something not right. Of course, lying came naturally to Yurovsky, just as he lied to the Romanovs."

"You're saying there was a cover-up?"

"Of some kind," Fomenko replied. "Let's face it, the Romanov case has always been shrouded by intrigue and conspiracy. No fewer than *five* of the original investigators died in highly suspicious circumstances.

"One of them a judge, Ivan Sergeyev, was assassinated after he admitted to a reporter that his investigations led him to believe that Anastasia escaped death. Someone obviously wanted to shut him up."

Fomenko sat back. "When I worked in the KGB archives, I heard rumors of files hidden in the secret party library in Moscow. Records that mention the Imperial family and involve foreign agents, and the survival of one or more of the children. All kinds of rumors and sightings circulated after the killings—the most prominent suggested Anastasia was helped to escape. I always found it ironic that her name, Anastasia, means the 'resurrected one,' or 'she who will rise up again.'"

Fomenko paused. "And then, of course, there's the famous mystery train. Shortly after three a.m. on the morning of the massacre, the Ekaterinburg stationmaster recorded that a train departed with its shutters drawn, after some kind of incident or other. In all the years afterward, no one's *ever* been able to ascertain where the train went. Or who was on board. It literally vanished."

"In your expert opinion, could any of the Romanovs have survived?"

Fomenko seemed amused. "How many times has that question been posed? Shall I tell you the truth?"

"Yes."

"Nobody really knows. Not even the experts. Logic and DNA samples tell us that none of the family *appear* to have survived—even though in Anastasia's case it cannot be confirmed with certainty. None of the bones discovered exactly match her age profile.

"And according to many experts, unless DNA is one hundred percent accurate, it means nothing. Anything else is just probability. In a famous seven-hundred-page judgment, a German court once concluded that there was no way the death of Anastasia could be conclusively proven."

He sat forward, eager to make his point. "It's well documented that there were at least three occasions that night when she could have escaped, despite the wounds she no doubt suffered. Eyewitness accounts stated that on two occasions after they thought she was dead she stirred and cried out."

He paused. "We also know that the *komendant* was highly distracted that night. He'd also been drinking. In fact, most of the executioners got blind drunk, if not before then just after the killings.

"Think about it. There must have been absolute chaos after the shooting, with blood everywhere. The air was thick with choking gunsmoke, the room covered in blood and bodily fluids. The half-drunk guards were deafened by the gunfire and their eyes were streaming from the smoke. The *komendant* admitted he had to lie down for half an hour after the killings because he felt so ill, and so he left his victims unattended.

"In fact, the guards were in no state to even transport the bodies to the woods—that was left to others, though the *komendant* joined them. As I said, even he got the body count wrong."

"So an escape isn't inconceivable?"

"It may seem unlikely, but in war, nothing's implausible. On two occasions the *komendant* claimed that Anastasia had to be finished off." Fomenko shrugged. "But was it really her they finished off? Were the guards sober enough to ascertain she was dead? Would they have even noticed if she was missing? And remember, all the girls had jewels and precious stones sewn into their undergarments for safekeeping, which was why the guards claimed it took so long to kill them. Their bullets and bayonets wouldn't penetrate the clothes; it's as if they were wearing bulletproof vests.

"Even those who disposed of the bodies gave completely differing accounts. Some said the bodies were pulverized to dust and bone fragments, and yet almost complete skeletons were found. Then there's the controversy over the tsar's remains—he once suffered a serious head wound with a sword, the result of an assassin's failed attack. Yet the skull declared to be the tsar's bears no such wound. A baffling mystery."

Fomenko was in full flow, thoroughly enjoying himself now. "Even Yurovsky's accounts of the killings are full of doubtful expressions like 'I don't recall when,' 'It seems to me,' 'I don't remember exactly,' and 'As far as I remember.' That doesn't sound to me like a man certain of anything. His reports were full of holes."

"What do *you* think really happened?"

Fomenko shrugged. "I think that either in the house or on the drive out to the Four Brothers mine area, something unusual occurred that was covered up. But I doubt we'll ever know what."

"Why?"

"Because there are still files on the period and on the killings that have never seen the light of day. And never will."

"Even after all these years?"

He made his point by touching a fingertip. "For one, the KGB and its successor were always a state within a state. Their kind run Russia now, for heaven's sake. How many assassinations have they carried out over the decades at home and abroad they've ever admitted to? Not a single one. Keeping secrets is their business."

He touched a second fingertip. "Two, do you *really* think they'd want to open up a hornet's nest by resurrecting such a bloody business from the past? I mean, to this day they've never even made public all of Lenin's papers."

Fomenko added, "If I've learned one thing, it's that anything is possible in Russia. Just like a Russian doll—you open up one part, thinking you've got to the end of it, only to find another part inside."

"Do you think we'll ever get to the bottom of it?"

Fomenko half-smiled. "No, I don't. But I recall an interesting little book published in America in 1920, titled *Rescuing the Czar*. Badly written, it purported to tell the real events of that night. But the U.S. government intervened and had the book rights withdrawn. I heard veiled whispers in the KGB that suggest some parts of the story may give a hint of the truth. Look into it, if you're interested."

"I'll do that."

Soon Fomenko's daughter arrived to drive him home. As she strolled on ahead to the parking lot, leaving us to have our final word, I said, "Did you ever hear of a man called Leonid Yakov?"

Fomenko smiled knowingly. "Yes, I've heard of Yakov. Also known as Michael Yakovsky, or Vassily Yakov. He had several aliases, as many Bolsheviks did in the early days, to avoid arrest. There were all kinds of stories about him."

"Such as?"

"That he oversaw the Romanov executions—that much is true—and crushed an attempt to rescue the royals. He was Lenin's white-haired boy after that and could do no wrong. But rumors said his heart wasn't in it anymore after Ekaterinburg. He faded into the background and later died in Moscow in 1976."

We reached his daughter's Volvo and Fomenko offered his hand. "It's been a pleasure, doctor. I hope I've been of some help?"

"One last question. The foreign plot you mentioned. Komendant

Yurovsky claimed it was one of the reasons for the execution. Was there really any truth to it?"

"Actually, only hours after the massacre, a telegram was sent to Lenin informing him that a 'serious' rescue had been foiled. And in an interview before his death in 1938, the *komendant* claimed he was aware of an attempt to snatch the family that night, and that it came perilously close to succeeding. But no sooner did the interview appear in print than it was withdrawn, as was the journalist."

"What do you mean?"

"The writer was executed in Stalin's purges. Another strand to add to the mystery. Shortly after, Komendant Yurovsky conveniently died, of stomach cancer." Fomenko smiled. "By all accounts, the executioner went to his death in agony."

The road to Kildare Stud Farm in Kentucky was hardly a road at all, just a blacktop track that wound up through emerald-green hills. It ended in a vast, sunny meadow of incredible beauty, on which stood a pretty house with several barns and lots of white-railed paddocks.

Constance "Connie" Ryan is a sprightly woman in her late sixties, and the youngest of Finn Ryan's four daughters—Lydia Ryan's nieces. When I saw her for the first time I felt stunned. Life sometimes offers up the near-same faces, generation after generation, and hers was no exception. It was as if I were looking at an older version of the young Lydia in the photograph taken with Uri Andrev all those years ago at Briar Cottage.

Connie Ryan had the same eyes, the same dark Celtic beauty. She was enthralled to hear my request to discuss the aunt for whom she had a lifelong fascination.

After we'd finished our introductions, she ushered me into a parlor, the walls covered in family photographs. "You said you were interested in Lydia's time in Russia as a governess to the Romanovs. That her name came up during your research into the period, Dr. Pavlov?"

"That's right. And I'd be grateful for anything else you can tell me."

"Let me show you some photographs that may interest you." She pointed to one of the snapshots with obvious pride. "This is Finn, my father."

I saw a young man with a mop of fair hair, and a freckled Irish face.

Connie said, "He sailed into New York harbor from Ireland on December 14, 1918, having lost his leg while gun-running for the Irish republicans. Quite a few Irish-Americans went back to the land of their forefathers to help in the fight for freedom, you know."

"Did your father talk much about those times?"

"He never really did. It was almost a taboo subject."

"Why's that?"

"I guess because of the fact that Lydia disappeared, presumed dead. It was something he never truly got over."

"Did he ever discover what happened to her?"

She frowned. "If he did, he never said. Toward the latter years of his life, he toyed with writing a book about their years together in Ireland. I even helped him type up some notes. But sadly, he passed away before he had too much written. I still have the notes somewhere. I kept them as a memento."

Connie moved along a wall covered with photographs: some in frames, others on shelves. She picked one up and passed it to me. "This is Lydia. She was quite a gal, apparently. Her father always called her *mo cushla*. That's Gaelic. It means 'the beat of my heart, the very breath of me.' My father loved that expression. He always said it summed up how he felt about Lydia. They were that close."

She handed me another snapshot, of Lydia in some sort of palace setting with the pretty Romanov children: the four girls, Tatiana and Olga, Maria and Anastasia, in white cotton dresses with satin ribbons. And Alexei, no more than eight, wearing his sailor's uniform, mischief in his smile. A stab of grief went though me; their image still hauntingly tragic when I thought of the savagery of that night.

Connie said, "My father always had a strong interest in the Romanov tragedy."

"Really?"

"I guess because of Lydia's connection to the family. In fact, he traveled to Russia shortly before he died, in 1977."

"Why?"

She handed me another photograph. It was of Finn as an old man, the snapshot obviously taken in Russia: a golden cupola in the background. "Ekaterinburg seemed to hold a particular fascination for him. This was before glasnost, of course, but he managed to get a tourist visa. The visit seemed important to him. I still miss him, you know."

I stared at the photograph, heard the pain in her voice.

Connie replaced the photograph on the shelf. "Perhaps you'd care to see the family plot where my father's buried?"

"I'd like that."

On a coffee table was a vase of yellow roses. She plucked two and led me on a short walk across some fields—the same fields where Lydia had learned to ride and shoot—until we came to a small, wire-fenced graveyard. It was the kind of family plot you often see in rural America, and in the afternoon sun it looked very peaceful, with a dozen or so granite headstones.

"This is my father's grave."

The black granite was inscribed simply, "Finn Ryan. A proud American who helped in the fight for Irish freedom. 1900–1977. Gone to lie in the arms of the Lord."

Next to it, another slab was inscribed: "Lydia Ryan. Born 1894. Died 1918." At the bottom of the stone it said simply, "Love never forgets."

I stared at the stone, stunned, and Connie said, "My father wanted to erect a memorial to remember her. What was it Freud once said? All depression is caused by the loss of someone's love. To tell the truth, he had his share of dark days after he lost her. He never stopped missing her." She knelt, placed a yellow rose on each of the two slabs.

I was tempted to tell her all I'd discovered, but something held me back. *Not yet. Not until I finally know everything.* "So he never knew what became of her?"

Connie stood. "No, but my father's cousin Frank spoke about some U.S. government men who came to visit my father in 1919. He claimed they told him that Lydia had perished and her body was never found. After the men left my father was pretty shaken. Whatever else they may have told him, he never spoke about it."

"Do you know anything more about the men?"

"Only what I recall among the notes I typed. One of them had an Irish name—Boyle, I remember that."

It was a cold morning in Dublin when I took a cab from my hotel to the Blackrock Private Clinic, near the city's southern coast. When I'd called Yakov's home number his housekeeper answered and said he'd returned to hospital. I found him in a private room overlooking the sea.

He shook my hand warmly. "Dr. Pavlov. It's a pleasure to see you again."

He seemed in good spirits, even if he did appear more gaunt, his eyes sunken, his bruised arms hooked up to drips. "Well, how did you get on?"

"It all fits together, everything you've said, each part of the puzzle fitting nearly into place. I'll give you that."

"But?"

"It's just . . . I don't know . . . mind-boggling. Don't get me wrong. All those strands you talked about. They fit, almost too perfectly. In fact, I've discovered amazing coincidences—about Boyle, Andrev, Lydia Ryan, and other players in the rescue that completely flabbergast me."

"Tell me."

I removed a thick notebook from my briefcase. "Take yesterday, for instance. I spent it checking archives in Dublin and reading up on Lydia Ryan."

"And what did you learn?"

"She certainly ran guns for the Irish republicans. And was much admired by the Irish rebel leader Michael Collins. In June 1918, after a skirmish with the British army, she vanished, and was never seen again. I'm still waiting for you to tell me what happened to her."

"We'll come to that. Please continue. What else did you discover?"

"Trotsky got what he deserved in the end. He fell foul of Stalin, was exiled, and later assassinated on Stalin's orders. Lenin didn't escape punishment, either. Six weeks after the events in Ekaterinburg, a woman named Fanya Kaplan shot and severely wounded him. Lenin's health was badly affected and he later suffered a stroke and died in 1924."

"And his assassin?"

"Lenin had her executed. And here's another remarkable coincidence—the woman, Fanya Kaplan, was believed to be one of Joe Boyle's Russian agents."

Yakov nodded. "Perhaps another reason why Boyle got that DSO, and never admitted his involvement. Lenin's Cheka would have hunted him down."

"The coincidences don't end there. In 1920 a book titled *Rescuing the Czar* was published in the United States. It claimed to tell the real story of the Romanovs' disappearance and detailed a rescue using the tunnels that ran under the Ipatiev House, and even made vague references to Ireland.

"But here's the astonishing thing: a deal was in negotiation for the film rights when the U.S. Secret Service had them mysteriously withdrawn from sale. As someone close to President Woodrow Wilson put it at the time, the withdrawal was 'a matter of great importance to the nation.'"

"It gets stranger and stranger, doesn't it?"

"It sure does. And then there's the aircraft, the Ilya Muromets."

"I was wondering when you'd get to that."

I checked my notes. "One crashed thirty miles from St. Petersburg on July 8, 1918. Turns out it had the same chassis number as one of the aircraft taken by Igor Sikorsky when he fled Russia. Sikorsky emigrated to America, where he died in 1974, a successful aircraft manufacturer. And guess what? He knew Boyle."

Yakov seemed faintly amused, but then his face became more serious. "And the nuns at Novo-Tikhvinsky—what did you learn about them?"

"The two young novices, Maria and Antonina, were later executed by the Reds. Sister Agnes was later murdered, too. The convent was closed and all the other nuns either shot or banished to labor camps."

"Did you discover any motive for their murders?"

"None that made any kind of sense, except their involvement in the rescue."

"And Hanna Volkov?"

"She survived her injuries but later sold her Irish estate." I checked my notebook again. "For decades, each anniversary of Boyle's death, a mystery woman would leave flowers on his grave. Some said it was the queen of Romania, with whom Boyle had a close relationship. Others suggest it was Hanna Volkov. She died of cancer in London in 1939."

I flipped ahead a few pages. "And now it gets *really* interesting. A Philip Sorg joined the U.S. State Department in 1912. A man of the same name spent six months being treated for laudanum addiction in a private Swiss hospital near Lucerne, until he was discharged in February 1919."

Yakov nodded silently and I went on. "A month later Sorg was listed as a passenger on the White Star Line, bound for New York. After that, he vanished off the face of the earth, never to be seen again. Just like Anastasia Romanov." I looked at Yakov. "But I think *you* know where he went. You know how it ended, don't you?"

"Yes, I know how it ended."

Questions tumbled impatiently off my tongue. "Did Anastasia live? What became of her? How did Lydia die? And what's the truth about Anna Anderson?"

Yakov put up a hand. "One question at a time. First, I should explain about Anna Anderson." He sat back. "After Anastasia escaped, the Brotherhood was fearful the Cheka would learn the truth and hunt her down. So one of their members, a psychiatrist, came up with a simple but brilliant plan. What if they had a substitute, someone expendable they could pretend was Anastasia? That way, if anyone tried to kill her, the real Anastasia would be safe.

"It took many months of scouring the mental hospitals of Europe, until finally they settled on a suitable candidate. The woman the world eventually came to know as Anna Anderson. She matched their criteria in terms of looks, and certain bodily features, like her ears and feet, that she shared with Anastasia.

"Scars were deliberately inflicted on her skull during surgery, to be consistent with wounds Anastasia suffered at the hands of the Bolsheviks. After that, it was a case of making an impressionable, mentally ill woman believe that she was Anastasia Romanov. Their deception began with Anna Anderson's supposed suicide attempt in a Berlin canal, and her amazing story was born."

"Anna Anderson was a *decoy*?"

"Pure and simple. To deflect the world from the truth."

"Do you really believe that?" I asked incredulously.

"My dear doctor, in over ninety years of mystery and intrigue concerning Anna Anderson, it's the only explanation that makes perfect sense. Consider this: the woman was a simple, mentally disturbed peasant. How could she have challenged and confounded some of the best legal minds in the world, as well as the most experienced investigators and journalists, for six decades, if not with powerful help?"

"The Brotherhood?"

Yakov nodded. "Only they could have drilled into her such intimate knowledge of the royal family—details known only by the real Anastasia, that convinced so many that she was the real royal princess."

"You're saying Anna Anderson was programmed by them, brainwashed?"

"Exactly. And many of the former Russian nobility who sheltered her during her life were part of the deception. There's no way she was just some insane imposter acting on her own."

I felt stunned. Yakov's proposition had a simple, but profound logic to it.

"And Anastasia? What became of her?"

A nurse appeared, ready to replace the drips.

Yakov hesitated, as if reluctant to speak further. "Perhaps you could meet me at my cottage this afternoon?"

"You're being discharged?"

"For a few days, to get my affairs in order. My housekeeper's coming to pick me up. I'm afraid the next time I leave here, it'll be in a box."

I felt jolted by Yakov's frankness, but he merely smiled. "Please, don't feel sorry. I'm an old man, ready to meet my maker. This afternoon, I'll tell you how this mystery ended."

■   ■   ■

When Yakov greeted me at Briar Cottage, I was again struck by how frail he looked. I wasted no time as he led me inside and gestured for me to sit by the fire.

"Tell me what happened to Anastasia."

"She didn't live a long life afterward, I'm sorry to say. Her wounds, mental and physical, caused her much ill health."

"Sorg joined her?"

Yakov shook his head. "I honestly don't know, even if I'd like to think so. Nor do I know where she was taken. All I'm certain of is that she was protected fiercely. And that her final years were a closely guarded secret."

"How do you know all this?"

"Uri told me much of it. As did Leonid Yakov. And on that, you'll simply have to take my word."

A good part of me believed him. Perhaps, like so many others haunted by the mystery of Anastasia Romanov, because I *wanted* to believe. "You say you met Uri."

"I arrived here not long before he died. Before my father passed away, he told me everything, you see. I was so stunned by his confession I was determined to try to track down Uri Andrev, if he was still alive. And that's what I did. It was an emotional meeting for us both."

"I can imagine."

"Actually, I doubt you can," Yakov said oddly, and went to add something but changed his mind.

"What became of Uri afterward?"

"He and Nina started a new life here, in Collon, among the small Russian community. She died some years before him. From what I hear, they lived quiet lives."

"Do you think he loved Lydia?"

"You know what they say—what has been joined, never forgets. He was deeply affected by her death, just as he was by his son's."

My questions tumbled out. "How did Lydia end up in a forest grave in Ekaterinburg? Why didn't Boyle rescue her?"

He hesitated, looked away into nothing a moment, before he replied, "For a time she hid out in Moscow with Yakov's daughter, where they were contacted by one of Boyle's agents. But Russia was in total chaos after the Ekaterinburg massacre. With the Red Army's retreat and the attempt on Lenin's life, Moscow became a city under siege. It was gripped by food shortages and disease. Thousands died. Lydia fell ill. To compound the problem she was carrying Uri's child."

I reeled, as if struck by a physical blow.

Yakov said, "Don't look so shocked. In wartime, faced with so much death, people often choose to affirm their belief in life. It's a natural, God-given instinct."

Yakov paused, then went on. "When Boyle's agent finally got in touch, Lydia couldn't be moved. She had a difficult pregnancy, so Zoba's wife took care of her. After the child was born, Yakov moved her to Ekaterinburg again, along with Zoba's wife, for the Reds had retaken it.

"From there, they would flee south over the border once the time was right. Yakov arranged their accommodation and returned to Moscow. He intended to join Lydia, with Katerina and Nina's parents, and for them all to escape together."

"What went wrong?"

"Lydia went out one day to buy medicine for her child and was caught in a roundup. The Red Terror was in full swing by then, the Cheka killing everyone they suspected. Innocent victims were being picked up off the streets, murdered, or thrown into jails.

"Lydia was held prisoner with hundreds of others in a disease-ridden camp outside the city. When Yakov learned this, he traveled to Ekaterinburg to have her released. But he was too late. Lydia had caught typhoid and died. They buried her in a mass grave, where you found her, along with other victims who perished."

I felt my throat tighten. "What happened to her child?"

"I survived, despite everything."

I felt so stunned by Yakov's words that my mouth fell open.

He saw my total shock. "I told you this was deeply personal, doctor. In many ways, my survival proved an irony. Yakov raised me—he was a good father to me—just as Uri's father raised him. It came full circle."

"Why didn't Yakov continue with the escape?"

"After Lydia's death, the Reds had the country in an iron grip. Even Boyle's network of agents fell apart. Escape became impossible."

I sat without speaking for several moments, thinking about it all. "How did Uri react when you told him who you were?"

"My revelations shocked him. It was a deeply emotional meeting, naturally. The knowledge that I was his son seemed to give him great joy. To know that his love for Lydia had a consequence, that it lived on despite her death—I think that meant a lot to him."

Still dazed, I removed the locket from my purse. "Tell me what the inscription says."

Yakov took the locket, rolled it between his fingers. "May I know you until the end of my days." He looked up. "It seemed fitting. Sometimes broken hearts never truly mend, do they? Love's wounds always twinge now and then, like shrapnel forever lodged in scar tissue. I think that's how it was for Uri. He did the honorable thing and took care of Nina, but his heart, I think, part of it forever belonged to Lydia."

Yakov stood with effort, one hand on his knee, his other hand gripping the fire mantel. "Let me show you something." He shuffled over to a shelf, took down an old metal biscuit tin. He pried the lid with bony fingers and removed an old sepia-colored photograph and handed it to me.

I held the snapshot so it faced the sun filtering through the window, as it burst from between rain clouds. I saw a young woman seated in the stern of a small boat that was tied up to a wooden promenade. In the background was a wide river or lake, with thick forest on the far bank. It must have been a sunny day because she shielded her brow with a hand as she looked out at the camera. From the look of her clothes, I made a guess that the photograph was taken sometime in the 1920s.

As I studied her features I felt my heart flutter. The young woman looked not unlike Anna Anderson, with the same facial shape and strong features. Her eyes looked bright but she wasn't smiling, a kind of detached calm about her.

"Turn it over," Yakov said.

I turned over the snapshot. Written on the back in blue ink it said in English: "With deepest gratitude. To a man of great courage and compassion. Bless you always."

Yakov said, "Now look again at the boat."

When I turned the snapshot over again, I saw the name on the stern: *St. Michael.* Anastasia's favorite saint.

Yakov said, "Uri gave it to me shortly before he died. He said it was passed on to him by Boyle."

As I looked down at the image my mind raced. I can only tell you what I felt. The woman certainly *looked* like Anastasia—a little older, more tired, a torment in her eyes, for certain, but then I knew nothing could ever erase the terror and the agony she had endured that night.

Finally, I looked up. There seemed nothing more to say.

Yakov met my stare. "And now you know the truth. The bright, shining truth, as they say."

Charcoal clouds threatened more rain as we drove to the graveyard. When we reached the tombstones, Yakov said, "Promise me that when the time comes you'll see to it Lydia gets a proper burial?"

"I'll do my best. Whatever I can."

"I know you will, Dr. Pavlov. I greatly appreciate it."

As we stood there together, I drew out the locket. I felt at that moment he needed this touchstone to the past far more than I did. "Why don't you take this, for now?"

He accepted, clutched it tightly. "Thank you."

Standing there, watching the old man bend his head in silent prayer, it finally started to rain again. The fine mist felt like velvet on my face.

I thought of Boyle. And of Sorg, and Yakov, and all the ghosts from the past. I thought about their bravery and their loss, their redemption and their self-sacrifice.

And I thought of Uri Andrev, and of Lydia Ryan.

And for some reason I thought how potent a creation love is—that although sometimes it exists for just a brief, glorious moment in our lives, the ghost of its giving and taking often weaves such an intricate pattern upon our souls, as delicate as lace, as strong as steel. That its spirit is something far too powerful for us mere humans to understand.

There was no complete answer to Anastasia's disappearance. Maybe there never could be, but I knew in my heart that there *was* a seed of doubt about her death. I had lifted a veil and glimpsed the shadows of myths and lies.

And who can say? Perhaps the truth of it all is far deeper than any of us can ever know.

Watching the old man standing over the gravestone, alone with his ghosts, I suddenly felt like an intruder.

The dead had spoken their truth.

I turned and walked back through the cemetery in the rain.

ACKNOWLEDGMENTS

In Moscow and Ekaterinburg, I'd like to thank Boris Nevaski, Leon Davis, John Wright, Pietor Ulyanov, Mariya Semenova; also Vadim Fomenko, Frank Evans, Maxim Petrovsky, and Peter Boyle. On the few occasions I had to twist arms to elicit help, I hope it didn't hurt too much.

To that certain lady in Kentucky who provided the missing link—thanks alone will never be enough.

My gratitude also to Jim Sherlock, Ray Kelly, and Paul Deasy, in Ireland; to Paul Higgins in Canada; and to the many others who expressed their opinions and theories, along with their wishes to remain nameless—I can only offer my appreciation for helping me weave the many strands of this story.

For the Gaelic purists: accept the phonetic.

I highly recommend the website www.alexanderpalace.org, run by Bob Atchison and his dedicated colleagues. It contains a wealth of information for those interested in exploring the lives of the Romanovs.

And finally to Peter, who first told me about the émigré Russians in Ireland, and Uri Andrev and Joe Boyle's involvement in the rescue plot.

I hope I've done an extraordinary tale some justice.

THE ROMANOV CONSPIRACY

Glenn Meade

Reading Group Guide

While on an archeological dig in the outskirts of the present-day Russian city of Ekaterinburg, Dr. Laura Pavlov discovers two perfectly preserved bodies in a mineshaft near where the Tsar Nicholas and his family were brutally murdered in 1918. Dr. Pavlov's discovery leads her on a journey across Europe to a small Irish town where she is told a story about a plan to rescue the Romanov family from execution—a story that crosses borders, languages, and centuries, and one that threatens to forever change the course of history. Alternating between a present-day Russia and the Bolshevik Revolution, *The Romanov Conspiracy* chronicles the mysterious circumstances surrounding the fate of the Romanov family—especially the spirited daughter Princess Anastasia.

Topics & Questions for Discussion

1. "I believe that the greatest secrets lie buried and only the dead speak the truth." (p. 3) In what ways does this quote set the tone for the novel? What does this tell you about Pavlov's character?

2. Revisit the scene on pages 24–25 when Yakov tells Pavlov that his father was responsible for the Romanov execution. What are

Yakov's motivations for revealing his family's secrets to Pavlov? Why does he trust her?

3. Consider the relationship of brothers Uri, Leonid, and Stanislas. In what ways are they a typical family? In what ways are they different?

4. On page 64, Yakov tells Andrev: "Sometimes unpleasant things are necessary for the common good." How does this statement become a maxim for Yakov's character? What are some examples of Yakov's sacrifices for the common good? Do you think he is misguided in his belief, or do you agree that sacrifice is always necessary for a larger freedom? Discuss your answer.

5. Discuss Andrev's character. What kind of role does he play in the narrative of *The Romanov Conspiracy*? What does his character symbolize to the other characters? Do you think his goodness is a standard by which his sons measure themselves?

6. Consider the structure of *The Romanov Conspiracy* and how the narrative shifts between both the present and the past. What effect does this have on the story?

7. Do you think that Andrev made the right decision by abandoning Stanislas's corpse in order to escape execution? What were his regrets? What would you have done if you were in his place?

8. Answer the question the hospital nun poses to Joe Boyle on page 127: "Who are you, sir?" Who is Joe Boyle? Why is he so powerful? What are his motivations for supporting the Russian Civil War? Did you have any remaining questions about him as a character?

9. What kind of role does privilege play in *The Romanov Conspiracy*? Consider Yakov, the Romanovs, Sorg, Uri, and Lydia in your response. In what ways does the pursuit of privilege influence these characters' decisions?

10. *The Romanov Conspiracy* has many characters. Ultimately, whose story is this? Is there one character you could name as the hero or heroine?

11. Why does Yakov have a change of heart in the end? Do you think it was because of Uri or in spite of him?

12. On page 400, Lydia says to Ryan: "You want to shut out the world and wait for the darkness to pass. But then when you open your eyes again you find nothing's changed. It never does." What kind of "darkness" haunts each of the characters?

13. Discuss Lydia and Andrev's relationship. Is their connection based in loneliness or do you think the two truly loved one another?

14. Did you like the ending of the story? Did it surprise you? Overall, did you find the novel "just like a Russian doll—you open up one part, thinking you've got to the end . . . only to find another part inside"? (p. 503)

Enhance Your Book Club

1. *The Romanov Conspiracy* explores a pivotal, tragic moment in history—the brutal execution of Tsar Nicholas and family. But the novel also explores the impact of personal tragedies or life-changing events: "Some events in our lives are so huge in their impact upon us that they are almost impossible to take in." (p. 13) Share a decisive moment from your own life with your book club members. How did you react? How do you think this experience impacted or shaped you as a person?

2. After an argument with Andrev, Lydia attempts to make peace by sharing with him one of her favorite poems called "When You Are Old" by the Irish poet William Butler Yeats. Find the complete poem online and read it aloud to your book group. Why was this poem Lydia's form of apology? What is the significance of this poem?

3. Speculation about what really happened to Grand Duchess Anastasia, the youngest Romanov daughter, has long fascinated historians and the public alike. Turn your next book club meeting into a movie night and watch the 1956 film *Anastasia*, starring Ingrid Bergman.

A Conversation with Glenn Meade

1. You have gained a reputation for being an author who does extensive research for your novels. Can you describe the research that went into writing *The Romanov Conspiracy*?

   I spent about a year researching the novel. It's sponge time—when you're trying to absorb everything you can lay your hands on that's relevant to the story. I read a lot during this period, including biographies of people who lived in Russia during the era to get a feel for the times. I spoke to local historians in the Irish village of Collon—where the grave of one of the main characters in the book is situated and which forms part of the opening of the story—and who met and remembered him. I also spoke to as many experts on the subject as I could get access to, from as far afield as Canada and the U.S., Europe and Russia. Sometimes it isn't easy to get access to the experts—it can take a little persuading. In the best journalistic tradition, on occasion I had to kick in a few doors to get the information I needed. I always try to travel to the main locations in my books. For *The Romanov Conspiracy* I spent a month in various locations in Russia. I rarely stay in hotels while researching, but prefer to stay in the homes of locals, which can usually be arranged through a bespoke travel agent. You'll learn nothing much about the city you're staying in while living in a hotel—but locals have the inside track and you can glean a heck of a lot of realistic detail about a city by spending time in the company of its inhabitants. Once the research is done, then comes the hard part—you roll up your sleeves and get ready to put your head through the wringer as you tackle the actual writing.

2. You write in a blog post titled "Anatomy of a Story: *The Romanov Conspiracy*" on www.glennmeadeauthor.com the following note to readers: "So, dear reader, much of what you will read in the story is true. The rest, but a small part, is fiction. As to which part is truth, and which small part is fiction, I will leave that for you

to decide . . ." Why do you think you are drawn to walk this line between fact and fiction in your writing?

Creating believability in a story is important—it's probably one of the most important techniques of fiction writing. I think it makes a story far more engaging and credible when a large part of it borders on the truth, don't you think? Also, for me, using my imagination to either muddy or clarify real events in order to give my particular take on those events, I think that's where the fun and pleasure lies in writing.

3. Do you have a favorite character in *The Romanov Conspiracy*? Was there any character that you particularly enjoyed writing?

Many of the characters in *The Romanov Conspiracy* are based on real people. Each is intriguing in his/her own way, so I guess this time it was a little more interesting than usual in terms of the writing. I particularly enjoyed exploring the characters of Andrev, Yakov, Lydia, and Sorg. Also, Joe Boyle is another real character I found pretty engaging. He was a truly larger-than-life figure, though so few people know about Boyle's incredible, real-life exploits during the Romanov era.

4. Whom would you consider to be your literary influences?

I've always loved Scott Fitzgerald and Hemingway, each for different reasons. More contemporary writers include Ted Allbeury, Elmore Leonard, and Harlan Coben. All are very different as writers, but I don't think that they necessarily influence my style in any major way—I write very differently compared to any of them. A writer usually writes the way he wants to be read—if that makes sense? Also, the writer's own character, for better or worse, shines through on the page, as does his tone of voice—you can't hide either in your writing, no matter how hard you try. As for influences, I think they're often a complex amalgam—they can go back as far as the kinds of books you read as a child.

5. The *Midwest Book Review* called you "a cross between Indiana Jones and Dan Brown" in a review of your previous novel, *The Second Messiah*. Do you agree? If you could write a blurb for yourself, what would it be? Do you characterize your writing as part of the thriller genre?

Gosh, that's a difficult one. Do I agree? I'm sure grateful for the compliment. Do I characterize my writing as part of the thriller genre? I certainly use thriller techniques. Usually though, straightforward thrillers are pure entertainment—nothing wrong with that. But I like to think my books offer a little more substance—the reader can expect to be enlightened as well as entertained. A blurb for myself? I'll take the *Midwest Book Review* blurb, thanks.

6. You've written several international bestsellers, all set in different time periods and locations. What inspired you to write about the Bolshevik Revolution and about the Romanov family?

I write about this in a blog on my website, www.glennmeadeauthor .com—a piece titled "Anatomy of a Story: The Romanov Conspiracy." I explain how I got the original idea for the book quite by chance. Also, Russia fascinates me—its people, its vastness, its history. I was acutely aware, too, of the enormous public interest in the Romanovs—so when I discovered early on in my research about a factual rescue attempt to save the royal family from execution I felt certain it would make a powerful and interesting tale.

7. *The Romanov Conspiracy* is your eighth novel. How have you grown as a writer from your first novel, *Snow Wolf*?

Actually, *Snow Wolf* was my second novel. *Brandenburg* my first, but they were published in reverse order in the U.S. Grown? I hope so. And I'd like to think I'm a little wiser but in truth my sensibilities probably haven't changed all that much. I share the major character trait of most fiction writers, who are essentially one half innocent and one half cynic; this Jekyll-and-Hyde flaw in their character is totally necessary in order for them to function—the innocent in them writes the first draft; the hard-headed cynic does the rewrites.

8. What do you hope readers will remember or take away after reading *The Romanov Conspiracy*?

The poignant tragedy of the story and the dynamism of the characters. The feeling that my interpretation of the Romanov mystery may offer a fresh take on the enigma surrounding the family's final hours, and on the role played by Anna Anderson. Above all, I hope that they both enjoyed and were moved by the story.

9. If you could go back in time and speak with one of the Romanovs, who would it be? What would you ask?

I think I'd be more interested in speaking with their executioners— I'd like to know what *exactly* happened on the night the Romanovs disappeared, and why different versions of the events were offered over the years.

10. What are you working on now? Can you share some details about your next project?

This is the part where the author runs like a scalded cat, trying desperately to avoid giving too much away. It's almost bad luck to discuss a story in the making, so let me keep it deliberately vague and just say that it's a powerful story of dark secrets, revenge, and redemption, which is set in the present, but with detours into the past. And yes, it does have a forensic archeological excavation as part of its plot.

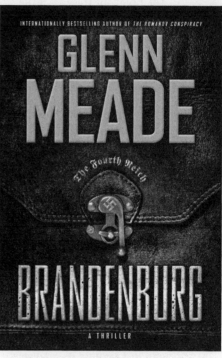